Fly fishing can be fatal

Osborne bent his knees to squat beside the corpse. "Lew, aim your headlamp into the mouth for me, please."

"Right. Something wrong?"

"I recall that Meredith had a goodly amount of gold work," said Osborne. "The gold is gone, Lew. Even in this light, I can tell you it was not politely removed."

"After death—or before?"

From the abrasions on the interior of this mouth—had to be after. Now I wonder if she drowned . . ."

"Are you saying this is not an accidental death, Doc?"

"I can't be sure . . . but it doesn't look good."

Lew looked at him, her eyes keen with appreciation. "Doctor Osborne, thank you," she said. "You just told me something very important that I might have overlooked. This changes everything."

And with that Osborne felt a swell of conflicting emotions: deep sadness for the victim, a young woman who had always been so pretty and gracious and full of life—and a school boy flush of happiness at Lew's words of admiration.

"A compelling thriller . . . populated with three-dimensional characters who reveal some of their secrets of trout fishing the dark waters of the northern forests."
—Tom Wiench, *dedicated fly fisherman and member of Trout Unlimited*

Dead Angler

VICTORIA HOUSTON

Adams Media
An Imprint of Simon & Schuster, Inc.
57 Littlefield Street
Avon, Massachusetts 02322

This work has been previously published in print format by:
The Berkley Publishing Group
A division of Penguin Putnam, Inc.
Print ISBN: 0-425-17355-0

For information about special discounts for bulk purchases, please contact Simon & Schuster Special Sales at 1-866-506-1949 or business@simonandschuster.com.

The Simon & Schuster Speakers Bureau can bring authors to your live event. For more information or to book an event contact the Simon & Schuster Speakers Bureau at 1-866-248-3049 or visit our website at www.simonspeakers.com.

Manufactured in the United States of America

ISBN 978-1-4405-8219-6

For Nicole, Steve, Amanda, Ryan, and Abby—
for being there when it counted

one

Dr. Osborne struggled for balance in the waist-high waters of the roiling Prairie River. With his new wading boots slipping and skidding over the algae on the rocks underfoot, he was glad he'd spent the extra dollars for chest-high waders.

Gusting winds whipped a warm crisp rain against his face while the icy currents surged, bubbled, and sprayed around him. He shook his head. The wild beauty and the absurdity of it. How on earth had he let Lew Ferris talk him into fly-fishing at midnight?

Well, it wasn't exactly midnight. But it *was* nearly eleven. The sky, black with a heavy cloud cover, smothered an intermittent moon. Osborne paused in his awkward casting to shout upstream, hoping his voice would be carried along on a sudden gust, "Lew? Lew!"

He listened for Lew's reassuring voice. Instead, his ears were filled with the soft roar of wind and rain through the tall firs. Moonlight flickered through the clouds for a brief instant. Enough so he could see that in this stretch of the Prairie, less than twenty feet wide, the brush of the forest crowded in from the bank. Bear crossed his mind. Bear and their affinity for fresh brook trout. He tried not to think about it. He was having enough problems already.

The route upstream was not only slippery, it was complicated with ghosts. Well, he admitted to himself, not exactly ghosts although that is how he planned to describe them to his fishing buddy, Ray Pradt, later. Ray, the musky guide and walleye expert, had tried to warn him off his return to fly-fishing.

"Too darn complicated," he'd said. "Don't you want to relax when you fish?" Then he said what he was really thinking: "So you like to fish with the pretty boys? Pretentious goom-bahs like Walter Mason?"

Osborne couldn't wait to tell Ray it sure wasn't Walter Mason and his state-of-the-art gear lurking in the woods tonight. Nor was "pretentious" the word to describe these fellows. Instead, an eerie crew of trout-fishing fanatics had stationed themselves along the tricky banks of the Prairie. As far as he could see, that was, and he wasn't seeing very far at all.

Figures kept emerging from the shadows. Other fly fishermen. Hidden by the dense brush and the dark. Concentrating. Very territorial. The first one he bumped into accidently, swooshing around a bend in the river bank and nearly toppling both of them into the water. This one he knew. Ted Frasier, a former patient, and a very genial man. Osborne had apologized profusely, backing off as Ted warned him away from the pool that Ted had been focused on for hours.

The next fellow wasn't so friendly. "Stop right there," grunted a raspy voice out of the dark to his left. The man was crouched on a rock close to the bank, smoking a cigarette, his fly rod resting over his shoulder. Osborne could barely make out his shape. "Git over to the other side," the voice ordered. He conveniently did not mention the big hole Osborne then stepped into, pitching forward and nearly losing his balance. Two down and how many more to go? Water, wind, rain, rod, and etiquette—in the dead of night?

Osborne seriously considered giving up the damn sport. But he had to admit the frustrations were his own fault. With practice, he'd renew the expertise he had acquired years earlier. He knew he would learn to love it again. No sport, except fly-fishing, can take you so close to the heart of water.

He was also intrigued by his instructor. He had arrived at the trout stream fully expecting a man, maybe even someone he knew, only to be greeted by a woman. And not just any woman but Lew Ferris, the Loon Lake Chief of Police. Sure, she held a man's job but still... *learning to fish from a woman?* He couldn't get over it.

Of course, Lewellyn Ferris had always puzzled him—even in the days when she was a patient he knew only from their brief chats during her six-month visits to have her teeth cleaned. And he had always found himself thinking about her after she left the office.

Her direct manner and fresh-faced vibrancy was so unlike his late wife and her coquettish, carefully attired, cosmetically-correct, female friends. Lew was hardly a beauty yet there was something satisfying in the healthy glow of her skin and the friendly snap of her eyes. Something earthy and attractive in the way she wore men's shirts and Levi's instead of ladylike blouses and slacks. When he had to construct a bridge for her a few months before his retirement, just seeing her name on the appointment calendar had brightened his day.

No sirree, thought Osborne in response to the momentary urge to give up, *I need to figure this out*. He meant the fly-fishing, of course.

Osborne grasped his fly rod with determination and forged ahead, bracing himself against the waist-high rushing waters. Slippery rocks, thunderheads, and all, fly-fishing had begun to look like it would beat the heck out of losing more cribbage games to Ray.

And all because he finally got around to cleaning the garage.

It was his first such clean-up since Mary Lee's death two years ago. She had been a fanatic on completely emptying and cleaning the darn place every winter, spring, summer, and fall. The result was a garage so clean he could have resumed his dental practice in the parking spot where her car used to be.

But when Erin, his younger daughter and the mother of his two grandsons, asked him to contribute items to the Loon Lake elementary school auction, he decided to explore the shelves in the storage area that ran along the back.

It had led to an afternoon of unexpected delights. With no Mary Lee to hurry him along, to insist that he keep throwing stuff away, he found himself having a great time. Gripping his old tennis racquet, he swung through a couple forehands and made a mental note to get back on the courts one of these days. Sixty-three is plenty young to win at doubles.

Reaching up, he pulled a dusty croquet set off a top shelf. He certainly couldn't give that away. Erin's oldest had just turned seven, the perfect age to learn the game. Looking for a place to set the rack of croquet balls so he wouldn't forget to dust them off, he bumped into a roll of leftover wall-to-wall carpeting that had been standing on end in one corner. The roll tipped and fell, exposing a tall metal sports locker he hadn't seen in years.

The minute he opened the locker door he knew why. Mary Lee must have shoved it back there on purpose: she had hated his fly-fishing.

Osborne reached for the first fly rod. Made of bamboo, it was light as a feather in his hand. A classic, handmade from split bamboo, it had belonged to his father. He set it aside carefully to pull out the second rod. This had been his favorite. The cork grip above the bird's-eye maple reel seat still fit his hand perfectly. The rod gleamed copper in the late morning sun, the guides glinted gold.

His creel rested on an overhead shelf. He pulled it down. Inside were tucked two boxes of trout flies. Behind the creel, Mary Lee had stuffed his fishing vest. Osborne shook it out, then explored its pockets with all the pleasure of a little kid on Christmas morning.

He got so involved sorting through the mix of clippers, forceps, bottles of floatant, trout flies, packets of leaders and tippets, an old fishing license, and all the other paraphaernalia packed into the vest's thirty-three pockets that he forgot to eat lunch.

It was mid-afternoon when he raised the garage door and walked out onto the driveway. Memories flooded back as he attached the reel, slipped line through the guides, tied on a trout fly and raised his arm. Up, back, and forward he flicked the rod. He had forgotten how delicate was the tip action, so unlike the heavy, weighted swoosh of his musky rod.

But the fly line flopped and pooled at his feet. It had been years since he had fly-fished. He had lost the muscle memory of the proper casting technique. And he had no one to ask for help. The elderly lawyer who had introduced him to the sport had long since moved on to more sacred fishing grounds.

Slowly, Osborne folded the fishing vest back up. With care and not a little regret, he wiped the rods clean with a chamois cloth and set them in the back of his station wagon. Then he packed the boxes of trout flies, the two reels, and his creel in a shopping bag. He would need an estimate before he turned these over to Erin. He hoped against hope she might want to keep them for her own children. But, like most women, Erin didn't fish. Nor did her husband.

Too bad, he thought as he drove into Loon Lake, fly-fishing with old John Wright had been one of the real pleasures of his life. Though a brief one. Mary Lee had been so unpleasant, arguing that he already had his bird hunting, his deer hunting, his musky and walleye fishing, not to mention angling for blue gills, crappies, and bass. As always, she was right. He didn't need another sport that took him away from home.

Nor had she had much use for his fishing partner. John Wright was a hard-drinking, steely-eyed trial lawyer who didn't suffer fools. Something didn't click between John and Mary Lee. It occurred to Osborne, as he parked in front of Ralph's Trading Post, that it may have been John Wright his wife detested even more than the fly fishing.

"You can't be serious, Doctor," Ralph Kendall, the trading post's owner and fly-fishing expert, had peered over his bifocals in astonishment, his piercingly nasal British accent so loud that everyone in the sporting goods store had stopped to listen.

"Why not?" Osborne asked, not a little taken aback by Ralph's vehemence.

He was fast regretting this decision to even enter the place. Since Ralph specialized in fly-fishing gear and Osborne had been focused on musky and walleye bait fishing for the last few years, he rarely stopped in. That plus the fact the man was always patronizing in a way that irritated Osborne. It wasn't like Ralph was a fly-fishing expert in *Montana*. This was the boondocks. This was Loon Lake for God's sake. Nope, a little bit of Ralph went a long way with Osborne. But he gritted his teeth and prepared to listen. The only alternative was a seventy-five-mile drive north.

"You want to *give* this equipment away? My god, man, bamboo rods like this aren't made any longer! I'll give you five thousand dollars for everything. Right here and now," said Ralph, slamming his fist on the counter.

"Really?" Osborne was flabbergasted. Five thousand dollars is a lot of money in Loon Lake.

"Your bamboo rod is worth half that alone," said Ralph. Both hands on the counter, he glared Osborne as if the retired dentist had just proposed to dump raw sewage in a pristine trout stream.

"Before you commit this crime," he said, his voice echoing down the aisles of fishing lures, "tell me why you are doing so. I do not understand. I have calls from around the world from people looking for rods like these. And your trout flies are exquisite."

"John Wright tied these himself," said Osborne feebly.

"I can place one phone call and sell every single one this afternoon," said Ralph. "But your creel—I'll keep that for my own collection."

"Really? Well. . . . ," Osborne stammered. "That creel belonged to my father."

"Now, Doc," Ralph lowered his voice, addressing him with the familiar title most Loon Lakers used for Osborne. His bushy eyebrows tipped up in sympathy. "Are you sure you want to give all this away?"

No, he wasn't. He felt foolish, but he also felt vindicated. Maybe he had been right to fly-fish all those years ago. With no Mary Lee to badger him, why not give it another try? Why not make up for lost time?

"Y'know, I'm not sure," said Osborne. "But I haven't gone fly fishing in so long that I . . ."

"Stop," Ralph raised his hands, his excitement growing with evidence of a crack in Osborne's resolve. "I admit I am a fanatic myself but I am not going to let you do this, Doc. Not without giving it one more chance. Let me call a friend of mine who just might have the time to take you out. What's your schedule like?"

The next thing Osborne knew he was booked to fish with a guy named Lou. At least that's what he thought until he arrived at the canoe landing on the Prairie River.

Lou was not Lou. Lou was Lew. Lewelleyn Ferris. Osborne had never in his life fished with a woman. But it was certainly a woman walking towards him, waving as he drove down towards the river. As he pulled up, the surprise on her face was equal to his.

"Well, Doc Osborne," she exclaimed. "Ralph never told me *you* were coming. He just said to expect some old guy in a Camry station wagon with beautiful equipment."

"I'm afraid I'm the old guy," said Osborne.

She caught the hurt expression on his face. A wide grin creased her friendly Irish face as she said, "Hey, don't take offense. You know Ralph."

No, he didn't. Not really. Osborne filed the insult away for future reference. If he ever did get to know Ralph better, he would definitely discuss this with him.

And so it was that, with his ego bruised and slightly daunted by his guide's gender Osborne had re-entered the world of fly-fishing. In fact, he was so stunned at the prospect of fly fishing with Lew Ferris that Sunday night that he neglected to mention a few pertinent details.

two

His first mistake had been not telling her it was at least six years since he last fly fished. Nor did he mention that he had never gone after dark. Instead, he allowed her to think he had not fished *this particular river before*.

"Why so late?" he'd asked Lew with a false casualness as he sat on the bumper of her beat-up pickup while clumsily pulling on his waders, trying to fit together the sections of his fly rod, adjust the hiker headlight on his forehead, and locate his old box of trout flies—simultaneously. And all in dim light with thunder crashing in the distance. Not the conditions Osborne usually found favorable for fishing.

Why am I doing this? he had badgered himself as he hurried to keep up. Isn't a 63-year-old retired dentist entitled to a life of grace and dignity? Dignity was out of the question as he plopped around in his boxy waders before confronting, befuddled, the jumble of trout flies that he no longer recognized.

He had forgotten that fly-fishing is an aristocratic sport, defined by conventions more confusing than a game of bridge. The angler is expected to command an arcane knowledge of nature, tempered with the ability to make a precise selection of the perfect fly to match the insect hatching at that very moment—not thirty minutes earlier. Musky fishing, even walleye fishing, presents much simpler options.

Lew sensed his hesitation and leaned over his shoulder, del-

icately plucked three flies from his box, then held them out in
the palm of her hand for him to take and hook onto his fly-
fishing vest. "Try these, Doc, they work for me," she'd said.
Then, her sturdy form efficiently encased in neoprene, her
crumpled khaki fishing hat thrust firmly onto her curly black-
brown hair, dark eyes ready but patient, she waited for him.

Moments later, he was lumbering after her while adjusting
his too-tight fishing vest, stumbling over marshy hillocks,
while desperately threading the tip of his rod through the maze
of branches closing in around them. Reality set in. Grace, too,
was not even an option.

He tried to keep all these thoughts to himself, but finally he
had it.

"Mrs. Ferris, is this wise?"

He aimed his words at her back as they both scrambled up
an embankment and onto an old farm bridge that crossed the
Prairie. Planks were missing from the bridge at random spots,
the holes black and threatening, reminding Osborne of a mouth
with too many rotten teeth.

"That storm's headed this way. Why don't we try another
night?"

Lew paused in the wet blackness. "Call me Lew, Doc. I
haven't been Mrs. Ferris in years. And trust me, this will be
worth it. Ralph told me they've used a muddler minnow the
last two nights just around this time. When the best fisherman
north east of Montana call the hatch, you are crazy to miss it.
Ben Kauppinen pulled a sixteen-inch brookie out of here yesterday. Fact is," she peered at him through the dark and leaned
forward to emphasize her point, "the bugs are hatching, the
fish are biting. You want to fish or not? I can guarantee that
if you're out here tomorrow in the noonday sun, you'll be
warm and happy and every trout in the river will be at the
bottom looking up . . ."

"You're right," Osborne held up a compromising hand. He
could sense, even in the dark, that she was giving him a dim
eye. Darn it, he kicked himself. Why did he have such a big
mouth?

His second mistake was hooking his trout fly on a high
branch within his first five minutes in the river. He had tried
to tie on a new one one, but the combination of the dark, the
rain, and the blood knot stymied him. After watching him
struggle for several minutes, Lew had come to his rescue,

briskly grabbing his line, checking the length of his tippet, and quickly taking over the situation. Within seconds, she had sliced off the tippet and whipped on a new one.

"Forget the blood knot," she had said with a bluntness that charmed him, "too complicated. Here," she plucked a fly off the fleece pad on her fishing vest, threaded the leader and worked magic with her fingers, "Ralph gave me two white caddis this morning. Use one of mine." She had been quick and kind, but, he was sure, through gritted teeth. "Follow me," she then said and promptly started upstream.

Osborne tried to stay close, but it was hopeless. She waded through the heavy current with the authority of having been there before, the authority of knowing, intimately, the rocky landscape underwater. Or was it the new job that lent her this air of knowing exactly where she was headed and why? Lew was four months into her new position as chief of Loon Lake's police department, a fact Osborne was well aware of thanks to the editorial page of The Loon Lake News. The appointment of the first woman ever to that position had generated debate within the community. Osborne thought to himself that on this particular occasion he, for one, was happy to follow Lew's lead.

But when she had disappeared around a bend, into the dark and the rain, he gave up. He opted to go at his own pace. That was what he loved about fishing anyway: it gave him time to think.

Osborne paused at one of the few quiet pools that didn't appear to be staked out by a ghostly competitor yet. Flicking his right arm up towards his forehead, he started the backcast, halting his movement as the line whipped back, then forward and out, running from his hand. Ah, grace at last. Of course, at no time could he see either line or fly. If it found a trout, he'd never know unless he felt it.

He really didn't care if he caught a fish or not. Right now, he was happy to be upright, dry inside his waders, and within shouting distance of Lew.

He still found it hard to believe he was fishing with this stocky, once-wed, once-divorced woman who pursued errant snowmobilers and jet skiers, not to mention out-of-control hunters and fishermen—while supervising the local jail. Fishing is, after all, something you do only with the best of friends.

And Osborne had never included a woman on his list of best friends—not even Mary Lee.

But, he mused, that could change. Only an hour into the river and he could see that Lew Ferris was not only an expert, she loved the act.

Osborne experimented with a false cast, which failed miserably. He was glad she hadn't seen it. On the other hand, he had a sudden mental image of her face if she had, Lew raising those no-nonsense dark brown eyes to his and letting the edges crinkle with humor. Yep, insult aside, he would have to thank Ralph—these few hours in the river with Lew had indeed changed his mind. The question was, how could he arrange for her to take him again?

Osborne checked his watch by flicking on the hiker's light attached to his fishing hat. Twenty minutes had gone by since he'd seen Lew head upstream. He sure hoped she didn't plan to fish much longer.

Although it was a humid August night, the drizzle chilled him—or maybe it was the cold rushing water swirling, at times, as high as his waist. Osborne edged forward with care. In spite of the thick felt glued to the bottoms of his boots, he continued to stumble and slide over the slippery rock beneath the surface.

The river felt so strange in the dark, challenging him with eddies and swirls and small rapids, one of which he stepped into now. He inched forward, legs wide apart for better balance. The roar of the water in his ears made him feel like he had a middle-ear problem as he tried to keep feet steady, rod and reel dry, and the white caddis fly out of the branches.

At last, he spotted Lew about sixty feet away. He could see her as if in a strobe light—whenever the moonlight flashed through the cloud cover—her fly rod arcing back over her head, then flowing forward with a grace Osborne envied. The wind and rain seemed to ease for the moment.

"Be careful, Doc," she shouted back as she moved ahead, casting upstream, "slight drop-off and a big log to the right off that bank in front of you. Take it slow." Once again, she left him in the dark.

Osborne waded as close to the bank as he could, hoping to avoid the log. That was silly. The Prairie, one of Wisconsin's premier trout streams and often less than twelve feet wide, is known for its treacherous drop-offs along the banks: holes scooped out by the relentless, roiling currents.

His foot went down and down and down. He felt it slide over the slippery log and continue down. He grabbed for branches hanging overhead. He missed. Water flooded into the top of his waders, the swift current pulling him under. Arms flailing, he let go of his rod as he tried to steady himself. Instinct brought his arms down to his sides as if to find bottom and push up. His hands met the slippery surface of the underwater log—then the cloth of its sleeve and the appendage at the end of that. Osborne grabbed, only to let go with a terrible understanding.

He found his feet somehow and shot up out of the river screaming.

That was no log. That was a body.

three

The sleeve was a pink sleeve. Fuchsia, according to Lew. Attached to the sleeve and its hand was the body of a woman dressed for fly-fishing.

"I've always thought it was a myth that your waders could fill and pull you under," said Lew.

"A frightening way to die," said Osborne, "but, boy, I can see how it happens. Trout streams like the Prairie are so dangerous when you don't know the terrain."

They sat on the river bank, side by side, still breathing hard. The body lay five feet away, face up, carefully laid out in a small clearing.

"Jeez, Doc," said Lew, "this is the third accidental drowning in less than a month. We better be careful or Loon Lake will be named the drowning capital of America."

Lew had already turned back when she heard Osborne's terrified scream. Both of them struggled to move as fast as possible, legs pushing hard against the resisting water. As Osborne pressed upstream, anxious to put distance between himself and the unexpected stranger underwater, he found himself back in his childhood nightmare: running, running, running, but unable to move forward more than an inch at a time.

Suddenly, the river bottom sloped up, and he was in shallows ankle-deep. As he lurched forward, still shouting but finally able to get some momentum, he nearly collided with Lew.

"Calm down," she grabbed his right shoulder firmly. "Take a deep breath," she commanded.

Osborne did as she said. As he inhaled, the panic subsided.

"Good," Lew relaxed her hold on his shoulder. She looked him over, and he was surprised to see the level of concern in her eyes. It had been a long time since he had such a sense that someone cared. He reminded himself it was all part of doing her job.

"Are you sure you're okay?" she asked after he had caught his breath. "Doc, before we go anywhere, let me help you get some of the water out of those waders."

Osborne looked down. In his panic, he had managed to travel upriver despite the fact he was carrying gallons of wa- ter—waist-high. He looked like the Pillsbury doughboy. To- gether they unhooked his suspenders and let the waders flop down, the water whooshing back to the river.

"I think I'll spend the extra ten bucks for a wading belt and avoid having this ever happen again," he said sheepishly as he pulled the rubber pants back up. "This is fine, Lew," he said. "I can manage with water in my boots. We've got to get back before that body floats downstream."

"Up on the bank," directed Lew, "there's a path up there."

"Now you tell me," said Osborne as he switched on his hiker's light so he could see where he was going.

They were back at the bend in less than a minute. The body was nowhere in sight. "Here," said Lew, handing him her fly rod as she jumped down into the river, "Let me check to be sure it's not lodged under that log." She leaned over, her arms searching through the water. Osborne did not mind in the least that she wasn't asking for his help.

"Got it," she shouted, "I got it. Boy, it's really stuck under here, too."

Osborne set both their rods against a tree and edged his way to the river bank. The clouds were clearing. Moonlight made it easier to see.

"That submerged log—want me to try to lift it?" asked Os- borne.

"Sure, but watch your back," said Lew. "I don't like to lose fishing partners if I can help it."

Osborne bent his knees and circled his arms around the

slimy old hunk of cedar. It lifted surprisingly easily, probably hollowed out from the steady hammering of the currents.

"Great," said Lew, her arms working in the water below her, "if you can hold it up for another moment or two . . . I've got the legs, but the waders are hooked on all these branch stumps . . . good, got it!"

He let the log down slowly. "Do you need help?"

"No, I'm okay." Osborne stepped back to watch Lew pull the body, face down toward the bank where they found a small clearing. "Now, I'll take the shoulders, Doc," she said scrambling up and backwards as she held tight to the pink-sleeved arms, "if you'll grab the lower legs."

They pulled and heaved and tipped it head down, the sodden figure weighing much more dead than it had alive, thanks to the gallons of water it, too, was carrying in its waders. At last, Lew rolled it onto its back and arranged the body as neatly as it would let her. She walked over to where Osborne was sitting on the ground, yanking off his waders so he would stop squishing every time he moved.

"It's a woman, Doc."

"Yep," he said, "I could see from here when you rolled her over. Does this trail lead all the way back to where we entered the river?" he asked her, "or do I need to pull these back on?" Lew threw herself down beside him.

"Gosh, I'm exhausted," she said. She glanced back at the body on the ground. "We sure as heck aren't carrying the victim back with us. Yeah," she looked at him in the moonlight. "We can take the trail all the way to the truck. I need to start carrying a phone, don't I? I have to call in and get Roger out here with the ambulance."

"Don't ever put a phone in the truck, Lew. Fishing and phones don't mix."

"What do you think?" she asked Osborne about ten minutes later. They stood together, studying the features of the corpse under the beams of their hiker's lights. They had rested briefly, broken down their rods, and tucked their reels into their vest pockets. Osborne had rolled his waders into ball, which he buttoned inside his shirt for the walk back. That left him with one hand to carry his rod and the other to keep branches from poking him in the eye.

He was relieved the rain had stopped and a warm August

breeze had replaced the gusty winds, as he was completely soaked from his khaki pants and shirt right down to his underwear.

"I think . . . ," said Osborne leaning forward to let the beam of his light fall across the face, then slide down the rest of the body, "this was a relatively recent accident."

"What makes you think so?"

"I was in the Korean War, Lew, assigned to forensic dentistry," he looked up at her. "I've seen a few too many corpses in my time."

"Hey, that's good to know, Doc. You could come in handy," said Lew with unexpected enthusiasm.

"Well . . . ," Osborne started to hedge, he was never happy around dead bodies. On the other hand, could this be his ticket to more fly fishing time with Lew Ferris? Backtracking quickly from his moment of hesitation, he said, "Just call me when you need me." And with that he determined to make the most of forensic skills he hadn't practiced in years.

Whether it was timing or the cold waters of the Prairie, the corpse showed just the earliest signs of decomposition and bloating. "She may have slipped and drowned earlier today—maybe even early this evening. The abrasions on her forehead and cheeks are probably from the body being forced through the shallows by the current . . ."

"You think so," said Lew. Her tone implied it was a rhetorical question.

"Those rocks and sand bars will do a nasty job on flesh."

After the roar of the wind earlier, the night was now so quiet Osborne could hear Lew clicking her tongue against the roof of her mouth as she catalogued details. She stood silently by his side for a good minute or more.ep "Tell me what you're thinking," he said.

"Blonde hair. About five feet six or so. Female, buxom. But no man goes fishing in a fuchsia shirt, anyway." Lew tipped her eyes up to catch Osborne's. "Just in case the Wausau boys need documentation on sex, " she chuckled.

"The Wausau boys?" Osborne asked, confused. Wausau was sixty miles away, a town ten times the size of Loon Lake.

"The stuffed shirts at the state crime lab down there. I have to report any death in my jurisdiction. They assign the forensic work-ups and dictate the final analysis," she said. "When . . .

if . . . they get around to it." Lew's opinion of the Wausau boys was obvious.

"That's a very pricey fly fishing vest and she's wearing ultralight waders. Tourist?" asked Lew. She waited.

Osborne didn't answer. He wasn't looking at vest or waders, but the facial features . . . something familiar . . .

"Doc—has to be a tourist. No one from Loon Lake would spend three hundred and fifty bucks on waders, would they? Not even someone from Rhinelander or Eagle River, do you think?"

"Lew," Osborne cleared his throat, as he always did before he delivered a pronouncement. "I recognize this young woman." By his standards, she was young anyway. Late thirties, younger than Lew.

"Really?" Lew waited. Her eyes searched Osborne's face.

"Meredith Marshall. She was a Sutliff growing up. A good friend of my daughter Mallory's. In fact, I believe she and Mallory saw each other from time to time in Chicago. Mallory lives in Lake Forest, you know." Lew nodded.

"She's from Loon Lake originally. The father died not too long ago, but he had retired to Phoenix. He managed the Rhinelander paper mill in the sixties," said Osborne.

As he spoke, he struggled to remember some recent gossip that been passed along during his regular morning coffee hour at the Loon Lake McDonald's, the informal men's club of early-risers, which included his neighbor, Ray Pradt, and several other fishing buddies. That was the one hour every day when any news, official or unofficial, in the fifty-lake region was likely to be heard. Usually accurate, the source was often only one to two parties removed.

"Now that I think of it, I heard she moved back from Chicago about six months ago. Divorced. Alicia Roderick is her sister," he said.

"Oh," said Lew. "Peter Roderick's wife. They own the big house over by the grade school."

"Right."

Lew knelt and gently unbuckled the suspender top of the waders on the corpse. "When was the last time you saw her?"

"Three years ago. She lost a filling while on vacation up here and dropped by the office. Just before I retired."

Lew folded the top of the waders back to expose a pocket sewn into the waterproof material, which she unzipped. From it, she pulled a sodden black leather French purse. She opened the side with credit cards and slipped out a driver's license. "You're right, Doc—Meredith C. Marshall. Still has an Illinois driver's license."

"Something strange about her," said Osborne reflectively. "I believe she married well, but for all her money, she had some of the crummiest dental work I've ever seen. I couldn't believe it."

"Really," Lew sounded only modestly interested as she resnapped the dead woman's waders, carefully slipping the purse into her own fishing vest.

"Yes," said Osborne emphatically, shaking his finger as if warning a class of young dental students, "this has always been a sore point with me, Lew. I never can get over the prices charged by some of these Chicago and Milwaukee dentists—and the third-rate work these guys get away with." As he talked, he bent down to pick up their rods, then he started toward the path, anxious to get them both on their way. Lew lingered over the corpse.

"Meredith, there, is an excellent case in point. Here was a woman with a good, healthy mouth but she had a problem on one of her incisors. Had it since childhood, I kept a "watch" on it when she was a teenager. Years later, this Chicago dentist gives her a porcelain cap, backed with gold and so poorly constructed that the backing *gleamed along the vertical edges of the tooth*. Made her look like a darn gypsy.

"A good dentist doesn't do that, Lew. Even though you can charge more for the gold work, you are responsible to your patient. When I commented on it, she said he never told her she had an alternative. Ridiculous. In her case, the dentist should have worked with porcelain exclusively, less expensive but tasteful. Something that doesn't flash, do you know what I mean?"

"I do, Doc," said Lew. She was still staring down at the corpse. "Show me what you mean. I don't see anything gleaming."

Osborne walked back over to stand beside her. He looked down. The mouth of the corpse gaped just slightly in death. "Lend me your forceps, and I'll show you," he said, referring to the small surgical tool that all fly-fishermen wear on their vests to use for ~~tying on flys and tippets~~, "I seem to have lost mine when I fell in." He touched his hand to his head. "Guess I lost my hat, too."

Lew handed him her forceps. Osborne bent his knees to squat beside the corpse. Gently, he pushed the right upper lip back to expose the incisor in question. He paused, then lowered himself onto his knees for a closer look.

"Lew, hold this, will you please?" He handed the forceps back up to her. With both hands, he grasped the jaws and forced the mouth open, his little finger expertly pushing the swollen tongue to the side.

"Aim your headlamp into the mouth for me, please."

"Right. Something wrong?"

"Very wrong. Someone has removed every one of this woman's gold fillings."

Lew dropped to her knees beside Osborne, her dark hair, curly in the humid air, so close he felt it brush his cheek. She dropped her voice as she asked, "what exactly are you saying?"

"I recall that Meredith had a goodly amount of gold work," said Osborne. "I did some myself when she was in her teens, and I remember noting that someone else put a good five thousand dollars-worth in after she reached adulthood. The gold is gone, Lew. Even in this light, I can tell you it was not politely removed."

"After death—or before?"

"From the abrasions on the interior of this mouth—had to be after. Now I wonder if she drowned . . ."

"Are you saying this is not an accidental death, Doc?"

"I can't be sure . . . but it doesn't look good," said Osborne. "I'd send her down to your experts in Wausau for a full forensic work-up."

Lew looked at him, her eyes keen with appreciation. "Doctor Osborne, thank you," she said. "You just told me something very important that I might have overlooked. This changes everything."

And with that Osborne felt a swell of conflicting emotions: deep sadness for the victim, a young woman who had always been so pretty and gracious and full of life—and a school boy flush of happiness at Lew's words of admiration. He was surprised, too, at how pleased he was to be recognized as a dentist again.

four

Lew slammed the gearshift into reverse to back the truck onto the grass. Then she yanked it into first gear, spinning rock and gravel as she cut straight across the highway and into the pasture on the other side.

"Jeez," Osborne grabbed the door handle as they lurched forward.

"Hold tight, Doc," said Lew, "we're going off-road. We can hit W back off this 40 acres, and that'll get us to the Thunder Bay Bar before they close. I gotta get Roger and get back here for this body before the mink and the 'coons get to it."

"Off-road?" Osborne asked, incredulous. "Lew, this little truck is going to come apart."

She tipped her head towards him. In the glow from the dashboard, Osborne could see a slight smile of pride on her face. "Trust me. Nellie and I are made for off-road. She's got four-wheel and I keep her well-tuned. A little short on the shock-absorbers, but what the heck—that's how we find the best trout streams, the best clear-cut for grouse, the best—"

Osborne interrupted her, "How old is Nellie?"

"Twelve and holding."

Given the confidence in Lew's voice, Osborne decided to drop the issue and just hold on for dear life. The red Mazda pickup with its white topper lurched up and down, rocking sideways over the gullies and berms that appeared in the head-lights seconds before Nellie took them on.

Suddenly the tires found a smooth universe of asphalt. The jarring stopped. Osborne took a deep breath of relief. "Now how on earth did you know we could cross that field to W?" he asked Lew. A devoted reader of the county gazeteer, the guide to all marked and unmarked roads as well as public and private lands, Osborne fancied himself an expert on back-woods byways. This was one route he would have never even considered.

"My ex ran a timberland recycling business, and I used to help him find acreage back in here," said Lew. "The state has a number of fields down in this area, set back plenty far from the river, where they restore the land that was over-lumbered back in the thirties and forties. I know the area pretty well, Doc."

"Does he still have the business?" asked Osborne. He was curious. From her patient records, he knew that Lew had been divorced many years ago, but he had never known a man with the last name Ferris. Unusual in Loon Lake, a town so small that everyone knows everyone, not to mention everyone's past and current partners.

"Not up here. He inherited the business from his uncle, took him only two years to bankrupt it."

Lew slowed the truck at the stop sign marking Highway K. As she turned to the right, she looked at Osborne, "I don't know what he does now. Haven't heard from him or about him in years. He's an alcoholic, Doc. I decided many years ago I don't have time for that."

Osborne looked straight ahead as he spoke, "You know, I went through re-hab over at Hazelden right after my wife died?"

"Did you?" She was quiet. So was Osborne. The truck sped forward in the dark. He could tell from the lack of surprise in her tone that she knew something about his problem.

Almost everyone in Loon Lake knew that the unexpected death of his wife had left Osborne a shaken and deeply lonely man. Less than six months after her death he had awakened one day to a knock on the door from his beloved youngest daughter, Erin, who said she couldn't stand it any longer. "Dad," she had said with tears streaming down her face, "you're in trouble. You are a serious alcoholic, and you're killing yourself. You're killing me, Dad."

Lew was an officer on the police force at that time, and Osborne dimly recalled she might have been one of the cops who drove him home in one of his drunken stupors. The kindness of Loon Lake residents can be deadly, Osborne had thought ever since, remembering how friends and other townspeople had been so helpful, protecting when they should have punished.

"Yep. Saved my life," said Osborne.

That was all he wanted to say about the six weeks that had rescued him from the swoon of loneliness and despair. He hoped the day would come when he could tell someone like Lew of the courage he had seen in Erin's face as she stood before him and told him, cleanly, clearly, how he was killing her love for him. Killing himself, killing a future with his grandson and grandchildren to come.

But it wasn't something he could talk about yet. Lew didn't seem to mind. She drove on, relaxed and easy with the quiet between them. That was so unlike Mary Lee, who always found silence a necessary hole to fill. In stark contrast, Lew made Osborne feel as though this mutual silence was a ribbon of warmth wrapped around simple companionship.

He felt so comfortable with her he made a mental note to consider offering to return the favor of taking him fly-fishing by giving her a few pointers in *his* area of angling expertise: musky fishing. A good musky fisherman doesn't invite just anyone into his boat. Stalking the huge trophy fish can take hours if not days of casting in near silence. Osborne had a very short list of men to whom he would extend that invitation. He had a hunch Lew was the only woman he knew who would appreciate the offer.

They made it to the Thunder Bay Bar a good half-hour before closing. Pickups, four-wheels, and a few flashy convertibles still filled the parking lot. Rock and roll blasted out the front door. Osborne shook his head as he looked at the neon bar signs in the windows. Thunder Bay was one Northwoods bar he had never entered. It was certainly the last place he had expected to find himself late this Sunday night.

"Don't worry, Doc," said Lew as they walked around the

truck towards the entrance. "Thunder Bay has been on my beat for years—they know me here."

Still, he felt edgy walking in. Thunder Bay might have the closest telephone, but that didn't change the fact that it was an infamous stripper joint, notorious for topless dancing, rumors of prostitution and excellent barbecue ribs—all of which made it a natural hang-out when "da boys" out of Milwaukee or Chicago decided to go north for a long weekend of fishing. On a hot summer night like tonight, counselors from the ritzy summer camps nearby and other young men without girlfriends or wives tended to drift this way if action was light at the more respectable taverns.

As the bar door swung shut behind him, Osborne wondered what his adult children would say when they heard he'd been seen in Thunder Bay, not to mention the razzing he'd get from the McDonald's coffee crowd. And they would hear, no doubt about that. He took a moment to survey the crowded room, left to right, for any familiar faces. Any former patients? None. At least so far.

"I'll call in from the pay phone," said Lew, "too loud around the bar. Would you get me a glass of water, please? I'm dying of thirst."

"Sure," said Osborne, though first on his list was the thought of dry clothing. Climbing out of the truck, the breeze chilled him.

He walked towards the busy bar, found an open spot and leaned over the counter. The young woman bartending looked frazzled. She didn't even glance up as she filled two glasses with water from the faucet over a sink full of dirty beer glasses. Osborne held his two up to the light to be sure they were clean. He'd seen too many cases of trench mouth over the years, the result of poorly washed bar glasses. These, he could see, were just fine.

"Doc!" Lew shouted at him from the pay phone next to the restrooms. He turned, glasses in hand. As he pushed his way through the crowd, he was keenly aware she was watching him as he walked towards her. He wondered how she felt about what she saw, sodden fishing clothes aside.

In this noisy barroom packed full of tanned, athletic young men in their twenties and thirties, did he stand out? Tall and lean, did he look younger than his sixty-three years? Distinguished with his black hair silvered at the temples, in spite of his bald spot? Handsome in his deep August tan, his skin still taut over the French-Irish cheekbones that carried a hint of his great-grandmother, the Ojibwa? He wondered and he hoped.

"I got Roger out of bed and he's arranging for an ambulance." Lew held her hand over the mouthpiece on the phone as she yelled over the music, then she raised the phone to listen again, a look of surprise crossing her face. Once more, she covered the mouthpiece. She shouted at Osborne, "Lucy Olson, my switchboard operator, had a call from Ray Pradt an hour ago—reporting you missing."

"*What?*" Incredulous, Osborne nearly dropped the glasses. "*Me? Missing?*"

Lew waved at him to be quiet while she listened again, then she smiled as she covered the mouthpiece. "It's okay, Lucy got him to back off. Seems he has an emergency of some sort, and he wanted us to help him locate you. You're to call him at home—no matter what time." Taking the water glasses from his hands, she handed the phone to Osborne, "Here—I had Lucy patch you through—he's on the line."

"Yeah, Ray?" Osborne grabbed the phone. "What on earth?"

"Doc—you seen my hat?"

Ohmygod, thought Osborne, nearly one in the morning, a likely murder victim in hand, and Ray's worried about his *hat*? Ray Pradt might be a good friend, an expert hunting and fishing guide, and a champion loon-caller but he could also be a major pain in the butt.

"No!" said Osborne emphatically, "No, I haven't seen your hat, Ray. It's August, you don't need a hat. What kind of foolishness is this?"

"Sorry, Doc, I'm real sorry, but I gotta find it tonight." Ray's concern was so intense that Osborne immediately regretted snapping at him. After all, Ray's hat was his signature garment: a large stuffed trout perched on top of an old, fur-lined leather cap with ear flaps that hung down loosely. The head and tail of the fish protruded on opposite sides over his ears. No one ever missed Ray when he walked through a door with that on his head.

"Okay, okay," Osborne backed off. "I'm sorry, Ray. It's just that it's late, I nearly drowned in the Prairie, and Chief Ferris and I have a dead body to deal with. I'm tired. But, no, I have not seen your hat. Why do you need it right now?"

"ESPN is coming tomorrow to shoot a promo for the Walleye Classic," said Ray. "I'm in charge of the boats, and I thought it would be a good idea to be the real me, y'know? I've looked everywhere, and I just can't find the darn thing. I thought maybe I left it at your place."

Osborne had an idea. Clearly, he wasn't going home yet himself. He had to help Lew get the body back to town. "Ray, I'm standing here at the Thunder Bay Bar soaking wet. But if you want to pick up some dry clothes for me, and give my place a quick once-over, you can check for your hat right now. If it's at my place, it'll be out on the front porch by your chair."

Even as he said it, Osborne was almost certain Ray's hat was there. The two men often shared a sunset cocktail, ginger-ale and ice, looking out over Loon Lake and commiserating over the day's wins and losses. Ray had a habit of carefully placing the prized hat on top of Osborne's leather-bound volume of Shakespeare. The one he inherited from his father and never read.

"Doc—I'll be there in twenty minutes. Thanks!"

But if Ray's gratitude was palpable over the telephone wire, Osborne's feelings towards his neighbor ran even deeper. Once upon a time, he had cursed the sight of the younger man in the trout hat. To his face, he had called him "a poacher and a lazy bum," but that was two long years ago.

Osborne had since learned Ray was many things. With his butt too often planted on a barstool, he was a talented raconteur who prided himself on knowing and embellishing the grim details of any local event—comedy or tragedy—for any crowd, whether it be the in-town Kiwanis wannabes or the bearded woodticks that hunkered in from the backwoods. Osborne had had to admit the man could tell a good story even if he did have the extremely annoying habit of stretching it out until his audience had to scream for the punch line.

Though he made his money as a hunting and fishing guide for wealthy tourists up from points south, Ray was so habitually short of cash that he often chopped wood, shot wildlife photos for local printers, and dug graves to make it through the long, fiercely cold northern Wisconsin winters. This career mix gave him access to excellent material for his barroom tales.

But Ray was not uneducated nor had he been raised in a wolf pack. His older sister was one of Chicago's top litigators, and his younger brother was a hand surgeon at the Mayo Clinic. No one knew why Ray chose a lifestyle one step above cave man, but to Osborne he seemed a happy man. He was an optimist. His arrival almost always brightened the day.

That did not mean, however, that Osborne did not still question some of his personal habits. Ray had launched their relationship by being the pain in the ass who bought a choice piece of lake-front property right next door to Osborne when an unexpected estate sale put it on the market while Osborne and his wife were at a dental convention in Milwaukee.

Osborne had arrived home to find a beat-up house trailer and an old blue pick-up with a door missing on the driver's side parked, not just illegally close to the lake, but in full view of Osborne's living room window. The view from this window had been a key architectural element, engineered at considerable expense during the building of Osborne's retirement haven. One shouting match later, Ray grudgingly backed up twenty-five feet.

A few months later, Osborne discovered that Ray had rigged his plumbing away from the city sewer system, which required fees for hook-up and annual use, to empty raw sewage just short of the property line and a little too close to Mary Lee Osborne's prized rose bushes. "Earth to earth" had been his smart-aleck excuse. Osborne couldn't lodge a legal complaint because he had a few violations of his own he didn't need checked out. Which Ray had known, of course.

Ray was not a stupid man. "The best goddamn huntin' fishin' guru north of Chicago" was how he introduced himself, and in Osborne's book he was right. He knew people, and he knew animals, and he knew how to horse trade. After the Osbornes got apoplectic over the poop in the rose garden, Ray made sure he had a tasty sling of fresh-cleaned blue gills hanging on their back porch every Sunday morning. That didn't appease Mary Lee, who crabbed at Ray every time he appeared on their property, but it satisfied the dentist.

And then there was the night that Mary Lee got sick. A blizzard was howling around the lake, the wind chill had dropped to 50 below zero and the blowing snow was four to five feet deep in drifts. Mary Lee woke at 3:00 A.M. with a bronchitis that had turned into pneumonia. Time was precious. Osborne called Ray for help. Within minutes, Ray had the plow on the front of his pickup and was pushing through the bitter blackness for a woman who'd ridiculed him. Mary Lee didn't make it, but Osborne was profoundly thankful anyway. No one could have gotten her to the hospital any faster than the two men did that night.

Mary Lee had been a hard woman to live with, and Osborne knew Ray understood that without the two men ever discussing her.

These days he was the one man Osborne was always happy to have in the boat. He could pull answers from places where few thought to go.

Osborne hung up the pay phone and turned towards the bar where Lew sat gulping her glass of water. Clammy in his wet clothes, he envied her: she looked quite dry and comfortable. Her ample khaki-clad hips spread with authority over the high bar chair. Above the open collar of her fishing shirt, her round face was relaxed, friendly, and, Osborne noticed as he took the bar stool beside her, surprisingly weathered. Did she fish year round?

"I have to wait for Roger to get here with the ambulance," she said, pushing the other glass of water his way, "shouldn't take more than a few minutes."

As he seated himself beside her, Osborne wondered if her job ever got really dangerous. He couldn't imagine crime in the northwoods beyond off-trail snowmobiling and drunken drivers. And, of course, the random body in the Prairie River.

She was the mother of three grown children who had gone through school with his own, and he had been as taken aback as anyone when the *Loon Lake News* announced her appointment to the force, the first woman police officer in the history of Loon Lake. He and his buddies at McDonald's had chewed on that for days. Mary Lee and her friends, who had never given a thought to full-time employment, were sure she had made a mistake giving up her "proper job" as a secretary at the paper mill. No one ever expected Lewellyn Ferris to be promoted to Chief.

Yet here she was a short seven years later. But then, Lew had always been a little different.

She was built like a linebacker. And walked like one, too. Well, maybe that was putting it a little harshly. She had broad shoulders, and she walked standing tall, shoulders back, tummy in, arms loose. She walked like an athlete. Osborne had to admit he found Lew Ferris more than a little intimidating. He could see why secretarial work didn't appeal to her.

The dancers must have been on break when Lew and Osborne first walked in because suddenly music started up again in a room off to the back of the bar. The crowd around the bar cleared, and most of the men drifted back to tables. From the corner of his eye, Osborne could see the small stage. Uneasy over what might happen next, he hoped Lew's deputy, Roger, would rescue them soon.

"So, Doc, how come Ray Pradt keeps such close tabs on you?" Lew lowered her voice. With the jukebox turned off and the music coming from the next room, they no longer had to shout to be heard.

"He's my neighbor . . ."

"Ray Pradt is your neighbor?" she interrupted. "You gotta be kidding. I thought that guy lived in a shack—in the woods—with the rest of the wildlife."

"No-o," said Osborne, smiling gently. "Ray's a good friend. He bought the lot next to mine three years ago. Out on Loon Lake. I take it you know him?"

"Of course I know Ray," she said, "better than I'd like to—may I say." She raised her glass and gave him one of those looks. Ray did not appear to be one of her favorite people.

Osborne could think of a dozen reasons why. He knew that over the years Ray had had more than his share of run-ins with local authorities. But the expression on Lew's face made Osborne worry he had done the wrong thing, asking Ray to bring him dry clothing. Quickly, he explained his friend's concern over his hat.

"He was so upset, he didn't even notice when I said that I was out here or that we found a body in the river," said Osborne. "Now that's not Ray. Under normal circumstances, he doesn't miss a detail. Know what I mean? And he knows darn well, I never come near this place. Something's going on . . ."

"It's TV," said Lew. "He's a nervous wreck over appearing on ESPN." She gave a big grin. "I would be, too. As far as Thunder Bay goes, he stops by almost every day, right around four in the afternoon. I'll bet it never occurs to that guy that respectable people don't like to come here."

"I don't know about that," said Osborne, feeling a surge of loyalty to his friend, "he's got a good business reason for stopping by. And he doesn't drink when he's here. He's recovering, too, y'know."

"Not from everything," she snapped.

Then Lew softened her tone, "I know, Doc. I'm just giving you a hard time. But the man can be a trial, y'know? He doesn't always make my job easy."

Osborne had a good idea of what she meant. He also thought it might be a good idea to drop the subject. God forbid she should think that he participated in any of Ray's legally marginal activities.

They were both right about Ray and Thunder Bay. It was a terrific place for him to pick up a guiding job when he needed it. All it took was a couple hours around the bar telling war stories. Then, four, five rounds of draft Michelobs later, and he could set his fee triple to quadruple what he'd charge the locals. Osborne knew this because Ray never hesitated to brag of his unique marketing technique to his prosperous neighbor. He'd had weekends he'd cleared over a thousand bucks in tips from "da boys from da cities" he'd met up there.

Aware that a dancer had jumped onto the stage in the darkened room off to his left, Osborne checked his watch. Just how long would it take that deputy to get out here? Meanwhile, as if oblivious to the activity in the other room, Lew asked for a refill of her water.

"How's that bridge I made for you?" asked Osborne, thankful for a noncontroversial topic of mutual interest.

"Fine, Doc." With that Lew reached into her mouth and whipped out the small piece of plastic, metal, and teeth. "See? Not a bent wire, nothing broken. You did good work, and that office hasn't been the same since you retired." She stuck it back in her mouth and smiled easily enough. It seemed she wasn't too annoyed with him over fact Ray Pradt was heading their way.

Osborne looked past her right shoulder. He could see several clusters of men sitting at tables near the stage. A few were paying attention to the young woman who had strolled out and was moving lazily to the dance music. As best Osborne could tell in the dim light, she was wearing a one-piece swimsuit.

He continued to watch the dancer from the corner of his eye. She seemed to have a friendly banter going on with the men at one of the tables and was casually pulling down the top of her swimsuit to reveal a set of pasties on her abundant breasts. Osborne answered a polite question from Lew, becoming more anxious by the moment, just sure that someone he knew would walk in.

"Isn't this stuff," he jerked his head toward the dancer, "against the law?"

Lew looked back and studied the woman who was now down to a G-string and bare-breasted, bobbing and weaving in front of a table of men. "So long as they don't violate Code 2116B, they're fine," she said matter-of-factly. "We haven't had any problems up here in, oh, six months or so. Tourist season is nearly over, and they don't want to risk getting shut down during peak season. Now, if this was late January and some of the Chicago snowmobile boys were laying down some big bucks, it might get pretty raunchy. That's when we step in."

Osborne watched the woman open her legs and semi-straddle one of the customers, her breasts deliberately sweeping his face. "That's not raunchy?"

Again Lew studied the action. "A little raunchy but that's table-dancing. She's wearing her G-string." Lew turned away, but Osborne watched for another few beats of the music.

"What would you say if one of *your* daughters did that?" asked Osborne, looking for a chatty way to fill the time and relieve his anxiety. He didn't really care if young women he didn't know danced naked or not.

Lew let his question hang in the air for a few seconds. She set her glass of water down on the counter quite precisely and crossed her arms. "One did, Doc. Suzanne."

"Oh." Osborne felt a slow flush move from his neck, up past his ears to his cheeks. *Now, why on earth did you have to say that, you dumkof!* he cursed himself silently.

"That's okay," said Lew, spotting his embarrassment and reaching over to give his hand with a friendly, forgiving tap. She had a brisk way about her, and it was clear she was ready to resolve this little issue and put it behind them as quick as possible. She slipped a small napkin under her water glass and leaned forward, her arms folded on the bar.

"Yep, Suzanne had a rough streak for a while there." Her tone was very chatty. Apparently, she didn't mind talking about it, which made Osborne feel a little better. "I don't know if you remember, but she married one of those Walker boys right out of high school, had twins four months later, a divorce six months after that and no money. Nineteen years old, no money, two kids, no future, right?"

Osborne nodded. "Those Walker boys" were three wiry little toughs who'd terrorized high school shop teachers, brandishing hammers when informed they weren't allowed to work on their cars during class time, and grew up to be weekly regulars in bar brawls. They were the kind of guys for whom he did full-mouth bridge work, including removing seriously decayed teeth and all paid for by welfare, only to have them die in drunk driving accidents—or brawls—a few months later. All that good dentistry right down the drain. Marriage to one of those jerks was worse than no future.

"The mill offered her a job, but she couldn't make enough to cover day care. Then, she heard what the Thunder Bay girls were making and ended up getting an offer she couldn't refuse. She worked the six to eleven shift, I watched the kids, and the money she made she saved. And she made *good* money. But she was a dancer, she was *only* a dancer," Lew said pointedly.

She lowered her voice, "I know people think the women who dance here are all hookers, but if they are, it's strictly on their own. The management does not allow it on the premises. That's what keeps Thunder Bay from becoming a real dive. The minute you let that other stuff happen, you've got problems with the mob, with law enforcement, with hysterical wives. You get an element you can't control. I've been doing this job for seven years now. *I* know what goes on.

"Suzanne worked here about a year, and the money made it possible for her get out of town and back to school. She met a nice guy down in Milwaukee, and she's married and doing just great now. She's a CPA—makes fifty-two thousand a year." Lew beamed.

Then she paused, took a slow sip from her can, and chuckled. "You never know, you know. Suzanne was my little one who played the Madonna in the Christmas play in third grade."

"I remember," said Osborne—and he sure did. "She got the part instead of my daughter Mallory—we certainly had the weeping and gnashing of teeth in our house over that. But Suzanne did a very nice job." Truth was, he knew Mallory never did understand how she'd lost out to Suzanne. Nor did her mother.

Osborne took a big gulp of his water. Life was so strange,

he thought, here was a woman whose daughter got off to rotten start but seems to have put together a decent life. Meanwhile, his Mallory, who didn't get to play the Virgin Mary, got everything else. The expensive degree from Radcliffe, the big wedding to the investment banker and the estate in Lake Forest. Mallory. The one who slurs her words on the rare occasion that she calls, and Osborne knows it isn't a problem with the phone line.

Lew had looked over at him and said, "We do the best we can as parents and then just hope for the rest, you know?"

Just as he opened his mouth to comment, Lew suddenly signalled with her fingers to be quiet. Turning quickly to his right, Osborne discovered why. One of his least favorite people in all of Loon Lake had advanced on them with the demented zeal of the dead drunk.

five

George Zolonsky of Sugar Camp was voted annually, by the McDonald's coffee crowd, most likely to die with the greatest number of DWI's to his name. Somehow, he stayed alive in spite of his allegiance to Wisconsin's leading export: beer. George was also a very bright man, an excellent deer hunter, and a talented ceramic tile layer. That's how Osborne first met him.

Mary Lee had thumbed women's magazines for years in preparation for the house they built on Loon Lake. For the kitchen and both bathrooms, she had insisted on ceramic tile. Only one man could do the job, and that was George. It was, however, a job that took months longer than estimated as George maintained an erratic schedule determined entirely by his drinking regimen.

When he was on the job, he was superb. He altered her kitchen design scheme to develop a truly stunning pattern of black and white tiles, which was showcased in the Milwaukee Journal newspaper. The publicity thrilled Mary Lee and lent her a status among her friends that no one could eclipse.

Osborne had noticed something interesting about George as he worked: not unlike dentistry, the expert tile layer worked with adhesives and tools demanding precision in time and movement, as well as the same delicate touch and brute strength required for work on the human jaw. Osborne had admired the quickness of the man's hands and his attitude of perfection. Once, a pattern had gone awry, only to be discovered after the grout had set like iron. Osborne had given George some of his old dental instruments to pry the tiny offending tiles from their wrongful spots.

For a short time, George had joined both Ray and Osborne and several of their peers in the room behind the door with the coffeepot. But George didn't really want to stay on the wagon and his stint with AA lasted only a few weeks. That was nearly two years ago. Osborne hadn't seen him in months.

"Hey, Doc, howthehellareyah!" hooted George, swaying at the bar with a beer bottle in his hand. A cigarette drooped out of one corner of his mouth, and he wore his Levi's just a touch too low over his bow legs. A young woman in tight Levi cutoff's and a tank top leaned against his right side, which Osborne figured was all that was keeping him upright.

The tragedy of George was that besides being talented, he was a fine-looking man. Lanky, cowboy-like in his style, he had prominent cheekbones under slightly bulbous eyes and straight sandy hair that gave him a rugged outdoors appeal. But he had his demons, and tonight Osborne did not want to hear about them.

Nor did Lew from the look she gave Osborne. Still, they were stuck waiting for Roger. Her eyes said she'd put up with George if he would. Osborne resigned himself.

"Fine, George, how's business."

"Pretty damn good! Got a new one goin.' " The whole bar could hear him.

"Really. What's that?" Years in the Northwoods had trained Osborne in dealing with his fellow man, drunk or sober, in ways that afforded all parties some semblance of dignity.

"Transport-sh."

"No kidding. Trucking, huh?"

"Yep. Got the contract shipping new boats outta the Milwaukee port. They bring 'em in on the boat from the Orient or wherever, and I truck 'em up here. Good money, Doc."

"Glad to hear it, George."

"George?" The young woman standing beside George cracked her gum loudly and wailed, "Ya gotta take me home now, George. Look, the bar is closing." She was right, the bartender was flicking lights to signal closing time.

"That's jus 'cause Miz Ferris Chief of Police is here," drawled George sloppily.

"That may be, George," said Lew firmly. "And I'd like to see your friend driving tonight, not you." George stood weaving in front of Lew, his eyes challenging.

"I'm not asking you, George. I'm telling you," said Lew. Her eyes drilled right back at him. Osborne watched the two of them. He knew better than to intervene. This was Lew's job and none of his business. Suddenly, as if something else had crossed his mind, George looked away from Lew.

"Screw it," he reached into his pocket for his keys and tossed them at the girl. They started to exit, just as Ray Pradt's six foot six frame appeared in the entrance.

"Hey, you!" he said to George, who kept on going out the door without acknowleging Ray's presence, even though he had to bump him slightly as he swayed past. "Where are my boats? You're two weeks late. George—?"

"Let him go, Ray," said Lew from the bar. "He's worthless tonight."

Ray had stopped to watch George go by. He looked at Lew and Osborne and the rest of the crowd at the bar, "Now doesn't that guy remind you of a mosquito?" he asked the group. "Bug-eyed and re-e-al annoying." He looked back at the door George had just exited and shook his head. Ray had a habit of making up his own jokes. Most were duds, he scored on occasion, and this time, in Osborne's opinion, he did okay. At least no one booed.

Osborne could tell that Ray was upset. Usually, he spotted his neighbor's belt buckle first. Thirty-six years of being close to the tallest person in Oneida County had taken its toll on six foot six Ray Pradt: he walked a loopy walk with his shoulders slightly drooped and his pelvis thrust so far foward that Osborne once told him his lower torso rolled into a room a full hour ahead of the rest of his body. "That, my friend, makes your hat—pride and joy though it may be—anticlimactic," the good dentist had said.

Not tonight, he was tense. He strode quickly to the bar and thrust the dry shirt and pants at Osborne.

"What a wise act," he said with disgust, again glancing back at the door that had swung closed after George. "I found out yesterday these boats we've been waiting on for the Walleye

Classic are being trucked up here by that goombah. Whaddya say we'll be lucky if they make it?"

Lew's dark eyes leveled with Ray's. "You better stay on top of that guy, Ray. He's got more action than he can handle these days. I had to book another husband overnight two weeks ago. I got a call he was out looking for George with a 30.06 in his front seat. Loaded. Poor guy. That was one night I had the wrong man in the cell." She shook her head.

"Word is," said Ray, "ol' George has something going with the wife of the chef at the Rainbow Inn."

"Something like that," said Lew, careful not to say too much. "Too bad, too. They've turned that place into a nice restaurant, and they've got three little kids."

"Are you serious? He's still at it?" Osborne leaned forward in his chair. George was a legend when it came to women. Ten years earlier, he had run off with the wife of a dentist Osborne knew in Rhinelander. That escapade was followed by stories of two or three more women. "I don't see what women find attractive in that guy," said Osborne. He looked at Lew, "Do you?"

"Oh, yes," she said. "I know exactly what they see in him. Unfortunately, they don't see past that until it is way too late."

"You'd think he'd grow out of it," said Osborne.

Lew gave him a curious look. She shook her head and glanced at Ray.

Osborne wasn't sure what she was thinking, but he thought she was trying hard not to laugh. He had a hunch, but he wasn't sure. He looked at Ray, who winked at him. Big help Ray was.

"Did you find your hat?"

"Right where you said, Doc."

The bartender walked up then, and Osborne noticed that the bar had emptied. "Chief Ferris," she said, "I need to close up."

"Sure," said Lew. "We'll wait outside. Darn that Roger, it's getting late!"

"I'll change quickly in the men's room," said Osborne and hurried off.

When he returned, he could tell from the look on Ray's face that Lew had shared the news of their catch in the Prairie River.

"Jeez, Doc," said Ray, shaking his head, "got your limit this time, huh?"

"Excuse me," said Lew, "I'm going to call in and see what the story is—this is getting ridiculous. I'll meet you out in the parking lot."

Ray watched Lew hurry over to the pay phone. "So, friend," he looked at Osborne, "you didn't tell me you were going fishing with the old chief here."

"You didn't ask." In the mirror behind the bar, Osborne caught a glimpse of the smug look on his face. As he turned towards the door, he relented, "I didn't know I was fishing with Lew Ferris until I got there tonight. Surprised the heck out of me, I'll tell ya."

" 'Lew,' huh? That's pretty cozy, Doc." As the two of them approached the door, Ray reached to hold it open for Osborne. "You've got some explaining to do, bud."

"Ralph Kendall set us up. He didn't tell me who, just said it was a good friend of his. I thought I was going out with some fly-fishing guide." The night air was still heavy with moisture from the storm.

"Ralph!" A funny look crossed Ray's face just as Lew came through the door behind them.

Now what's that all about? wondered Osborne. He was reluctant to say any more in front of Lew.

"Lucy said Roger's on his way. Should be here any second."

The three of them walked out into the parking lot. Ray's fishing truck was pulled up next to Lew's. As they neared their cars, Roger pulled his Honda Civic into the lot.

"Sorry, Chief," Lew's deputy rolled his window down. "They ran the ambulance over to Tomahawk. Head-on collision on Highway 51. I got some tarps here so we can put it in the trunk, maybe?"

They all looked at Roger and his little car. The very thought was appalling.

"Chief, I just cleaned up my truck for the TV crew tomorrow," said Ray. "It's real clean, and a little blood and guts won't hurt it anyway. Do you want to use it?"

"Well . . . I guess that's better than trying to cram the poor soul into my Mazda, which is full of fishing gear. Okay, let's do it. Roger, you go home. Ray and Dr. Osborne can help me finish up."

"So, Chief Ferris," Ray looked out over the rushing river as they trudged back down the trail together, "did you have any luck?"

"Gee, I almost forgot," said Lew. "Yes, I did. I had a good night. I got four brookies. About twelve to fourteen inches each one. Released 'em all."

"Are you always 'catch and release'?" asked Ray.

"These streams have been so overfished, I have to," said Lew. "I feel guilty if I don't."

"Too bad," said Ray, "I love the smell of brookies in butter—y'know? With a light dusting of fresh-ground pepper. Umm."

Lew ignored him. Osborne appreciated the fact she wasn't a "catch-and-release" fanatic like some of fly fishermen he knew. One of those guys would've done a Rumpelstilskin dance at Ray's comment.

"Ray, think I've got a chance of finding any tracks after all this rain we had tonight?" asked Lew.

"I dunno, Lew," said Ray. "If you mean tracks in the grass along the banks here, that'll be real tough. You won't tomorrow morning I can guarantee you that. Not in the grass anyway. Probably too late already."

"Damn," said Lew. "I'm roping off 500 feet each direction from where we found the body. I was hoping for some signs of a fight or—"

"You gotta problem, Chief. I'll bet you and Doc walked this way less than an hour ago, right?"

"We did."

"But there's so much moisture in the soil tonight. Doncha know it's rained off and on all week, so any grass you two tromped on has sucked it right up and, pop, is right back in place like only your ghost blew through," said Ray. "I can look for broken branches, but this brush is so dense most folks enter the river at a clearing. Sorry, Chief. I'll take a look for you, but don't count on anything.

"How far are we from the body?" he asked.

"Five minutes."

"Okay. I'll run on ahead and see what I can see. It's getting late, y'know, I need to look good tomorrow."

That said, Ray's lanky frame disappeared into the blackness of pine and aspen running along the river bank. He was shaking his head in disappointment when they met up with him at the clearing. "Nothing a deer didn't do," he said. "On the other hand, this area is pretty damn popular. I'll bet if you didn't have all the rain, you'd have found plenty of tracks right here."

"Including our own," said Lew drily, accepting Ray's answer. Osborne knew, despite other opinions she might hold of Ray, Lew had to agree with one voiced by a member of the McDonald's coffee crowd in Ray's absence: "That asshole can track a snake over a rock."

But if Osborne thought the clearing by the river looked startlingly different in the moonlight, to Ray it was quite familiar.

"You found the body here?" Ray asked, raising his voice so they could hear him against the relentless roar of the Prairie.

"Under that log," hollered Lew, pointing. The three of them walked down to the water's edge to look in the direction she indicated. Black water capped with pale froth rushed towards a bend in the river where it poured down between two hillocks that couldn't be more than five feet apart.

"A log? Did it feel real smooth with horizontal striations?" asked Ray.

"Yeah," said Lew, "runs right across the opening at the bend—right there."

"That's no log, Chief," said Ray. "That's a rock with a "keeper," a hole that's formed in the rock where the river flows over and reverses itself." He gestured with a swoop of his hands. "Maybe the smoothness made you think it was a log, but I know that rock real well. Too well.

"Can you keep a secret?" Ray shouted, peering at Osborne and Lew. His eyes were twinkling in the moonlight, his left hand pulling thoughtfully at his beard. Osborne recognized all the signs that Ray was about to launch one of his long-winded tales of bad behavior in the North Woods.

"Ray—" The exasperation in Lew's voice made it quite clear she wasn't in the mood for a twenty-minute discourse.

"C'mon, Ray," scolded Osborne. "You're the one needs a beauty sleep."

"All right, all right," Ray raised his hands in surrender. "Rock, hole, whatever. We used to call this spot 'Bill's Place,' after my old buddy Bill Barstow. Remember Billy, Doc?"

"Sure do." Bill Barstow and Ray had been terrors in their late teens, good-hearted youngsters but a little too familiar with the marijuana dealers out of Madison. Ray had managed to stay just an inch on the right side of the Loon Lake cops, possibly due to his generosity with strings of blue gills in the

dead of winter, but Billy ended up doing time. These days he
ran a used furniture store that was a front for an illegal pawn-
shop. Osborne's McDonald's buddies defined Billy as a good
guy with a twisted sense of business ethics. His father had
been an orthodontist and a partner in Osborne's hunting shack.

"Well ol' Bill used that hole for his stash," said Ray. "Then
one day he found a six-pack of Bud in there and realized some
high school kids knew about it, too."

"You think a lot of people know about it?" asked Lew.

"Hard to say, but if anyone does, it'll be a local, that's for
sure."

Lew turned back towards the clearing. A bright half-moon
lit the final few yards and seemed to cast a halo over the
woman's body, which lay undisturbed just as they had left it.

"Who is this?" asked Ray as he knelt with Osborne to lay
the tarp alongside the victim, his voice gentle with concern.

"Do you remember Meredith Marshall?" asked Osborne.
Together they rolled the body onto the tarp, then folded the
rubber sheets over and back until they had a neat sling.

"Oh, sure—about three years ahead of me," said Ray. "She
had a sister who was quite a bit older, didn't she?"

"Alicia Roderick," said Osborne.

"Oh yeah? The dachshund's wife," said Ray.

"The who what?" Lew gave Ray a quizzical look.

"You know that really rich guy with the Range Rover who
sells lighting fixtures—he looks like a dachshund. That's Peter
Roderick, Alicia's husband," said Ray, "Once a year I take
him up to Canada for walleyes. Now there's a guy travels a
lot—every week almost."

"I wonder if he's home tonight. I'm afraid I need to wake
up his wife," said Lew.

"Alicia was a good friend of my late wife's," said Osborne.
"Would you like me to come along?" he asked, feeling more
presentable in his dry clothes.

"I wouldn't mind," said Lew. Then a look crossed her face
as if she was about to get bad news. "Doctor Osborne . . .,"
she hesitated, tightening her lips, "I have a problem. In order
for that dental exam to be official, which I need it to be . . .
Well, Jack Pecore is on vacation all week," she referred to the
Loon Lake coroner whom Osborne knew and despised, "and
to make this official I need to deputize you right now. In fact,

"Fine," said Osborne.

"Really?" Lew stopped short in surprise. "But I might have to keep you on for a week if that's okay. With Pecore gone, I'm stretched to the limit over this Labor Day weekend. If the autopsy confirms criminal activity, I'm going to need extra help. You know the family and you have all that military experience . . ."

"Whatever I can do, just let me know," said Osborne. "My schedule is wide open." Not to mention his life. The thought of being a professional again, of working around a woman as interesting as Lew, had a sudden, intriguing appeal.

"The department will pay you for your time."

"Don't worry about it." Osborne had an idea. "We'll barter. You give me some more pointers on my fly-fishing, and I'll help you out with whatever you need over the next few days."

"You've got a deal," said Lew, extending her hand to grasp his in a firm shake.

"Just don't ask me," Ray raised his hands, "I'm up to my ears with the Walleye Classic—"

"Not a chance, Ray," laughed Lew. "Not with your record. I don't mind your untimely toking, fella, so much as your total lack of remorse. I'll tell ya, Ray, you're the kinda guy," she shook a finger at him good-naturedly, "I never know what you're gonna do next."

Ray shrugged. Some things he just couldn't help. He wouldn't be Ray if he could.

Lew eased up, "But I'm impressed you're chairing the Walleye Classic, huh? That's a big job!"

Ray cut his eyes in a "ya gotta be kiddin' " look. "Me? Heck, no," he said. "That's *work*. I'm just in charge of the boats for the pros."

And his image, noted Osborne with amusement. For the first time in years, Ray had been to the barber. His distinctive head of rich, reddish-auburn curly hair and chest-length, very curly auburn but greying beard had been stylishly trimmed.

Lew noticed, too. "What's with the class act, Ray? Something wrong? Death in the family?"

"Jeez, Chief, didn't Doc tell you? We've got ESPN coming in, we've got a hundred thousand dollar purse—lots of excitement." Then he rolled his eyes in an expression of total frustration, "but now that damn George Zolonsky is late delivering our boats!"

six

It was two o'clock in the morning when Osborne and Lew climbed into the police cruiser to drive the short mile from the hospital and its tidy six-body morgue to the Roderick home. They had been lucky to find space for their victim. The Highway 51 accident had been bad: four dead.

They left Meredith in a drawer, her naked body resting on cold steel. Osborne had found it mystifying that her torso and extremities were nearly free of contusions. Even at that, the few random bruises he did find on her arms and legs appeared to be days older than the massive skull fracture that may have killed her.

"In my opinion," Osborne had said, leaning over Meredith to study a mark just below her right knee, "these bruises on the arms and legs are perfectly normal, Lew. Like the ones we all get from everyday banging around." He looked up to emphasize his point. Lew leaned against the wall in the brightly lit examining room, her arms crossed, her dark eyes intent on watching Osborne work.

He wasn't having an easy time of it. Meredith's body was that of a young woman in her prime, a woman who had been physically active, who ate a healthy diet, a woman who kept herself prepared for life, not death. A woman like his own daughters. It must have registered on his face as he withdrew the Shepherd's hook explorer from the victim's mouth.

"Are you bothered by the body?" asked Lew softly.

"Is it that obvious?" said Osborne, peering at her over the rims of his glasses. "I can't help thinking this could be one of my own daughters." Osborne sighed as he lay his instruments on the nearby metal tray and started to remove his gloves. "Do you ever feel this way?"

"Hah!" Lew pushed herself away from the wall. "More than you can imagine. I bailed that son of mine out so often, I tried so hard to tell him what he was doing to his life—when I see that same arrogant look on the faces of some of these young kids . . ."

"Really?" said Osborne. He struggled to remember what he knew about her son. "Amazing they survive, isn't it? What's he doing today?"

"Pushing up flowers in St. Mary's cemetery," said Lew with a tight little grin. "He was knifed in a bar fight, Doc. Bobby Fallon went up the river for that one. That's the first I met your friend Ray—he dug Jamie's grave."

"Oh," Osborne gave himself an internal kick in the shins. How did he always manage to make such terrible faux pas around this woman? Why did he always forget she hadn't lived the same Loon Lake life he did? Why did he have to sound like such a middle-class jabone? He changed the subject as fast as he could.

"The only good news is the fillings were definitely yanked out after death. That I can tell from the angle of the scratches on the enamel and bruising on the interior of the mouth. She had to be unconscious or dead for someone to manage this. They might have used a drill, but I can't be sure. But I will say, whoever it was took great care to get every iota of gold."

"Just a fomality, Doc," said Lew, "but would you say for certain that this was not an accidental death? Strictly on the basis of the missing fillings?"

"No. Not just that. I'm convinced this body did not travel far down the Prairie. That current is vicious. Throw in all the loose timber and branches and other debris pounding through there from the storm . . . ," his eyes scanned Meredith's form one more time, ". . . the *entire* body should show serious contusions, not just the neck and the back of the head."

Silent and thoughtful, they had both stood staring down at the naked dead woman. Lew looked up at Osborne as if to see if he would change his mind. He would not. "Foul play, kiddo."

"Good," said Lew. "The Wausau boys may argue but this is one autopsy I'll log on their budget."

That said, she had marked the drawer holding the body, indicating it was to be sent to the forensic investigators in Wausau for an autopsy immediately following an ID from the family.

"Let's stop by Pecore's desk," she said before they left the building, "I'll leave two notes. I don't need that dimwit sending our Mrs. Marshall over to Johnson's for embalming with the accident victims or have his dogs destroy any evidence. You and I both know he's entirely capable of screwing this up. Pecore is one big reason I would love to have you on board to help me out, Doc."

The local coroner was not exactly respected in the town. A pathologist of questionable skill, he had irritated the townspeople when they discovered he let his two golden retrievers roam unrestricted in his lab. Truth was the dogs probably minded their own business but Loon Lake residents were appalled. Since every death in the community had to be run by Pecore, many families had taken to accompanying the bodies of loved ones through the entire process just to be sure the canines didn't lick Grandma.

Now the cruiser moved silently down a side street, turned right to pass the baseball park, then left onto Ojibway Drive. Osborne cracked his window for air. He stared out at the sleeping town. The storm had blown through Loon Lake around midnight, leaving a trail of broken tree limbs, some heavy with leaves, strewn across the street and yards. Loon Lake was used to violent weather. By mid-morning the evidence of howling winds would be gone.

"Quiet out there," he said softly, "I don't even hear an owl hooting."

"Yep," said Lew. He could tell she was thinking about something else. Probably how to break the news to the Rodericks.

They passed the modest frame houses that lined the streets close to the hospital, their windows dark. The night was moonless, the only illumination the soft pools thrown by street lamps. As they neared the Rodericks', the houses grew taller, the front yards deeper, wider and landscaped. This was the east side of Loon Lake, the prestigious side by Mary Lee's standards. Here lived the doctors, the lawyers, and the paper mill executives.

Osborne pointed off to their right, and Lew slowed to turn. An imposing stone manor anchored the corner of one of the town's oldest and loveliest neighborhoods.

"That's it," said Osborne. "See Peter's Range Rover in the drive?"

"I'll turn around at the school and park in front," said Lew.

Directly across from the Roderick home was Loon Lake's original elementary school, a two-story red brick building erected in 1910. The Rodericks' front door faced a quiet street, bounded on the far side by a tall, dense hedge of lilacs that guarded the schoolyard, nearly blocking the building and its grounds from view.

"Just look at those lilacs," Osborne said in a low voice, making small talk to keep his mind off the pending confrontation, "they must be eighty years old, Lew. What a sight they are in the springtime."

"Umm," Lew agreed. Everyone in Loon Lake agreed. The Carlton School lilacs were the pride of the entire town.

"I think this is the biggest house in Loon Lake," said Lew as she swung the cruiser around, pulled up to the curb, and turned off the ignition. "They must have a hell of a heating bill in January." She had her way of stalling, too.

"The old Martin house around the corner may be larger," said Osborne. "I know this was originally built by old man Daniels in 1891."

"I thought he died in the twenties," said Lew. Everyone in Loon Lake knew about the man who founded the paper mill, the life blood of the little town for fifty years.

"Yes, you're right. But his widow's family kept it for a long time. I think she died here. Peter told me the kids would come up from Alabama for the summer, close the place down for the winter. One day he and Alicia rang the doorbell and made them an offer. That was right after their marriage, a few years before Mary Lee and I met them."

"When I was a kid I always thought the people who lived in houses like this had perfect lives," said Lew.

"Umm," said Osborne.

Lew reached into the back seat for her briefcase, "well . . . ready?"

"Not really."

They looked at one another, then out at the dark windows of the manor. On the second level, four bedroom windows running along the front of the house appeared to be half open to catch any breezes. At ground level, a series of tall French casement windows, which Osborne knew opened into the front hall and the dining room, had been cranked open, too. But the moon, still hidden behind clouds, did not help illuminate any more details. Not even the corner street lamp with its hazy glow made a difference.

As they braced themselves to enter the stately home, the night air grew warmer, heavier. Osborne rolled his window down all the way. He reached for the door handle, then paused.

"Listen . . . ," he said. "I hear music . . ."

"Odd this time of night," said Lew, rolling down her window. "I do, too. Tony Bennett. 'I Left My Heart In San Francisco.' Is it coming from the Rodericks'?"

"I can't tell," Osborne strained to listen.

Lew cleared her throat gently. "Doc, you know Alicia, right?"

"She was a close friend of my wife's," said Osborne. "I know her husband better."

"Would you mind telling them?"

"Well . . . okay." Osborne didn't move. He felt his shoulders slump slightly.

"Doc . . . if you don't want to . . ."

"No, no, that's all right." Osborne still didn't move, ". . . Jeez, y'know, Lew, I just remembered something. This won't be the first time they've gotten news like this. Their only child, their son, committed suicide."

"Oh . . . ," said Lew. "Recently?"

"A good ten years ago. He had just finished med school and started his internship. It was a real shock. Mary Lee came over that day to help out . . . ," Osborne shook his head, "I forgot all about that until just now."

"I assume you weren't the one to deliver *that* news . . ."

"No, fortunately . . ." Osborne sighed and braced himself. "All right, Lew, I'm ready." He stepped into the night, closing the car door behind him. The faint strain of music could no longer be heard. A flagstone walkway led up to an imposing front door.

"Remind me to tell you about this door later," muttered Osborne as he reached to press the doorbell.

A massive slab of dark wood, it was adorned with a single square of leaded glass into which was etched a delicate design of a fairy princess. The door had been shipped from England right after Peter and Alicia moved in, a non-negotiable "surprise" purchase that Alicia had made in spite of her husband's horror at the price. The door and Peter's inability to reverse his wife's decision had been the talk of Loon Lake husbands for years.

Osborne pressed the doorbell and listened to the chimes pealing in the distance. Though at least three years had passed since he'd been to this house, the musical notes instantly reminded him of the time, nearly thirty years ago, when he first met Alicia. He met Peter then, too, but it was Alicia who left the indelible first impression.

Their lives had first intersected at a dinner party hosted by the couple about two years after the Osbornes had moved to Loon Lake. For Osborne's wife, the invitation to that dinner party had been like winning the lottery. It meant she'd been chosen.

Alicia and Mary Lee were introduced at a bridge club luncheon, when Mary Lee was asked to substitute for a regular. While Mary Lee recognized immediately that Alicia was a woman she dearly wanted as a friend, Alicia was more guarded.

She let outsiders into her circle slowly, carefully. Only those women whose husbands had a certain kind of professional status, only those women who clearly demonstrated that they had taste and the means to afford it, were chosen by Alicia. Osborne had found it curious to discover that Mary Lee admired this kind of discretion. It was something he hadn't expected in his wife. But she found Alicia classy and sophisticated. She described her once to Osborne as " 'old' Loon Lake, you know," as if a community founded in 1885 and boasting a total population of 2657 could pretend to an aristocracy.

One day, Alicia chose to elect Mary Lee as a regular in the Wednesday bridge group. This meant excluding someone else, so it was an occasion of note among young Loon Lake matrons. Then, months later, came the golden dinner invitation. From that time on, the two women were the best of friends. Only much later, years later, did Osborne understand why.

In the early days of their marriage and their life in Loon Lake, he was too busy building his dental practice and developing his own network of hunting and fishing buddies to pay much attention to the woman Mary Lee was becoming. So it wasn't until a number of years into their life together that he became aware of traits his wife shared with her friend that he really didn't like.

The first was an insatiable drive to acquire. They devoured the women's magazines, constantly lobbying their husbands for the latest in everything from wallpaper to curio cabinets to six-burner stoves. The friendship between Osborne and Peter initially grew out of their mutual frustration with the many ways their wives could find to spend hard-earned dollars and the women's ability to make their husbands feel bad for not being able to afford it all.

The second trait was an equally intense need for their children to be the first and the best in everything. Fortunately, Alicia's only child was male and one year older than his elder daughter, Mallory, so the two never competed. Osborne did not even want to consider the consequences if they had. As it was, he had often felt left out and not a little resentful of the attention showered on his firstborn.

But he knew none of this thirty years ago. Instead, that first dinner party was great fun. Osborne was more than a little bowled over by Alicia. He found her lovely to look at, smoothly charming and, at times, a wonderfully witty woman. She had a magnetism that took over the room. And when she wanted, she could make you feel like you were just as fascinating. Alicia was the first and only woman Osborne ever had a crush on during his marriage, news he was wise enough not to share with Mary Lee. Over time, he learned that he wasn't the only man in Loon Lake to fall under Alicia's spell.

Peter seemed content to play back-up, to provide the stage setting for his vivacious wife. Older than Alicia by thirteen years and quite well off financially, due to his success as a manufacturer's rep for an industrial lighting company out of Chicago, he adored and indulged her.

•   •   •

Osborne pressed the doorbell again. As they waited, he thought of Ray's description of Peter Roderick earlier. The man was as homely as his wife was lovely. He was built low to the ground, thickset, with a head that was truly unusual: from the cheekbones up, it was egg-shaped and almost totally bald, while the bottom half was pulled earthward by cheeks that swung loose and low, just like the ponderous ears of a dachshund. Darn Ray, now he would never be able to think of Peter without that image in mind.

Not that that influenced Peter's own taste in dogs. He was the proud owner of two undisciplined, hyperactive springer spaniels who went everywhere with him—in the fishing boat, bird hunting. When one dog would die, he would rush to replace it with another. Osborne and his early morning coffee buddies would often grouse over how Peter and his springers were a little too synonymous: you couldn't invite one to fish without getting 'em all. That would be okay except, barking and jumping, the darn dogs were guaranteed to scare away any fish, not to mention overturn the boat.

On the whole, though, Osborne liked Peter. The man was always happy to see him, eager to hear how Osborne had raised a musky or flushed a partridge. He was a fanatic fly-fisherman and generous with hot tips on the latest hatch. When weather was bad, he would stop by McDonald's to see who he could persuade to tour the flea markets with him—his abiding passion.

After that first dinner party, Osborne grew to know Peter as a man whose natural earnestness and sweetness of nature were the key to his success as a salesman. He was an optimist who firmly believed that everything would always work out. After all, he was a homely guy who had snagged a beautiful wife, wasn't he?

If Alicia could make you feel fascinating, Peter could make you feel good. Safe. Yet, in Osborne's opinion, his optimism was also his undoing. Two years into their friendship, Osborne discovered he had good reason to feel deeply sorry for Peter Roderick.

seven

Suddenly, an outside wall sconce switched on. Osborne glimpsed Alicia's eyes behind the fairy princess in the leaded glass. She flung the heavy door wide open.

"Paul?" Alicia stepped forward, surprise and concern in her face and her voice.

She was wearing a long, black dressing gown, the kind Mary Lee had worn when they vacationed at nice hotels. The stark color of the gown set off her honey-streaked brown hair, which fell soft and loose to her shoulders. Tall, slim, and fine-boned, Alicia's face was deceptively open with a classic, sculpted nose, prominent cheekbones and a wide mouth that could smile graciously when it wanted to.

Her wide-set dark brown eyes glittered for an instant in the golden stream of light from the sconce. She looked, Osborne thought, as she always did: much younger than her years and simply stunning.

"What—?"

The eyes had widened as they shifted from Osborne to take in the meaning of Lew standing beside him, official in her long-sleeved khaki police uniform, black briefcase in her left hand, black holster on her right hip. Alicia stepped back, closed her eyes and thrust her hands in front of her as if forbidding them to be there.

Eyes still closed, she spoke. Her words quiet, deliberate.

"Peter . . . A plane crash? A car accident?" She held her breath.

"Not Peter," said Osborne. "Your sister Meredith. We found her in the Prairie River several hours ago, Alicia. She's dead. We aren't sure—"

"Meredith!" Alicia's eyes flashed open. "No! Paul, that can't be." Then she closed her eyes tightly, crossed her arms and hunched forwards, clutching her body as if to keep herself intact. The gutteral vehemence in her voice made each word painful to hear, "No . . . No . . . No! Not Meredith, Paul. Not my baby sister. She *just*—she can not be dead. No."

"Alicia . . ." Osborne crossed the threshold. Taking her elbows gently, he pulled her towards him. Still clasping herself tightly, she let him fold her into his arms.

"Alicia," he said over her head, "this is Chief of Police Lewellyn Ferris. She has to ask a few questions . . . and . . . we can take care of the rest in the morning. I take it Peter's away?"

"Yes," said Alicia, her voice smothered in his shoulder. "He's in Osaka on business. Due back Saturday. I almost wish . . . ," she stopped. Osborne couldn't help but wonder if she had been about to say she wished it had been Peter's body they had found.

As she pulled away, he could feel her body vibrating with tension. Then, she took a deep breath.

"You better come in," she said hoarsely. She gave Lew's hand a cursory shake and turned away to flick on the entrance hall chandelier.

"This way." Her voice was curt. Osborne stepped back to let Lew enter first. They followed in silence as Alicia walked swiftly through the entrance hall, her back to them as she marched towards the formal living room.

Osborne noticed she leaned forward as she walked, a slight hunch to her shoulders. Whether it was that or a weight gain since he'd seen her last, he could see, too, as she paused and turned slightly to adjust a rheostat lighting the living room, that the elegant dressing gown could not disguise a slight pot belly. This was new, she had always been a woman who kept herself in excellent physcial shape.

Lew, in sharp contrast, walked erect behind her, head high, shoulders back, tummy flat. While everything about Alicia exuded femininity, including a faint trail of perfume behind her,

Lew was the opposite—her square Irish face free of make-up, her hair a short, black no-nonsense cap of curls.

Woodsmoke, pine bough, and fresh air were the only scents likely to be worn by the Loon Lake Chief of Police, especially in August when, she had complained to Osborne earlier that evening, she spent too many of her non-fishing nights crashing underage beer parties. The parties were easy to spot since their adolescent hosts always opted for the same venues: beachside campfires burning a little too close to stands of brush where the fire hazard is highest in the late summer.

Osborne was struck by other differences between these two women who lived in the same small town. One was defined by money and the soft luxuries it could buy, the reality it could buffer. The other was tuned to the wind, the forest, and the water, the rawness of life. A rawness that extended to her work. He shook his head, amazed not only by how different Lew was from women like his late wife but how much he enjoyed being around her.

Entering the lavishly-decorated living room, Alicia paused several times to turn on table lamps. She continue to look straight ahead, saying nothing, not even glancing back.

At first, Osborne wasn't sure if it was grief or anger she was experiencing. He was open to anything. Sixty-three years had taught him one of the few certainties in life: death hits everyone differently.

He would never forget his own reaction to the unexpected news of Mary Lee's death—a feeling of standing alone on a road with a massive immovable boulder before him. His grief had been slow to surface, more potent for its lateness. But in those first moments he felt no anger, not even sorrow, just a vast sense of nowhere to go.

The young emergency doctor had placed a sympathetic hand on his shoulder, but Osborne hadn't said a word. And he was forever grateful to Ray, who had been sitting beside him and who had said nothing either. Ray had waited while he called his two daughters from the nurses' stand, then driven him home in an understanding silence. Like now, that death had occurred deep in the night with nothing to be done until daylight.

As they followed her into the living room, light from the lamps and recessed wall lighting illuminated the reflection of Alicia's face in an ornate wall-to-wall floor-to-ceiling gilt-framed mirror that anchored the far end of the room. Now Osborne could see in her eyes and the fierce set of her jaw exactly what she was feeling: anger. A black, swirling anger.

"I know. . . . ," he offered, flinching at the inadequacy of his words. He felt he should be able to do something to help but he had no idea what. "Alicia, I—"

"How did it happen?" Alicia cut him off with the demand, her back still turned.

Anger at death—that's a fair response, thought Osborne. Ineffectual but fair. He wondered how long it would take her to work through the initial emotion so they could talk.

As long as it took her to turn around apparently.

She spun towards them, her face drawn but less tense than the mirrored image of a moment earlier. The dark fury in her eyes had vanished.

"I'm sorry, Paul. I'll be okay. Please . . . ," she gestured towards a long, English-style leather sofa beneath the mirror as she seated herself opposite them in a dark green wing chair, "everyone sit down."

"We won't know exactly what happened until after the autopsy," said Lew with quiet authority as she opened her briefcase to pull out a narrow reporter's notepad and a ballpoint pen. She flipped the notebook open as she talked, her eyes on Alicia's face.

"We found her body in the Prairie River around eleven this evening. Doctor Osborne and I were fishing. It appears she was fishing, too. She was wearing waders and a fishing vest but no sign of her rod and reel. Yet, that is. I've got a good thousand yards or more of the river roped off so I expect we'll find her equipment in the brush along the banks at some point."

"My sister was an expert *fly*-fisherman," said Alicia, with careful emphasis on her last word. "She studied with Joan Wulff on the east coast. The famous Joan Wulff—the champion caster, *the* foremost expert on fly-fishing." She spoke in a blatantly patronizing tone as if fly-fishing alone would be news to Lew.

Osborne shifted his position on the sofa. He would be surprised if Lew didn't knew exactly who Joan Wulff was—even he knew that. He found it interesting she said nothing to counter Alicia's condescension. Having seen Alicia go after many unsuspecting, kind-hearted females in years past, Osborne found himself not unhappy that she might be picking on the wrong one this time.

"That's one of the reasons she moved back here. She was fanatic about fly-fishing. I warned her about fishing the Prairie at night. I told her that was very, very foolish."

As she spoke, Alicia had carefully arranged her gown over her knees, then propped her right elbow on one arm to rest her chin in her hand as she leaned towards them, an expression of intense concentration on her face.

"Uh huh," said Lew, making a note. "Why else did she move back here?"

"What time did she drown?" Alicia ignored the question.

Lew ignored the rudeness. "Well . . . at first, we thought she drowned, of course, but Dr. Osborne's initial exam showed her head was quite battered. That and a few more details—"

"Like what details?"

"We found very few bruises on the rest of her body. If she had been in the current for any length of time, there should be significantly more bruising to match the head."

"That's it?" Alicia's tone was ever so slightly scornful.

"Yes," said Lew. "Anything you wish to add, Doctor?" Lew gave Osborne a look that indicated she did not want to share the details of the missing fillings.

"Paul—how on earth did you get involved with this?" demanded Alicia. "You're not a coroner."

"Doctor Osborne is deputized to help me with forensic dental exams when Doctor Pecore is tied up," said Lew matter-of-factly—as if they had been working together for years, not hours.

"Alicia, I did some forensic work during the Korean War though I'm certainly no expert," said Osborne, "Like she said, I just help Chief Ferris on an as-need basis. But I can tell you, Alicia, this was no drowning. Chief Ferris sees at least one drowning a season out of rivers like the Prairie, and those bodies exhibit stresses on all extremities not just—"

"Well—you're both wrong," said Alicia, waving her hand and a snide tone of dismissal in her voice. "Everyone knows the nightmare currents of the Prairie River. No one in their right mind fishes that river in weather like we had here tonight. Don't you think Meredith might have slipped and fallen and hit her head on one of those submerged boulders? I mean, really. I fly-fish, Mrs. Ferris, I know how dangerous a rushing river can be."

Osborne caught her deliberate refusal to use Lew's official title. Classic Alicia, he thought, still nasty after all these years.

"There is something else," said Lew, reluctantly. "Please keep this confidential?"

"Absolutely," said Alicia, leaning forward more intently and dropping her patronizing tone.

"Meredith's body was wedged under a log. Deliberately wedged—no question about it."

"I see . . . ," said Alicia. She sat in thoughtful silence for a long minute, then she sighed deeply and stood up. "You know, I could use a drink—can I get anyone anything? I can make up some coffee . . . ?"

"No, thank you," said Lew.

"Nothing for me," said Osborne.

Alicia left the room. Lew and Osborne looked at each other but said nothing. They waited. Lew doodled on her notepad.

"You know, on second thought, I could use a glass of water," she said, jumping up and following Alicia back to the kitchen. Five minutes later, they returned. Lew with a tall glass of ice water and Alicia with a goblet of white wine in one hand, a plate of Wisconsin cheddar and Ritz crackers in the other. She set the plate on the coffee table in front of them.

"I'm sure you're right," she said rearranging herself in the chair, "I just find it so difficult to imagine anyone wanting to kill my sister."

Her attitude had changed markedly. Her tone, her manner, made it clear she had decided to be cooperative. Very cooperative. But if she had changed her attitude, her tension level was still tuned high. Osborne could almost see the vibration he'd felt earlier.

He was ashamed of his next thought, but knowing Alicia as he did, he wondered what she had up her sleeve.

"And you *are* sure it's Meredith? I know that bodies can change in the water. . . ."

"Alicia," said Osborne, shifting his position on the sofa to lean forward on his elbows, hands dropped between his knees, eyes fixed on hers. "I know your sister. Remember, she grew up with my oldest daughter. I did all her dental work until she went away to college. Even in recent years, when she was visiting in the summer, she would drop by the office if she had a problem, a loose filling usually. I wish I could say otherwise, but I know the victim is Meredith."

"The body appears to have been in the water a very short time, plus the Prairie runs cold," added Lew. "In spite of Doctor Osborne's certainty, I do need you to identify the body, Mrs. Roderick. And I'll need your permission for the autopsy."

"Hmm," Alicia was thoughtful. "An autopsy? What a shame." Then she started up from her chair, "Tonight? I better change—"

"No, oh no," said Lew. "In the morning will be fine. We'll set up a time to meet at the hospital morgue."

Alicia settled back and took a sip of her wine. She turned to Lew and waited expectantly. "You have questions, Chief Ferris?"

"If you can give me a few details, Mrs. Roderick, we can go over much more tomorrow. But any personal background you think is important may help me jumpstart this investigation," said Lew. "First, some nitty gritty. Her age. Does she have children? Did she work? Daily routines? Any fishing partners?"

"Meredith was fourteen years younger than me," said Alicia. "So that makes her thirty-eight. We were half-sisters. My mother died when I was six, and Pop didn't marry again until I was about twelve."

"Your father was John Sutliff."

"Yes. Pop was chairman of the mill until his retirement. He passed away about eighteen months ago, which may interest you. Our father was quite wealthy and he left everything to us—me and Meredith—we're his only heirs."

"How much are we talking about?" asked Lew.

"He left an estate of six million dollars to be shared between us."

"That's a lot of money," said Lew, jotting notes.

"Yes it is," said Alicia, "with her inheritance, my sister had a net worth of close to five million because she had money of her own already."

"Children?"

"None. She never had time. My sister was a remarkable woman, unusual from the day she was born," said Alicia. She took a sip of her wine. "As a child, she was absolutely beautiful. Blonde curls so thick you couldn't get a comb through them." Alicia smiled, "She looked like Shirley Temple. The children's shops in Rhinelander would always ask Dorothy if she could model for them . . ."

"Dorothy?"

"My stepmother. She died of cancer just after Pop retired. Meredith's mother. She always dressed Meredith like a storybook doll. I'll never forget: I would come home from school for the weekend and there would be this picture-perfect little kid, so pretty and so sweet. I was like her second mother."

"So you were the big sister baby-sitter?"

"Not really. I would show her off to all my friends, but I didn't baby-sit. Dorothy wouldn't leave Meredith alone with anyone."

"What do you mean when you say you came home on weekends. Didn't you go to school here in Loon Lake?"

"Heavens, no." Something in her tone made it clear Alicia couldn't believe Osborne had not told Lew that she was one of the favored, one of the few to attend a prestigious private school. "I went to Holy Cross, the private Catholic girls school down in Merrill. Pop sent me from first grade until I went to college. He believed in quality education."

Osborne let the remark go. Sometimes he couldn't believe this woman. Honestly. Did that mean that sending his girls to Loon Lake High School meant he and Mary Lee *didn't believe* in quality education?

"Did Meredith attend Holy Cross?"

"Heavens, no. Dorothy wouldn't let her out of her sight. She was an obsessive mother. Of course, that's probably why Meredith came back. She loved Loon Lake," said Alicia, swirling her wine glass, a slight smile on her face. "She loved her friends from here, she loved our lake house. She was Loon Lake High Homecoming Queen her senior year," said Alicia with quiet pride.

"She was also a National Merit scholar," added Osborne.

"Yes, that too."

"She sounds like an All-American, bright, happy young woman growing up."

"Then she met Ben," said Alicia, her eyes narrowing slightly. "Ben Marshall. Big man on campus—Northwestern. Merry was a freshman, he was a senior and, boy, did he change her life."

"Really," said Lew.

"Nothing was the same after Ben."

"You sound . . . regretful?"

"I think he killed her."

Lew looked up from her notepad. She waited. Alicia's statement hung in the air. Her eyes shifted from Lew to Osborne and back to Lew.

"In more ways than one, he killed her."

"Tell me about it." Lew's voice was gentle, understanding.

"Ben's a commodities broker on the Chicago Board of Trade. Winter wheat, pork bellies. He runs the family business. They married right after he graduated and moved into the family compound in Lake Forest. Big fancy Chicago Irish Catholic millionaires. At first, as long as Meredith took care of all his needs, it was great. That was the first five years.

"Then they find out they can't have children. Bored out of her mind, Meredith wants to back to school, she wants to be a biochemist, which drives Ben mad. Takes wa-a-y too much time away from filling his needs.

"Ben, you see, is a big game hunter and a fly-fisherman only he has to go to South America, to Russia, to Africa. God forbid he ever fish in Wisconsin or Michigan. Meredith couldn't take that kind of time off from school. So they compromised. She quit school and took up cooking."

"Cooking?!" Lew and Osborne exclaimed simultaneously.

"Don't ask me where it came from," said Alicia, "Dorothy was a lousy cook. But Meredith was a natural. French and Italian cuisine were her first loves. She went to France to study, to Italy. She became a superb chef. I'm not exaggerating. She was phenomenal. Pretty soon she was running her own catering business up and down the North Shore. She loved it."

"And Ben?"

"This did not suit him. Also, by now Meredith is seeing a shrink and starting to stand on her own two feet. Then she decides she wants to open a restaurant."

"How long ago is this?" asked Lew.

"About eight years ago." Alicia set her wine glass on the table and crossed her arms over her chest. "She opens a restaurant in Evanston, then one in Winnetka. Within two years, she's a huge success. Fortune Magazine writes her up as one of the top ten chefs in the country. And—*and*—she writes two cookbooks. The little wife has become big business."

"I think I'm getting the picture," said Lew.

"The magazine piece runs, the book deals come along, Meredith is thriving. She never looked better, she's happy . . . when Ben drops his bomb." The smirk on Alicia's face was a giveaway.

Lew sighed, "I know what's coming . . . the secretary?"

"Bull's eye," said Alicia pointing her finger at Lew. "The 'personal assistant.' Age twenty-six, blonde, honkers out to here, slimy little bitch named 'Tiffany.' Need I say more?

"Meredith took it on the chin. She took responsibility for it. She did her best to put their marriage back together. That's when *she* learned how to fly-fish. She didn't just learn, of course, she became an expert. She hired Joan Wulff for two weeks of private lessons. Then she and Ben took three months off to travel. Fishing, a safari, Paris and Rome. When they got back, she sold her restaurants. She loved Ben, she wanted to stay married to him. She forgave him. She also made a couple million selling those restaurants."

"This is now—three years ago?"

"Right. But it was too late. Ben was still seeing other women. The final blow came when Ben left on a business trip. The next day the airlines delivered 'Mrs. Marshall's lost luggage' to their home, only they were not Meredith's bags. She wasn't the 'Mrs. Marshall' he took on that trip. That was it. She told me she's since heard from their friends he had dozens of girls. He's a creep. A real creep."

"Is Ben an attractive man?"

Alicia looked at Lew and gave her a sly grin, "He has money . . ."

"Tall, short?"

"Oh, he's good-looking," said Alicia reluctantly, swinging her foot. "He's a little on the beefy side these days, but tall, ruddy-faced. Real Chicago Irish with red hair, y'know? Yes, I'd say women find him attractive."

"Have you met him, Doc?" Lew turned to Osborne who nodded that he had not. He saw Alicia's eyes widen at the familiarity with which Lew addressed him but she said nothing.

"So no children, no heirs that you know of."

"Well—that's the interesting part," said Alicia. "I don't think that Ben knows the divorce was final last week. He thinks he's her heir."

"How could he not know it was final?"

"He was out of the country last week. Meredith was trying to reach him."

"But if he has money, why—"

"First, she got a nice chunk of his assets in the divorce, then his company made a bad call in the copper markets. He told her the business was looking at Chapter Eleven. That's why she was trying to reach him. Pop's estate was settled a couple months ago, and Meredith had decided to take less money in the divorce. Actually, she wanted to do a trade."

"That sounds pretty big-hearted, given what you've told us."

"That's Meredith. She has been so happy up here. She didn't need the money. She told me she wanted a fresh start and no bad feelings from Ben. She was determined to set that whole chapter of her life behind her.

"But she wanted one thing from Ben. He kept a family heirloom of ours, a diamond brooch that belonged to our grandmother. Pop gave it to Dorothy, and Dorothy gave it to Meredith. Ben had it in the bank vault and refused to return it until the divorce was settled. I want that brooch, Chief. You can tell Ben for me I consider it stolen."

"You don't care much for Ben, do you?"

"Would you?" Alicia swung her foot harder. Suddenly, from the rear of the house, they heard a light bang as if a door had swung shut.

"What's that?" Alicia looked startled, alarmed. She rushed from the living room. Lew and Osborne followed. They ran out of the living room, down the hallway to the kitchen and through another doorway into a rear laundry room. An inside wooden back door stood wide open exposing the outside screen door, which opened to the garden and garage.

"The screen door is unlatched," said Osborne pushing against the outer door frame. "Was it locked?"

"I never lock my doors," said Alicia. Then she looked at them, fear crossing her face. "What if it's not Ben?" she said. "What if someone's after both of us? Peter's not here. I'm all alone."

"No one came in," said Lew looking down at the gleaming white ceramic tile that covered the kitchen and laundry room floors. Her eyes scanned the open shelving in the room carefully.

"With the mud and wet grass from the storm tonight, anybody trying to walk in here would leave plenty of footprints on this white floor of yours, Mrs. Roderick. This place is buffed clean. Maybe your door slammed in the breeze or blew something off one of these shelves. Maybe it was this mop that fell over." Lew righted a sponge mop that had tipped over beside the washing machine.

"Do you have any reason to think someone might be after *you*?" asked Lew, backing into the darkened kitchen.

"I'm . . . I'm not sure . . . ," Alicia paused, looking down and thinking. "Something odd happened earlier this week. I didn't think much about it at the time . . . I thought it was one of the neighbor kids . . ." She looked up. "I was in the garden weeding, on my hands and knees, when I was sure I heard the front door slam. I got up and walked in—sometimes a neighbor will stop by with iced tea or to chat, y'know. But no one was here. I know I left the front door open. Someone had to shut it. Slammed it shut."

"The mailman?"

"No, it was late afternoon."

"Where were you tonight around suppertime?" asked Lew.

"I went up to the country club with Carlyn Sandeman and her mother-in-law for cocktails and a salad. After that, we played bridge at her house. She lives next door," Alicia gestured towards the garden that separated the two large houses.

"I better start locking my doors," Alicia walked back to peer out the screen door towards the silent garden.

"I would if I were you," said Lew briskly. "Until we get this cleared up, you should be careful, Mrs. Roderick. Particularly if many people know the kind of money you and your sister inherited. Some of these backwoods idiots we have around here might think you keep cash in the house."

Alicia pushed the back door shut and slipped a deadbolt.

"You are so right, Chief Ferris," she said. "I'll be very careful. Are we finished?"

"Just another question or two," said Lew. "I'm sorry to keep you up so late. Can we go back to the living room? I left my notes on the sofa."

"Right now having you two here is all that's keeping me from having a nervous breakdown," said Alicia, "Please, however long it takes . . ."

eight

"Did your father have enemies?" asked Lew as they walked back through the hallway.

"I imagine," said Alicia, "he ruled hundreds with an iron fist but Pop was retired over twenty-five years. He was ninety-two when he died. I doubt too many people from his era are still around."

"Ah, so he was older when Meredith was born," said Lew as she sat back down on the sofa.

"Yes. Dorothy was forty-two. She'd been Pop's secretary," added Alicia. "*My* mother was a Claywell from Farmington, Connecticut." Osborne almost chuckled. Alicia's inflections left no doubt as to her opinion of Dorothy. Poor Dorothy, thought Osborne, Alicia would have been serious competition even as an adolescent.

"What has Meredith been doing since her return?" asked Lew.

Alicia's eyes brimmed with tears. She reached for one of the paper napkins she'd set out on the plate with the cheese and crackers.

"We . . . ," she bowed her head and crunched the napkin to her eyes, then she inhaled deeply and looked up, fighting back the tears. "We were business partners," she said. "That's how I know about the divorce and the final dates. We signed the incorporation papers this week after waiting until the divorce was final so Ben could have no claim against our business."

"Which was—?" Lew's voice held an edge of fatigue. Osborne didn't blame her for trying to rush Alicia along. A glance at his watch had shown him it was nearly 3:30 in the morning.

"We've been catering for the last six months," said Alicia. "A select clientele from Manitowish Waters and Land o' Lakes. We planned to open a restaurant in early October. Meredith was the chef, the creative genius, while I am—was—the business manager."

"So that's why she bought The Willows?" asked Osborne, remembering now all the speculation by the McDonald's crowd over Meredith Marshall's purchase of the property. The old estate, built in the 1930's by a Chicago mobster, was a mansion on a magnificent peninsula in Cranberry Lake that came with many legends attached. Legends and, according to Loon Lake lore, ghosts.

"Yes. Meredith has been remodeling the boathouse, turning it into The Willow Inn," said Alicia. "Now . . . all our plans are . . . dead, I guess." She emptied her wine glass and started to stand up.

"Was Meredith living at the Willows?" asked Lew.

"She moved in two months ago. She didn't close on it until last week."

"I see," said Lew, tapping her pen on her notepad. "Alicia, is there anyone besides Ben who might have had an unhealthy interest in your sister?"

"If you put that way, yes," said Alicia. An odd expression crossed her face, an expression that struck Osborne as a mix of indecision and delight.

"She was dating—actually, she was intimate with this creep from the Lac Vieux Desert casino up in Michigan," said Alicia, picking her words with ladylike care. "Supposedly he's a gardener and she wanted him to landscape The Willows."

"I take it you have your doubts about this fellow?" Lew's pen worked busily across the page.

"I told her she was crazy to even talk to the jerk," said Alicia, rolling her eyes in disgust. "But he has these cheap good looks. She thought he was cute."

"He's a landscaper?"

"He's a waiter at the casino who says he's a master gardener. Frankly, he's a gigolo," said Alicia. "And his name, for the record, is Clint Chesnais."

"French Canadian?"

"Indian. Off the res up there. Creep."

"But what could he possibly get from your sister?" asked Lew.

"Money. She opened a landscaping account and put him on as co-signer," said Alicia. "I told her not to but she did it anyway."

"How much money is in the account?"

"I have no idea. That was her personal business, not connected to the restaurant."

"Mrs. Roderick," Lew stood up and flipped the narrow notebook closed, "If you are up to it, I would like to take a look at your sister's house tomorrow."

"I think that would be all right," Alicia nodded, standing. The three of them walked back through the living room towards the front hall.

"Let's meet at the hospital at nine for the identification, if that's all right with you," said Lew. "Then we can go to the house immediately afterwards."

"Oh—could we do that later in the afternoon?" asked Alicia. "I have a doctor's appointment at one and I'll have all the burial arrangements . . ."

"I understand," said Lew. " Would three o'clock work for you? At the Willows."

"That's fine."

"Wait for me in the driveway," said Lew. "And please, don't enter the house if you arrive before I do."

"Don't worry," said Alicia. "I won't. See you tomorrow morning, Chief Ferris," she said, shaking Lew's hand as she opened the front door for Lew to leave. Then she turned to Osborne, brushing his shoulder lightly with her hand to stop him. She let the door close behind Lew, watching her as she went, then stepped back into the hall.

"Paul, you'll keep some of what you heard tonight confidential?"

"Of course, Alicia, I'm deputized to work with Chief Ferris on this case. Everything is confidential."

"Oh fine then," said Alicia. She turned her face up to him with a tight little smile on her lips, "You know, someone should tell Mrs. Ferris that girls with bottoms that broad really shouldn't wear khaki ... know what I mean?" She winked as if Lew's bad taste was to be a private joke between them.

"Good night, Alicia," said Osborne curtly. "I am very sorry about your sister."

"I just remembered something very interesting," said Osborne as he opened the door of the cruiser, "Ray mentioned earlier tonight that Peter Roderick has been travelling a lot lately, but the last time Peter and I fished together, he told me he was retiring this summer."

Osborne could hear himself talking a little too loudly and too fast, but he was hoping against hope that Lew had not heard Alicia's snipe.

"You didn't mention she was an old girlfriend of yours, Doc," said Lew, not letting him off the hook.

"She's not," said Osborne, "what do you mean?" He was trying to figure out why he felt guilty as he spoke.

"I heard her through the open windows," said Lew, pulling the car away from the curb. "She made sure to say it just loud enough."

"Don't take it personally, Lew. That's Alicia. She's always had that nasty side to her—"

"That was more than nasty, Doc, that was a warning to me: 'hands off.' " Lew turned to him, a half-smile on her face, "you don't get it, do you?"

"I guess not," said Osborne, unsure if he could possibly feel more embarrassed.

"I may be a cop, Doc, but I'm also a woman. Women have signals. Unmistakable signals."

Osborne said nothing. Little did she know how aware he *was* that she was a woman. Better she shouldn't know.

"Wait until you hear how she talks to her husband," said Osborne, anxious to change the subject. "You played her well, Lew. You played her like those brook trout you caught tonight."

"Hah!" Lew snorted. He loved her snort—it said it all.

"What do you mean, Doc?" He knew she was fishing for the compliment.

"You know exactly what I mean, Lew," Osborne looked out the window as he spoke. "You teased her in, you let her run, and you teased her again ... The only thing missing in that

living room was a double taper fly line running from the sofa
to Alicia's chair."

Lew chuckled. "Actually, I needed thirty pound test, Doc. I
felt more like I had a musky on the line."

"You fish musky, too?"

"Oh sure," she said, "right after trout season ends next
month, I'll be out row-trolling for that 'ol' shark of the
north.' "

"No kidding." Osborne liked the sound of that. Ralph Kendall wouldn't know beans about muskies. Osborne made up
his mind, he would definitely invite Lew to fish his weed beds.

"But, Doc," Lew interrupted his thoughts, "there's a big
difference between Alicia Roderick and a musky."

"Oh yeah?"

They headed down Ojibway Drive again, this time towards
the jail and Lew's office where Osborne had left his car.

"Yeah. One *is* a shark. Something I don't understand, Doc,"
said Lew, "how can a woman be so pretty, have all that money
and security—and be so damned unkind? Was her sister like
that?"

"I don't know. I'll have to ask my daughter."

Lew swung the cruiser around a corner. "What was it you
were going to tell me about that front door of theirs?"

"Oh that. Right," said Osborne, nodding happily, "That door
was Alicia's first and, possibly, most famous stunt as Peter's
wife. Now that you've met her, you'll understand. Right after
they were married, she ordered that thing from England. Never
said a word to Peter until it was here and was hung. So he
admires it, opens it, closes it. He finds out the damn thing is
something like 250 years old. So he asks how much it is. Alicia
tells him and he can't believe she did it. He told her it had to
go back."

"Which it obviously did not."

"That door cost $20,000 in 1964," said Osborne. "Can you
imagine spending that kind of money on a door?"

"Guess we know who's boss in that family," said Lew. "She
seemed to think she was running the investigation for awhile
there tonight."

"I'll tell ya," said Osborne turning to Lew and shaking his
head, "I know more about antique radios thanks to that go-
dawful woman—"

"Now why's that?" Lew glanced at him, "what on earth are you talking about?"

"Peter Roderick. He's got this antique radio fetish—he drives hundreds of miles to find them. And if you have the misfortune to sit near him at a dinner party or the fish fry at the Pub, you will hear every detail. Which I have.

"Actually," Osborne raised his hands in a gesture of surrender, "I have done so on purpose, Lew. You feel so sorry for the poor guy—the way Alicia takes him apart in public.

"I'm not the only one. A number of us go out of our way to listen to the man, strictly out of sympathy. He's good-hearted, but brother can he be a bore. There are times, I tell ya, when I've been fishing with the guy, I've been desperate to get out of the boat. Between the minutae of the radios and those crazed dogs of his—"

"Say, Doc. What about the dogs? Where were they tonight?"

Osborne looked at Lew. "Good question. Now that's odd, Lew. If Alicia's so worried about someone breaking in? Why doesn't she have the dogs around?"

"Back to Peter, Doc. So all these years he's taken all this abuse? Been humiliated in front of his friends? Why would a guy do that? Why wouldn't he just walk out?"

"Those of us who know Peter have speculated on exactly that issue for years, Chief," said Osborne. "To the point that the one time he stood his ground, we gave a party. We all went out to Rick French's deer shack for some poker to celebrate."

"Really," said Lew.

"Did you notice that mirror in the living room?" asked Osborne.

"You mean the mirrored wall," corrected Lew.

"We call it Peter's Revenge," said Osborne. "Everyone knows it came out of an old brothel up in St. Germaine. He picked it up for about twenty bucks at the auction when they tore the place down, then he forced Alicia to hang it in the living room. Absolutely put his foot down. She fumed over that for years."

"I'm starting to wonder if someone murdered the wrong sister."

Lew angled the cruiser into a parking spot beside Osborne's station wagon. It was still dark, not quite 4 A.M. They opened their doors and got out.

Osborne fished his car keys out of his pocket and had turned towards his car when Lew's soft voice stopped him. She stood behind his car, her briefcase swinging in her left hand.

"So, Doc," she said, "I think it's time we go home and get ready for bed, don't you? I don't know what your plans are. I thought I'd put on a little make-up, my best nightie, some hair-spray. Whadda think?"

Osborne stood in stunned silence, his car key in his hand. What on earth? Then the note of irony in her voice registered. "Lew. You're right. I thought Alicia was looking pretty good tonight. It never occurred to me—"

"Of course not, Doc. It takes a woman's eye." Lew leaned back against the cruiser, cradling her briefcase in her arms. "When I followed her back to the kitchen, I could see she had that wine bottle with two glasses and the cheese and crackers already set out. She wasn't happy that I walked in on her either."

"Just who do you think she was expecting?"

Loon Lake was still dark when Osborne pulled his station wagon into his own driveway. He could hear Mike barking a wild welcome inside the house. He was such a good dog, Osborne was sure there had been no accident, even though he should have been back to let Mike out hours ago.

He hurried through the back porch and opened the kitchen door to let the bounding black Lab through. "C'mon, guy, let's go down to the lake." The dog rushed by. Osborne stepped into the dark kitchen to open the refrigerator. He reached for a can of ginger ale, poured it into a tall glass, added an ice cube, then turned to follow the dog down to the dock.

That's when he saw the sheet of yellow note paper tacked over the sink: "Doc, I need you in the morning. The ESPN guys asked me to bring a client who can demonstrate while I talk walleyes—you'll make me look good. Pick you up at nine. Love you forever, Ray."

Stinker, thought Osborne. Ray knew darn well he wouldn't be getting to bed much before dawn. On the other hand, it made him feel good Ray would single him out for the TV thing. It would be fun. Something to talk about at McDonald's.

Osborne shut the screen door quietly behind him and followed the dog down to the lake. As Mike busied himself, Osborne sipped at his ginger ale. He looked west over the still-dark lake. The tall tamarack that ringed the eastern shore delayed the early light of dawn, especially in late August as the days shortened. Osborne didn't mind, he loved the absolute stillness. A soft forest breeze drifted across from the far shore.

Life was so funny. In less than a year, he'd gone from being a man whose empty days and hours yawned like an abyss to someone whose life overflowed with friends and family and unexpected excitement. Poor Mary Lee was fast becoming a faded, rather crabby, memory. He was happier now than he'd ever been, he thought.

Even the prospect of getting up to go fishing in less than four hours didn't bother him. Years of rising at 3 A.M. to go duck-hunting had conditioned him to short nights for the sake of great sport.

What did bother him were the missing fillings. He swished the ginger ale in the glass as he mulled over that situation. Alicia's blatant accusation of her ex-brother-in-law didn't fit, thought Osborne. A business man whose company sees revenue in the millions would not be desperate for a few extra thousand in gold inlays.

Or would he? A memory that had tugged at the back of his mind ever since he examined Meredith's mouth suddenly came into focus. Richard Campbell. The resort magnate from Manitowish Waters. Of course, thought Osborne. Why hadn't he remembered earlier?

The Campbells had moved up from Chicago in the late 60s, buying one of the North Woods' finest and largest resorts with money made in the stock market. Richard's wife had had some of the softest teeth that Osborne had ever seen. Even though the days of gold inlays were fast coming to an end, Richard had insisted on the best for Harriett. Just a year after Osborne had finished all that work, she died. Breast cancer. Richard had called him from the hospital.

"Paul," he'd said, "I can't bear the thought of all that money six feet under. What can we do about it?" Osborne had helped him out, of course. Richard wasn't desperate. Richard was frugal. It was how he made his fortune in the first place.

Osborne called to Mike. Slowly, he and the dog ambled back up to the house. Could Ben be that kind of guy? Osborne figured, conservatively, Meredith's mouth had held ten to fifteen thousand dollars worth of precious metal. Maybe. Made more sense if a man with a lot less money was involved.

Osborne slipped off to sleep instantly, deeply. But when he woke to the ringing of his alarm at 8:30, the dream was as vivid as if he were still in it. The cold body on the steel drawer. The lean, well-toned body with its pale breasts. Only this body carried not the face of Meredith Marshall, but a face he knew intimately: Mallory Osborne Miller.

Osborne whipped off the alarm and jumped to his feet. Ray would have to wait a few minutes. He had to call his daughter.

nine

Twenty minutes later, teeth freshly brushed, coffee perco-
lating in his battered old Mirro pot and the party line finally
clear so he could have a turn, Osborne stood in his kitchen,
by the wall phone, and geared himself up to talk to his oldest
daughter. He hoped his neighbors would accord him some privacy and not listen in.

Osborne let the Lake Forest line ring and ring. Finally, Mallory's answering machine kicked in. Whispery clicks on the
line made him fairly certain someone was listening. Oh well,
Loon Lake had to hear about the tragedy sometime. He waited
for the beep, "Mallory, it's Dad. Please call me as soon as you
can. It's urgent, hon," Osborne started to hang up. Suddenly
he heard Mallory's real voice.

"Dad? Hold on, let me turn this off." As Mallory dealt with
her answering machine, Osborne let his breath out in relief.
Her voice was spirited and clear, not the slurred, slow cadence
he'd come to expect when he called in the evenings. Mallory
worried him these days. She appeared to be following a family
tradition, one he was reluctant to discuss with her. Close as he
was to his youngest daughter, Erin, he had always been distant
with Mallory. She was Mary Lee's child. It had always been
so.

"Dad—you caught me running out the door for a tennis
match. What's up?"

"I've got some sad news, kiddo."

"O-o-h . . . ," her voice tightened. He could feel her prepare herself, "not Erin or Mark or the baby, Dad?" She named her sister's family.

"No, no, everyone is fine. An old friend of yours, Meredith Marshall, died yesterday."

"Dad! That's not possible. Tell me that's not true—Meredith! We had lunch just a few weeks ago. She looked like a million dollars. Was she sick? What happened?"

"I found her, hon. I was fly-fishing the Prairie River last night, and I slipped and fell and stumbled over Meredith's body . . ." Osborne paused. He hated saying even that much not knowing who was listening.

"Oh-h-h, she drowned, Dad. That's just awful," Mallory's voice slowed as she processed the news. "And she was so happy. She had the divorce behind her. She told me she had a new boyfriend, a new business. She had this great joke, y'know. She said she had what every woman needs—a good lawyer, a good shrink, and an excellent hairdresser. She said she had it all. We had such a good time that day. Gee, Dad, I'm stunned."

"It wasn't an accident, Mallory," said Osborne, "that's as much as I can say right now. Don't forget I'm stuck with a party line on this darn phone." Looking out the kitchen window as he talked, he saw Ray's truck pull up in the driveway.

"Meredith murdered?" Mallory's disbelief was palpable over the phone line. "Dad, I'm catching a flight today. I'm coming up. She was one of my dearest childhood friends."

"So you two have really stayed in touch?"

"Dad, we lived in the same town here. We belonged to different clubs, but, yeah, we've stayed pretty close."

"What do you think of Ben—?"

"Ben? Well . . . I don't know. Let me think about that. I know he's got a cheap, sleazy girlfriend, but I don't think Ben's the type to kill anyone. Boy, now that's something to think about. Oh darn, Dad, I've got to go. I'll make some plane reservations."

"Honey, there's no reason for you—"

"Dad. I'll be there. See ya."

"Wait—Mallory!" Osborne tried to keep her from hanging up.

"What? Sorry I gotta rush, but I'll call you later."

"One question—does the name Clint Chesnais ring a bell?"

"Nope, never heard it." Mallory hung up, and a series of two more clicks followed.

"Gosh, I hate this party line," said Osborne grimly, setting his phone back on the hook. "I'm surprised it doesn't put the Loon Lake News out of business."

"Hey, old buddy, it's a glorious day out here." Ray shouted through the open kitchen window as he walked towards the back porch. An entirely new version of Ray that was heading his way. The distinctive loopy walk that always seemed to roll his torso into a room minutes ahead of the rest of his six-foot-six frame was the same, but this Ray Pradt was clearly dressed for success.

This was not the grave-digging Ray, the minnowing Ray, or the leech-harvesting Ray—but the "Ready-for-ESPN Ray." Resplendent in chestnut-colored rhinohide fishing pants and a long-sleeved heavy cotton shirt to match, Osborne fully expected to see a leaping walleye embroidered in gold over the left pocket.

But the pièce de resistance was the hat. No one in the world had a hat like Ray's. Due to the warm weather, he had tucked the ear flaps up under the battered leather cap, which sported the large stuffed trout, head and tail protruding over both ears. Draped across the breast of the fish, like a jeweled necklace, was an old wood and metal fishing lure, its silver disks glinting in the sunlight as Ray crossed Osborne's yard.

Ray paused in front of the jalousied porch windows to study his reflection. He tipped his head to one side, then tweaked the angle of the hat ever so slightly. Only then did he saunter up the steps and into the house.

"Whaddya think?" he said, spreading his arms in a grand gesture, turning first this way, then that.

Osborne laughed in amazement. He *did* have a walleye embroidered over the left pocket. "My god, Ray, where on earth did you get that walleye patch?" he asked, squinting to see it better as he took a sip of his coffee. Just then the phone rang. "Excuse me." Osborne picked up the receiver. It was Lew.

"Doc?"

"Yeah."

"I'm in the office. Alicia's due in a few minutes—"

"Lew," Osborne interrupted, "I'm on a party line out here—

you should assume you're talking to at least three of me, know what I mean?" Two clicks confirmed his suspicions.

"Thanks for telling me," Lew's tone changed, "I hate party lines. We'll have to do something about that."

"Good luck, I've been trying for years."

"At any rate," she continued carefully, "I was wondering if you could drive up to the reservation with me later today. To see that fellow—you know who I mean."

"What time were you thinking? I'm Ray's guinea pig this morning for his television debut."

"I'd like to be heading up there by one if we could. I see Alicia again at three. I think this gives us enough time . . ."

"Be happy to, Lew. I'll be at your office by one." He hung up.

"Donna sewed it on for me this morning," said Ray. "Pretty neat, huh?"

"Yet another reason to wed the woman," kidded Osborne. It was a running commentary between them. Poor Donna. She helped the guy out time and time again, even though she was plenty busy herself as sales manager of Loon Lake Trailer Homes. Practical, no-nonsense, Donna might have a lot of rough edges, but she overflowed with kindness and good humor.

Once, when Osborne pressed Ray on why he hadn't married Donna after nearly six years of off-and-on courtship, Ray had offered an excuse Osborne found lame yet telling, "Doc, she's a very sweet woman, but whenever I take her somewhere, she always wears the wrong thing."

Then there was Ray's insistence that he still carried a torch for his high school sweetheart who'd fled Loon Lake to become a fashion model in New York City and marry a real estate tycoon. The torch was just an excuse, Osborne figured, Ray's way to insure his independence. And Osborne thought he was probably wise to stay single. A married Ray just wouldn't be the same. What wife would put up with ice-fishing at midnight in the icy winds of the North Woods winters? He was certainly safe from any involvement with his old girlfriend. What fashion model would be seen with a guy wearing a fish on his head?

"What's new with the Chief? Any leads?" asked Ray.

"Yeah, Alicia thinks either the ex-husband did it or a fellow

off the Lac Vieux Desert reservation by the name of Clint
Chesnais. Ever heard of him?"

"No-o-o. Know a lotta guys up there, too."

"Yeah? Funny you don't know him." Osborne did find that
unusual. Ray knew everybody. Particularly around the casinos
where he frequently unloaded his guiding clients after a long
day's fishing. "Lew asked me to go with her to see him later.
Want to come along?"

Testy as she might be with Ray because of his intermittent
habit of smoking dope, Osborne knew he could argue one
simple reason for including the guy: his vast network of contacts throughout the North Woods. Everyone liked Ray, men,
women, locals, tourists, teenagers, old folks, priests and nuns,
felons. Knew him, trusted him, talked to him.

Osborne was no longer surprised by this. Over the last couple years, as the two had grown closer, he had learned a lot
about Ray. He knew that his neighbor might appear to be a
numnut with a fish on his head, a man not to be taken seriously, but that wasn't exactly the case—though it certainly was
what Ray wanted people to think.

Why was that, anyway? Osborne had consciously mulled
that over while sitting on his front porch in the cool lake
breezes and warming his hands with a hot cup of coffee. To
date, he'd probably spent several hours of his life musing
about Ray Pradt.

He still didn't know the answer. He did know that the real
Ray was a canny son of a bitch. Alert to the eagle's whisper
on the wind, quick to see the fault in a beaver dam, Ray had
the eyes and ears and intuition of a deer. Just as smart as his
siblings, he'd told Osborne over black coffee one dawn that
the difference between him and them was "real simple: I'd
rather barter with the river than some asshole right-winger any-
day." Given what Osborne had learned over the years, who
was to say he wasn't the wisest of the three.

"Doc, I can't go," said Ray, "I'm on Zolonsky's butt for
those boats right after we do this TV thing. I'm goin' nuts. I
got two pros flying in tonight that are expecting to pre-fish
tomorrow. I have to track George down this afternoon if I'm
going to nail those suckers."

As Ray was talking, Osborne filled his thermos with coffee.
He set out some fresh water for Mike and opened the door to

hurry Ray back to the truck. "You take your truck, and I'll follow," said Osborne.

He knew better than to rely on Ray, much less Ray's vehicle, to get where he needed to go.

When you drove with Ray, you took two risks: one physical, the other existential. Since the passenger door on his truck was frozen shut, you exited by climbing out the window. That meant you had to be fit enough to crawl through a 22 X 22 inch opening. You could crawl across the seat but the gear shift was perfectly situated to do serious harm to any male hoping to continue to propagate his kind upon the earth. That hazard ran parallel to a time frame so wide open to circumstance that Osborne had learned on more than one occasion you might not get home for days.

Ray Pradt lived in a world measured by what Osborne and his morning coffee buddies called "Ray time." That meant a world defined not by hours, minutes and seconds, but by whom you stopped to chat with on the street or the county road, how deep your truck got stuck in swamp muck, how hard the ground was frozen when a grave had to be dug, and whether or not there was a yard sale or a flea market on the way to anywhere.

"So, Ray, where're we going?"

"Follow me."

Osborne knew that signal: Ray was planning to poach.

"Of course, I've got some funny business planned," said Ray under his breath. Osborne had quizzed him as they got out of their respective vehicles in the Pine Valley Resort parking lot. "These people want to see some fish caught, right? Trust me, Doc. And don't worry. Okay? Don't worry."

Osborne did worry. But he understood the problem. He doubted if the TV crew would, however.

A shiny van from Rhinelander's Channel 12 was parked in the lot, its front passenger-side door standing open as they walked towards it, rods in one hand, tackle boxes in the other. "I thought you were ESPN," said Ray to the open door.

"We are—we just borrowed the equipment from a local crew," said a female voice. From the door popped a round face capped with sleek, short dark-brown hair that fell over her brow and crowded her chubby cheeks.

"I like the hat!" A smallish woman, she had a figure like a

good-sized tree trunk, straight up and down and pretty darn
solid. She wore crisp Levi's and a shirt to match, neatly belted.
Osborne was happy to see little evidence of flapping purse
straps or eye make-up. The woman was dressed for the outdoors and ready for business. He like her immediately.

"Whadda know about walleye fishing?" asked Ray, extending his hand.

"Not a thing. I flew in from LA yesterday. What do you
know about producing talk shows?" she said, pumping his
hand. "My name is Marilyn, and this is my crew," she jerked
her right thumb over her shoulder. "Rich works the camera
and Wayne the mikes."

As she spoke, two men emerged from the back of van, arms
full of cords and black boxes. Tall and slim, Rich wore baggy
shorts, an over-sized black T-shirt and a buzz cut that made it
tough to determine what color hair he had. Osborne guessed
him to be in his late twenties. Wayne was a good ten years
older, as chubby as Rich was skinny, and sporting a thick,
unruly mass of black hair. He wore a dun-colored T-shirt
tucked into well-worn Levi's that rode low but safe on a pudgy
torso. A beer belly tested the buttons of his 504s.

"Talk show? I thought this was a fishing show," said Ray.

"A *fishing* talk show."

Ray looked at her, slightly taken aback, "That's a conversation stopper." Then shook his head and grinned. "You're the
boss. Where do you want us?"

"I have a lovely boat from our sponsor," said Marilyn, herd-
ing them towards the boat landing where a red Toyota Landcruiser had backed a boat trailer down into the water. Ray
looked at the sleek fiberglass rig and whistled.

"My audience is wannabes, and my advertiser wants to sell,
sell, sell—so I need you to talk boats for a few minutes, then
we hit the water, and you show us how to catch a fish. We
have two hours. Okay?"

Marilyn handed Ray a glossy brochure, "Here's the info on
the boat." He took it, scanned it carefully, then walked over
to check out the boat. He looked over at Osborne, nodded
approvingly as he pointed to the positioning of the rod holders.

"Okay, except for one small item," he said finally, turning
to Marilyn, who had been giving directions to Rich and
Wayne. He raised both his hands in front of him. Ray had a
way of spreading his long, slender fingers when he was making

a point that reminded Osborne of a concert pianist attacking a keyboard.

"That item is this . . . ," said Ray, showcasing particular words for effect, "no . . . walleye . . . will be biting in . . . this lake . . . this morning. Walleyes in this lake don't even begin to bite until sunset."

Marilyn looked at him, her face set, intense. "That won't work, Mr. Pradt, we need daylight to shoot. This is a perfect day."

"Call me Ray, Marilyn. Now listen . . . all I said was the walleyes aren't biting on *this* lake."

"You have a better idea?"

"Better than discussing it with the fish. Follow me."

Twenty minutes later, the Landcruiser backed down a grassy bank that had seen little trailer traffic and prepared to unload its eighteen thousand dollar cargo. Osborne, unmiked, positioned himself in the cushioned chair at the front. He was happy to be Ray's silent student. He was even happier to see that the huge log home off to their right appeared to be dark.

"Don't worry, Doc," Ray had whispered as they drove over in the van with the crew, "the caretaker is a good buddy of mine."

Ray, miked, stepped forward to angle his lanky frame into the driver's seat in front of the console, then leaned to open a storage unit, and carefully stowed his hat. Marilyn and Rich settled into the back of the boat.

"Ray, let me tell you what I'd like you to do," said Marilyn, a clipboard clutched to her chest, a headset clamped over her glossy hair.

"Not necessary," said Ray, waving his hand to Wayne who backed the Landcruiser a few more feet, allowing the the big boat to ease off its trailer into the lake. "I've watched ESPN fishing shows plenty. Let me do it my way, and you see what you think. With all my clients, I do the same. See? We get out into the water. I know right where we're going . . . then I give the good dentist my BJL routine—that should do it. You just sit back and watch the fish fly."

"Well . . . The BJL?" Marilyn was clearly uneasy with Ray taking command of her production. Osborne minded his own business. He'd watched Ray tell the CEOs of blue chip companies what to do when. And when they listened, they scored. Marilyn was in for an adventure.

" 'Boat-Jig-Leech'—Ray Pradt's winning walleye technique—five minutes to your five-fish bag limit." Osborne turned his head away so they wouldn't see him trying hard not to smile. Ray was, of course, neglecting to mention the key to their pending success: illegal fishing of a private, heavily stocked lake.

"Jig I know, but leech?" A quizzical but amused look crossed Marilyn's round face. She might say she didn't know fishing, but watching her cheery, no-nonsense face made Osborne certain she'd researched bait fishing enough to have some idea what to expect. Like most non-fisherman, though, she'd probably neglected to notice that walleye fishing was quite different from fishing for bass or panfish, not to mention musky or trout.

"Leech?" She said it again as if the very sound of the word gave her the creeps. Then she threw her head back and laughed a hearty, robust laugh. It was a laugh so spontaneous and gutsy, Osborne's first thought was how much it reminded him of Lew. "I like this," said Marilyn. "What a great lead for this story. Go right ahead, guy."

"Ready, Rich?" Ray looked at the cameraman who hoisted his rig. Rich looked at Marilyn.

"Go ahead," she said, "let's give it five and see what we get. Dr. Osborne, don't even think about us back here. We'll voice over that he's guiding you so you'll just keep your eye on him or doing whatever he tells you to."

While she talked, Ray had turned the ignition key, the motor purring preciously beneath them.

"Whoa, listen to that lovely hum. Exquisite. Of course, for eighteen thousand bucks it ought to tuck you in at night," he said as the button on Rich's video camera glowed red.

"Fellas," said Ray, addressing Osborne as if he was one of a large crowd, "The boat is critical to successful fishing. The boat must be an extension of you for everything to work right. Yet every boat has its own personality. Your challenge is to psych it out, to find the boat that fits you, the boat that *is* you.

"Me? I love my Stratos 219CF," Ray patted the steering wheel on the console in front of him. "This mother has a modified V-hull, a good 19 feet 3-inches with a 91-inch beam. And because you don't ever, *ever* wanna underpower your hull, I keep a 175 horse power engine with a 25 kicker for heading into the wind.

"Now this is strictly personal, fellas, but *my* interior features one livewell and two baitwells, one forward of my console and one at the splashwell. This single-side console works best for the type of guiding that I do, though you yuppies can get a double if you must. You just better fish good enough to make a double console make sense, or don't even show up at the bar, know what I mean?"

Marilyn gave a big thumbs up from the back of the boat.

"What distinguishes this particular boat," the lake was smooth enough so Ray could rise slightly from his seat and point, "are the low sides. This makes it easy for me to fish weed walleyes or I can fish musky—very important up here in the northwoods. Bottom line? I need flexibility and Stratos makes it happen for me, y'know. I've had this boat up on Lake Erie, and I wanna tell ya it stays right on top. No wave crashing in this honey.

"Now, the Doc here is getting ready to go for ol' bubble eyes." As Ray spoke, Osborne swiveled his seat and readied the spinning rod that Ray had handed him.

"Our walleye warrior, in case you don't know, is a fish of a certain and unique charm. A handsome fish. Eyes like fine crystal, a dorsal fin so erect . . . ," Ray winked at Marilyn. Osborne hoped like hell he wasn't about to launch into one of his eminently tasteless jokes.

"But," he paused and raised his concert pianist fingers again, "nothing separates a good walleye fisherman from a goombah walleye fisherman than his jig." Osborne breathed an audible sigh of relief: Ray's star turn was still on track.

"Frankly, fellas, choosing the right jig weight can make you or break you. The secret is this: quit trying to make a fish strike you. Change your attitude. Keep contact with the bottom. Okay?" Ray's voice slowed to emphasis his point: "You must present as close to the structure as possible. What's structure? The contour, the rockpile, the bottom where the fish are feeding—"

"Doing great, Ray," Marilyn interrupted. "Don't show a jig right now, we'll do B-roll and shoot some sponsor jigs in the studio. Just keep going."

"But . . . ready, Doc?" Ray signaled to Osborne to open the bait box he'd brought on board and slipped into the baitwell.

Osborne followed directions, the slippery bait greasing his fingers.

"What makes a great walleye fisherman, guys? Not good, but great? What gets you past that tiny two-pounder and up to the five pound range? Forget crankbait. Forget crawlers. The secret? Le-e-eches." Ray rolled the word off his tongue. He turned to look at the camera, his face alive, eyes sparkling brighter than the waves around him.

"The absolute best walleye-getter is the leech. Tough, durable—Doc, hook one on.

"See? Watch the good dentist, you goombahs."

Osborne raised his arm, fifty years of spin-casting kicked in to give him a soft, smooth roll. If only he could do that with a fly rod.

"See how hard you can cast?" he heard Ray over his right shoulder. "That leech will keep on swimming for hours. And you can't beat 'em below slip bobbers . . ." Osborne cast again. "Treat yourself to the most seductive sidewinding action you'll ever—hey! Doc's got one on!"

Ray shut up and moved aside as Rich crept forward to let the camera zoom in on the action. Osborne played the fish as close to the boat as he could. As he worked the fish, Ray talked, "Now you see why the thrill for the real walleye guy is catching this fish in shallow water. Five feet deep or less. I know fellas will drive hundreds of miles to fish bubble eyes in shallow water."

Snap! The walleye flipped high into the air, flashing green and gold. The white-tipped tail flung a rainbow of crystalline raindrops around it. With an expert flick of his wrist, Ray scooped it in. Grabbing the gills with two fingers, he held the flashing, gleaming fish high, "Good work, Doc. You got seven pounds of pure gold. Okay, let's go again."

As Osborne slipped another leech on, Ray continued, "The problem you'll run into with leeches is cold water. They curl up tight when the water is under 41 degrees. Other than that the only hazard is storing them in your home refrigerator. Before you do it, you better be sure you got an okay from your family members, fellas, or you'll be paying psychotherapy bills for years . . ."

"What?" Marilyn asked from the back of the boat.

Ray looked towards her, which actually put him looking into Rich's lens, "How would you like to reach for the pickles and get an eyeful of these?" He whipped his hand up to thrust a quart jar full of leeches at the camera.

Four huge walleyes later, Osborne looked back at Marilyn. Ray wasn't going say anything but Osborne drew the line at poaching. He was not going to break state law, too. Not even for Ray's television debut. "We got the bag limit," he said. "Do you want to keep going?"

"No, no, this is great stuff," said Marilyn. "We're fine. Rich? Shoot some B-roll of the shoreline, the boat, and get our walleye guys from a couple angles, please." With that, Ray throttled the motor and turned the boat back towards shore.

"Say, Ray," Marilyn yelled over the roar of the motor, "those livewells are huge. Do people really catch fish that big?"

"Aways hoping," Ray yelled back. "Lot of fishermen have trouble estimating the size of their future catch. Same problem they have estimating the size of certain personal appendages—"

"Ray—" Osborne stopped him. Ray had managed to stay relatively tasteful in his remarks so far. Was he going to ruin it now?

Ray smirked at Osborne. He knew what the good dentist was thinking.

"Gives a guy a chance to think positive," he finished.

Marilyn threw back her head and laughed, "I'd like to keep *that* in the show."

"Gee, doesn't look like many people fish here," commented Rich a few minutes later as he stepped carefully from the boat, handing his camera over to Wayne.

"Yeah, folks get spoiled on the big lakes," said Ray casually as he stepped onto the shore. "I prefer the small ones for early morning fishing."

"It's the *only* early morning fishing," said Osborne, following Rich from the boat. He was pretty excited himself over the catch. Why hadn't Ray taken him here before?

"Gee," said Marilyn. "I never thought you'd get your limit. This is great footage. Now where do we say we were fishing, Ray?" She held her pen ready over the clipboard.

"Oh, no. We never say that," said Ray. "Fishing holes are top-secret."

"Ah," said Marilyn, "I like the way you put that. Good, I

see you're still miked, I can use that, too. But I do need you both to sign some releases, please."

She handed the clipboard with the release forms over to Osborne, then stuck her hands in her back pockets and walked down to the water's edge. Rich walked alongside her, a smaller videocam on his shoulder scanning the horizon, the lens zooming in and out as he turned. Marilyn inhaled deeply as she gazed across the lake.

"God, the air is great up here. What incredible scenery—ohmygosh! What kind of duck is that?" She pointed towards the middle of the lake where a dark distinctive shape had popped to the surface.

"That's no duck" said Ray as he was stepping out of the boat, hat in hand. He set his hat on his head and walked his loopy walk down to where Marilyn stood on the shore. He looked past her, then straightened up, cupping his hands to his mouth. Rich caught the movement and shifted the lens towards him. Osborne noticed Ray still wore the small black mike clipped onto his shirt pocket. Miked and ready for stardom.

His eyes serious over the carefully brushed and trimmed beard that reached to his chest, the stuffed trout hat cocked jauntily over his ears, Ray seemed to remember Donna's constant nagging that he stand up straight and pull in his gut. Throwing his shoulders back, Ray looked out across the lake toward the dark figure rocking in silence on the glassy surface.

Osborne closed his eyes and held his breath.

The haunting call of the loon started low and distant as if far across lake waters at dusk. Then the bird swept closer, its dark tones echoing over the reeds and gentle waves. That's when Osborne heard the impossible: he heard the mate answer and the two call back and forth, each distinct in tone, one overlapping the other. No sooner had the crescendo risen than the birds fell still. Marilyn and her crew stood in stunned silence, waiting. A low flutter of sound rose with mounting urgency, then a hush . . . and a final aching cry to the wind. With exquisite control, Ray gave voice to the autumnal call of the male loon: the call to travel south.

Osborne exhaled slowly. He opened his eyes.

"That's no duck," said Ray with a happy grin, "that's a loon."

"That was no loon, that was Ray," said Osborne.

"Did that—did the loon call back to you?" Marilyn was clearly dumbfounded.

"I wish," said Ray, "I did that, too. Fooled ya, huh?"

"Ray is a champion looncaller," said Osborne.

"Wait, wait, let me take notes," Marilyn reached for her clipboard. When she had her pen ready, Osborne continued, happy to finally be able to return a small favor to the man who had helped him through so many dark and lonely hours.

"Every June there is a loon-calling contest in Mercer, a little town northwest of here, that draws people from Canada and all across northern Minnesota and Michigan. He always finishes first or second," said Osborne. "The old guides say Ray Pradt is the finest looncaller they've ever heard."

"That was a showstopper, Ray," said Marilyn. "Thank you. You're giving me great stuff. I have one last question, though. What do you do with all these beautiful fish?"

"Ah, hah," said Ray. "What time do you have?"

Marilyn glanced at her watch, "Eleven-fifteen."

"I'll tell ya what," said Ray. "You absolutely cannot understand walleye fishing until you've tasted it. Since Doc's not due in town 'till one, and since I recently acquired a pound of fresh butter, I think it's time we go to my place.

"No, no, not to worry," he raised a finger at the look of doubt on Marilyn's face, "you'll be heading south in 45 minutes, I promise."

Osborne was surprised to see Marilyn look over at Wayne. The man gave a slight nod. Osborne was taken aback. Why was Wayne, the silent sound man, suddenly giving permission?

ten

Twenty minutes later, after stopping for Ray and Osborne to pick up their vehicles, the TV van lurched its way down through towering Norway pines to Ray's trailer. Ray's truck followed, and Osborne, who had driven ahead to park at his own place and let Mike out, walked down the drive after them.

Ray had definitely planned ahead. An old bait pail was perched on a tree stump just outside the screen door, bursting with pink petunias that cascaded to the pine needle carpet. Off to the left, behind a wire deer fence, Ray's two golden Labs observed the rush of activity, their huge black eyes polite but curious. As a backdrop, Loon Lake shimmered in all its late morning blueness.

"Ray, your place looks downright bucolic," said Marilyn as she jumped out of the van. "This is Northwoods wilderness?"

"Yes and no," said Ray, walking towards her. The string of walleyes dangling from his right hand. "If you want a true wilderness forest, you have to drive about forty miles due north. All this pine and oak and birch that you see back here," he swept his left arm towards the road behind them, "all that was logged in the late 1800s. Most is second growth. But these white pines along the lake here? They saw the white man come."

"Magnificent," said Marilyn looking up.

Ray allowed only a moment of admiration, "C'mon inside,

folks. You might want to watch me clean ol' bubble eyes."

The day was warming up, but with the thermals off the potato fields blowing steadily across Loon Lake, the air stayed comfortably cool. As he entered the house trailer ahead of everyone, Ray threw all his windows wide open, filling the neat, comfortable interior with sunny fresh air.

Ray's mobile home might look tacky from the outside, but inside it was spacious and quite clean. The living room held a plump, over-sized dark blue corduroy sofa and matching recliner against cream walls with curtains to match. One corner held the jukebox, Ray's pride and joy; the other an antique wooden phone booth with a working rotary phone. A round oak table filled the kitchen.

Ray walked through the trailer to a back door. He opened it, letting in the two yellow Labs who sniffed everyone politely, then focused all their attention on Ray, wagging their tails until he had set down two large bowls of dog food.

"Good-looking animals," said Wayne. "Ducks or grouse?"

"Both. 'Rough' and 'Ready' got the softest mouths in the county," said Ray. "They can scoop a mallard without moving a feather."

"Make yourselves at home," he said, waving towards the refrigerator, "Sodas in there; ice cold water on tap; mugs on the first shelf."

"I can't believe I was having lunch at Spago's on Sunset Boulevard just yesterday," said Marilyn, seating herself at the round kitchen table, "and now I'm sitting in a trailer in a town called Loon Lake? What kind of job do I have anyway?"

"You might want to watch Ray fillet those fish," said Osborne, tapping her on the shoulder. In all his years of fishing, he had never been able to wield the fillet knife with the finesse of Ray Pradt. And so the four of them gathered around the kitchen sink to watch Ray work his magic.

"I got this from an old hermit friend of mine," he said, brandishing a long narrow blade with a wooden handle that looked as old as the white pines girding the lake outside the trailer. "Herman the German's his name. He migrated down here from Canada in the 30s. I believe his father or his grandfather made this. Herman's in his nineties, so you gotta figure this blade's been around awhile. I keep it sharp—Wayne, you soundmeister, feel that edge." Ray held the blade out for an appreciative, very careful touch.

With an expert flourish, he sliced open the bellies of the five fish. Entrails landed with a soft thwop on a brown paper bag sitting on the counter. Grabbing the tail of each fish, he slid the knife just below the surface of the skin, adding each sheer strip to the entrails. Then, tipping the edge of the knife at a slight angle. he whipped slice after smooth slice until ten perfect planks of shining walleye rested on a chipped green Fiestaware dinner plate.

Less than five minutes had passed. Meanwhile, a cast iron frying pan already boasted a half pound of butter sizzling over a gas flame. Ray turned around to lower the heat. He grabbed a beat-up cream-colored mixing bowl, threw a cup of flour into it, shook his big silver salt shaker over that and deftly ground a teaspoon or more of fresh black pepper onto the mix. In went the fish, over that a towel, and Ray flipped the bowl over and over, shaking it up and sideways. The butter sputtered. Less than two minutes had passed.

"Hey, Rich," said Ray, as he laid the dusted fish gently into the pan, "open that drawer right behind the table there and grab those paper plates and napkins. Doc, you know where the forks are. Marilyn, make sure everyone's got something to drink. And, Wayne, put the salt n' pepper on the table, will ya?"

The smell of Ray's cooking filled with room with an aroma Osborne had only ever found one word for: "Heavenly."

In short order, everyone was seated. Soon, five chipped Fiestaware plates colored red, cobalt, yellow, green, and orange, boasted identical lightly sauteed pieces of walleye. Two per each. "Wait," said Ray, "there's more." He went to the refrigerator. From it he pulled a large orange bowl full of potato salad. "Homemade by my dear friend, the esteemed Mrs. McEldowney," he said as he set it in the center of the table.

"And for dessert," he reached back into the refrigerator— "The finest lemon merigue pie you'll find north of Chicago, made by yours truly and featuring his grandmother's perfect pie crust." The half-eaten pie went onto the table beside the potato salad.

"A toast to the Northwoods," said Ray, raising his glass of ginger ale as he seated himself at the head of the table, "Life doesn't get much better than this."

"Wait," said Marilyn, her fork poised. She stood up and

raised her mug of ice water, "Ray, I have never asked a man
this question before but I have never met a man of your talents
... Ray Pradt, will you marry me?"

"Now how can I turn that down," said Ray. He touched his
mug of ginger ale to hers. "Make me a star and we got a deal."

A look of ecstasy crossed each face with the first bite. "And
I don't even like fish," said Marilyn, rollling her eyes in disbelief. "This is fabulous."

"This is what it's all about," said Ray. He turned to Osborne,
"Y'know, Doc, you are a superb walleye fisherman. I just
don't understand why you insist on that damn fly fishing when
this is all a man needs to be happy."

"I need the challenge, Ray," said Osborne, winking at the
crew around the table, "it keeps me young. One of these days,
you'll figure it out ... when you grow up."

"Don't do it, Ray," said Marilyn. "Don't you dare grow up."

"Well," Osborne stood up and walked over to the sink with
his plate, "while you folks counsel Ray on his future, I have
an appointment to keep."

"He's working a murder investigation," volunteered Ray as
he chewed.

Osborne was astonished at the sudden change in the faces
around the table. All three—Marilyn, Rich, and Wayne—
stopped chewing, their forks frozen in midair. Something hard
and still had entered the room.

"Really," said Wayne. He had said little all morning. Now
he spoke with a tone of quiet authority. "Can you tell us about
it?"

"A little," said Osborne and relayed everything he was sure
was likely to appear in the *Loon Lake News* later that day. He
did not mention the missing fillings. He did tell them he was
deputized to help Lew because she was short on local man-
power.

"Sounds like the ex-husband to me," said Rich when Osborne had completed a synopsis of Alicia's allegations.

"Dr. Osborne," said Marilyn, "I am what I say I am—a
television producer. And Rich really is a free-lance cameraman
from a Milwaukee station, but our pal Wayne here. For one
thing, he's my brother-in-law. For another—Wayne, don't you
think you should tell them?"

"Undercover. Chicago Police," said Wayne with a half-

smile on his face and an edgy look in his eye. He didn't seem
real happy with Marilyn's decision to tell them who he was.

"Why?" said Ray.

"Rich and I are hanging around for the weekend, catching
up on the action around here," said Wayne. "Rich is my cover.
I don't need to tell you it's impossible to blend with the locals
in this area. But the walleye tournament gives me a great excuse to hang out."

"Why?" repeated Ray. Osborne checked his watch, then
crossed his arms and leaned back against the sink. He had an
hour before he had to meet Lew. This was getting interesting.

"I'm not sure I . . . ," said Wayne, brushing crumbs off the
table with a large white hand as he stalled, "Oh, what the hell.
We're up against the wall, Ray. We know we've got a pipeline
of drugs heading north from the Chicago port. We know the
source, and we know the stuff is surfacing up here and all the
way into the Upper Peninsula. But even though we know it's
being moved into Wisconsin, we haven't been able to determine exactly how. Since we've been working from the bottom
up with no luck, we thought we'd try from the top down and
see what might surface.

"This walleye tournament being a big, big weekend around
here, I thought I'd hang out and see what I can dig up. See if
any of the dealers around here might give me some leads."

"You mean drug dealers," said Ray. "Any local names?"

"Sure," said Wayne with a chuckle, "Ray Pradt."

"Ya gotta be kiddin," Ray stood up and reached into the
cupboard by the sink for a small cup of toothpicks. When he
sat down, his eyes were dead serious. "That's ten years old. I
have no felony arrests, only misdemeanors."

"Yeah, I know that," said Wayne."

"Now I'm not going to say I don't smoke, but only on
special occasions."

"Like opening day ice fishing season?" The entire county
had heard about Ray's quandary that day: to celebrate the success of his new jig technique—he had his limit in less than
two hours—he indulged in little something with a distinctive
aroma, an aroma that happened to drift by an off-duty sherriff
who was fishing with his teenage son. Unfortunately, it was
the son who noticed. Ray's day did not have a happy ending.

"You heard about that?" A sheepish grin spread over Ray's
face. His eyes twinkled.

"Yep, I heard about that little caper," said Wayne. That's why you can help me, Ray. You're trusted up here."

"Yes I am, and I want it to stay that way. Wayne, I'm not your man. I've got my hands full. I'm under more stress than you can imagine," said Ray, crossing his legs and swinging his foot. "I *have* to deliver ten humdinger boats for the pros fishing this tournament. The boats were to be here last week— but the jabone delivering the damn things is late. Real late. Today late. Until those boats are here, I'm not doing anything for anybody."

"No boats, no fishing, hey," said Rich.

"You got it." Ray tapped his toothpick on the table. "I am not a happy man." A look of despair crossed his face suddenly, "Does this mean you're not really doing this ESPN thing?"

"Oh, no, no. This is for real," said Marilyn. "You were fabulous. The show is on. Not to worry. Rich and Wayne— I'm making Wayne pay for his cover, see—are going to shoot more B-roll for me during the tournament. But, Ray, you're my story. I promise, you are the star."

"Let me think about it, Wayne. Okay?"

Ray unfolded all six feet six inches to tower over the kitchen table. He reached forward to gather up the paper plates. "Just one question, you guys. What the hell is this B-roll you keep talking about?"

As Marilyn started to describe the background visuals and sounds that she needed, Osborne rose to leave. He shook hands around the table, then opened the screen door. Ray walked out with him, "Thanks again, Doc. You heading up to the res with the Chief?" Osborne nodded. "Then what?"

"Meredith's home. The Willows. Alicia's meeting us at three."

"I might be by, Doc. I've always wanted a look inside that place."

"They say it's haunted," grinned Osborne with a wave.

"I'm sure it is."

When Osborne got to his house, he let Mike back in and checked his answering machine. He had two calls. The first voice, constricted and stammering, was halfway through flight arrival times at the Rhinelander airport before Osborne recognized it was Mallory. She sounded like she was gasping for air. This was not the first time in recent months that she had sounded so tense. Tense or drunk. He doubted it was grief that had her so strung out. Osborne was relieved that her flight wasn't due in until early the next morning. He needed time to prepare for her arrival—in more ways than one.

A crisp-voiced Lew followed, instructing him to meet her up at the casino. No need to drive all the way into town and back out again. That suited Osborne fine—gave him time for a nap.

As he set his timer for thirty minutes, he tried to guess which of the nosy neighbors on the party line, whose soft clicks he heard on the machine after Lew had hung up, would gossip that he and the Chief of Police had a bingo date. Probably the Anderson sisters, the old biddies.

Ah well, he thought as he closed his eyes, small towns may offer a simpler life but no less an observed one.

eleven

A heavy summer haze swamped even the electronically controlled interior of the Northern Lights Casino. Pressing in through windows and open doors, it washed out the vivid lighting and damped the ringing slots to a steady drone. Nevertheless, Osborne's eyes had to do a fancy two-step to adjust to the neon messages flashing along the perimeters of the room like lurid fishing lures adorning a sport shop wall.

He strolled slowly down the wide entry corridor. To his left was a casual sandwich bar–type restaurant, a sea of dozens and dozens of formica-topped tables stretching back to a distant shore of silver-domed serving centers. To his right, a formal French Café with white linen tablecloths, muted lighting, and tuxedo-clad waiters poised to serve the slot winner, the blackjack champ, the casino-courted high roller. He scanned both for Lew.

No need to look far. She was sitting to his left at a small round table, a paper cup in front of her. Legs crossed, right arm propped on the table, she was studying a sheaf of papers in her hand. She looked up as he walked towards her.

"Have you been waiting long?" asked Osborne.

"No-o-o, maybe five minutes. Say, Doc, how're you doin'? That was one long night we had." She set the papers down to look at him, eyes friendly and concerned.

"As a matter of fact, I got a nice nap before heading up

here, thank you," Osborne pulled out the chair across from her and sat down.

"Me, too. Grabbed a peanut butter sandwich and closed my office door for a cat nap. I feel quite refreshed. Guess what?" She leaned forward, eyes sparkling with anticipation. "Ralph said the Deerskin tonight. Between seven and nine. The tiny blue-winged olives will be hatching. I'm going up, and I was hoping you might like to come along. I've still got all your gear in my truck, y'know. But if you're too tired, Doc, I can hook up with Ralph. He'll be fishing the Deerskin tonight for sure."

"Oh no, I feel great," said Osborne.

Even if he didn't, he was damned if he'd have Lew fishing with Ralph. Ralph! If he had to hear that pretentious expatriate Londoner's name one more time, he swore he'd break out in hives. For some reason, he was growing increasingly irritated each time the subject of Ralph came up. Not only had he had to endure being patronized in front of all Ralph's customers when he walked in for that estimate on his fly-fishing equipment, but then Ralph had the nerve to describe Osborne to Lew as the "old guy in the Camry" that night they fished the Prairie. After all, Osborne was only—what—ten, maybe twelve, years older than Ralph?

Then, he had had to hear how Ralph was "the best fly-fisherman east of Montana," "the best" to call the hatch, "the best" to tie the fly. Hell, thought Osborne, let's all-around fishing. Let's talk musky fishing. Now there's the measure of a good fisherman—he bet Ralph couldn't cast a crankbait fifty feet.

No sirree, the only "best of" he would give Ralph right now was "pain in the butt." But what really irritated him most was not understanding why he let the guy bother him so much.

If Lew sensed his animosity towards her other fishing buddy, she didn't let on. She seemed pleased Doc was up for fishing the hatch.

"Well, good. We'll head over right after our meeting at the Willows. It's only twenty miles from town. I left my truck in the jail parking lot."

"Maybe we can get a bite along the way?"

"How 'bout we take some sandwiches from here?"

"Good idea."

"Okay, Doc, that's set," Lew slapped her hands on the table as if the fishing plan made her entire day.

"Time to check out this Mr. Chesnais." She turned to wave at a young waitress who was passing by. "Excuse me, miss," said Lew. "We're looking for Clint Chesnais?"

"Oh sure," said the girl with pleasant smile. "He works over in the Café. You won't miss him. Look for the cute one."

" 'Cute?' What can be 'cute' about a middle-aged man?" said Lew in a low tone to Osborne as they walked towards the French Café.

The Café was nearly empty. Once Lew explained that her visit involved a personal matter regarding a serious accident, the maitre d' had nodded in understanding and said he would send Mr. Chesnais over immediately.

"Take all the time you need," he'd said, directing them to a banquette at the back of the restaurant that offered some privacy.

"No need to cause anyone to lose their job or generate any more friction up here," explained Lew to Osborne after the maitre'd walked away. "If he's not our man, we don't need the tribe to think we singled him out without good cause. Tribal relations are delicate enough what with the spearfishing situation."

Osborne knew exactly what she meant. When it came to spearfishing, the facts were simple but emotionally charged. When Native Americans, in this case the Ojibwa, sold their land to the U.S. Government so many, many years ago, they did not sell the hunting and fishing rights. They retained the right to hunt and fish wherever they please, whenever they please. In the Northwoods, unfortunately, there is a small segment of sport fishermen who resent the Native Americans' right to fish any time of the year. Some people call that white male minority "redneck." Osborne called them "misguided." Whatever you call them, they are vocal and difficult and, sometimes, dangerous.

The face of the man who crossed the room towards them, slipping gracefully between the tables, carried a quizzical expression and obvious evidence of his origins. Osborne recognized the same Metis bloodline that ran in his mother's family. Though Osborne could find only miniscule evidence of his heritage in his own features, Chesnais was clearly second generation.

Osborne guessed him to be the grandchild of an intermarriage between a Chippewa and a French Canadian. Unlike the broad-shouldered, heavy-boned, fullblooded Chippewa native to the Northwoods, Chesnais had inherited a slighter, more delicate frame. Of medium height, slim, and darkly handsome in his black tuxedo, he walked towards them with the bearing of an aristocratic Parisian.

The Meteis are exceptionally attractive people, and Clint Chesnais was a fine example: his dark, tanned complexion offset by a classic oval-shaped head that would catch the eye of any sculptor. A cap of lightly thinning black hair, greying at the temples, was cut close at the sides but left to curl stylishly long in the back. If you didn't know he was a waiter, thought Osborne, you would think he was on his way to a black-tie dinner party. He wondered if that was what had attracted Meredith.

Chesnais spoke as he neared their table. The voice was reedy and dark, careful in its diction: "Are you looking for me?" An expression of guarded surprise crossed his face as Lew displayed her badge.

"Mr. Chesnais," Lew rose and extended her hand. "I'm Chief Lewellyn Ferris of the Loon Lake Police Department. This is my deputy, Dr. Paul Osborne. Please sit down."

Chesnais looked alarmed. "One of my kids?" he asked.

"No, no," said Lew. His face cleared, and he sat down. He placed his left arm on the table and leaned forward, waiting. Osborne couldn't help but notice the man's distinctive eyes, moss green and set above high cheekbones under a wide forehead. The satin smooth skin of his face was free of age lines, the bone structure feminine in its graceful lines. Years of studying faces up close had tuned Osborne to what was natural and classic and compelling in the human form. This man was quite good-looking.

"I have some news," Lew emphasized her words, "you may find disturbing. A friend of yours, Meredith Marshall, was found dead last night."

"Dead?" Chesnais was obviously taken aback.

"In the Prairie River. Possibly drowned. Possibly . . . foul play." Lew paused.

"Oh . . . I'm sorry to hear that." Chesnais seemed saddened

by her words, though his reaction was subtle. Just a slight tipping of his head as he looked off to his right, his eyes cast down ever so slightly. It could be that the news did not genuinely surprise him, thought Osborne, or he was a man who had experienced so many losses that one more no longer had much effect.

"You did know Mrs. Marshall . . . ," said Lew.

"That's why you're here, isn't it?" Chesnais's eyes connected directly with Lew's. The message in his clipped response was clear: You know I know her. If you've got something to ask me—get it on the table. His attitude made Osborne wonder if Chesnais was accustomed to being under suspicion.

"How well did you know her?"

"We've been seeing each other for several months. I've also been doing some work for her. This isn't my only job." Chesnais gestured towards the empty tables.

"I'm a master gardener, and I was about to restore several areas of plantings on some property she recently bought. I moved back here from Minneapolis last spring, see, and I'm just starting up my business. But, yes, I have been seeing her on a personal level if that's what you're—"

"Mr. Chesnais, I'm sorry to pry, but I need to ask some personal questions." Lew kept her voice low and very polite.

"I understand."

"Have you been intimate?"

"Yes."

"How recently?"

"Two nights ago. How—"

"How did you meet Mrs. Marshall?"

Once again, Osborne noted Lew's style of interrogating was as relentless and targeted as her casting for a sly trout.

"She bought some perennials from me at the Farmer's Market in Loon Lake last June. We got to talking about what she was hoping to do with her property. She invited me out to look at the place. We went to dinner and then . . ." Chesnais stopped, chewing the inside of his cheek. Lew's earlier words had finally sunk in. His eyes brimmed with tears.

Osborne, still fascinated by the greenness of the man's eyes, saw another subtle change in his expression, a slight start as if an unsettling thought had crossed his mind. Whatever it was lingered, making him appear preoccupied as Lew continued her questioning.

"Where were you last night, Clint?" she asked gently.

"Huh? Oh, sorry. Here. I was here. I came on for the late shift from four to midnight. Chief Ferris, when . . . how did Meredith die? She was an expert fisherman."

"We don't know yet."

If it had occurred to him that he was a suspect, Clint Chesnais seemed unperturbed by the prospect. Both his elbows rested on the table, his hands resting calmly in front of him. He remained serious, serene, waiting. Suddenly, he looked up, the maitre d' was waving to him from across the room.

"Excuse me for a moment, I seem to have a phone call."

Once he was out of earshot, Lew turned to Osborne. "Now that is a hauntingly beautiful man. Did you see those eyes?"

"Yeah," a soft well of disappointment filled Osborne's heart. Hauntingly beautiful? Was this the kind of man that attracted Lew?

"I've seen it before," she continued. "He is exactly the type to get a summer woman in trouble. Good-looking, bohemian lifestyle, and very experienced in handling a woman—in every sense of the word. A dangerous type to have around when you're vulnerable. At seventeen, you get pregnant . . ." Lew paused abruptly, Chesnais was heading back their way. Osborne wondered if she would have finished, ". . . at thirty-eight, you get killed." He made a mental note to ask her to complete that thought later.

Meanwhile, he felt a sense of relief. Even if Lew had acknowledged Chesnais' good looks, her cynicism reassured him. She read deeper than the surface.

"Just a few more questions, Clint," she said as he returned to the table.

"Certainly," said Chesnais. "That was another one of my gardening clients. I oversee two estate gardens up in Land o' Lakes. I'll be there tomorrow if you need me."

"I may. But right now what I'd like to know is . . . ," Lew leaned forward and looked hard into his face, "were you aware of anyone ever threatening Meredith? Do you know anyone who may have wanted to harm her?"

Chewing the inside of his mouth again, Chesnais sat quietly, thinking. "I've known her less than three months," he said finally. "I never met any of her Chicago crowd, but she didn't imply any problems with anyone. Early on, she talked about some difficulties she was having with her husband and their divorce, but she seemed to be working those out."

Lew remained silent, letting him think out loud.

"See, Meredith and I didn't get into much personal stuff. We shared some common interests—gardening, food. I'm a pretty good cook myself, so we talked about food quite a bit. We were designing a kitchen garden for her to start this fall.

"I'm kind of a jack of all trades, see, so I was able to do a few odd jobs around her place that made her happy. And she liked people, y'know? She was basically a happy person who enjoyed good conversation. She told funny stories, she was fun to do things with. I didn't have a sense that she thought people didn't like her or anything. No threats, nothing at all like that."

"Did she seem worried about anything?"

"She was very caught up in this new restaurant and the catering business with her sister."

"What do you think of Alicia?"

"Never met her. Well, maybe she came by my truck at the market that day I met Meredith, but I don't recall meeting her per se. Meredith and I didn't really go out, see. We'd do some gardening around her place, then cook something up together. I might stay over once or twice a week.

"I work some pretty wicked hours here at the casino. It's not easy building a business, y'know. I'm not bankrolled like Meredith is. Was."

Chesnais sat up straight in his chair and crossed his arms over his chest. "Let me think about it. I'm still . . . I'm so surprised by all this. Meredith was a very nice person. Very nice . . . you know . . ." Again, the look of distraction crept into his eyes.

Lew glanced at her watch. "Oh, boy, it's getting late. Clint, if I need to talk with you further, is there a home number where you can be reached?"

"Certainly," said Chesnais and gave it to her. "I have a house trailer outside Clearwater. But I'll be here until eight this evening." Then Chesnais raised a forefinger and paused, as if remembering something critical, "speaking of Meredith being worried about something?"

"Yes?" said Lew.

"She was worried about her brother-in-law. His state of

mind. We were at the grocery store in Eagle River one night, and we ran into him. Seems he was supposed to be out of the country at the time, so she was quite surprised to see him. He'd been drinking."

"Is this Peter Roderick?"

"Yeah. Nice enough fella, I think. But having some emotional problems or so it seemed. She invited him to stay at her place."

Lew nodded thoughtfully, "You mean at The Willows."

"Um hum. Seventeen bedrooms. She had plenty of room. Room for lost souls." Chesnais gave an embarrassed little laugh.

Lew gave Chesnais a slight smile, "Like you?"

"Aren't we all sometimes?" he said softly. "I will miss her."

"Thanks, Clint," said Lew as she and Osborne stood up. "I'll be in touch. Here's my card if you think of anything else."

A few minutes later Lew and Osborne, sandwich bags in hand, walked out the casino doors in silence. They headed toward the parking lot. Suddenly, they both stopped and turned to each other saying almost exactly the same thing simultaneously: "Why on earth is he waiting table?"

"You wonder, don't you?" Osborne stopped by his station wagon, his hand on the door handle, "the man is well-spoken, obviously very bright. Why doesn't he have a regular job? Lew, I find this very peculiar . . . ," Osborne paused, thinking.

"Maybe he wants to live life on his own terms, Doc."

"But what on earth would attract a woman like Meredith Marshall to a man like Chesnais? Just look at her—a successful restauranteur, a bestselling cookbook author, the wife of a prominent businessman. Well, ex-wife. It had to go deeper than looks, Lew. I don't think Meredith Marshall was what you call a 'summer woman.' Why wouldn't she choose—?" He struggled for a description of the kind of man that would be right for a woman like Meredith.

"Choose what?" said Lew, "a hard charger like herself? Think about it, Doc. She did once. And look where that got her. As far as wanting to be with a man like Chesnais . . . ."

"Oh, Doc," Lew's voice changed. A soft seriousness crept in, "I think the answer is a simple one. Divorce is as painful as a death in the family. You know what I mean?"

She looked at him. Yes, he knew that loneliness too well.

Until now, he'd never heard another human being admit they'd been there, too.

"That would make her very vulnerable wouldn't it?" he said.

"What makes you vulnerable makes you strong."

Osborne looked away so she couldn't see what was in his eyes: her understanding made him love her. Lot of good it would do him. But it sure helped him recognize what it was he felt for Ralph: jealousy. Pure, unadulterated jealousy. Oddly enough, the two emotions mixed together made him feel years younger. Alive.

As Osborne got into his car and turned the ignition key, he considered again what it was that had distracted Clint Chesnais. Each time the preoccupied look had crossed the handsome face, it was almost as if someone had entered the room and signaled him to shut up. Strange.

twelve

Osborne turned left off Highway 17 onto Birchwood Road immediately behind Lew's cruiser. Birchwood Road, wide at this point, skirted the shoreline of Cranberry Lake. Close to the highway, the property values were reflected in multiple driveways, marked with signs proudly welcoming visitors to "Our Little Piece of Heaven" or "Larson's Lair," which lead to modest year-round houses visible from the road. Every house backed up to a dock, and every dock held at least one boat.

Just two miles down the road, such plentiful access to the lake disappeared. The road narrowed and the pine forest closed in. Soon the lake was so hidden that only random slivers of light escaped through the dense woods.

The two-story and split-level lake houses gave way to scattered log cabins, weathered black and nestled deep under the trees, often only a roof line visible. Several recently-cut private roads led to the type of architect-designed log and stone mansions that were popping up more and more frequently on the bigger lakes. No Trespassing replaced the Welcome that had marked earlier entrances. These were expensive lake properties whose owners did not want to see anyone uninvited.

Soon, even the sunlight disappeared, and the blacktop gave way to a gravel lane that twisted deeper and deeper into the gloom cast by an umbrella of ancient maples and oaks with a scattering of pine. Now the No Trespassing signs were scattered more and more nervously, as if to fend off not just hunters but mountain bikers and cross-country skiers whose trails crisscrossed the road at several junctions.

As the lane snaked and forked, Osborne's hands swung back and forth with the steering wheel. His chest tightened. He'd forgotten that Meredith's estate was at the end of a drive where he had nearly lost his life.

One fiercely cold January night, he'd chosen the wrong fork on the way to a Ducks Unlimited meeting. Driving in circles down identical snowbanked lanes, road signs long since buried under the snow, it was nearly two hours before he was able to find a lighted residence where he could ask for directions. Even today, four years later, he could recall the minutes of mounting panic, the frightening realization that he might be spending the night in his car with a very real threat of freezing to death in the 30 degrees-below-zero weather.

Lew's brake lights came on, and the cruiser slowed under a canopy of white birch and Norway pine. As Osborne rounded the curve behind her, massive lannon stone pillars confronted them. An eight-foot tall iron gate stood open to a freshly-paved drive. Overhead, etched in wrought iron script and definitively marking the end of the road, floated two words: "The Willows."

Beyond the gate, the road dropped down and down, corkscrewing through a final stand of forest that grew so close that pine boughs brushed the top of Osborne's station wagon and scraped against his windows.

Suddenly, the trees dropped away. The drive swept up a small hill to end in a breathtaking sight: straight ahead to the west, the brilliant blue of Cranberry Lake surrounded a peninsula of perfectly-mown lawn dotted with manicured spruce and hemlock. Sunlight dappled across the grass. In swampy bays along the shoreline, long-leafed branches of weeping willow swayed with consummate grace in the lake breezes. Misshapen at heart, the willow trees masked their gnarled trunks and twisted arms in flowing capes of emerald green.

The drive had crested in a small parking lot bordered on the left by a long, low, six-car garage. Osborne parked his car near the garage and got out.

He could feel the thermals from the distant potato fields working their late afternoon magic, banishing the heavy haze with sweet lake breezes. Osborne took a deep breath, determined to shrug off the tension that had crept through his muscles, determined to appreciate this scene of perfect tranquillity.

Off to his right was The Willows' main house. Norman Gothic in design, the entry was marked with a flagstone walk leading up to a gated stone balustrade and a balcony that led, in turn, to a carved mahogany door. The door was shadowed from the left by a tall stone turret that peaked just below a sheltering Norway pine.

The mansion of gray lannon stone had been designed to burrow back into the rocky hillside. Though the turreted entrance was imposing, the rear wing seemed to sag under its heavy slate roof, ending up either half buried underground or hidden behind elegant cones of arbor vitae. Up close, The Willows struck Osborne as less a home than a dark and mammoth cave.

Off to his left, he could see the old boathouse. Totally different in design, the boathouse was as exposed as the house was hidden. Cantilevered out over the water, its exterior of burnished brown cedar shake shingles captured the late afternoon sunlight to glow as if painted in gold leaf. A magnificent sleeping porch wrapped around the building. Thousands of panes of leaded glass studded walls of French doors trimmmed in forest green.

Osborne understood instantly why Meredith Marshall had wanted to open a restaurant here: the views of the lake and evening sunsets would be unforgettable, even more so when enhanced by exquisite cuisine and fine wines. Yes, he could see how the boathouse had captured the imagination of the talented chef. What a loss. His pleasure in the view turned to sadness. He looked for Lew.

He didn't have to look far. In the circle drive fronting the main house, she had pulled in behind another cruiser. Roger, the deputy, was leaning against his car, arms crossed, head down. He peered up as Lew got out of her car. Osborne got the distinct impression Roger was expecting something unpleasant. He looked like Mike, Osborne's black Lab, had looked after eating the remote control for the television set—uneasy.

Lew started to walk towards him, then she stopped. Osborne followed her eyes. Yellow police tape lay on the ground, torn away from the balcony posts that fronted the flagstone walk-way. She turned to Roger.

In front of Roger's car was parked a black Mercedes, which Osborne recognized as Alicia's. Ahead of that a small red van.

As Osborne neared Lew and Roger, he could hear her voice, low and insistent: "What do you mean they're in there? Roger, I told you to be here by six this morning and to let no one inside. No one."

Roger looked very, very unhappy. It had to be a moment when the former life insurance salesman wished he had never made a career change. "I was a little late, Chief. I got here at six-thirty or so, Mrs. Roderick was already in the house. She told me you said it was okay because she's family. You know, she's a former client of mine. I respect her, Chief. I respect she lost her sister—"

"I hear you, Roger. What's with the van?" Lew's eyes had darkened but her voice was level, almost jocular.

"Mrs. Roderick—she took the housekeeper in with her, Chief. But I told 'em both, they couldn't take nothin' off the premises. I told 'em and they haven't, Chief. Not a thing."

"The *housekeeper* is in there?" Though Lew kept her voice low, a note of incredulity had crept in.

"Roger . . . ," Lew gave a long pause, "Why didn't you radio in to check this out with me?"

"Well—Chief, y'see—," he stammered, "There was no way I—I'll tell ya, Chief, I woulda had to pull my gun to keep her outta there."

"Fine. What do you think it's for? Mourning doves?"

"Mrs. Roderick isn't the kind of person—"

"I know, I know, she's a former client of yours. Roger, you are not selling life insurance, this is a murder investigation."

Osborne suppressed a smile. He knew exactly how Alicia would have intimidated the elderly deputy. Railroaded right over the old guy whose crime-busting credentials were limited to issuing traffic citations. He must have stewed here for hours, hoping against hope that Alicia would leave before Lew arrived. Poor guy, his face was dead white.

"Okay, okay," the tone in Lew's voice was calming, "how long have they been here?"

"Like I said, Mrs. Roderick was here when I got here this morning, Chief. Just coming out. Then she left and said she was going to see you. That's why I thought everything was okay. She just got back about an hour ago."

"And the housekeeper? How long has she been here?"

"Well, jeez," Roger winced, "I dunno. Maybe Mrs. Roderick let her in before she left. She's been here all day—but, Chief, most of the time she's been over at the boathouse."

"I see. Well, Roger, you saved me a major budget item. I sure as heck don't need any fingerprint tech driving all the way up from Wausau now, do I? What's a fingerprint likely to be worth now? I mean, we've got people coming and going in every direction—right? Opening doors, closing windows, wiping things off . . ." Lew was quiet for a long minute, making sure Roger understood the ramifications of his mistake.

"Roger, Roger, Roger," she continued, "Do I have to put you in time out?" The humorous singsong in her voice did nothing to undercut the look she leveled at him. Lew waited for his eyes to meet hers.

Roger shifted nervously and uncrossed his arms. He glanced up and then away. "I'm really sorry, Chief. I guess I'm not very good at this, y'know. I shoulda radioed in, I know I shoulda."

"Okay this time, Roger," Lew reached over to pat him on the arm. "But if you *ever* ignore my orders again—without checking with me—you are off the force. Permanently. Understood?"

Roger nodded.

"Go on now. You've been here long enough."

As Roger pulled his cruiser out of the drive, Lew looked over at Osborne who had been standing by in silence. "Doc, what do you think?"

His first thought was that Lew didn't seem all that disturbed by Alicia's actions. As if reading his mind, Lew answered her own question, "I find this very interesting, don't you? You heard me tell that woman to wait for me in her car. I distinctly told her not to enter this house. When she met with me at the morgue this morning, she never let on that she'd already been out here, that she had already done *exactly* what I told her not to do."

"That's Alicia," said Osborne. "She does things her way. Always has."

The two of them started up the walkway towards the front door.

"Brace yourself," said Lew. "Time for the next two-year-old."

"You don't seem too upset by this."

Lew shrugged. "I apply reverse psychology, and it works. Oh, bless me," she grinned, "these predictable human beings."

And with those words Lew gave him a quick wink. She lifted the large brass pine cone that passed for a knocker on the massive front door.

thirteen

Before Lew could lower the brass pine cone, a loud "H-o-o-nk!" sounded from behind. Ray's old blue pick-up had joined the crowd of cars in the drive, double-parked alongside the Mercedes. His hood ornament, a foot-high musky frozen in a permanent leap, glinted psychedelically in the sunlight. Beneath the musky, the bug-catcher, a narrow plastic shield across the shattered grill of the old truck, declared its owner: "Gravedigger."

"What on earth is Ray doing here?" said Lew. "And who's the presidential candidate with him?"

She raised a hand to shield her eyes as she studied the two men in the truck. Then she shook her head, "Doc, much as I like that man—and I do like Ray—he's got some mighty bad habits. One big one is his tendency to hang out with types who pursue less traditional ways of making a living, if you get my drift. Until they can prove otherwise, anyone who consorts with Ray Pradt, outside of hiring him as a fishing or hunting guide, has only misbehavior in mind." She dropped her hand and turned towards Osborne.

"The latter does not include you, Doc."

"Thank you," Osborne was relieved to hear that. "You want me to talk to him?" he asked, stepping back. He checked his watch, "You go ahead with Alicia?"

"No, no, Doc. I want you with me when I talk to her. You

know her, I don't. Let's see what Ray's up to first, I've got a favor to ask of him anyway. I hope he's got time."

"Hey, how's it goin?" Ray leaned forward in the truck, talking past the chest of his passenger at Osborne and Lew as they walked up. "Meet my buddy, ol' Wayne, here.

"Doc, you remember 'ol' Wayne" from this morning." Wayne lifted his hand in a slight wave of recognition. "Ol' Wayne" looked as pudgy and hairy as he had then, but with the addition of a five o'clock shadow and a beery look in his eye. That plus the crumpled khaki fishing hat with the beat-up brim now sitting askew on his sweaty brow certified him as an official North Woods bearded woodtick. Yep, thought Osborne, if he kept this up, "ol' Wayne" would fit into the bar scene just fine.

"I thought you were going after George and the boats," said Osborne, leaning his elbows on Wayne's door.

"I was. No sign of the razzbonya. So I'm gonna take ol' Wayne here up the Cisco Chain tonight. He isn't exactly Mr. Walleye, y'know. Gotta teach him how to talk the talk if he wants to hang out with the fishing boys this weekend. Thought we'd drop by Thunder Bay later," Ray grinned. "Whaddya think, Doc? Chief? Care to join us?"

"Thanks, Ray, once was enough," said Osborne.

"Don't push your luck, bud," said Lew, giving Ray and his invitation her cut the crap look. "And keep your nose clean. I could use your help when you have a little extra time. Fact is, Ray, I could really use you right now. Are you a registered volunteer fireman?"

"Sure am," said Ray, "have been for the last four years that I've been living on Loon Lake Road. Why?"

"Then I can draft you as a deputy on a short-term basis, get you an hourly rate for the effort."

"Don't worry about that, Chief." Ray's face dropped its bantering expression. "We've got time this afternoon. That's why I drove up. George is gone, due back tomorrow morning with those boats. The warehouse manager told me they're loading his rig this afternoon. All I can do is wait, y'know. We've got some time right now." Ray checked his watch, then the sky. He looked at Lew. "I don't plan to start fishing until after six. What's up?"

"We?" Lew's eyebrows shot up. "Who's *we?*" Drawing herself up like a disapproving schoolmarm, she assessed Wayne with a look that made it clear she had no intention of drafting him as a deputy. "Excuse me? Ray, this is official business I'm talking about."

"Oh, sorry, I forgot to introduce you," said Ray, a tone of mild amusement in his voice. As always, he loved putting someone on. Especially someone with a low tolerance level for his humor: Lew.

"Chief Lewellyn Ferris, meet Detective Wayne Harper from the Chicago Police Department."

Lew looked Wayne up and down again. "Oh yeah? Nice to meet you, Detective. Got some I.D.?"

"Certainly," said Wayne with a sheepish smile. He seemed more than a little embarrassed by Ray's performance. He reached for his wallet, opened it, and handed it over to Lew. "I'm working a drug investigation. Ray is helping me get set up to do some undercover work this weekend."

"Really?" said Lew, handing the wallet back. "Not in Oneida County?"

"Oh yes, Oneida and Vilas," said Wayne.

Now it was Lew's turn to lean into Wayne's side of the truck. "Y'know Detective," she said, her tone as hostile as Osborne had ever heard it, "I do not appreciate the cooperative manner in which one law enforcement organization is willing to share information with another. You are on my territory. I am personally responsible for dealing with criminal activity here.

"Do you think you or one of your superiors could be so kind as to call ahead and inform me as to your intended activities in my area of jurisdiction? To tell me you have evidence of drug traffic heading our direction? Or am I supposed to find out the hard way when one of my officers gets wounded in a surprise drug bust that we may have staked out, too. We aren't clueless, you know. How do you think I will feel if a drug bust goes down and I know nothing about it. I will be publicly embarrassed, sir.

"Explain this to me, Detective. Or is your mission to teach us backwoods idiots how to do our jobs?"

"Well . . . ah . . . I'm very sorry about that," Wayne's face had grown redder and redder as she spoke. "You're right, of course. We should have been in touch. But, you know, very few departments share . . . not that we shouldn't but—"

"But it's the American way," Lew finished for him. "Every

man for himself. Get the bad guy, grab the glory. Hey?"

"I'm real sorry about this."

"So am I." Lew dropped her head and stared at her feet as if considering whether or not to kick him out of the county. The tension was thick in the silence around the beat-up old truck. Osborne cleared his throat. Ray looked the other direction. Finally, Lew raised her eyes to Wayne's. "You better tell me what's up."

Briefly, Wayne repeated what he had told Osborne and Ray earlier, the bleary look in his eye replaced with intense sincerity. ". . . And that's as much as we've been able to determine so far," he finished.

"I see," said Lew. "You should stop in my office and check our computer records. I've got a part-time college kid who is quite good with data analysis. He's set up a grid that may interest you. We're seeing a pattern of drug activity running up both Highways 51 and 45. We always have drugs in some form moving through here thanks to all the tourism from the cities, but this isn't quite as random as it has been in the past. Two years ago, for the record, we had one of the biggest designer drug busts in the country right outside Stevens Point. That's only ninety miles from here.

"Now all I ask, Wayne," Lew raised a cautioning finger, "is you keep me informed. Okay? Right now, I've got my hands full with a homicide. I'm due inside here as we speak to conduct a search. That's why I was hoping Ray could help me out but—"

"Whatever you need, Chief," said Wayne, eager to accomodate. "Ray and I can fish tomorrow just as easy."

"I need a ground check. The victim owns about forty acres running back from the shoreline in that direction," Lew stepped back from the truck and pointed. "The gazetteer shows a good portion is wetland, but I was hoping Ray could walk the property for me, let me know if you see anything."

"What are we looking for?"

"No idea. I just don't want any surprises. Those state boys will be up from Wausau to do their best to second-guess me." Lew looked at Wayne. "You'll find no one better in the woods than Ray Pradt, Detective. No one. You ever need an expert tracker—he's your man."

She slapped the hood of the truck with her hand, "Thanks, fellas. Appreciate it. Look for me inside when you're done, will ya?"

fourteen

Back at the entrance to The Willows, Lew lifted the brass pine cone again. This time she let it fall. It hit with a loud thud. She waited, raised it again, dropped it. Still no one answered. The matching brass door knob was unlocked. She pushed the heavy wooden door wide open. Osborne stepped in behind her.

The hallway they entered was dank and musty-smelling, reminding Osborne of the root cellars of his youth. Straight ahead, he could barely see the outlines of a lodge-like room with a vaulted ceiling. Bulky shapes, probably furniture, were shrouded in gloom.

"Dark enough for you?" whispered Lew over her shoulder.

As they got closer to the main room, they could see that heavy curtains closed off any light that might filter through the fifteen-foot windows. Still no sight or sound of anyone. "Place is a tomb," muttered Osborne.

Lew veered to the right towards a set of doors closing off the back wing of the house. Osborne followed.

Suddenly, from over Osborne's left shoulder, a huge black bat came flying at him. "Duck!" he shouted running forward and pushing Lew ahead of him. Together they stumbled down the hall. Lew grabbed at the parlor doors, which refused to open. Osborne, heart pounding, suddenly realized he heard nothing behind them. Whatever was coming had stopped. Silence.

Lew turned around first. She chuckled. "It's okay, Doc. I think we'll survive."

Once his eyes adjusted to the blackness in a far corner, Osborne could see it wasn't a bat at all. They had passed a darkened anteroom that lead up into the turret. The huge shape that had startled him was, in fact, a full suit of thirteenth-century armor guarding the darkened stairwell. Looming, yes, flying, no.

"Jeez, Lew, I'm sorry. Scared the living daylights out of me. I hope you didn't hurt yourself."

Just as he spoke, he heard a key turn. One of the parlor doors swung open and Alicia Roderick stepped out.

"Oh, Paul! Chief Ferris. I didn't realize it was three already. Come in, come in. I hope you weren't waiting long. I wasn't expecting you to come in that way."

She backed into a brightly-lit, brand-new and fully-equipped all-white kitchen, drawing them forwards. The only color contradicting the brilliant whiteness of the high-gloss walls and ceramic tiled floor was the stainless steel surface of the five-foot wide commercial stove anchoring the opposite wall of the spacious room. Osborne recognized it as a Viking, the stove Mary Lee had coveted for the lake house kitchen but that they could never afford.

The contrast between the light-filled state-of-the-art kitchen and the musty aura of dankness and decay on the other side of the door was startling. It was as if Meredith had planted her heart in this room with a long-term plan to rebuild The Willows starting from this radiant source of warmth and energy.

An exuberance of overhead lighting flooded the room, washing the color out of Alicia's face and emphasized a pale redness around her eyes. Dressed in trim-fitting Levi's and a pale blue cotton blouse with short Peter Pan sleeves exposing her long arms, Alicia had pulled her hair straight back into a silver clasp at the back of her neck. She looked tired, she looked feminine, but more than anything, she looked all business.

"Did you knock? I didn't hear you." Her tone was forthright and her dark eyes concerned. It was clear she had been interrupted: her right hand was raised with a ball-point pen pointing to the ceiling, the other held vinyl-sleeved checkbooks. "This place is so darn big—we all use the kitchen entrance. That door has a bell ringer you can hear anywhere in the house."

Alicia paused, her eyes darting back and forth between them. "What? Chief Ferris?" The alarm grew in her eyes. "Paul? You both look . . . is something wrong?"

"Yes," said Lew briskly as she marched past Alicia to a long pine baker's table in the center of the large kitchen. She set her briefcase down at the end of the table with a flourish that asserted her command of the room and everyone in it. She turned to face Alicia.

Osborne watched Lew as she stood there, authoritative in her crisp, long-sleeved khaki shirt and pants, the official summer police uniform. Even though she was shorter and stockier than Alicia, as she stepped forward with her shoulders back and her head high, she gave the impression of taking up just as much space. Her full breasts pushed politely against the front of the man-tailored shirt. The khaki color of the uniform highlighted the warm ruddiness of her fisherman's tan and her close-curling mop of dark brown hair gleamed under the lights. She looked arrestingly healthy.

Sexy, thought Osborne with surprise. Sexier, oddly enough, than the willowy, wheat-haired society matron confronting her anxiously.

"Something is very wrong." Lew's tone was even.

"What is it?"

Osborne stepped back against the wall, thinking it wise to stay out of the line of fire.

"I told you to wait for me out front. Not to enter the house until I arrived."

"Oh *that*," said Alicia, emphasizing her second word as if it was a relief to find the problem was such a small thing.

"I'm so *sorry* about that, Chief. I had no idea Meredith had scheduled the cleaning woman today. She was here when I got here. So I came in to be sure nothing you needed would be disturbed. That's why I'm in here, Chief," she said waving her right hand with studied nonchalance as if to dismiss the issue. Osborne wondered if she had rehearsed the moment. It all seemed a little too pat.

Lew nodded in silence. She stood there, saying nothing, arms crossed, feet set slightly apart. Osborne watched the two women closely. Just how would Lew play out the line this time? And what would she use to tease, to draw in the crafty Alicia?

"You asked me not to disturb any of Meredith's things," said Alicia, nervously filling the silence in the room. "So that's why I'm here. To be sure nothing is touched."

"Mrs. Roderick—that's no excuse. I specifically told you to wait in your car in the driveway. Instead, I hear from my deputy, you let yourself into the house early this morning before he arrived."

The look in Alicia's eyes was worried but insistent. "I—he's wrong. Like I said, the cleaning woman was here already, and I thought this would be the better way to—but you're right," she raised her hands in surrender, "I should have waited. I didn't think. I'm a little upset with all I have to do right now, Chief. The arrangements for Meredith. And I have a business to run—"

Lew looked down at the papers organized in a series of small stacks across the table, papers that Alicia had obviously sorted through.

"Not until I say so, Mrs. Roderick," said Lew firmly. "May I see those checkbooks you have in your hand?"

It lasted but an instant: a flash of fury across Alicia's face. Then it was gone, replaced with fatigue and grief. She handed the checkbooks to Lew.

"The top one is for the restaurant," she said calmly. "I am a co-signer. I needed to see if we had any bills due. That's what all this is on the table. We were due to open in four weeks, you know. As we speak, ads are running in the Chicago and Milwaukee newspapers. I have to decide if I'll go ahead with the business.

"The other one is Meredith's personal checkbook. You'll find something quite interesting in that one, Chief . . ." She waited while Lew studied the first checkbook.

"I see a check for fifteen thousand dollars . . . to George Zolonsky?" Lew asked.

"Yes," said Alicia, nodding as if there was no question about that check nor the amount, "he's been tiling the new bathrooms and the restaurant kitchen in the boathouse."

"I see a check to you for thirty-five thousand . . . ?"

"Last week, yes. I have been purchasing all the supplies, the food and equipment."

Osborne thought Alicia was talking a little too fast. Perhaps to make up for her major mistake?

"But, Chief, forget the restaurant—take a look at the checks written in her *personal* checkbook. Last page of the register."

Lew flipped the second checkbook open.

She whistled. "Fifty thousand dollars to Clint Chesnais?"

"Yes!" said Alicia. "Look at that handwriting. I don't believe my sister wrote that check."

Just as she spoke, a phone rang in the distance. It had the party line sound to it: a distinctive series of long and short rings. Osborne found himself listening to hear if it was for him. It wasn't, of course.

"Excuse me," Alicia disappeared into a small office off the kitchen. They heard her answer, then she called out, "This'll take a few minutes, Chief. Father Vodicka from St. Mary's needs to talk to me about the funeral Mass and the burial arrangements. Do you mind?"

"Take your time," Lew tossed the second checkbook at Osborne.

He looked at the check register. The Chesnais check had been entered in a handwriting quite different from all the others, no doubt about it.

Just then another door to the kitchen swung open. A petite female figure backed towards them. She wore a pair of beige bermudas and a short-sleeved black T-shirt. A vacuum cleaner hose hung around her neck, her left hand carried a sweeper unit and her right hoisted an Electrolux canister. Once through the door, she swung around.

"Cynthia!" said Osborne, surprised.

"Hey, Doc!" the pixie face with its scattering of freckles under the short spiked black hair looked at him in equal surprise. "What are you doing here?"

"I'm . . . just helping out," said Osborne, unsure exactly how Lew would want him to describe his role to someone like Cynthia.

Cynthia Lewis was the wife of Bud Lewis, a surgeon at Sacred Heart Hospital and one of Osborne's long-time deer shack partners. Cynthia and Bud were two of the oddest people in Loon Lake. Though they had lived there for years and raised three children, they were a couple that kept to themselves.

Bud did not fish, making deer season the only time that

Osborne saw much of him. Even then, he was a quiet man who hunted only the one or two days necessary to get his buck. Unlike the other hunters, he didn't linger at the shack to enjoy the camaraderie. Cynthia, Osborne rarely saw now that he was retired. Even when he was her dentist, he only saw her for her annual check-up. Saw her to talk, that was.

Cynthia might be the only woman in Loon Lake who never wanted to be in Mary Lee and Alicia's clique. The two women had been astounded when she actually turned down their invitation to substitute at one of their bridge parties. They made sure never to invite her again—to bridge or any other social event.

Cynthia lived in her own world: an avid tennis player, a bicycle racer, and a dedicated kayaker, she had carved out a Loon Lake life quite unlike the wives of the other professional men. She was the only wife of a professional man who insisted on working.

"Doc, it is important to me to be self-sufficient," she told Osborne when he had asked her, during a dental appointment years ago, why she did what she did. "You never know what's going to happen in life, y'know."

Further confusing her peers, Cynthia did not choose socially acceptable jobs. At one point, when her children were in high school, she waitressed at an Eagle River supper club. Loon Lake couples shook their heads in wonder: Bud made more than enough money.

One thing really bugged Osborne about Cynthia: her grin. The woman had a huge gap between her two front teeth that should have been corrected years ago. When she smiled, that was all you saw: not the perky black eyes and the quick charm of her smile but the gaping hole. One day Osborne couldn't stand it any longer. "It's very easy to fix, Cynthia. Maybe six months or less in braces with a retainer to wear at night. And not expensive."

She had just shrugged, "Sorry, Doc, the only thing I hate worse than snakes is the dentist's chair. I will get my teeth cleaned but that's as far as I go. It doesn't bother Bud so it doesn't bother me."

Otherwise, Cynthia was a striking woman in terrific physical shape. Small and wiry, dark and not a little pugnacious in her manner, she could be mistaken for sixteen rather than forty-six. On more than one occasion, Osborne had driven by her

as she bicycled through Loon Lake, thinking he was passing
a high school kid, only to look back and see Cynthia pedalling
furiously with a driven look on her face.

"What are *you* doing here?" Osborne returned her question in
kind.

"Cleaning," she said brightly. "I started my own cleaning
service a year ago." Suddenly, she peered around the kitchen
edgily. She dropped her voice, "Is she gone?"

"You mean Alicia Roderick?" asked Lew. She jerked her
thumb toward the back room where Alicia was on the phone.

Cynthia nodded, keeping her voice low. "Yeah. Boy, you
guys, bad news about Meredith, huh? That's who I've been
working for, y'know. Not that piece of work." She rolled her
eyes towards Alicia's location.

"Cynthia," Lew stepped forward to extend her hand, "I'm
Lewellyn Ferris, Loon Lake Chief of Police. I just took over
from John Sloan."

"We've met," said Cynthia, shaking her hand. "I waited on
you up at the The Timbers a couple times. You and that En-
glish guy whatshisname."

"Ralph," said Lew.

Osborne didn't like the sound of this.

"So you two are here about Meredith?" said Cynthia, "I
have to say—I was really shocked to hear about it. I liked her.
She's very different from Mrs. Tight-Ass back there," she
tipped her head again towards the room where Alicia was still
on the phone.

"How long have you been cleaning out here?" asked Lew.

"Several months. Since before she moved in," said Cynthia.
"We've been working the last two weeks getting the boathouse
kitchen ready to pass the health inspection . . ."

Cynthia stopped suddenly and swallowed hard. She took a
deep breath. "What a shame. This was going to be so neat and
now—" Her voice caught and her eyes brimmed with tears.

"Here, Cynthia, let me help you," Osborne walked over to
lift the vacuum cleaner equipment from her shoulders.

"I keep everything in here," Cynthia wiped her eyes and
walked across the room to open a closet. Taking the equipment
from Osborne, she put it away, then reached into her pocket
for a Kleenex, and blew her nose. She looked at the two of

them. Alicia was still on the phone. "Have you seen the house?" she asked.

"No," answered Lew. "I've never been here before."

"You're in for a treat," said Cynthia, holding open the door through which she had entered, "C'mon, while she's on the phone, I'll give you a tour. I grew up down the road, I know this place like the back of my hand." She started through the doorway and motioned for Lew and Osborne to follow.

As the door swung closed behind them, they found themselves at the foot of a dark, narrow staircase. Cynthia laid a hand on Lew's arm. "In case you haven't noticed," she said with a grim smile, "I have no use for Alicia. I am supposed to be in charge of the wait staff when the restaurant opens, but I refuse to work for that woman. So whatever I say, just know I detest her. Prejudiced witness." She winked and started up the stairway.

"So . . . who do think killed Meredith?" said Cynthia as she hopped lightly up the stairs.

"That's what I want to ask you," said Lew.

"Alicia's convinced the ex-husband did it," said Cynthia. "She must have told me that six times today. She insists he's been calling Meredith trying to reconcile ever since the money from their old man came through. But I don't know if that's right. I've been around here quite a bit these last few weeks, and I never heard him call. Meredith didn't say anything to me either, and I think she might have."

Cynthia paused near the top of the stairs, keeping her back to them, "I didn't want to ask Alicia. I can barely stand talking to her . . . do you mind if I ask . . . how *did* Meredith die? I want to hear she didn't suffer—"

"Bludgeoned," said Lew. "I doubt she knew what hit her. Someone worked hard to make it look like a fishing accident."

"Oh my god," said Cynthia turning around, a mix of sadness and shock on her face. She shook her head, taking her time before she answered, "Meredith didn't deserve this. She was very kind and a very interesting woman. I will help you any way I can."

"You liked her," said Osborne, well aware that when it came friends, Cynthia's list was short.

"Oh yes," said Cynthia. "I thought she was very smart. Unpretentious. The opposite of Alicia. One of the few women to get out of Loon Lake and do it on her own." She sighed, "But

you can't win, y'know. She told me that was the reason Ben
had all his affairs. She was more successful than he was. He
couldn't stand it. He said she emasculated him."

"You and Meredith talked a lot?"

Cynthia had reached the top of the steep stairwell. The upstairs hallway stretched ahead of them, dark and dank. Osborne
shivered.

"We hit it off," said Cynthia. She pointed towards a landing
about fifty feet away. Slowly, the three of them started walking
in that direction. "Bud works pretty late, and I don't have kids
at home anymore, so we'd hang out here for a glass of wine
and a late dinner once or twice a week." She laughed, "We
talked men and work. What else matters, y'know?

Then her demeanor sobered, "I considered Meredith a good
friend, very much so. And a business partner. She put a little
money into my cleaning service. Made it possible for me to
buy that van."

Cynthia answered the question on Osborne's face, "I refuse
to take money from Bud. This is my business. But Meredith
was different. She came to me, and said she'd like to be a part
of it. I didn't ask her. It was her idea to market spring and fall
cabin clean-ups, which is going quite nicely. We have forty-
one booked for October already. *We.* Listen to me.

"That damn Alicia!" Cynthia stopped suddenly, "Would you
believe—first, she has the nerve to call me at the crack of
dawn and demand I get over here ASAP. Then, I kid you not,
she gives me a demonstration on how to clean. Gives *me* instructions," Cynthia shook her fist, "I wanted to bop her in the
nose.

"What did she demonstrate?" asked Lew.

"Germ removal. Alcohol on the banisters and knobs, bathrooms pristine enough for surgery."

"Did you do it?"

"I did what I thought necessary."

"Oh no," Cynthia groaned and raised her eyes to the ceiling,
clapping a hand to her forehead. "Does this mean she inherits
Meredith's share in my business?"

"What's that?" asked Lew.

"There's no will. That makes Alicia next of kin. Meredith
told me she had the will on her 'to do' list. The divorce was
settled just days ago, and she didn't want to use the same
lawyer because he was a friend of Alicia's or something like

that. She told me she needed privacy for her personal matters
so I recommended a friend of ours."

"Cynthia, did Alicia give you any other instructions when
you got here today?" asked Lew.

"She made it clear I was not to touch Meredith's room, her
desk, any of her papers. She didn't want me near any of that
until she looked through it first. I'll tell you something else,"
Cynthia kept her voice close to a whisper. "She's been back
and forth to her car a dozen times. I figure the sterling flatware,
the jewelry, the small expensive stuff will never see probate.
Know what I mean?"

"That's not atypical after a death in a family," said Lew.
"I'm not saying it's right, but I see that pattern all the time.

"Clint Chesnais. Do you know him?" asked Lew.

Cynthia reacted strangely to the question. She dropped her
head as if considering long and hard what to say, as if measuring how much she could trust them. Then she lifted her
head, her eyes staring off into the distance. The expression on
her face reminded Osborne of Clint Chesnais. She had that
same haunted, preoccupied look as if someone had entered the
room and was cautioning her to keep quiet.

"Yes, I know Clint," she said finally, her voice soft. "Meredith had a crush on him. He's a sweet man. Just what she
needed at the time. I have no doubt Alicia's dumping all over
him, too. Right? She didn't like his being around here at all.
See, Meredith was like her property. This whole Boathouse
Restaurant project was her ticket to becoming a big cheese.
She didn't want me or Clint horning in. But Meredith needed
us. Alicia sure as heck wasn't going to clean, she wasn't going
to do the landscaping, the bartending. Clint and I were testing
recipes for Meredith. You think Alicia even knows how to
cook? Know what I mean?"

"So he and Meredith were pretty close?" asked Lew.

"I don't think it was marriage if that's what you're asking,"
said Cynthia. "Meredith was still pretty bruised by the divorce.
She told me Clint was fresh air for her. He is a quintessential
North Woods man, and she loved that. She was learning a lot
from him, too."

"Like what?" asked Lew.

"Oh stuff we all take for granted. How to clean her shotgun,
where to fly-fish for browns if you're tired of brookies, who's
got the best deal on plumbing supplies . . . and . . . ," Cynthia

gave them a coy look knowing the next comment implicated her, too, "who to talk to if you want to roll a joint."

"Ah-h," said Lew. "Did she smoke a lot?"

"Not really. But she got a kick out of it. She told me she hadn't had any since college and she enjoyed it—but I'll bet three times is as much as she did it that I know of."

"She's a very wealthy woman," said Lew. "Did that play into the relationship?"

"Hard to judge," said Cynthia. "Clint is a man of meager resources. He couldn't afford to take her to a movie even, but they fished together. All that costs is a six-dollar license. As far as I know, they didn't go places or do things that cost money, which was just fine with Meredith.

"If you look at the guy from a traditional point of view," said Cynthia, "he is not what you would call a success. I don't think he even has running water at his place. I know he doesn't. Meredith loved that. She said she had known enough 'big picture' guys with their corporations and their private jets. Guys who were overbearing because they had the bucks, guys who were always in a rush. Clint would pull his truck to the side of the road for half an hour just to show her a wild iris. One wild iris."

"You like him," said Osborne. He was starting to like the man himself.

"Yes I do. I got a real kick out of watching the two of them together. One day last spring, over by the boathouse, he had her on her hands and knees, head down, smelling the arbutus. It's what we try to teach our kids, Doc," said Cynthia, "how to see beauty in the little things in life. Know what I mean?"

Osborne understood exactly what Cynthia meant. Few fragrances rival the wonder of arbutus, queen of the North woods. A secretive wildflower whose beds are tough to spot. The bloom is very brief, and if you want to savor it, you have to seize the moment. Osborne himself had made a top-dollar offer on his lake property hours after stumbling over an unbelievable patch of arbutus close to the shore. Mary Lee had criticized how much they'd paid, but Osborne knew the arbutus plus the view made it worth every penny.

"And he cooked for her. Made great stir-fry. Now how many people would dare to cook for Meredith? But Clint didn't care. He's a simple guy. So he was good for her, I think. He's going to be upset when he hears about this," said Cynthia.

"We better hurry if you want to show us the place," said Lew, checking her watch.

"Right," said Cynthia, waving them forward.

They walked to edge of the balcony and, elbows on the pine railing, leaned over. Cynthia stood to the side. Osborne sensed her watching them closely.

Below was a scene straight out of the money years of the North Woods, the years of the lumber barons and the fortunes they harvested from the wilderness forests: a huge room defined by massive beams of white pine from which hung chandeliers of black cast iron festooned with racks of buckhorn.

The vaulted ceiling was planked and doweled, reaching thirty feet high. At the far end, the room was anchored, corner to corner and up past the vaulted ceiling by a fireplace hand-made of river rock. Both sides of the long room were windowed from floor to beams. At least windows were hinted at though they were hidden behind yards of damask that pooled on the floor.

"I imagine you can see the sun rise and set from this room?" said Osborne.

"Yes," said Cynthia with quiet satisfaction, "it was designed with that in mind. My grandfather built the fireplace. The original owner brought in craftsmen from Norway to carve the beams."

The room was an artifact, a relic of artistry that money can no longer buy: white pine of such remarkable girth is no longer found in the forests, not to mention the antique hand tools needed to chisel every inch of the logs in distinctive patterns.

"I don't think you can find a stonemason today who could design and build a rock chimney of that width and height," said Osborne.

Yet the magnificence of the room was undermined by the inexplicable presence of dozens of sofas and overstuffed chairs.

"What's with all the furniture?" said Lew, "this place looks like a cross between a cathedral and a convention center."

Cynthia's laugh pealed through the room. "Isn't it schizoid? Try cleaning it. I spent the first week moving families of wolf spiders."

Lew turned around, sniffing the air, "What is that smell? Is there a deer carcass around here somewhere?"

Osborne smelled something, too. "Or mold?" he asked.

"That odor is driving me crazy," said Cynthia. "I have used buckets of bleach up in this back wing, but I cannot get rid of it."

Then, Cynthia leaned down over the balcony to listen. They could hear the hum of Alicia's voice. "She's still on the phone," said Cynthia. "You know . . . ," a look of uncertainty crossed her face, "I'm not sure how much I should be telling you. Oh, hell—." She started to walk quickly down the long hall off the balcony. "Hurry," she broke into a half-jog, "I have something to show you I don't want Alicia to see."

fifteen

The odor grew stronger as they walked away from the balcony and down the long hall of the bedroom wing. Doors stood ajar, opening to empty rooms on both sides. Osborne caught glimpses of faded wallpapers and wooden floors, but otherwise the rooms were bare. He noticed the stench was definitely stronger in the rooms with windows facing east.

"The Willows was built in 1928 by Joseph Daniels, a wealthy industrialist from Chicago," said Cynthia, striding along with the energy of a young dancer, shoulders back, arms swinging, toes pointed slightly out. "Seventeen bedrooms and twelve baths, not counting the guesthouse."

"I've always heard there was a big fire here," said Osborne.

"Yep. Almost exactly one year after it was built, the whole place burned down. To the ground. The architect forgot he was building miles from city water mains and fire hydrants. By the time the volunteer fire department got here, it was too late. All that was left standing was that fireplace in the lodge room. But Daniels rebuilt immediately. Only this time, he put in his own water plant and pumping station. As a result, the soil between the main house and the shoreline holds more water, which is why the willow trees grow so well."

As she was talking, Osborne had begun to wonder about the wisdom of Meredith living alone in this monstrous residence.

The hall and its dozen-plus bedrooms seemed to go on forever, empty, moldy and not a little spooky.

"The Willows was sold in the early thirties to Mike Galvin, a mobster pal of Al Capone's," Cynthia said as they hurried past more empty rooms.

"That fits," said Lew. Everyone knew the Capone crowd had hung out at the Jack O' Lantern Club, driving Eagle River property values up. Capone, Dillinger, and many other Chicago mobsters were the first of "da boys" to hide out in the Northwoods.

"At first, Galvin used it as a summer home and . . . ," Cynthia stopped to give them one of her little half-smiles again, "a convenient location for keeping his enemies closer than they ever wanted to be."

"Ah," said Lew. "Are we talking burned out cars on the back forty?"

"Yep. Bud and the kids and I counted three within a mile of here last winter. My son uses one for a deer stand. But when I was a kid, I swear there were a dozen or more back in there. We used to scare ourselves silly searching for bones."

"Long gone," said Lew, "the forest eats 'em up."

No one said anything. Every local knew the backwoods of the North Woods, aside from the recreational draw of its cabins and lakes, had provided great cover for the misdeeds of the Prohibition kingpins. Just a five hour's drive north of Chitown, and you could park a car when it wouldn't be found for months, if not years.

"Where on earth did Meredith sleep?" Osborne asked finally. The eerie solitude of the bedroom wing, stench aside, was getting to him.

"Not up here," said Cynthia. "Didn't Alicia show you? Meredith turned the dining room off the kitchen into her bedroom. She didn't even consider using one of these rooms—too costly to heat in the winter. On the other hand . . ."

They had reached the end of the hallway. One last door to go. One closed door. Before opening it, Cynthia motioned for them to stand back. She knocked softly. No answer. Slowly she turned the knob and slid the door open. She stepped back. Lew and Osborne peered in.

The room was fully furnished. A cheery yellow and blue checked quilt covered a double bed. At the foot of the bed, the planked wooden floor was warmed with a cobalt blue hooked rug, which matched the quilt. The walls had been freshly painted white, and the knotty pine wood trim around the door and windows gleamed as if freshly waxed.

Still, the room smelled.

"Oh, oh," said Osborne, expecting the worst.

"No," said Cynthia immediately, "the smell isn't coming from here. As I said, it has been an ongoing problem. Believe me, I've checked everything. It comes in the window."

She was right. The odor was carried on the breeze blowing in through the open window above an antique oak dresser at the far end of the room. "And I've checked outside twice," she said. "But both times I didn't get to it until late afternoon. When the wind dies, you don't smell anything. Today, it's really bad.

"I'll leave the door open so we can hear if Alicia comes," whispered Cynthia as she followed them into the room. She opened a closet door and pointed. Two expensive-looking men's business suits were carefully hung on wooden hangers. A pair of leather hunting boots stood alongside felt slippers on the floor.

"Those are city suits," said Lew, "this can't be Clint Chesnais's room." She turned to Cynthia, who had been anticipating the moment.

"Peter Roderick."

Osborne was stunned.

"Does Alicia know?" asked Lew.

Cynthia cracked a thin smile. "No. He tells her he's traveling on business, and then he comes here."

"But Alicia—she comes out here, too, doesn't she?" asked Osborne. "How can he hide?"

"Alicia is one of those people who only sees what she wants to see," said Cynthia. "In fact, she doesn't come out here all that often. A lot of what Meredith asked her to do kept her in Loon Lake working with vendors out of Rhinelander and Wausau. When she does come, she's either in the boathouse or the kitchen. She never comes upstairs. She has no idea that Peter has been hiding out here."

"But why?" asked Lew. "What is he doing here?"

"Not much that I can tell. He keeps to himself. He keeps his car hidden behind the guest house—and he drinks. Last week, he scared the daylights out of me. I found him down in the laundry room, sitting on the washing machine in his underwear. Totally schnockered."

"But why . . . ?"

"I have no idea," said Cynthia. "Nor did Meredith. She ran into him a month ago. He was hiding out in some cabin up in Land o' Lakes when he was supposed to be in Japan. She insisted he come here and tried to get him some help. Obviously, the guy is sick. Meredith thought that letting him stay here might help him get back on his feet."

"Cynthia, are you serious?" said Osborne, "this does not sound like the Peter Roderick I know."

"Isn't it strange, Doc? I wasn't going to say anything. I'm sure he's harmless, but the more I thought about it, I figured you should know——"

Just as she spoke, they heard someone running up the stairs at the far end of the hall. Quickly, they turned to leave the room. Cynthia pulled the door closed behind them and, as if conducting a guided tour, and made a show of ushering them into the nearest empty room. She positioned herself at a window, raising her voice and gesturing animatedly as Alicia appeared in the doorway. She pretended not to see her.

"See over there, Chief? You can get a glimpse of the building from this angle," said Cynthia, as Lew and Osborne made a show of crowding in behind her to see where she was pointing.

"We've always called it 'The Stone House.' It cost a million dollars to build in 1929, which was a lot of money back then. My grandfather built it for old man Daniels after the big fire. He said they made it big enough to service a town the size of Loon Lake. He also warned us as kids not to play around there ever. Gases build up in the storm sewers that can kill you."

"Like the tragedy in Wausau last year?" asked Lew. "Did you hear about that, Doc? Two city workers went down to do a regular inspection of one of the city sewer mains and they were overcome like that," she snapped her fingers, "dead in thirty seconds."

"You're kidding," said Osborne. "I never heard of such a thing."

"Chief's right," said Cynthia. "My dad drew Meredith a diagram so she could the vent the system properly. There are two separate drainage routes. All the toilets and sinks discharge into a septic system and drainfield, but the rest of the water—like from the laundry, the sprinkler system, the storm sewers—is carried separately. That water can be used for an emergency. Meredith had Clint get the system up and running. Right now, it's used to water the landscaping that's going in around the restaurant."

"That must explain why she got such a good deal on insurance," chimed in Alicia from the doorway. "My god, what smells so bad?"

"Hey—what's Ray Pradt doing here?" Cynthia was still looking out the window. "He just walked down the walk towards the kitchen door."

"Ray Pradt? Why is he here?" Alicia echoed Cynthia. An unmistakable edge crept into her voice as she said Ray's name.

"I asked him to walk the property," said Lew.

"Ray Pradt?" Alicia sounded dumbfounded. She waited as if she expected Lew to explain this absurd directive.

Lew ignored her as she strode hurriedly back into the hallway and headed toward the back stairwell to the kitchen. Everyone followed her. "Cynthia," she asked as she ran down the stairs, "Why is the lodge room so crowded with furniture?"

"That was the previous owner," said Cynthia, "the Galvin estate sold The Willows in the early sixties. The new owners ran a hunting and fishing lodge up here until ten years ago. They packed this place with the junkiest furniture you can imagine, crap from garage sales, used furniture stores. The place looked like an attic upstairs and down. When they went broke, the bank took over the buildings and everything in them—"

"I'm ready to show you around," interrupted Alicia.

"Not necessary," said Lew, handing the checkbooks back to her. "Cynthia gave us a tour. I would like to look through your sister's personal things and her bedroom but that may have to wait until tomorrow. Right now, I have to see Ray. Oh—Alicia, one thing. That second checkbook you handed me, that's *not* a personal checkbook. I'd like to see the personal checkbook when you find it. Okay?"

"But I won't be here tomorrow morning—"

"Cynthia, can you help me tomorrow?" Lew's tone was brisk.

"In the morning? Certainly."

If Alicia was planning to argue, it was too late. Ray was waiting for them, arms crossed, leaning against the baker's table in the center of the room. His lanky form relaxed but his eyes serious over his tanned cheekbones.

"Got a few minutes, Chief? Wayne and I found some eagle bait you need to check out."

"Another victim?"

"In a manner of speaking," he said, twisting a lock of his beard absently as he spoke. "It's a lit-tle dis-turbing," he enunciated his words with studied deliberation as he always did when he was in control of vital information. If Osborne found it frustrating when Ray pulled this, he knew it made Lew grit her teeth.

"You may want to limit the number of visitors until you have observed the situation," he said, rolling his eyes towards the sound of shoes clattering down the stairwell to the kitchen.

"Give me a clue, Ray," demanded Lew. Osborne waited for Ray's response to her obvious irritation. But you couldn't hurry Ray.

"One hundred sixty-five million."

"O-o-kay . . ." The testiness in Lew's voice escalated another level. Someone was pushing their luck.

"That's the *minimum* number of dry flies you'll be able to tie with what I'm about to show you." Then he straightened up—"C'mon, you two."

sixteen

As Ray pulled his truck over, Wayne stood up from where he had been sitting on an old kitchen chair that had been reincarnated as a deer stand. He walked towards them with his hands thrust deep into his pockets, shoulders hunched, eyes drowsy. The summer heat had put a shine on his face.

"Yo. Not a sign since you left," he said to Ray, looking back over his right shoulder. Osborne followed his glance down the dirt path that continued past the clearing. Wayne seemed more than a little reluctant to move in that direction.

"You two go on ahead, don't wait for us." As he waved them on, Ray busied himself with something in the back of his truck. A certain smugness in his manner made Osborne feel like he was on the wrong end of a poker hand. At the same time, Ray wasn't his usual light-hearted self, which worried him. Plus the drive along the wide-cut cross-country ski trail that got them here had been made in complete silence. Another ominous sign.

Osborne made sure to stay just ahead of Lew as they walked briskly down the dirt path. He felt in his bones an urge to protect her. Of course, if she knew what he was thinking, she'd probably kick him in the shins. He tried to be subtle, hoping his long legs would give him a good twenty-foot lead.

He rounded a curve in the path. Just ahead, black with age, was an old log hunting shack. The path ran off to the right of the shack, leading up to huge old jack pine that towered over a dense stand of young aspen trees. Not until he was right in front of the trees could he see that they were hiding a shed cleverly constructed of wooden planks with the bark still on. Almost impossible to see against the heavily wooded forest.

As he waited for Lew to catch up, the wind died so suddenly that the stench hit his face like a filthy rag. In the same instant, he realized the path at his feet changed color the closer it ran to the shed: grassy ruts turned to sodden black strips laced with ribbons of red glinting in the sunlight. Coagulated blood.

"Oh boy," he heard himself saying, "what do we have here?"

The three-sided shed was floored with a concrete slab angled for run-off. Inside to the left stood a rusted oil drum stuffed full of severed deer limbs jutting out all directions. To the right of the barrel, against the back wall, he could see a heap of hides, crusted and bloodied along the edges. Overflowing from a small wooden bin in the corner were buck tails.

"Pretty nasty, huh?" said Ray from behind. "I told Wayne we call this open-air taxidermy."

"Tell Wayne I call it poaching," said Lew, "friends of yours?"

"I don't think so. My friends go for meat not mounts."

"Ah-h," said Lew. "You're right, Ray. Brother, talk about a license to kill . . . this may be the biggest poaching operation I've ever seen."

Wayne finally appeared, walking the perimeter of the path, careful to keep his shoes out of the bloody muck. "Pretty recent butchering, isn't it?" he asked.

"Recent and rushed," said Ray. "I found hoses in the back, which makes me think they usually do a better clean-up than this. I think somebody was hard at work until daylight today. Skilled cutter, too. Very nice job on the hides. Been working their way through quite a few deer."

"I imagine they knew exactly what they were doing," said Lew.

"Oh yeah," said Ray. "Feeding station and deer stand right behind the shack, drawing from a deer yard I'll show you back there. This time of the year, the bucks still travel in groups. Easy pickings."

"Whew! That August sun doesn't do this place any favors," said Wayne. He looked nauseated. "If it carries like I think it does, this stench could be tough on the restaurant business. "

"The smell isn't from the shed," said Ray, "I found some pits out back where they've been dressing the carcasses."

"The odor is being carried over to house," said Lew. Cynthia said it's been a problem off and on. I'll have to find out when she first noticed it."

"I guess we're talking some good money, here?" asked Wayne.

"A mature mount with a 12-point rack will go for three thousand dollars easy," said Lew. "If the poachers got a pipeline to dealers on the East Coast, they can get two or three times that."

"Wow," said Wayne. "All because people love Bambi?"

"Deer are beautiful animals," said Ray, "now . . . my girl friend isn't bad looking either but . . . I'm happy with photos."

"That's an old joke, Ray," said Lew. "Why don't you work on your timing, y'know?"

"I'm sorry, I'm sorry," Ray waved his hands up by his head, "couldn't resist."

"To answer your question, Wayne," said Lew, "we get these jabones from the cities that like to think they're big game hunters. Either they hunt on the game preserve with the prey driven smack onto their laps, or they buy their trophies like they buy their wives.

"Just last month I arrested one idiot who shot a bighorn ram as it was standing in a pen. The poor animal had been retired from a zoo, and this jerk paid five thousand bucks to shoot it. Why not hunt cows in the barnyard?" Lew shook her head in disgust. "Maybe I shouldn't complain—this is exactly what keeps us North Woods cops in business."

Wayne looked a little taken aback by her vehemence. Osborne just fell in love with her all over again.

Lew walked the perimeter of the shed once more. Finally she spoke, "They're certainly dropping these bucks at peak season. Their racks are fully grown, they can skin the velvet easily. If the area hasn't been hunted for five or six years, they will be trophy-size racks. I'll bet they took some beauties out of here. Where's that feeding station, Ray?"

Ray pointed, and Lew started towards the back of the log cabin. "What're they using?"

"Shotgun with deer slugs. You can do that when the poor suckers are fifty feet away."

"Great," said Lew. "All we need is the gun, match 'em up, and we got our man."

"Lew?" Osborne hurried after her, "I find it difficult to believe Meredith Marshall would sanction anything like this on her property."

"She would have been too busy with the restaurant to take the time to check it out," said Lew. "This entire operation, including that shed, can be put in place in just a few days. And it isn't exactly easy to see."

"But the smell," said Wayne, "isn't that a giveaway?"

"Only if you have bad luck," said Ray. "This time of year the wind generally blows out of the southwest. It's a fluke to have it blowing towards The Willows." He and Wayne shuffled along behind Osborne. "We didn't find it by smell, did we?"

"You spotted those turkey vultures," said Wayne.

"Yep. But first we headed this way because it's the most remote section of the property, remember? No snowmobile trails. You and I figured if anybody had something to hide this would be the place. Then I saw six turkey vultures circling, and I knew we had serious carrion. Didn't hit the smell till we were right on it."

"Brilliant, Ray. Brilliant," said Lew, almost effusive with appreciation. The pleased smile on his friend's face told Osborne Lew had just sealed a friendship for life. He wouldn't be surprised if, in the future, Ray would pass on any lucrative guiding, grave-digging or snow-shoveling jobs if and when Lew needed him. Osborne sensed that Ray liked Lew Ferris almost as much as he did. For some reason, that made him feel good.

"Whoa, look at that!" Ray pointed. Off to their right, less than twenty feet away, stood a bald eagle, unmoving on its golden claws. It was an old bird, nearly three feet tall. They advanced, but the bird ignored them, cocking its head arrogantly to pluck another strip of intestine from its prize. They were now so close they could see the elegant layering of each dusky brown feather: disk upon disk edged with silver, a pattern as delicate as the embroidery on a Japanese obi. Finally, disgusted with their insistence on interrupting his meal, the magnificent bird spread his immense wings to spiral up and away.

"I've never been that close to an eagle," said Wayne, mesmerized.

"He's not anxious to leave," said Osborne, watching the bird circle overhead.

Lew picked her way carefully in the direction of where the bird had been feeding. A cloud of black flies buzzed over the spot. Everyone else hung back.

"Doc? Ray?" Lew called to Osborne. "Do you mind taking a look at this?

"Do I have to?" Osborne walked forward reluctantly. "Decomposing deer guts are not high on my list today."

But it wasn't guts he saw. Lew stood over the rotting carcass of a doe and two young fawns.

"Why on earth . . . ?" she turned to Osborne with troubled eyes.

Ten minutes later, after scouting the remaining clouds of flies, they added it up: for sport the poachers had killed at least three doe and five fawns. That wouldn't include any wounded animals that might have run off to die in the forest.

"Nothin' like a guy who knows how to mix business with pleasure," said Ray.

"This is nauseating," said Osborne. "Poaching is one thing—but what kind of person does this?" He had a hard enough time each year shooting one buck or doe for the venison, which he loved to eat. The death throes of the animals had often been so disturbing that more than once he had considered giving up the sport. This might just do it.

Lew knelt over the last group of deer carcasses. "Ray, do you notice anything unusual with these fawns?"

"Well . . . they're all about three to four months old," said Ray. "Oh, I see what you mean—no bullet holes. Now that is interesting." Osborne stepped in to look. Sure enough, he could see no sign of bullets or slugs on the small decomposing forms.

"The does were shot," said Lew, looking around, her hands on her hips. "But these fawns—how did they die?"

Wayne had been kicking around in the tall grasses along the edge of the woods. He paused and bent over. "I don't know if this means anything," he stood up with a sawed-off limb in his hand. "Somebody's been cutting wood back here." Ray walked over to where Wayne stood.

"O-o-kay . . . so you cut down a stand of spruce, shave off the branches and chop it into four-foot lengths," Ray observed outloud. "Now why would you do that? This wood is too green

to burn but . . . ," he grabbed one length with both hands as if
it was a baseball bat and swung.

"Boom. Batting practice. You know what I think, Lew? I
think this was used to kill those animals. The does were shot,
maybe the fawns stayed with their mothers long enough for
someone to come up from behind and break their necks."

Lew shook her head sadly as she examined one of the limbs.
"Ray, you sure this is spruce?"

Ray examined the chunk of wood he held in his hands.
"Black spruce. Pretty sparse around here these days. Wood-
workers keep an eye out for black spruce because it's good
for railings on stairs and balconies. It's a pretty wood. Light-
colored with streaks of brown, which is why it's called *black*
spruce."

He studied the trees along the edge of the field where they
were standing, then pointed. "See that stand over there? The
trees with the very slender, uniform trunks? Those are black
spruce." Ray walked in that direction. "Someone has really
been cutting back here," he said. "Here's another stack. My
guess is our poacher is also in the home building business. At
least he knows good wood when he sees it."

"I'll take one of those," said Lew, reaching down to pick
up one of the cut limbs. "Never know when it'll come in
handy."

Osborne reached to pick one up. "Gee," he said, "this is
surprisingly heavy, isn't it?"

"Yeah," said Ray, "conifers are considered softwood, but
black spruce is one of the denser, harder woods. It's a good
wood, Doc."

"And a weapon all right," said Osborne, speculating on the
miserable human beings who turn nature's beauty against itself.

"I guess we better scratch the fishing, huh?" said Osborne as
they got out of Ray's truck back at The Willows.

"Are you kidding?" said Lew. "Follow me in your car."

"But I thought you said you want to see Clint Chesnais right
away."

"I do, Doc. We're going to scream back to Loon Lake for
my truck, then up to the casino. We'll hit the Deerskin on our
way back."

Well, of course, silly me, thought Osborne as he pressed
down on the accelerator. When she hit the highway, Lew

turned on her siren and they did 75 MPH all the way back to town. While Osborne parked his car next to hers, Lew dashed into her office. She was back out in less than ten minutes, dressed in fishing shorts, a long-sleeved cotton shirt, and her fishing hat.

"I got twenty-three phone messages that can wait until morning," she grinned. "Except one. Ralph called in on his cell phone to say the tiny blue olive hatch is outrageous."

Osborne could feel her excitement as he climbed into the passenger seat of her truck. "I admire you, Lew. Very few people could run a police department and a murder investigation and still have the energy to fish."

"Ya gotta realize, Doc, the only thing that keeps me sane in this job is time to unwind with the old rod and reel."

Osborne knew the feeling. Over the years of practicing dentistry, an occupation that locked him into a permanent sitting position until his back ached, he had learned the pleasure of relaxing into the roll of a drifting boat, casting and stretching and breathing in the cool evening air after a day in a stuffy office. This was time devoted to teeth that closed rather than opened.

The only drawback had been Mary Lee who made a federal case out of the time he spent on the water. What a pleasure it was to know a woman just as intrigued as he with the canny creatures lurking below the black surface.

The casino was looking lively when they arrived, the neon asserting itself against the darkening sky. A quick check with the cafe manager and they learned that Chesnais had checked out early, pleading a migraine. A hastily-drawn map sent them north again.

"Ah," said Lew with satisfaction as she spotted the right fire number. She turned off the highway onto a dirt road that ran back to a small house trailer. In the dusk, Osborne could see that the trailer, smaller than Ray's, was tidily kept with a modest but well-tended garden laid out across the front and protected from deer with chicken wire. To the right was a vegetable plot overflowing with mature bean and tomato plants. To the left, a flower garden was bordered by enough arbor vitae shrubs that it looked like a commercial operation.

The trailer had an awning across the front. In a director's chair directly beneath, feet up on a tree stump, sat their man.

He had changed into Levi's and a forest green shirt, open at the neck.

Clint remained where he was as they got out of the truck. "Mr. Chesnais?" called Lew.

"Oh, it's you," he said, his voice mellow in the night air. Osborne noticed the man gave off an aura of quiet calm. "I wondered whose truck that was."

"Yep," Lew said. Several lawn chairs were scattered about, and Chesnais half-stood to pull two forwards for them. "It's us." She sat down and looked around. "Nice evening."

"That depends," said Chesnais. "I've been feeling pretty bad since you left this afternoon. I begged off work. I needed some time alone . . ."

"Well . . . she was a good friend, right?" said Lew.

"Meredith was extraordinary," he said.

"In what way?" Lew's questions were direct but delivered in an easy tone. Almost seductive thought Osborne.

"Oh, jeez, how can I put this . . . she accepted me, she actually *liked* me for being the bum that I am. From the beginning, I assumed we wouldn't last as lovers, but I felt we would always be good friends. And I felt okay about that."

"Does that have anything to do with why she wrote you a check for fifty thousand dollars?"

"I wrote the check."

"You did? In her checkbook?"

"I should have told you earlier. It was on my mind the entire time we were talking this afternoon. But I didn't know how to say anything without having it sound—"

"Yes, it looks funny." Lew looked over the trees that surrounded the little trailer and inhaled the summer night. "Nice place you have here."

"Thank you. I have two hundred feet of lakefront back behind us. I'm trying to start a nursery here. Meredith wanted to invest a little in the business—she bought that truck you see back there." Chesnais twisted in his chair to point to a white Toyota pick-up parked behind the arbor vitae rows. "Once I got that, I was able to sell nursery stock at the Farmers Market every Wednesday and Saturday morning."

"How's business?"

"Better than I expected. Meredith gets the credit. It was her idea."

"Tell me about the check."

"Meredith opened an account to be used for landscaping The Willows, the entire property. We put together a five-year plan, and she decided she wanted to keep that cost separate from all expenses for the restaurant. For tax reasons, I guess. I'm not into high finance so I don't know exactly why she did it that way. But she put me on the account as a co-signer so that I could buy plants and materials without have to run every detail by her. I was due to leave next week on a buying trip to Vermont—they have a new rhododendron out there that I thought might winter okay in this region."

"Clint—did you plan to use any of this money for drugs?" Lew's voice was matter of fact. Her question went unanswered for several beats.

"No."

"Do you do drugs?"

Chesnais shifted uncomfortably in his chair. He cleared his throat and nodded, "A little dope . . . from time to time."

"And Mrs. Marshall?"

"On occasion. Maybe twice."

Lew stood up and walked slowly around the garden, studying the plantings. "Did you see Peter Roderick at The Willows?"

"Yes, he's been there the last two weeks."

"Why didn't you tell us this afternoon?"

"Because I learned the hard way, many years ago, to answer only those questions asked. If you want my opinion, I feel sorry for the guy. Something's wrong there. But I don't think he's your murderer."

"Cynthia Lewis. You know her?"

"She's terrific. Meredith counted on her. If you want an opinion on Peter, talk to Cynthia. She's been closer to the situation. All I know is he was drowning in booze, and Meredith thought she could help."

"Umm." Lew sat thoughtfully in silence. "Cynthia talked about Peter, but she didn't say much more than you just did. She certainly doesn't care for Mrs. Roderick . . ." Lew left Chesnais room to comment but he said nothing.

"So . . . you'll stay around, right?" Lew said, leaning forward as if she was about to stand up.

"I imagine I'm suspect number one, aren't I?"

"It might be wise to return the money."

"Certainly. Just a minute." Chesnais rose from his chair and went into the trailer. Seconds later, he returned with the check in his hand. "I didn't deposit it. I always thought it was too good to be true. Meredith was too good to be true."

Now Lew and Osborne did stand up, ready to leave. Chesnais gestured awkwardly back towards the door to his trailer, "Did you want to see my place? I apologize, it's a bit of a mess."

"Might be good to take a look, thank you," said Lew. She opened the door and stuck her head in. Osborne was very surprised when she didn't step inside. Instead she closed the door, stuck her hands in her pockets, and turned back to Chesnais.

"That's a pretty sinister piece of property down there, don't you agree?"

"The Willows?" Chesnais was surprised. "I think it's beautiful. People are sinister—not the land."

Lew nodded thoughtfully at his answer. "Did you happen hear any gunfire around The Willows?"

"Off and on. That guy who was laying all the tile in the bathrooms and the kitchen. The one her sister sent over—whatshisname—George Zolonsky? He made a big deal of his target practice the last couple weeks. Said he was trying to buy a new deer rifle and needed to try some out. But he stayed off in that north quadrangle so it wasn't too bad. You barely noticed, really."

"Clint, is there anyone you think might have had it in for Meredith?"

"Did Cynthia talk to you about Ben?"

"The ex-husband? She didn't say much. Why, what's your take?"

"Meredith told me how he left her. I thought it was pretty strange behavior for a guy who's supposed to be worth a lot of money. Funny, I thought Cynthia would have told you about that."

"We were short of time. Tell me what you know."

"Only that he moved out on her. Moved in with his girl-friend, y'know. A month later, while Meredith is up here staying with her sister, he pulls up to their home with a moving van and takes almost every piece of furniture and art out of the place. He took her china and silver. He took the stove. He took everything. It's not like he couldn't go out and buy his own stuff. So why steal from a woman he's already been cheating on?"

Chesnais chuckled, "This is why I've never made it as a businessman. I just don't think like they do. Meredith's lawyer made the guy return the stove on the grounds that it was how she made her living. This wasn't your run-of-the-mill stove either. It was a custom-built AGA that cost twenty thousand bucks. According to Meredith, that pushed him over the edge. He came over to the house during the delivery and made quite a scene."

"But that was months ago?"

"Just before she moved up here."

"How did she feel about the other things he took?"

"She told me she didn't miss it. She was happy to pare back. She was happy to be without all the crap."

"So she buys The Willows with its six dozen sofas?" Lew laughed.

Chesnais laughed, too. "Like I said, she was extraordinary. She was giving those away, you know."

"Clint," said Lew extending her hand to shake his. "You've been a big help. I'll return this check to the estate tomorrow morning."

"Lew, is that guy for real or just a good salesman?"

"Let me put it this way, Doc. He never goes home alone." Lew caught the slightly confused look on Osborne's face and hastened to explain her remark as she pulled the truck back onto the highway. "Even without the tuxedo, that man is very easy on the eyes. I know women, and I can see how Meredith found her way here."

"Well okay, so he's handsome, he's genial, he was helping her out . . . still Lew, he's just not the type of man you would expect her to fall in love with."

"Love, schmove. Doc, I deal with broken hearts and angry spouses every day. Trust me—love affairs are impossible to judge from the outside. Now, not to change the subject but what time is it?"

"Nine."

"Good. Let's go fishing." Lew's eyes twinkled. "I need a dose of fun."

Osborne settled back in the seat as she drove. He was having a hard time erasing the images from his mind. The broken bodies of the fawns, the broken skull of Meredith Marshall. He could try for fun but he felt haunted.

seventeen

Osborne stood, fly-rod motionless in his right hand, entranced by the sight of Police Chief Lewelleyn Ferris dancing in the moonlight. Body and fly-rod arcing forward and backward in rhythmic patterns, fly-line shooting against the night sky with consummate grace.

Her movements were soundless against the murmuring rush of the river, making it easy for him to concentrate on every swoop of arm and rod. Rod tip down, she plucked the dry fly from the surface as delicately as if it dangled from a spider's thread, leaving not a whisper of movement to spook a trout. Right arm whipping a series of false casts high in the air, she rocked on her feet like a jazz dancer: from back to front, toe to toe. Then both arms pulled in graceful opposition, executing a double haul that Osborne swore shot the line a solid seventy feet. He'd never fished with anyone, male or female, who could shoot that far.

Jeez! Here he was still working to develop a decent backcast, much less a double haul. How on earth did that woman learn to cast like that? And she made it look so easy. He planned to tell Ray after fishing with Lew tonight that she is the one reason he is willing to tackle this sport one more time—she is the first fly-fisherman he knows who makes a deliberate effort to keep her fishing free of technical frustrations.

"Lewelleyn's Rule #1," she had said earlier when he pulled two full boxes of wet and dry flies from his vest, "never, ever carry more than five flies." So he set one box aside and slipped the other into the front pocket of his fishing vest even though it held a dozen flies. Lew had raised a critical eyebrow. Seven too many.

"Lew," he'd complained, "it's tough to choose. Whatever I don't take will be the one I need."

And so, together, they had sorted quickly through his box to select one Royal Wulff, two tiny Blue-Winged Olives on #22 and #24 hooks respectively, a Pale Morning Dun, and an outrageous Salmon Stone Fly. The latter pushed on him by Lew who said: "You just never know what you'll see out there, Doc. Ralph laughs at my Salmon Stone Fly, but I've caught many fine trout on this little lover. Tied it myself," she said with pride, grinning as she hooked one of the fluffy buggers onto his lambswool pad, then patted his shoulder to velcro down the khaki safety flap.

Critical though she might be of his fly selection, Lew had made no comments on his casting, which he knew to be marginal at best. Tonight, however, after watching him lay down a few roll casts, she pointed to a bubbling seam less than 15 inches from the bank.

"Lewellyn's Rule #2," she said, "see the riffle—cast the cover."

"Good point," he responded. He knew she was right. Every good trout fisherman knows the biggest, the brightest, the wisest trout lie in the deep sheltered pools, safe from eagles, otters, and other predators. It's just doggone hard to cast there without hooking brush or submerged branches.

Egged on by Lew, Osborne cast closer to the bank, sneaking his fly under an overhanging alder that protected a deep crater carved from the rocky shore by the current. An immediate strike! Drats, he had too much slack in his line. Osborne fumbled, losing the fish before setting the hook.

"Good try," said Lew, ignoring his awkwardness. "If I were you, I'd stay with that pool. We know they're rising. Next time, lift that forearm and fly reel as if they're glued together and keep it that way. Try to lose the wrist action, Doc, and stay tuned to your line hand. Now I'm getting out of here before I bug you to death." And off she had waded, up and to the left, taking care not to disturb any water heading his way.

Thirty feet later, her felt-bottomed waders balanced on two submerged boulders, Lew tipped her hat back to signal she had spotted another tantalizing pool, overhung with black brush, outlined with bubbling seams, a beauty of a hangout for the elders of the stream. That's when Osborne dropped his rod to watch.

Outlined against the reflection of the moon, he could see the fly line as it carried its weightless treasure forward to land with the ethereal grace of the mayfly spinner it was designed to duplicate. Again it flew and dropped. Again . . . once again. Suddenly, the dupe worked.

He saw the strike and Lew's instant tuck of slack that set the hook. Then she surprised him, parting with tradition to let the monofilament run loose, to give the fish a slack line. Osborne's jaw dropped. This was not standard operating procedure. But yes! She fooled the fish a second time. With the pressure off, the hooked trout lingered in its pool, now a false haven of safety.

She edged around her unsuspecting prisoner to set up a downstream run. The fish took the hint. Letting the line run out, controlling it with her left hand, disguising it with current, Lew followed the action. Her face was soft and eager in the moonlight, concentration and pleasure playing across her features.

Not once did she make the mistake he always did—a yank of the rod so high and so far back that it would wobble under pressure, snapping the line. No such rudeness for Lew. She stripped more line and let it run with careful control. Her hands were intuitive, caressing the fish so no membranes ripped, her hook a gentle jailer.

She had moved downriver, closing in on the tiring fish. Now her shoulders and torso rocked and swayed, dancing her prey closer and closer until the trout was inches from her legs. Feeling her excitement in his bones, tensing as if he were the one with the pulsing rod, Osborne understood the mystical draw of fly-fishing: you become one with the water and the finned creature, one with the body and the blood.

Lew's line hand reached behind to pull her net from the clip at the back of her vest. She dipped the wooden handle into the shallow river to scoop up her prize, an expert nudge of her finger displacing the hook. Setting her rod aside, she reached for the glistening body and held it high in the moonlight for him to see: "A beautiful brown, Doc. Nineteen inches, maybe. Three pounds or more." She held it for seconds only, then bent to release her catch, guiding it tenderly with her hands until it flashed into the watery black.

That's when Osborne conceded that Lew just might outfish him in these waters. If Ray knew lakes like a walleye, Lew knew this river like a trout. She could sense who was hungry and who was not. Better yet, she could drop a fly into precisely that pool where the hungry lurked. But more important—of all the trout swimming beneath her, she could find one she could fool.

Just maybe, thought Osborne, that's what made her a good cop, too.

Lew straightened up, reattached her net and picked up her rod. "What did I tell ya, Doc? Location, location, location. We've been in this water less than ten minutes, and already we got two strikes. Life doesn't get much better." The happiness in her voice traveled easily over the gurgling black riffles.

"Where did you learn to double haul so well?" asked Osborne. "I'm jealous."

"Ralph. The man casts like an angel," said Lew over her shoulder as she waded upriver. "He taught me everything I know. You should talk to him, Doc. You'd like fishing with Ralph. You'd learn a lot."

Over my dead body, thought Osborne.

"I'll think about it," he said to her back, knowing full well he would not. He despised the man. Ralph Kendall was the son of an Englishwoman, a widow who met and married the owner of Loon Lake's only sporting goods store when Osborne was stationed abroad during the Korean War.

Though Ralph had lived in the Northwoods since his early teens and worked for his stepfather for twenty years or more, the McDonald's coffee crowd agreed with Osborne that it was curious how Ralph's pretentious British accent grew more pronounced with time. Nor did the McDonald's crowd appreciate the fact that the accent only seemed to enhance Ralph's standing as Loon Lake's most eligible bachelor.

Osborne had to admit, grudgingly, that the man had never done anything to offend him personally. He was always forthcoming with solid information on fishing gear, whether musky lures, walleye jigs, or trout flies. But it seemed to Osborne that he was a little too abrupt with male customers. Not only that, you had to know what to ask, he didn't volunteer extra helpful information. And when he didn't have an answer, he would beg off with a weak, "That's how the Brits do it," excuse.

Yet he appeared to be the God of Fly-Fishing for Lew. Maybe for ladies in general. Having heard earlier in the day that Cynthia had served dinner to Ralph and Lew, Osborne was even more irritated with Ralph. Just hearing the name caused his jaw to tighten. *Stop*, Osborne said to himself, *just stop thinking about the guy. Don't let it ruin your evening.*

Oblivious to Osborne's emotional distress, Lew continued to edge forward in the water. She waded with care, moving slowly, sliding over the rocks, her body angled so the trout would see only one leg and assume she was a tree.

"I'm going upstream, Doc, you move down." Osborne nodded and stepped back a step or two. He waited until she disappeared around the bend in the river, then looked about him. He had no intention of going anywhere. He was quite comfortable standing right where he was with two feet solidly planted in less than eight inches of water at what appeared to be the widest, most shallow spot in this branch of the Deerskin. Here the river was a managable twenty feet wide, narrowing as it curved north into the night.

Last night's terror still lingered: the plunge into unknown waters and the panic that gripped him when the current swept his feet out from under him. Granted this river appeared much more benign at the moment, he just didn't trust appearances.

So he decided to give himself a break and enjoy the night rather than try to be Fisherman of the Year. Content with the Royal Wulff that he had tied on, he focused on the one square inch in the pool where he had had the first strike and initiated a series of short casts. As per Lew's instructions, he tried to tuck the fly reel under his forearm in order to keep the wrist from bending back. It seemed to work. But after a few more casts and no luck, he put his casting arm and line hand on automatic pilot, happy to let his mind wander.

This spot in the river was one of Lew's secret places. He was flattered she would share it with him. Not that he could ever find it again. She had pulled the pickup off-road about five minutes away, then bounced them down a narrow stretch of meadow under power lines with poles marked "Keep Out: Danger of Explosives." Lurching up and down until he thought he would need dentures, Osborne was relieved when Lew finally braked at a patch of dirt that showed signs of other vehicles.

"If you live north of Bruce's Crossing," she said of the tiny Michigan town where they had stopped at a gas station for Osborne to buy a one-day fishing license, "you can catch a back road into here, but this is the fastest way in from the south—and, you know, it's getting a little late."

It was nine-forty-five when they waded into the river. A dark nine-forty-five even though a three-quarter moon overhead lit the riverbank. Spires of balsam and stabbing arms of white pine stood out against the night sky with the clarity of silhouettes cut from black construction paper.

Osborne found this river to be milder in tone than the Prairie, burbling, gurgling, and quite shallow. As he looked about, he could see that the surface grew more complex over the rocks that lay downriver. His gaze picked up the eddies and riffles and deep pools illuminated by the moon.

The pools were the source of his greatest anxiety. He had learned the hard way how those still surfaces could mask treacherous holes. Holes rich with fish but deep enough to swamp your waders even if they were only inches from the bank. Holes requiring polarized sunglasses to gauge in daylight, thus impossible to judge in the black velvet of the August night.

Osborne's arm grew tired. It had been a long day, what with the bait casting for walleyes. Ironically, it was much, much harder to cast the fly-line with its weightless fly than it was the weighted jig.

Reeling in until he could hook his fly onto the rod, Osborne eased himself onto a chair-sized boulder. He slumped into the curve of the rock, relaxed and happy. The truck was a short distance away, maybe fifty yards. An easy walk. He let his eye wander over the riverbank.

That's when he saw the bear scat. A large fresh clump. Too fresh. He stood up and sniffed the air. Bear breath is worse than a pig's. He'd know if one was close. The air was fresh, but now that he listened, he was sure he could hear muted crashing back in the woods. Blackberries, he thought suddenly, his chest tightening. How close were they to the ripening berries? Inches perhaps? Inches away and fourteen thousand berry-hungry black bear prowling the neighborhood.

Osborne moved back into the river, sliding his feet diagonally across the current. Better to stand out here and practice casting than get into a negotiation he couldn't win. With his luck, any bear would end up between him and the truck. One thing gave him a small measure of confidence: the bear was more likely to be afraid of him. Particularly once it got an eyeful of his miserable casting.

Osborne gauged the distance between him and each bank carefully, parking himself in the center of the stream. Forget seams and pools, riffles and eddies, all he wanted was plenty of non-threatening space between him and the berries.

Jeez, it was dark. Lew, Lew, where are you? Not a little desperation crowded his thoughts. He decided to think of something else before he worked himself into a real panic. Okay: Mallory. He focused on the need to get back and prepare the guest room for her before he went to bed tonight. And the bathroom. God forbid he forget to set out clean towels. Ohmygod where was Lew?

After what seemed like hours but was really only ten minutes, Lew's shadowy figure rounded the bend. Slowly, slowly, she moved toward him, casting downstream, mending her fly against the current. Her movements so rhythmic, he found them hypnotizing. His anxiety over the bear faded as she approached. He wasn't sure why, but having her near made him feel safe.

"Any luck?" he asked, deciding not to tell her about his most recent brush with panic.

"Four little brookies, nothing more than ten inches. Tired?"

"Beat. Call it a day?"

"Sure," her voice soft and agreeable as she reeled in her final cast, then sat down, knees spread, on a flat-topped boulder close to the bank. Leaning forward on her elbows, she gave a deep sigh, closed her eyes and lifted her face to the cool night air. She seemed reluctant to leave the raw beauty of the river and the moonlight.

"Well, Doc, nights like this will be in short supply soon. Thanks for coming."

"Thank you for including me." He waited, but she made no move to stand and leave.

"Are you going to the wake tomorrow?"

"Yes. Mallory and I will probably go over with Ray. His folks were good friends of family. Would you like to join us?"

"Oh, I don't think that would be appropriate. I didn't know the family. But I would very much like you to keep an eye on Peter Roderick," she said in the same tone she had used to direct his cast to the deep hole under the cover.

"I plan to. I'll certainly be talking to him at some point."

"Be careful what you say, Doc. I don't want him to know I'm aware he was staying at The Willows."

"I guess you have to consider him a suspect?"

"Maybe . . . I find it difficult to imagine a motive. If we had the lovely Alicia in the morgue, yes. But a woman who was being kind and helpful? His own wife just inherited a ton of money, so what would he have to gain?" Lew shook her head. "Ask him how business is. Let's see what he says."

"Speaking of business, I've been meaning to mention something relative to Ben Marshall."

"Oh yeah?" Lew stood up and together they swished through the water toward the riverbank. "You think the ex-husband did it?"

"I wouldn't go that far. Though it's crossed my mind he could have hired someone."

"I've been thinking about that, too, Doc. But a man of Ben's means—he wouldn't be concerned with gold fillings."

"That's what I wanted to talk to you about," said Osborne. "I'm not so sure about that. I had this patient about twenty years ago, a resort owner who retired up in Manitowish Waters. Richard Campbell was his name. His wife had the softest teeth you can imagine. She had had years of gold work already, and I ended up putting even more gold in that woman's mouth. In those days, once you started with gold, you stayed with it. But that was fine with Richard—they could afford it.

"Well, a couple years after they moved up here, Harriett died of breast cancer. Before the funeral, I got a call from Richard who asked me to meet him over at the funeral home. He wanted me to remove the fillings."

"He did?" Lew looked at him in astonishment as she began to break down her rod.

"That was my reaction, but he was adamant. So I did what he asked. Then I had them melted down and sold on the secondary market for him."

"Why on earth?" said Lew.

"He was one of those people—every penny counted. He was frugal."

"To put it mildly."

"People are funny, Lew. Ray has a great story about a family that forgot to remove the hearing aid from Grandma and made Ray dig her up so they could get the deposit back."

"You gotta be kidding."

"No-o-o I'm not," said Osborne. "You know . . . ," he paused thoughtfully, "I've been mulling over the story about Ben Marshall and the moving van. What would a millionaire need with another VCR? What possesses a man to do that?" asked Osborne.

"Divorce does funny things to people," said Lew. "I see it all the time. To me that break-in wasn't about theft, not even anger. That's rage, pure rage."

"And rage can lead to murder."

"Most definitely . . . you know, Doc. I watch Alicia. I see people's reactions to her. I keep wondering if someone made a mistake and killed the wrong woman."

Twenty minutes later they pulled into the Bruce's Crossing gas station once more. This time for gas.

"My turn," said Osborne, reaching for his wallet as he jumped from the truck.

"Thanks, Doc," said Lew. "I'm going to call in quickly, see if I have to worry about anything tonight."

"Don't call—you need a good night's sleep."

"I know, I know, but it'll be waiting for me at home if I don't check now."

"Big news," she said as they climbed back into the truck minutes later. She looked at Osborne, raising her eyebrows and letting a grin play across her face. "The switchboard reports six hysterical calls from Alicia Roderick—Ben is flying in for the funeral."

Then Lew laughed heartily, "What flaw in my personality makes me actually look forward to this?" She looked at Osborne, her eyes twinkling—"This job is always interesting, y'know?"

He smiled back, happy to be along for the ride.

eighteen

At eight A.M. Tuesday morning, the tiny Loon Lake airport
bustled with tourists and camp kids in spite of a threatening,
dismal grey sky. Osborne checked his watch as he leaned
against a post near the empty baggage carousel. If Mallory's
United flight was on time, they would have a little over an
hour to get to St. Mary's for the funeral Mass.

A sudden bustle of activity over at the Northwest counter
caught his attention: another commuter flight was arriving
from Minneapolis. Osborne watched as the prop plane taxied
up, swung around, and finally dropped its stairs for the passengers to descend. Down the shaky stairs came an elderly
couple, taking each stair very slowly. Behind them, stepping
patiently, came a man Osborne recognized instantly in spite of
the tiny sunglasses sitting like black dots on his oversized face:
Ben Marshall.

The wide pale Irish face capped with thinning white-blond
hair stood out like a beacon in the grey morning. Ben was a
big man, broad across the shoulders and tall, a good six foot
four. Heading across the pavement toward the lobby, face in-
scrutable behind the glasses, a strapped Western-style leather
briefcase swinging from his left hand, he walked the insouciant
walk of a man with money.

He was dressed casually in Levi's and a muted plaid short-
sleeved shirt. The latter bulged slightly over a turquoise belt

buckle so large Osborne could see it from where he stood. Ben had no butt to speak of, his figure tapering down from wide shoulders to skinny legs.

Osborne knew that physical type well—the result of too much rich food, more than a few cigars, and spare moments of exercise acquired by walking from golf club to golf cart. He might be dressed like a cowboy, but to Osborne he looked big city. Big city likely to experience at least one cardiac incident before age fifty. Ray liked to kid about the big city guys, describing a special "two-for-one" offer: a day of serious fishing with a cheap grave chaser. On more than a few occasions, he almost had a deal.

Ben paused before the lobby entrance, fumbling in his shirt pocket for a cigarette. He lit up, then looked back to wave at a small blonde woman headed his way from the plane. She wore tight white jeans and a black halter top. Gold gleamed around her neck and both wrists. Osborne pegged her to be in her late twenties and, like so many of the summer women, over-tanned and over-accessorized. As she beamed up at Ben, Osborne caught the flash of bright white teeth and wondered which whitening toothpaste she used. If she wasn't careful, she'd scar the enamel.

Osborne straightened up, thrust his hands into his pockets and wondered if Ben would recognize him. The couple sauntered in behind the rest of the passengers. Without even glancing around, they drifted toward the luggage carousel. Ben set down his cowboy briefcase, inhaled deeply on his cigarette, and placed a casual hand on the right haunch of the blonde. She snuggled closer to stand touching him. Ben inhaled once more, then flicked the cigarette onto the industrial carpeting of the airport and ground it out with his foot. He hitched up his jeans absent-mindedly and looked around at the other travelers. That's when he saw Osborne. He straightened up instantly.

"Dr. Osborne," he left the blonde and walked over to Osborne, his hand out. "Good to see you, sir. What a sorry occasion . . ." He waited as if expecting sympathy returned.

"Hello, Ben," Osborne shook the extended hand. "Yes, sad news about Meredith . . . how's your family, Ben?" And with that he launched into the funeral patter he had perfected over the years of burying patients, good friends, and one wife. He decided to let Ben find out from someone else who discovered Meredith's body.

Six years earlier, he had done an emergency root canal on
Ben. Since that time the flat, round face had become etched
with red-blue veins, especially around the nose. The pale
brown eyes seemed weary and bloodshot. No parting a Chicago Irishman from his hard liquor, thought Osborne. Ben also
sported a carefully trimmed white-blond mustache. He exuded
the jaded, affluent, but genial manliness of a Northwoods
weekender.

When they had run out of small talk, Osborne explained his
presence: "I'm waiting for Mallory. She's due in on the next
flight."

"I know," said Ben, his voice husky, "she called me with
the news yesterday. Tough to get flights up here. I had to fly
west to get east." He chuckled at his witticism. "See you at
the church, then?"

He waved a hand, then stepped back toward the blonde and
his brief case. With a nearly imperceptible nod to her as he
walked by, he picked up the briefcase and moved to stand at
a distance from the woman. When the baggage carousel finally
rattled by, she grabbed her own garment bag and walked off
without a glance at Ben. If Osborne hadn't seen them earlier,
he would never have known they were together. Ben caught
Osborne's eye to wave conspicuously as he left. Alone.

Just as he disappeared through the electric doors, activity
picked up at the United counter. The two young women who
had been checking in travelers left the desk and ran outside to
greet the plane. When it stopped, one moved to unload the
luggage, the other to fuel the plane. Finally one remembered
to open the plane's passenger exit. Mallory was the third person down.

From a distance, Osborne thought his oldest daughter looked
good. Tall and slender, she wore an ankle-length, sleeveless
celadon-green cotton dress. Simple and pretty. Her dark hair
was cut in soft bangs and a youthful page boy, which she
tucked behind her ears. Given they were the same age, Osborne thought it curious that Ben Marshall looked every inch
a man in his late forties while Mallory appeared to have barely
broken thirty. At least to her father. She picked up a soft-sided
bag from the rack outside the airplane, slung its strap over her
shoulder, and headed toward him.

"Dad," she smiled slightly she came through the doors. Her
serious black eyes always reminded Osborne of his own

mother, who died when he was six. Her eyes and her wide, generous smile made Mallory the daughter who looked like her father. Osborne pecked her on the cheek and took her into his arms for a gentle, if distant, hug. A soft redness stippled the skin around her eyes and the end of her nose was chapped from sniffling.

"Any more luggage, kiddo?"

"No, this is it," she said. "How are you doing, Dad?"

"I'm fine, Mallory. It's good you've come." Though he had the urge to keep his arm around her shoulders, he stood away from her. He always felt so stiff with this child. "How are you?"

Mallory looked up at him. She opened her mouth as if to respond automatically, then wordlessly her face crumpled, and she burst into tears. "Oh, Dad," she sobbed. People standing near them tried to look away.

Osborne didn't know what to do. He pulled her toward him again and slipped the bag strap off her shoulders. "There, there," he tucked her face into his chest above his heart and patted her left shoulder blade. She felt fragile, bony under his hand. He could feel her rein in her sobs, trying for control. "There, there . . . take a deep breath." He patted some more and the sobbing eased. "We have plenty of time, hon. We're going to Erin's so you can freshen up. Do you need to change before Mass?"

Mallory stepped away, wiping her cheeks with the back of her hand and fumbling in her straw basket of a purse for Kleenex. "Yes, I'd like to, Dad. Sorry about this."

"Understandable, kiddo. Say," he dropped his voice, "Ben Marshall arrived on the flight just before yours."

"Oh yeah? I'm sure Meredith's sister will love that," said Mallory. "Tell her it's my fault. I called him after you called me. I knew she wouldn't. I never thought he'd come."

"Who's the woman?"

"A woman? He brought his girlfriend?!" Mallory's face freshened up at the news like a garden after a summer storm. "Dad, I don't believe it. What an arrogant pig that man is. Actually, I do believe it, given everything else he's done."

Walking over to Osborne's station wagon, Mallory peered into the empty crate resting in the back of the car: "Where's my buddy? Where's my favorite, Osborne?"

"Mike? He's waiting for us in Erin's backyard. He's got his ball all slobbered up—just waiting for you," said Osborne, relieved she was feeling better.

Moments later, as they pulled onto Highway Eight toward Loon Lake, Mallory said in a business-like tone as she adjusted her dress, "I'm leaving Steve, Dad."

Osborne didn't answer right away, but he felt something lift from his shoulders. It was Ray who put it best during one of their sessions behind the door with the coffee pot: knowing the terror defuses the tension. He was surprised and yet he wasn't.

"Do you want to talk about it?" he said softly.

"Later." Her voice was firm. He glanced at her. Her mouth was trembling. He thought of the slurred messages on the phone, their infrequent, clipped conversations over the recent months. Mallory was in trouble, but she wasn't asking for help. So far, unlike her mother, she wasn't whining.

She looked out the windshield at the gloomy sky, "Great day for a funeral, Dad."

Osborne pulled the wheel to the left as he turned up Erin's street. Great day for a funeral, great day to hear of the death of a marriage, great day for a chat with a killer. Heck of a Tuesday.

nineteen

Ten minutes later, Osborne parked his station wagon in front of Erin's big white Victorian house. His heart lifted at the sight of the open porch with the bright yellow and green trim. Petunias, pansies, and fuchsia overflowed from hanging baskets and clay pots that crowded the stairs. His youngest daughter had a way of making everything around her seem sunny.

The house was the oldest Victorian in Loon Lake, and Osborne could never get over how much hard work had gone into restoring it—and how much of it Erin and her husband Mark had done themselves. He was always impressed with the energy level of his younger daughter. Wife, mother of three, president of the Loon Lake school board, gardener, cook, and furniture refinisher. And she taught part-time at the Rhinelander Montessori school.

They were close, he and Erin. They had breakfast together once a week, and he thoroughly enjoyed hearing about the frustrations of daily life in a small town, the kids in school, her husband's law practice. He'd developed a strong friendship with this daughter ever since Mary Lee's death. Through her he'd learned it wasn't the money but the listening that counted. *She* was happy in her life. He knew that.

Erin stepped out the front door as they started up the sidewalk. She was dressed for the funeral in a fitted navy blue linen jacket buttoned over a softly gathered creamy skirt that reached to her ankles. Her long blonde hair hung down her back in a braid, and she balanced one-year-old Cody, Osborne's first grandson, on her hip. While Mallory's darkness reflected her grandmother's Meteis bloodline, Erin's fair skin and white-blonde hair was evidence of the Norwegian grandfather.

"Hurry on in before it rains," she waved. "Come share the dregs of the coffee pot, you guys."

They followed her into the long, airy living room. The sisters embraced. Osborne loved the picture he saw: his lively eyed, slender-bodied daughters plopping down on an old overstuffed sofa in a room full of interesting and colorful things. Not expensive, traditional stuff like Mary Lee had always wanted, but what Erin called "funky." Old furniture and antiques, comfortable sofa and chairs, nothing young children couldn't clamber on. The room was full of life. Erin was full of questions.

"You can change in a few minutes," she instructed her elder sister. "We got thirty minutes until we have to be at the church. So tell me—do you think Ben killed Meredith? Why did they split anyway? Does he have another bimbo?"

"Hold on," said Mallory, "first I get to hold Cody, then I get coffee, then I talk."

"Okay, okay," Erin jumped up, dropping her son on her sister's lap. The child promptly rolled off in the direction of a wooden train set scattered across the rag rug under their feet. Erin returned immediately with two cups of hot black coffee. "Not really dregs," she said, "just brewed in honor of your visit. So—talk!"

"Well, here's what I know," said Mallory, relishing her role as primary source.

"I remember when Meredith met Ben. They were still in school, and he was a cute guy. Much thinner, of course. And a real party animal. He liked her because she was blonde and she was pretty—"

"In that order?" interrupted Erin.

"Pretty much. Personally, I think she married him because he was cute and rich and . . . ," Mallory paused for effect, ". . . the first man she slept with."

"Ah hah, the 'good Catholic girl syndrome,'" said Erin.

"Tell me about it," said Mallory, and the two sisters hooted in laughter. Osborne laughed along, so happy to be sitting and listening. He wasn't often privy to these sisterly performances so he forgot they shared a directness and a ribald sense of humor that they certainly did not inherit from their mother. Where it came from he had no idea, but he loved it.

"They did fine until Meredith complained because he went on all these guy trips all the time with his buddies. You know, the usual hunting, fishing, gambling, and drinking rituals that go with being Irish and a commodity trader."

"They go with being male and stupid," said Erin.

"Do you want to hear the story or not?"

"Sorry."

"So she goes back to school then gets diverted into the cuisine career, etc., etc.—you know all that, right?"

"Right."

"About five years ago, Ben makes some bad trades in the copper market and loses a lot of money. He then decides to make up for it by churning some family accounts. Unfortunately, he picks a brother and sister who find out what he's doing, complain to the old man and—boom—Ben's out of the family business."

"I didn't know this," said Osborne, sitting forward in his chair. He pulled a pen and a small notebook from inside his sport coat. Mallory looked at him in surprise.

"Mal, didn't you know Dad is a part-time cop these days?" said Erin.

"I knew he found the body," said Mallory.

"He's working this case," said Erin, a broad grin spreading across her face as she added, "I think he has a crush on the police chief."

"I do not," Osborne protested, feeling silly.

"He doesn't know it, yet," said Erin. "Trust me."

"Ooohh, Dad," said Mallory. "We have to talk."

"Hey, the good side is this could cut down his time with the stuffed minnow hat," said Erin, referring to Ray. Both his daughters were edgy about his friendship with Ray, whom they considered a serious loose cannon.

"Back to Meredith," said Mallory, glancing at her watch. "I have to change in a minute. After about six months, Ben finds another firm that will take him in, but he has to invest some of his own money to get the job. By this time, Meredith is making very good money on the restaurant and the book deals. Ben asks her to back him with her cash—and she refuses. I know this because she came to Steve for advice."

"Why did Steve tell her not to?" asked Osborne.

"He's never liked Ben. He thought the churning was a crooked thing to do, and he basically told Meredith to expect Ben to screw her, too. So she said no, and he got himself a girlfriend."

"Did she know that?"

"Not right away. But she knew saying no would damage her marriage. She was ready to get out. Ben finally wheedled the money out of his mother."

"If all this happened four years ago, why didn't she leave him then?" asked Osborne.

"She was just too darn busy, Dad. She had two restaurants going, she had the books to write. But when her father got so sick, she realized she was going to have even more money, and she didn't want Ben to get any part of it. And who knows? Meredith had a weird side to her, too. She told me that before they were married, Ben had a fling with Alicia."

"Really," said Erin, quietly. "Up here?"

"Yep, the first time Meredith brought him to meet her folks. I don't know the whole story. All she told me was Alicia came onto Ben in the swimming pool at her place, and there was some kissing, but that was that. She was infatuated with him in those days so she let it go."

"Funny she trusted Alicia to go into business with her."

"Family meant everything to Meredith," said Mallory. "In the long run, once she knew the real Ben, she probably thought it was all Ben's fault."

"Jeez," said Osborne, "Alicia is what—fourteen, fifteen years older than Ben?"

"Dad," said Erin, a tinge of disgust in her voice, "how many years do you have on Miss Police Chief?"

Osborne started to protest then quit. Time was running out before Mass, and he wanted to know one more thing—"Mallory," he asked, "why do you think Ben would take a moving van and break into their house?"

"Control, Dad. She said she was leaving him, and he showed her he could walk back into her life anytime he wanted. He's not a very nice guy. End of story—where can I change?"

"Use my bedroom," said Erin, standing up. "By the way, how's Steve?"

"Mr. Sunshine?" said Mallory, a teasing tone in her voice.

Erin's room was just off the hall. She left the door open as she changed, calling out to her sister.

"C'mon," Erin called back, "how often do I have to apologize for calling him that. He's just a little dour sometimes, y'know."

"He's real dour these days," said Mallory. "I filed for divorce yesterday."

"Are you serious?" Erin threw a look of grave concern at her father.

"Quite," said Mallory. "I'm going back to school. I start next week."

"Mallory—why haven't you called to tell me this?" said Erin.

"I don't know," said Mallory walking back into the room. She wore a tailored black silk short skirt and jacket. "It's been a hard summer." Her eyes suddenly brimmed with tears. Erin reached out to wrap her arms around her.

"Look," said the younger sister, "I'll send the kids over to Mark's mom's place tonight. Why don't you stay here with me? Okay?"

"No," Mallory shook her head, the tears rolling down her cheeks. "No, I want to stay with Dad. I have to talk to Dad."

Oh my God, thought Osborne. Oh my God. Erin's eyes caught his. She had been the daughter who forced the intervention that saved his life. The things that were said during that time had been so painful. The damage wreaked by Mary Lee and his inability to stop it had shamed him. Would he have to face the pain again? Erin's eyes told him he must.

twenty

Osborne, Erin, and Mallory hurried down the sidewalk that ran along the side of the church. The sky was still threatening, and Osborne thought he felt a few drops. Rounding the corner, they rushed up the steps into a crowd of dark-suited men. Over their shoulders, Osborne caught a glimpse of the flower-draped casket.

"No you don't!" he heard a high-pitched woman's voice, dangerously close to hysterics.

"Yes . . . I . . . do," came the gruff, uncompromising answer. "This is my wife. Now get out of the way, Alicia."

Gregg Anderle, owner of the funeral parlor, backed away from the crowd to turn a reddened face to Osborne and throw his hands up in despair. "We'll never get this show on the road," he whispered in a hoarse low tone. "I may need two more caskets before this is over."

"Ben, be understanding . . . ," Osborne recognized Peter Roderick's voice.

"Make that three—," said Gregg.

Osborne jockeyed for a full view of the scene just as Father Vodicka appeared. "What's the brouhaha?" The priest's measured question prompted simultaneous responses from Ben and Alicia.

"All right, one at a time," he said. "Keep your voices down please. This is a house of worship."

"It is not appropriate for my sister's *ex-husband* to be a pall-bearer," said Alicia, teeth gritted.

"Whoa—the venom in that voice," whispered Erin into Osborne's ear. "Why doesn't she come right out and accuse him of murder?"

"I am not her ex-husband, Father," Ben faced the priest calmly, though Osborne could see an artery pulsing across his right temple. "Yes, a divorce was in process . . . ," he turned to Alicia, "I have been trying to explain that I have received no signed papers. Until then, I am legally wed to the deceased." Ben looked back at the priest, his face drawn and tight, "My wife and I—I had hoped we could reconcile, Father, and I think it highly appropriate that I be allowed to assist here today. I loved this woman . . ."

"Oh, give me a break." This time it was Mallory who whispered in his ear.

Father Vodicka bent his head in thought. He had been the pastor of St. Mary's for nearly forty years and, Osborne knew, had had more than his own share of run-ins with Alicia.

The year Alicia and Mary Lee had been co-chairs of the holiday art auction had been a nightmare for the poor priest who had had to deal with dozens of calls from irate parishioners whose contributions were sneered at or rudely refused by the two women. "One more duck painting and I'll vomit," Alicia had exclaimed in front of a well-known regional artist, member of the church, and potential donor. *Yep*, thought Osborne waiting the decision, the good priest knew the score.

"Alicia," said Father Vodicka softly, "take your place in the family pew, please."

Alicia stayed right where she was, glaring at him. She wore a full-skirted black dress with a crisp white silk collar, giving her a distinctive Mother Superior look, a look exaggerated by her haughty expression.

"Alicia . . . ," the priest refused to be intimidated, his feet planted like tree trunks under his black vestments, hands folded and unmoving. The set of his jaw implied he had faced down Mother Superiors before, and he could do it again.

As if she knew she had pushed as hard as she could, Alicia gave one more round of dirty looks then huffed down the center aisle toward the altar.

"Peter," the priest pointed to the front of the casket, "you take the right side, Ben, you take the left."

"O-o-o-h, Round One to Ben." This was a male voice that whispered in his ear, and Osborne turned to face the entertained eyes of Ray Pradt. "Let's hope he comes to the wake, huh? Par-r-r-d-e-e-e-e."

Leave it to Ray to see humor in this horrific situation, thought Osborne. He knew Ray was already thinking of the terrific story he could tell around the bar if Ben was so brazen as to challenge Alicia on her own ground.

Another male voice spoke up from behind Osborne, "Father, I would like to be included, please." Clint Chesnais stepped forward. Father Vodicka nodded, and Chesnais moved into formation behind Peter Roderick. Osborne saw Peter catch Chesnais' eye and give a slight nod of recognition. The fourth and final pallbearer was an elderly man whose name Osborne could not recall, though he knew the gentleman had been a manager under Meredith's father.

At last, Meredith was allowed to proceed to the same altar where she had been baptized, received the sacraments of Communion and Confirmation, been wed and would now be blessed in death.

Blessed? Osborne questioned the concept. What was blessed about that ugly moment when someone, possibly someone attending her funeral today, slammed the life from her eyes? What was blessed about the rage that simmered between the people who had known her best?

The small church was nearly full. As the guests proceeded forward to take Communion, Osborne let his eyes wander across the lines and beyond to the pews behind him. Cynthia Lewis was there with her husband and children. The fellows from the hunting shack and most of the McDonald's coffee crowd.

Other familar faces were folks who would have known the family over the years, maybe attended high school with Meredith or Alicia. A smaller group, easy to spot because they were a little too casually dressed, had to be the curious. Those who had heard that foul play was an option and wanted an up-close view. The same idiots that always rushed to the scene of a car accident.

More interesting, he thought, was who didn't attend: George Zolonsky, recipient of a very healthy check from Meredith. When he pointed that out later, Ray responded that George's absence was a good sign: "Means he's on the road with my boats, Doc. Pre-fishing begins 8:00 A.M. tomorrow. If he's not here, he sure as heck better be there."

Planning to drive himself and his daughters out to the cemetery for the interment, Osborne left the family pew a few minutes early in order to bring his car around to the front of the church. He walked quickly back down the aisle to the front of the church and through the swinging doors into the vestibule. At the same time, the doors on the other side swung open, and a young man in his early thirties waved at him.

"Dr. Osborne," he said. "May I speak with you for a moment?"

"Certainly," Osborne kept moving out the main doors. The man ran down the steps alongside him.

"I'm Tom Chandler, a lawyer here in town," he said. "I don't think we've met, but I understand you are working with Chief Ferris on this case. I had a case on the docket at the Court House yesterday and heard about it through the grapevine."

Osborne stopped to look at him. He wasn't surprised. The Court House adjoined the jail and Lew's office. Since all the cigarette smokers took their breaks at the same spot, any news in any office spread instantly through both buildings. "Yes, I'm somewhat involved. Why?"

"I'm a fly-fisherman, and I was fishing the Prairie that night, too. I think I might have waded that stretch where you found the body about two or three hours before you did. I always park near the old bridge and work my way down and back."

"Really? I didn't see any other cars . . ."

"I left before you got there—I don't like to fish in stormy weather."

"I learned the hard way," said Osborne with a wry chuckle.

"At one point, I climbed out of the river to take a short break. I walked back into the brush about forty feet—I needed a little privacy, y'know. And I found something back in the bushes that I didn't think much about at the time, but since I heard that the victim may have died from a blow to the head, I thought you should see it. My car is behind the church, which way are you going?"

"Same direction," said Osborne. The car was parked in the direction of Erin's house. "Let's take a look."

The two men hurried over to Chandler's Jeep. He opened the rear door and pointed. Osborne looked down at a four-foot length of wood nearly identical to the slender trunks he'd seen the day before. "My fiancée and I silkscreen fish prints, and I love to use this particular wood for the frames, which is why I picked it up in the first place.

"It's black spruce," said the lawyer. "I was pretty delighted to find it. But see how it was hand-cut? That's strange. I'll tell you something else—I have never found black spruce growing along the Prairie. And I look for it all the time."

"May I have this?" asked Osborne. "And I'd like Chief Ferris to hear what you have to say, too."

"Of course."

The burial at the cemetery proceeded without incident, Ben keeping his distance from Alicia and Peter. Osborne and the girls stood off to one side with other family friends. From that distance, Peter Roderick appeared to be his old self though maybe a touch more grizzled and hang-dog than usual.

A luncheon followed, served by the church ladies in the school cafeteria as was the custom after a funeral Mass. As was the custom, too, Father Vodicka had invited everyone attending the funeral service, so the cafeteria was crowded.

Lunch was simple: tuna fish casserole, Parker House buns, a watery coleslaw, and chocolate pudding for dessert. Ben elected to sit with Osborne, Mallory, and Erin. Everyone dedicated themselves to polite discourse, avoiding all mention of murder, mayhem, divorce, and adultery. Osborne was particularly proud of Erin's restraint, as he knew she was bursting to drill Ben. He was grateful, too, that Ray, responsible for filling in the gravesite, did not appear. Who knows what he would have said to Ben.

Across the room were Alicia and Peter. Osborne kept trying to get a glimpse of Peter, but the constant parade of sympathizers shaking either his or his wife's hand made it difficult. He gave up and resolved to wait to talk with him at the wake.

Just as they were finishing up and Osborne was enjoying the last spoonful of pudding, a beefy man with a rugged face under his sandy crew cut, tapped Mallory on her black silk shoulder. She turned, a look of pleasant surprise crossing her face.

"Randy!" she stood up to take a warm hug from the man.

"Dad, you remember Randy Nuttle. He took me to the Jun-

ior Prom. We double-dated with Meredith and Jeff Danner.
Gee, Randy, you're looking good . . ."

As she turned back to Randy, chattering enthusiastically,
Osborne caught Erin's eye. They knew Randy Nuttle too well.
He was the new owner of Thunder Bay Bar. Osborne knew,
too, that Lew's drug dealer "tip list" for Wayne would likely
have one name right at the top: Randy Nuttle. Osborne remembered his relief years ago when Mallory's interest in
Randy had finally fizzled, but only after she left for college.
Until then, he'd been worried, and Mary Lee had been furi-
ous—Mary Lee's fury serving only one purpose, of course: to
goad Mallory on.

Suddenly, pushing Randy aside and speaking in a sharp
shrill voice that reminded Osborne of his late wife, Alicia
loomed over their table, shaking a finger at Ben: "You've got
Mother's diamond brooch and I want it back."

As if he'd seen her coming, Ben looked up from his pudding
with no change of expression. "I have no idea what you're
talking about," he swallowed the spoonful and slowly dipped
for more. Osborne thought Alicia was going to take a swing
at him. She stood there, her eyes fixed in fury. "I want those
diamonds, Ben—and I want you out of here. Now!"

Ben stood up, shoved his chair into the table. He faced her
off, his eyes pinpoint black, the artery throbbing at his temple.
"You want too much, Alicia. You always have. Now you've
got it. But you've lost the only person who ever truly loved
you." He wiped his lips with his napkin and threw it down on
the table, "Meredith loved you in spite of your nasty little
habits. I never understood why. But she did—ain't life crazy?"

Alicia opened her mouth to retort, but Ben raised his hand,
"Don't say a word. I'll see you at the lawyer's tomorrow. If
those papers weren't signed, you won't see a penny, babe."

With that he walked from the table and out the swinging
doors of the cafeteria. The entire room was silent after as he
left. Then a polite buzz picked up. Alicia turned to Osborne
and his daughters, her face pale but set, "You'll join Peter and
me at the house, won't you?"

One hour later, Osborne was glad of one thing: the Rodericks'
house was air-conditioned, the only Loon Lake residence that
was. Outside, the threatening storm had continued to build, air
growing heavier by the minute, the humidity so high that

nearly everyone arriving for the wake entered patting fore-
heads and temples with handkerchiefs or Kleenex.

Loon Lake loved wakes. The house was already crowded
with friends and neighbors eating and drinking. Osborne and
Mallory stood munching brownies in the cavernous dining
room as Erin chatted nearby.

"That cost plenty," said Mallory, surveying the brass chandelier that hung over the long mahogony table. "She must have
picked it up in Chicago. It certainly isn't early Shultz," she
laughed, referring to Loon Lake's only furniture dealer.

Erin waved them over to a side table in a small alcove where
Alicia had set out a leather-bound family photo album and a
silver-framed photograph of Meredith that must have been
from her college graduation.

"Hey, Mal," she said, flipping the album open enthusiastically, "I'll bet you're in some of these—weren't you and Meredith best friends in junior high?" Osborne watched over their
shoulders as they turned pages carefully. "Yes! Look," said
Mallory, excitedly. "Girl Scout camp. Oh my gosh, aren't we
funny looking?" Erin held the album page up so Osborne could
see.

Mallory continued turning the pages after Erin drifted off to
talk to another friend. Most of the photos showed Meredith
with her mother, but several were of the senior Sutliffs with
the two girls: Meredith around age five, blonde and angelic,
Alicia in her late teens, stick thin and looking awkward.

"Is it my imagination," Osborne asked Mallory, "or does
Alicia look unhappy in these? Look—" He took the album
from Mallory and flipped back to a shot of what appeared to
be the family at Thanksgiving dinner, everyone smiling at the
camera except Alicia. "And here, see this?" He paged ahead
to a summer photo taken at a cabin somewhere. In both pictures, Meredith and her mother looked happy and relaxed. Not
Alicia. Staring straight at the camera, she glowered, a sullen
anger evident in her features. The photos had faded slightly,
but her eyes burned right off the page.

"Isn't that interesting," mused Mallory. "I didn't know Meredith until junior high so I don't remember much about Alicia.
She was already out of college and married to Peter. But I
never liked her. I still don't. I always thought it was funny she
and Mom became such good friends."

"That was partly because Peter is my age," said Osborne.

"So they socialized with an older crowd. Speaking of Peter, I need to find him. Excuse me, Mallory."

Osborne moved through the clusters of chatting guests, shaking hands and exchanging remarks. The group seemed a little more subdued than usual, perhaps because of the questions surrounding Meredith's death. Peter was nowhere to be seen. It occurred to Osborne to wonder if the man was deliberately avoiding him.

Just then he heard his name called and looked over the crowd to see Alicia waving at him. He made his way through the crowd toward her. "You have a phone call, Paul," she said. "Do you mind taking it in the kitchen?"

"Not at all." He stepped into the kitchen with her. She pointed to a wall phone near the back door. Several women were at the kitchen sink, cleaning up platters and plates.

"Hello, Doc, it's Lew. How're things going over there?"

"Pretty calm," he turned away and dropped his voice, aware that Alicia was hovering nearby, wrapping leftovers with Saran Wrap. "A few things here and there."

"Talk to Peter yet?"

"Nope."

"I got the lab report from Wausau this morning. They confirmed your reading—a single blow to the back of the head killed her. She sustained two, but the first one did the job. They took some slivers from her skull and sent them down to the Center for Wood Anatomy Research in Madison. They can tell us what type of wooden object was used by the killer, they may be able to ID the specific piece of wood even. Be several weeks until results however."

Osborne cupped his hand over his mouth. Alicia, now putting away glassware, had parked herself about three feet away. This was worse than trying to have a private conversation on his home party line.

"Any news on Peter?"

"Still working on it," he muttered.

"What? Oh . . . you can't talk now, can you."

"No."

"Maybe we should tonight?"

"We better."

"Okay. I was hoping you might have some time to compare notes. I know your daughter is in town—"

"She's having dinner with her sister," said Osborne, taking

his hand down from his mouth. "Why don't you come by my place about six, Lew. We'll cast a few flies from the dock. Maybe you would coach me on my double haul."

"You want to fish?" her voice picked up in delight. "Let's check out the Gudegast. It's only five minutes from your place. We'll just go for an hour or so."

"That'll be fine," said Osborne, letting his voice return to a normal register. "I don't expect Mallory home until eight or so. See you at six, my place."

Alicia gave him a nervous smile as he hung up the phone. "Was that Chief Ferris? Any news?"

"No," said Osborne, deciding it was Lew's choice when to share the news, "just confirming a fishing date."

Alicia gave him a shaky smile and reached toward him with both arms. Osborne gave her as impersonal a hug as he could manage, then drifted back into the party. The woman was really getting on his nerves.

A small but lively crowd had gathered at one end of the living room, some in chairs, some standing, drinks or bottles of beer in hand. Hearing everyone burst into laughter, Osborne recognized a familiar scene: Ray was holding court. As he approached, he could hear Ray's voice, rising and falling as he built the momentum of his story, pausing for audience appreciation. On cue, everyone laughed again. Then Ray must have delivered the punch line as several people turned away, laughing so hard they had to wipe tears from their eyes.

Mallory was one. Sitting off to the right in a chair alongside the sofa where Ray was ensconced, she was tuned to every syllable, an open-mouthed grin across her face. Osborne could not recall when he had seen her so happy. Sometime in her childhood maybe? The day she caught that big walleye? Osborne stopped at the edge of the group. It was a story he had heard many times.

He watched his daughter. The laughter lingered on her face, and her eyes remained fixed on Ray, even when someone else entered the conversation.

Ray looked remarkably good. Having his hair and beard professionally trimmed for the ESPN appearance had inspired him to outfit himself appropriately for a change. Gone was the stuffed minnow hat and the fishing khakis. In their place, dark brown gabardine slacks and a nicely fitting slubbed silk tan sport coat. A crisp white shirt, open at the neck, highlighted his deep tan. The star fishing guide and stalwart grave digger looked almost like a college professor. But it was a big "almost"—he wore a fuchsia tie emblazoned with a brilliant lime-green leaping walleye.

Tearing his eyes away from the lurid fish on Ray's chest, Osborne realized with a start what that look on his daughter's face meant. As he watched her, Mallory stood up, reached for Ray's empty glass and left the room. She returned with it moments later. Setting it down in front of him with her left hand, she let her right hand linger on his shoulder. There was no doubting the significance of the touch. Ray appeared not to notice, until she turned away to sit down again. The look on Ray's face told Osborne his hunch was right: Mallory was flirting with Ray. And Ray was as surprised as her father.

Surprised and concerned. Much as he loved Ray and considered him one of his closest friends, he knew Ray's faults. And he sure as heck didn't favor having him as a family member.

Osborne mulled over a few tidbits he might share with Mallory to curb her interest. For example, he could bring up Ray's long-standing liason with Donna, the faithful standby who mends his shirts. Or his obsession with the high school girlfriend turned fashion model, the elegant beauty who flies back every summer in her private jet to visit her mother . . . and doesn't sleep at her mother's every night.

Osborne's eyes had drifted up to the mirror over Ray's head. Suddenly he realized two deep-set, unhappy eyes had been staring at his reflection from the back of the room. He turned and walked back quickly, determined to greet the man face to face.

"Pete, I am so sorry about Meredith. Alicia seems to be holding up okay. How 'bout yourself? I hear you just got back from Japan to all this."

"Thank you, Doc," said Peter. He might be the well-dressed host, but he smelled like one of the old whiskey stills they uncovered back behind the deer shack. Osborne backed off ever so slightly. "Is there anything I can do?"

"Gee, I don't think so," Peter looked around the room vacantly, shaking the ice cubes in his empty glass. "Alicia's got it all organized, y'know."

"As always," offered Osborne in a friendly tone. "You

know, Pete, I was surprised when she told me you were traveling. I thought you retired a few months ago."

"I did." Peter's weary eyes avoided Osborne's. His cheeks
seemed to hang lower than ever, the mouth was pursed. "I had
some opportunities that were too good to pass up," he said,
pushing enthusiasm into his voice.

As if to tell his old friend he didn't believe him, Osborne
said, "Pete, you look tired." It was an understatement. He
looked dead. "Come by McDonald's tomorrow for coffee."

"I'd like that," Peter raised his glass. "I need a refill." He
started to walk away, then he stopped. Without looking up, he
said simply, "This is not a good time, Paul. Not a good time."

Osborne turned back to Ray's crowd, but Mallory had disappeared. He found Erin in the dining room, wrapped up in
earnest discussion over the pending school budget referendum.

"Erin, where's Mallory?" asked Osborne.

"She left, Dad, said she was going to visit an old friend.
Don't worry, she'll be at my house for dinner at six. We'll
drive her out to your place later."

twenty-one

Osborne walked from the Rodericks' house back to Erin's sweating all the way. Gray clouds laced with feathers of white scudded so low to the treetops that he kept an eye out for funnels. The air had turned the peculiar green that telegraphs tornado activity.

Not surprised to find the interior of his car blistering hot, he quickly lowered all the windows, hoping the sky wouldn't open up while he was inside getting the dog.

Erin's babysitter had all the windows and doors wide open. As Mike barreled toward him from the kitchen, he shouted a warning back toward the family room where the teenager was watching television with his grandchildren.

"Trish, you better be ready to close everything up. If you hear sirens, take the kids down to the basement . . ." She waved at him and leaped up to follow his instructions. He wasn't worried. She was a responsible kid and tornado warnings were a familiar phenomenon over Loon Lake summers. Osborne and Mike headed home.

It was four-fifteen when he turned down Loon Lake Road and coasted past the year-round homes that had replaced cabins over the years. At Greystone Lodge, one of the few remaining resorts, he slowed to check out the cars parked in front of the main lodge and the housekeeping cottages.

At his own driveway, he stopped the car, leaving the motor

running, and got out to let Mike into the house. He headed back toward Greystone. Seconds later, he pulled into the parking lot. Chances were good he might find Ben Marshall at the bar, since he and Meredith had often stayed there in the past.

Just as he stepped out of the car, Julie, the owner's daughter ran toward him from the entrance to the bar. Even in a white tank top and cut-off shorts, she looked hot and unhappy. A chubby brunette in her late twenties, Julie's face was red, loose strands of dark hair plastered damply to her forehead.

"Dr. Osborne," she called, "are you in the volunteer fire department?"

"No, why?" Osborne, walked toward her and the bar.

"Oh shoot." she said. "Do you know anybody who is? We've got a guest missing. I just hope we don't have a drowning. I tried Chief Ferris, but she's out and both deputies are tied up, so I have to call for volunteers. Oh good, here comes somebody now. They musta heard me on the phone."

Like Osborne, the lodge was tied to the party line serving all the residents along the shoreline. More than one household managed to eavesdrop pretty steadily on conversations. Whenever Osborne thought he was being too mean-spirited in suspecting such busybodies, something like this would happen and confirm his suspicions.

A battered black Jeep pulled in behind Osborne's car, the yellow signal beam identifying a volunteer fireman flashing behind the windshield. Julie ran to talk to the driver while Osborne opened the door to the bar.

Julie's father, Larry Snowden, was behind the bar on the phone. "Calm down, sweetheart, everything's going to be okay," Osborne heard him saying. A shrill female voice echoed from the phone, which Larry now held away from his ear, raising his eyebrows in frustration. He let the screaming go on for about ten seconds.

"Look sweetheart, cursing me out isn't going to find your boyfriend any faster. I'll tell ya what, you come up here to the bar . . . no, no, just come on up. We need you anyway to give a description."

Then he hung up and turned to Osborne, "Jeez, I'm gonna cancel the rest of these damn Chicago reservations. These people are impossible. Can't walk from their cabin to the dock without getting lost. And the abuse from their women—un-

believable. What can I get ya, Doc? The usual?" Larry was
already reaching for a mug.

Osborne was contemplating his frosty mug of ginger ale
when the woman slammed through the doorway. He hadn't
had a chance to ask Larry if Ben Marshall was registered there.
Now he didn't need to—the woman on the edge of hysteria
was the same blonde he'd seen with Ben at the airport. She
was wearing a variation on her theme: low-cut black top, tight
white slacks. Only this time she looked upset.

"Listen, big guy," she drilled her words at Larry, "I demand
you call the state police this instant. I'm going to stand here
and watch you do it, damn it. You have exactly two people
out looking for Ben, and that is not enough!" She banged her
fist on the bar. "He's been missing for hours, he's dead, he's
drowned."

"He went for a walk, Miss. We know he's not on the water.
He's been a guest here before. I assure you he's off enjoying
himself somewhere like you do when you're on vacation—"

"Don't 'Miss' me, you . . . you . . . ," she stammered. "I may
be blonde, but I'm not a bimbo. I . . . I'm a purchasing agent!"

"Wait—Ben?" Osborne interrupted, looking from Larry to
the blonde and back to Larry. "You aren't talking about Ben
Marshall, are you?"

"Yes!" the blonde almost landed on him with both feet. She
thrust her face into his, "Have you seen him?"

"At lunch at the church."

"Oh," her face sagged, and she backed off.

"When was the last time you saw him?" asked Osborne,
standing up. "Maybe I can help."

"Sit down, Doc." Now Larry interrupted, "I got it under
control." His back to the blonde, he rolled his eyes so only
Osborne could see.

Larry Snowden was a short, wizened man, bald with a blunt
beard that made him look like one of the Seven Dwarfs. He
was a long-time friend of Osborne's and one of the few bar-
tenders who not only shut him off when he'd had too much
during those terrible months after Mary Lee's death, but on
more than one occasion drove him home and somehow got
him into bed.

"Here, young lady," he shoved a whiskey straight-up at the
blonde who had settled two stools down from Osborne. "On
the house. You cool your jets for ten minutes until the rest of

the search team gets here. Then you brief everyone on what he's wearing and so forth and so on. They'll take it from here because we know he's not on the lake."

"How do we know that?" she demanded. "He said he was going fishing."

"I told you before. No one takes a boat out without signing for it. I do not have Ben on the list for a boat. See for yourself." He shoved a yellow legal pad at her.

Just then a huge crash of thunder rattled the building. And the sky that had been threatening all day burst. Sheets of rain blew across the lawn that ran down to the swimming beach, visible through the big picture window at one end of the bar. That did it for the girl, she burst into tears. The two men just looked at each other. Osborne knew what his eyes said, and Larry's seemed to match his: "Summer women—a little always goes a long way."

Larry kept wiping the bar slowly while he handed over a box of Kleenex. Rain thundered on the roof, lightning flashed rapidly outside, and the blonde kept weeping. Osborne sipped his ginger ale and waited patiently for her tears to let up. He had a couple questions he wanted to ask.

"Are we in a tornado?" the blonde finally sobbed from inside a clutch of tissues she had mashed against her face.

"No-o," said Osborne, gently, "just a good Wisconsin thunderstorm." He introduced himself. She shared the fact her name was Karen. Osborne was mildly surprised. Alicia had alleged she was named "Tiffany." But then, when it came to Ben, Alicia did not hesitate to exaggerate.

"Did you know Ben's ex-wife?" she sniffled. "This is such a small town, I'll bet everyone knows everyone." She seemed relieved to talk.

"Yes, I did," said Osborne. "In fact, I stopped in here to see your friend. I was a little concerned for him after the luncheon. Did he seem okay when he returned?"

"No. Not at all. He came back mad. Then he called home and got madder." Conversation was calming her down. "He's been waiting for his divorce papers, and it turns out they arrived last week but nobody told him."

She downed the shot of whiskey like a pro, pushing her glass forward for a refill. A good match for Ben, thought Osborne.

"The truth is he was at my place all last week, and his

housekeeper doesn't open his mail, so she couldn't tell him they had arrived. It wasn't her fault. But he was mad. And then this idiot police woman calls and tells him he has to be in her office at the crack of dawn tomorrow. So he starts to holler at me, I holler back—none of this is my fault, for heaven's sakes—then he ran out the door. That was four, five hours ago."

"Three," said Larry. "I'll tell ya, sweetheart, he's in town at one of the bars on Main Street putting away the booze. I would be." Then he reached over to pat the young woman's hand, "Now you stop worrying, we'll find him. Julie's checking the local bars and the entire volunteer fire department will be here as soon as this rain lets up.

"Hey, look—here comes someone," said Larry, pointing through the screen door to a masculine figure, head hidden under a rain poncho, running up the path from the marina.

"That's Ben!" shouted the blonde. She ran to the door.

She was right. The rain poncho tipped back and the heavy face of Ben Marshall looked around bar. "Who-e-e-e! Excitement out there. But I got a 37-incher in the livewell. He hit me hard about fifteen minutes before the sky opened up. I was way up on Fifth Lake, too. Hell of time getting back against that wind."

"Hey, man, I didn't have you down for a boat," Larry said. "You were s'posed to sign out."

"Oh, yeah?" Ben gave the shrug of a man who didn't think it necessary to follow the rules. "Sorry about that. Nobody was down there, Larry. I took that new Ranger you got. Thought I'd see what 150 horsepower could do."

"What're you drinking?" Larry dropped the subject, but his body had tensed. Osborne knew why. Ben had taken a boat that belonged to one of Larry's friends, not one of the resort rentals. It was a very expensive boat, and if anything happened to it, Larry was liable. Liable and, right now, irritated.

"C'mon, honeybunch, shush now," Ben kissed the blonde's forehead as she started in exclaiming her worry over his absence. He laid a finger over her lips, "You go back to the cabin and get ready for dinner. We have reservations at six-thirty. Get beautiful, huh?" She resisted, but he put both hands on her shoulders and nearly shoved her toward the door. "Hurry, the rain let up a little."

Still, she resisted, "Let me finish my drink, Ben."

"Karen." The banter became a warning. She got the message and banged out the door almost as hard as she had coming in.

"She was worried about you," said Osborne when she was gone.

"Yeah, well, I was worried about me, Doc." Ben slipped onto the stool next to him. "That damn Alicia."

"I thought you might like to talk."

Ben laughed a mirthless laugh, "Hell, talk is just what I shouldn't do. What am I? Suspect Number One?"

The two men sat in silence. Larry leaned back against the bar a short distance away. He remained silent as well.

"I knew those papers were signed," said Ben after a long pause. "Meredith's lawyer called a few weeks ago on final details . . ."

"Were you hoping to reconcile?"

"No. I said that to yank Alicia's chain. She sure yanked mine plenty over the years. No, I figured the papers were signed, but I hadn't seen them. When I got the news from Mallory yesterday, I did hold out a little hope there had been some kind of delay . . ."

"Why?"

"Why, Doc?" Ben looked sideways at him with a slightly incredulous look on his face. "Six million bucks why. That's what she inherited from the old man."

"Is that why you came up?"

"Partly. Partly that since it wouldn't hurt to appear bereaved if the will could be challenged. But partly . . .," and with that Ben sighed deeply.

He looked over at Osborne. The smart-aleck attitude had disappeared. The eyes Osborne looked into were the eyes of man in pain.

"I love it up here," he said. "I love going up that stretch of the channel where you don't see a house or a cabin for miles. I love the tamarack against the sky. I loved my wife . . . we were together for fifteen years, Doc, and nine of those years were probably the best years of my life . . ." He stopped. Osborne waited.

"What happened?"

"I don't know, Doc. People change, marriages just get old."

Osborne nodded over his ginger ale, "Yep, they do."

"So I figured the funeral was the last excuse I might ever

have to come up here. And, to be perfectly honest," he said, as if in answer to the expression on Osborne's face, "I do have to meet with the authorities. Better sooner than later, I figure."

He stood up. "What do I owe you, Larry?"

"You got that boat back in one piece?" Larry didn't smile. "Five bucks."

"For Karen, too?"

"She's on the house. Just keep her out of my hair, okay?"

Ben started toward the door, then he stopped and came back to the bar. He leaned forward on his elbows and stared into Osborne's face.

"I didn't kill her if that's what you're wondering."

"I believe you, Ben," said Osborne, and he did. "But who do you think . . . ?"

"I can't imagine. Maybe a nut, huh?" Ben stood erect. "One other thing. I have no recollection of this diamond brooch that Alicia accuses me of keeping. I do not have it, I do not remember ever seeing any such item from her family. I gave Meredith diamond earrings as a wedding gift. They should be with all her other jewelry."

Osborne believed him. He had a sudden thought, "Ben, do you keep old records like your personal articles insurance policies from years back?"

"I should."

"Why don't you look through those when you get back and give me a call."

"Sure, Doc." He looked a little puzzled but agreeable. "Oh, I see, a good check against what's listed in the estate?"

"Something like that. See if anything jumps out at you. Here's my phone number," said Osborne, scribbling on a bar napkin and shoving it over.

"Doc, something you should know since you said you're helping Chief Ferris," said Larry as Osborne stood up to follow Ben out the door. "That Meredith Marshall? I ran into her two or three times this past month way back in the woods behind the Starks potato fields. Now what do you suppose she was doing back there?"

"Starks?" Osborne was puzzled. "I take it she was driving?"

"All by herself in that Jeep of hers. Only plum-colored one in town, hard to miss. I buy eggs from a fella's got a chicken farm way the hell out," Larry gestured toward a gallon jug of pickled eggs that rested on the bar. "Usually do some dumping when I'm back there, too. So I was back on one of those unmarked dirt roads by Kubiak's Landing when she went by going the other direction."

"What time of day?"

"Late afternoon. I thought it was kinda odd because nobody you wanna know lives out there. You get out past Kubiak's and you redefine the words 'trailer trash.' Know what I mean? Unless you're into seed potatoes, why would you drive the backroads of Starks?"

"The people who live out there do tend to be a little strange," said Osborne.

"When you can find 'em. I think they all live under rocks. I wouldn't want my wife or daughter on those back roads. Night or day . . . Just thought you'd like to know."

twenty-two

Two minutes before six, Osborne pulled into his driveway. He scrambled into his fishing clothes and threw two cups of dog food into Mike's dish, hoping to be ready before Lew arrived. Just as he finished a quick brushing of his teeth, he heard the crunch of tires across in his gravel driveway.

"Come in," he shouted at the knock on the back door. He grabbed his fishing hat from the fireplace mantel and bent to zip shut his duffel. As he straightened up, he glanced through the kitchen window to the driveway.

To his surprise, it wasn't Lew's truck he saw parked behind his station wagon, but Peter Roderick's black Range Rover. Only it wasn't Peter at his back door.

"Hi, Paul," Alicia chirped, smiling up at him from the back stoop. She was dressed for fishing: khaki long-sleeved shirt with the sleeves rolled up and polarized sunglasses hanging from the open neck, a fly-fishing vest that look brand new, and a pair of bermuda shorts that matched her shirt. A bright red baseball cap with a beige brim completed the ensemble.

"Alicia?" Osborne was taken aback. Did Lew invite her and forget to leave him a message? Then he remembered he hadn't taken the time to check phone messages. "Oh, I'm sorry, I'm standing here like a big dummy."

Not for long he wasn't. Alicia stepped right up, backing him into his kitchen as she strode past him. Osborne followed her with an invitation after the fact, "Please, come in, Alicia. Have a seat. Lew isn't here yet."

As she plopped herself onto a kitchen chair, Alicia grinned sheepishly, "I know this is a surprise, Paul. I decided to invite myself fishing with you two. Hope you don't mind."

She took off her hat and set it on the kitchen table, tipped her head back to run both hands through her hair. Then, bracing her elbows on the table, she dropped her face into her hands. And remained in that position saying nothing.

"Can I get you something to drink?" Osborne asked after a moment. He wondered if she was about to cry.

"No, no, I'm fine. I'm trying to relax. I think my cheek muscles are going to crack from all the smiling I did today." She pulled her hands away and looked up at him. Osborne could see the strain and fatigue in her face. In spite of her make-up, she looked exhausted. Why on earth was she here?

"Paul, I just needed to get out of the house and away from Peter and all the phone calls. You're an old friend, I hope you don't mind."

Of course not, thought Osborne, *aside from the fact you just ruined my evening.* He was about to compliment her on the wake, but before he could open his mouth, he heard another set of tires in the drive. This time it *was* Lew. He watched her saunter toward the back door and excused himself to let her in.

"You've got company?" she asked as Osborne opened the screen door, shifting his eyes in such a way that she would know he couldn't say much. Lew gave an understanding nod and stepped inside.

"Alicia Roderick stopped by," he said. "She'd like to fish with us tonight."

"That's nice," said Lew, walking ahead of him into the kitchen. "Mrs. Roderick, you must be exhausted."

"Exhausted and all wound up simultaneously," said Alicia, throwing her hands up and laughing. It struck Osborne she was determinedly cheery. "I've always found that fishing is the best way ever to unwind, so I hope you don't mind my tagging along. And, please, Chief Ferris, call me 'Alicia.' "

"Glad to have you," said Lew graciously. "You should come more often."

Her enthusiasm helped Osborne relax a little about the situation, though he suspected she was faking it.

"I brought a cooler of beer and soda, and some leftovers from the wake," said Alicia. "I thought we could take my car."

"Thanks, but I'll follow you two in my truck," said Lew. "I need to have it along for the radio—just in case someone from the department has to reach me."

Liar, thought Osborne, vividly recalling Lew's determination to never have a car phone or radio in her fishing truck. On the other hand, he was relieved they would not be wholly hostage to Alicia. The big question in his mind at the moment was whether or not Lew would follow through on their initial plan and share her secret spot on the Gudegast now that Alicia was along.

Continuing to tweak the truth, Lew honed in on that very subject with, "So, Alicia, where do you suggest we fish? Doc and I were planning just an hour off the dock here on Loon Lake—"

"Well, if you'd like," said Alicia, matching gracious for gracious, "Peter and I have a membership at Silver Bass—if that's close enough." Lew looked at Osborne for his input.

Silver Bass was an exclusive hunting and fishing club located twelve miles outside of town. As far as Osborne knew, Peter Roderick was the only local who was a member of the club, which was rumored to have an annual membership fee of ten thousand dollars and an initiation fee triple that.

Members got their money's worth if you liked your sport dumped in your lap: Silver Bass Lake was the best-stocked lake in the region and one Ray Pradt delighted in poaching when he was short on time but hungry for a mess of bluegills, lightly breaded, sauteed in butter. Ray could pull thirty fish out of there in less than an hour.

One secret to his successful poaching was leaving a percentage of his catch at the door of the club manager, a gentleman who did not mind inventory abuse of his neurotic, complaining club members so long as he shared in the benefits. The other secret was that Silver Bass Lake, being private water, was darn difficult to find.

Osborne checked his watch, "Fine with me so long as you ladies don't mind that I have to be back here by eight to meet my daughter."

"C'mon, Cinderella, you're on," said Lew, leading the way out the door.

*   *   *

Twenty minutes later, Alicia pulled the Range Rover off the highway onto a paved road running due south. She must have been counting the number of unpaved lanes running off it as she suddenly swung right onto a one-lane drive that had no marking, not even a fire number that Osborne could discern.

She had turned so quickly, she had to stop for a minute to let Lew, who shot past the turn, reverse and catch up. This lane ran back and back, the Range Rover living up to its name as it heaved and pushed its way over boulders and slash that had blown onto the road. The forest changed dramatically as they drove along.

What appeared to be millions of slender maple trees reached high for the sun, their leafy canopy allowing enough sun through to blanket the forest floor with the rich green leaves of saplings. This light and pretty forest gave way to the rough bark and dark, twisted shapes of ancient pines. Down into the cavern of this uncut woods rocked and swayed the two vehicles.

Pulling to one side of the lane, Alicia cut the engine. "We park here and walk the rest of the way," she said. Osborne got out of the car and looked around. He whistled softly, caught Lew's eye and pointed.

"These white pines must be well over a hundred years old," he said. "Just look at the trunks on those trees. When was the last time you saw a tree trunk five feet wide?"

"The hemlock. I haven't seen hemlock like these in years," said Lew.

"Nor have I," said Osborne, struck by the vast openness beneath the overhead branches. The towering fine-needled trees filtered out sunlight, leaving the forest floor exquisitely spare. No slash, no underbrush, not even a mushroom grew from the soft decades of needles. No birds sang, no breezes whispered through the eerie stillness. And all was in shadow.

Looking past the massive trunks into the gloom, Osborne refused to let his imagination work overtime. Logic told him the looming figures with limbs stabbing into the dark silence were only moss-covered timbers. It wouldn't be for another hour that a thought grounded in reality would occur to him: no one knew where they were or with whom.

twenty-three

"We call this 'the hemlock cathedral,' " said Alicia. "Isn't it beautiful?"

"Thank you for bringing us here," said Lew softly. "I had no idea such a magnificent uncut forest could be found so close to Loon Lake."

Following Alicia's example, they gathered up their gear and walked after her about a hundred yards to where a clearing opened to a bog. The brush grew thicker, closing off the forest. Someone had built a planked walkway, which they followed over the bog to the shore of Silver Bass Lake. It was a small-ish, lake, long and narrow.

The storm had cut the oppressive humidity. A light, cool breeze blew toward them from the west, causing ripples on the lake surface to shimmer gold as the sun dropped behind the tall pines. The club kept the shoreline undeveloped except for the massive log and stone lodge at the far end. The result was a scene of pristine beauty, of nearly perfect wilderness.

"Well," said Lew, "well, well." She looked back to admire the towering hemlock and white pines ringing the lake behind them. She thrust her hands into her pockets and inhaled deeply. "What a magnificent forest."

Alicia was quite pleased that her fishing site was appreci-ated. "This end of the forest was protected by the founders when the club was established in 1882," she said. "They made a deal with the state. Unlike most of the other forests around here, this one has never been clear-cut. Only selective cutting ever, if that."

She pointed off to her right, "I like to wade the north shoreline down to the lodge."

"No wonder you fish here," said Lew. "How often do you get out—a couple times a week?"

"Heavens no, I haven't fished in years," said Alicia, apparently forgetting her earlier statement. "I sent Meredith over last month with that weird friend of hers. That Chesnais creep. Boy, do I hope you've questioned him . . ." Her tone had turned derisive and pushy, ruining the spell of the moment, and she looked to Lew for a response.

"Really. So much for how often *you* need to relax, huh?" said Lew lightly, catching her in her lie and ignoring the not so subtle probe. She turned away, carefully set down her rod, and prepared to pull on her waders and boots.

Unaware that Osborne was watching, Alicia stared at Lew's back. An angry, calculating expression flashed across her features, reminding him of the face he had seen in the photos of the adolescent Alicia earlier that day. It was, he realized, the same expression he had seen in the mirror when she was dealing with the news of Meredith's death.

Lew was right. Alicia Roderick was a bully of a woman. Her aggression might be indirect but no less damaging: gossip and innuendo can kill as effectively as a bullet.

"I think I'll try a 'Dancing Frog,' Doc," said Lew, her back still turned as she slipped the straps of her waders over her shoulders, "it's the only bass fly I've ever used. What about you?"

Before Osborne could answer, Alicia interrupted. "Say, Chief," she said brightly, now fitting her rod sections together, "what did you hear from Wausau on cause of death?" She kept her head down as she attached her reel. The studied casualness prompted Lew to throw a quick glance Osborne's way, a signal not to say anything.

"Nothing yet," said Lew, matching brightness for brightness. Osborne had to tuck his head to hide a grin. Lew was going to look like Pinocchio if she wasn't careful.

Osborne pulled a long purple bass fly from a box he found at the bottom of his duffel. "Hey, ladies," he held it aloft, "check out my 'Whitlock Hare Grub.' I oughta see some terrific action with this."

"I don't know, Doc, that's awful fancy," said Lew. She gave him a big grin and winked. Like himself, she had decided to treat this as a lark rather than serious fishing.

Alicia busied herself pulling up her waders. Again, the studied casualness as she cinched her wading belt: "Did you talk to Ben Marshall today, Chief?"

"Uh, uh, tomorrow morning," said Lew. She looked directly at Alicia, "Today was my day to go back up to The Willows and take a few hours to look through your sister's place."

"Oh?" That caught Alicia off-guard. "I thought you were going to let me know..." Osborne saw her hands start to shake. "So, really, you went in, huh. Find anything?"

"I'm not sure," Lew tone was noncommittal. "Your sister was an exceptionally well-organized woman. Her bedroom, her dresser drawers, even her desk was quite tidy. Unusually tidy for someone going fishing on the spur of the moment. Most of us leave clothes around, papers stacked here and there, a coffee cup in the sink. Know what I mean?"

Lew braced her rod against her shoulder and doubled her fly-line to thread it through the guides. "Of course, you had Cynthia Lewis in to clean and you went through a few things..." All three of them knew exactly what she was really implying: Alicia searched and reorganized everything Monday morning before Roger arrived.

"My sister was a compulsive organizer. That's how she got so much done." Alicia's voice had taken on a slightly defensive tone. "So... you did find something?" She stepped in front of Lew, blocking the path down to the water, demanding an answer.

"I'm not sure. It may be nothing," said Lew, shrugging and walking around Alicia. "But I don't want to discuss it until I've been able to question Ben Marshall... and your husband."

"My husband?!" Alicia's voice cracked on the last word, and she coughed. "Excuse me, I swallowed a bug." Osborne knew she didn't swallow anything. "Why on earth do you need to talk to Peter? He wasn't even in the country when this happened."

"Alicia, do you always wear a red hat when you fish?" asked Lew, changing the subject.

"I dunno. Why?"

"A little bright in my opinion." If Lew had full-scale torture in mind for the woman, she was doing a great job. Alicia was going to rue the day she barged in on this little get-together, thought Osborne. Rue the day. Lew was loading on so much innuendo, the woman would toss and turn all night trying to figure out what was happening with the investigation. *Yep,* thought Osborne with satisfaction, *Alicia was finally learning to keep her nose clean, the hard way.*

"Alicia, do you *have* to wear that hat?" chided Lew as Alicia kept walking toward the water. "I think you'll spook the fish."

"Oh, phooey. That's an old wive's tale," said Alicia, "fish are color-blind."

"That's not what I've heard," volunteered Osborne in a lighthearted tone, but Alicia was in no mood for humor.

"Oh, hell," she said, marching back up to the open window of the Range Rover. She yanked the offending hat off her head and threw it onto the front seat of the car. Again Lew winked at Osborne. She was having a great time.

Hurrying after them, Alicia waded into the lake with the grace of a rhinoceros, stirring up the mucky bottom as she pushed weeds and water noisily out of her way. No one said a word, but any fisherman knows fish can hear. Lew just shook her head and moved forward and away from Alicia as quickly as she could.

If any doubt remained about Alicia's fishing prowess, her technique said it all. Her casting was a marvel of loose-elbowed jerkiness, and Osborne had to admit he wasn't entirely unhappy to watch the wind knots multiply exponentially on her leader. More than once, her fly flew alarmingly close to his head. For all the money she may have spent on fishing equipment, she spent precious little time on etiquette or skills.

But none of this bothered the Silver Bass Lake fish. All Osborne could imagine was they were used to klutzes. Over-accessorized fishing klutzes. Maybe they were paid to bite! The monsters practically jumped into her pockets. Osborne swore he saw Alicia hook bass of varying sizes at least every five minutes. His estimate was conservative. Forty-five minutes later, she announced with grim pride that she had caught and released seventeen fish.

Osborne didn't do so bad either, releasing eight. Lew counted thirteen.

"Bet this beats your trout streams, doesn't it?" said Alicia.

"Sure does," said Lew. "Nothing like a stocked lake."

"I like my fishing quick and easy," said Alicia. "Last time I was here, I caught forty-two fish in ninety minutes. What's the most you ever caught, Lew?"

"I guess I'm a little less into the numbers and more into the challenge," said Lew. "I like to work on presentation."

"Boring. I like to score." Alicia struggled out of her waders. She appeared to have given up on getting anything out of Lew. She no longer looked so determinedly pleasant, nor did she seem at all relaxed.

"I'll catch a ride back with Chief Ferris," said Osborne.

"Fine," said Alicia.

Minutes later, he was standing a few feet away as she tossed her waders into the back of the Range Rover. Just as she slammed the door shut, he glimpsed a long, rust-colored padded case: a shotgun. A shotgun out of season. The forest seemed suddenly darker and their location very remote.

"I do hope," she looked at Lew grimly, "as the family member in charge of this entire situation that you will keep me informed at some point. And I cannot fathom why you have to question Peter."

Osborne saw a shadow pass behind her eyes. He wasn't sure if it was that, the sight of the gun, or an unexpected cool breeze that sent a shiver down his spine. But he was doubly happy Lew had her truck along and had left Alicia with the impression she stayed in touch with her department.

"Alicia," said Lew in a patient tone, "I have to answer to Wausau. I need clearance from them before sharing details of the investigation with the public. They call the shots, they can overrule my decisions. Any conflict between Wausau and my department can have serious budget ramifications. I'm sorry, but we are a business like any other."

Now that was not a lie. During his exam of Meredith's corpse, Lew had made it clear just how frustrating that relationship was. Because she was held hostage to their crime lab services, the Wausau officials tended to behave as though they were the decisionmakers. They were not. Lew was. Nor did she report to them. Her bosses were the mayor of Loon Lake and the town board. Period. Still, there were times when she was unable to rebuff their meddling.

"Alicia," said Osborne hastily changing the subject, "do you have any idea why Meredith would have been driving around Starks these last few weeks? I saw Larry Snowden today, and he told me he'd seen her back in there recently, way back by Kubiak's Landing."

"Starks?" Alicia sneered. "Meredith had no business in Starks. He must have seen someone else."

"He's positive it was Meredith."

"Well, I'm just as positive it wasn't."

"Come on now, Alicia," Lew countered in a reasonable tone, "you weren't in a position to know every move your sister made, were you?"

"Of course not. But Starks? She had no reason to go there. None."

"But you could be wrong," said Lew.

"I doubt it," snapped Alicia.

"So much for going home relaxed," said Lew as the Range Rover's tires spun out of the clearing.

"You didn't exactly give her what she wanted."

"I refuse to be bullied, Doc. She can do it to her husband, maybe to her friends, but I don't buy that routine." Lew opened the door on the driver's side of her truck as Osborne climbed into the passenger seat. She backed out and pulled Nellie up onto the road in the direction of Loon Lake.

"She had a shotgun in the back of her car."

"Really? In a case?"

Osborne nodded.

"Nothing illegal about that, Doc."

"This is an odd time of year to be driving around with a shotgun."

"Maybe she had it in for cleaning and just picked it up. Anyway, it's her husband's car, maybe it's his gun."

"All I know is I didn't like it, Lew. No one except Alicia knows we're back in here. Keep an eye out."

This time Lew didn't argue. She drove slowly, watching for signs of tires that might have pulled off the lane. "The ground is soft enough after this rain, Doc, we'll spot anything unusual." But it wasn't until they reached the highway that Osborne felt the tension leave his shoulders. Lew's soft exhalation told him she felt it, too.

●   ●   ●

"Do you mind if I ask if you did find something up at The Willows today?" asked Osborne, once the truck was on the highway.

Lew looked at him, a hint of a smile betraying her satisfaction, "Not at all. I found Meredith's personal checkbook, and I think Alicia missed it."

"Really?"

"I think that's what she was looking for yesterday. Meredith kept a brass box up on one corner of her desk in that room off the kitchen. It was full of bills for the house and the construction on the boathouse. I pulled out the phone bill to check her long-distance calls—and found the checkbook. It must have fallen or been accidentally shoved into the envelope with the bill."

Lew looked over at Osborne, "During the two weeks before she died, Meredith wrote three checks to Alicia, each for twenty thousand dollars. That's a lotta cash, Doc.

"Then, upstairs, I found a file that Peter Roderick left behind. Actually, he was keeping it under his mattress. It's a loan application completed a month ago. The man is broke. Stone cold broke. A bank out of Minneapolis has a lien on that house of theirs. If that loan didn't come through, he was looking at receiving an eviction notice any day now."

"The Rodericks evicted? That's unbelievable. Do you think he's been hiding this from Alicia?"

"Your guess is as good as mine, Doc. Now what was all this about Starks?"

As they neared Loon Lake, Osborne filled her in on his conversations with Ben Marshall and Larry Snowden, finishing up just as Lew pulled into his drive.

"Something else important, Lew," said Osborne. "Wait here." He ran over to his station wagon and retrieved the length of black spruce that the lawyer had handed him after the funeral. "You should talk to him for a better description of exactly where he found it," said Osborne. "You know that territory better than I do."

Lew looked at Osborne. "Given what we learned from Chesnais, George Zolonsky is a little too close to the action. At least, it's starting to look that way. Does he fish trout?"

"I have no idea."

"When does Ray expect him with the boats? I want to be included in the welcoming party."

"But why would Zolonsky—?"

"Who knows what a creep thinks."

Suddenly, through the kitchen window, he heard his phone ringing. "Oops, I'll bet that's Erin and Mallory wondering where I am."

"Answer it, Doc," said Lew. "I'll get your gear out of truck."

Osborne dashed through the back door to grab the phone.

"Doc," Ray's voice was on the other end, shouting over the blare of rock and roll music. "Where've you been?"

"Fishing," said Osborne. "Where are you?"

"Me and Wayne are up here at Thunder Bay," said Ray. "Time for you to join us."

"You're kidding," Osborne wasn't amused. "I've had a long day, Ray, and the girls are due back here any minute."

"We-e-ll, I dunno know about that, Doc. Doesn't look to me like she's moving too fast."

"What do you mean?"

"I . . . mean . . . she's . . . here." Ray always delayed his delivery when the news was hot.

"Who's where?" Osborne didn't believe what he was hearing.

"You know who . . . at Thunder Bay. Hey—Doc—we're talking on a party line . . ." Ray's voice grew serious.

"I'll be right there." Osborne hung up the phone, checked the dog's water dish and ran back out to the drive where Lew had gotten back into her truck. His rod, waders, and duffel were waiting for him on the grass.

"That was Ray," he said, leaning in the passenger door window. "I have to meet him at Thunder Bay."

"You don't look so good," said Lew. "What's wrong?"

"I don't know. I guess Mallory is out there." Osborne tried to resist a feeling of panic. He looked down at the ground, thinking. Then he looked up. Lew was watching him, concern in her dark eyes.

"Get in," she said. "I need to get in touch with Ray as soon as possible anyhow."

"I just don't know . . . ," he started to say, struggling to understand why on earth Mallory was at the most notorious stripper bar in the Northwoods.

"We won't know until we get there," said Lew. "She's a big girl, Doc."

"She is and she isn't," said Osborne, "and I don't understand her. Any better than I ever understood her mother."

He didn't realize he was tapping the fingers of his left hand nervously on his knee until Lew reached over to cover his hand with hers.

"She's a big girl," she repeated, "and you can only do so much."

"I know she's been drinking too much," he said, as if excusing whatever they would find. Turning away, he stared out his window, a hot flush of tears pressing against the back of his eyeballs. He blinked, set his jaw, and they drove silently into the night.

twenty-four

The last place Osborne had expected to find himself that Tuesday night was on the road to a rendezvous with Ray and his older daughter at the Thunder Bay Bar. Beside him, silent as she drove, was the one person who had been with him on his only other visit to the place. Lew accelerated into the darkness. Watching the fog drift into the windshield as they flew down back roads, Osborne wondered where on earth his life was going.

The little fishing truck followed the curve of the narrow road running parallel to the backwaters of the Wisconsin River. A final dip and curve, and the neon lights of Thunder Bay Bar came into view.

Tuesdays are not the most social nights around Loon Lake. Plus it was still early, not quite nine. The club was less than half full, though the music was pounding away. Osborne spotted Ray and Wayne immediately, sitting at the far end of the nearly empty bar, chatting with the bartender. Ray was still in his sport coat and slacks, looking handsome. Wayne, in T-shirt and sunburn, looked like he'd been out in a boat all day. No sign of Mallory.

Ray, cigarette in hand, waved his right arm, beckoning Osborne and Lew in his direction. As they neared, he threw a guarded glance back off to his right. Osborne stopped to look in that direction. Lew walked on into the bar.

Thunder Bay Bar was, in fact, a bar and a dance hall. The room with the bar was spacious with a jukebox, a pool table, and a small area for dancing. Through a wide doorway to Osborne's left was the second room, which held a small stage surrounded by formica-topped tables of varying sizes and stages of cleanliness. More than a few needed to be cleared of empty beer bottles, overflowing ashtrays, and crumpled napkins. Wooden chairs, kitchen chairs, and shaky folding chairs were scattered between the tables.

At first, all Osborne could see through the dim smoky haze was a dancer writhing on the small dance floor, dollar bills tucked into strategic sections of her costume. Five men at a nearby table were keenly interested. A couple of other tables held clusters of men in twos or threes, most talking among themselves. As Osborne's eyes adjusted, he could make out two other women, sitting among the tables and dressed to perform. At least he assumed they weren't planning to visit Wal-Mart in their pasties and G-strings.

Tucked back into the far corner of the room, he saw who he had come for: Mallory. Deep in conversation with Randy Nuttle. Randy must have said something funny. Mallory leaned her body into his, laughing, then gave a mock punch to his chin. He caught her hand affectionately. A little too affectionately for Osborne. He could see Mallory was hanging on every word Randy was saying, a loose grin on her face. Pulling her hand away from Randy's, Mallory took a deep swig from a mug of beer.

"Don't stare," Lew nudged him from behind. He obeyed and took a bar stool two down from Ray and Wayne. "Ray said Zolonsky is due to deliver those boats sometime tonight. Now don't you worry about that, Doc. I'll catch up with him in the morning. You take care of your daughter."

"How long has she been here?" Osborne asked.

"She was here when we arrived an hour ago," said Ray. Old Mal is one shnockered unit, Doc," said Ray, "but I've got it under control."

"Really, Ray," said Lew, sliding onto the bar stool between Ray and Osborne, "how's that?"

"You'll see."

"All I see is that Mallory and Lew are the only women in here not working," said Osborne grimly. "I'll tell you something else—I don't like what I see. I don't like my daughter

being seen here, particularly with Nuttle." Osborne was well
aware that everyone knew of Randy Nuttle's career path,
which had included showing pornographic films to high school
boys, five dollars each. This was at another crummy bar Nuttle
owned over on Clear Lake. "And I really don't like Mallory
drinking so heavily."

"None of this is anything you can do much about, Doc,"
said Lew.

Ray tipped back on his stool, the warm bar lighting giving
his face a healthy glow. "So, Doc, I got a duck joke."

"I'm not in the mood, Ray." Osborne was curt. Wayne
raised his eyebrows and shook his head. Apparently, he had
already heard the joke.

"What's the difference between eroticism and pornography?"

"Ray . . ." Osborne's tone was one of warning.

"Eroticism is when they use one feather, pornography the
whole bird." Ray chuckled heartily. "Not bad, huh?" Osborne
gave him a dim eye.

Lew had taken the stool between them. Osborne lowered his
head and leaned to talk into her ear, "Now *why* does he tell a
joke like that? This is hardly the appropriate moment."

"C'mon, Doc," Lew muttered back with a slight grin. "Does
Ray do anything at the appropriate moment?"

"The man's got problems, Lew."

"Anyone who spends half the year with a fish on his head
isn't normal."

Osborne had to chuckle.

"On the other hand," said Lew, "he's not stupid."

Ray leaned around in his chair to study the two figures in
the back corner. The music from the other room had stopped
pounding as the dancer took a short break.

"One small detail," said Ray to Osborne and Lew, "Randy
does have a wife."

"That's supposed to make me feel better?" said Osborne.

"She works the ten o'clock shift. Means we don't have
much time."

Osborne gave a great sigh and rubbed his forehead. He had
no idea what to do next.

"Let Ray handle it," said Lew calmly. "That look in his
eye—he has a plan."

Ray smiled in appreciation. He stubbed out his cigarette.

Both hands extended in front of him, Ray swung away from the bar.

"Here's what I think, Doc. Ol' Wayne here knows how to find his way home. My vehicle is outside," the first two fingers of each hand gestured gracefully as he spoke. "You will return to your place with the good Chief, and I will give Mallory a ride to my place."

"Your place?" Osborne almost choked on his words.

"Where you will join us," added Ray. "I have thirty-seven blue gills filleted and waiting. We'll sober the kid up."

"But how do we get her out of here?"

"Just you watch," said Ray, raising his eyebrows and a finger. "Trust me, Doc."

Osborne tried to. He was well aware of the many times Ray had given him excellent advice. Upstairs, behind the door with the coffee pot, he'd given good counsel on basic human survival. Sitting on Osborne's porch as the sun set over Loon Lake, he had changed Osborne's twenty-year mindset on musky fishing. The funny thing he had noticed over the two years of their deepening friendship was that Ray's fingers articulated the air identically, distinctively, regardless of whether he was dispensing advice on how to change your life or your lure.

At the moment, the same fingers were scooping up quarters from the bar. Coins in hand, Ray unfolded his lanky frame from the bar stool and ambled over to the jukebox. Without even looking at the selections, he punched in a combination. The voice of Frank Sinatra singing "I Did It My Way" filled the bar. Ray walked into the other room toward the back table.

Osborne sipped from the plastic cup of water the bartender had placed in front of him, staring straight ahead. After a few moments, Lew poked him with her elbow. He turned his head slightly to the right. Ray was dancing with Mallory, holding her close, dipping and swaying to the lyrics but keeping her back to Osborne. He gave a quick nod. Osborne, with Lew close behind, stood up, skirted several newcomers to the bar and left. Mallory never saw him.

The fishing truck snaked back along the river toward Loon Lake. Lew had taken a short cut north of town on their way out, now she passed the turn-off and continued straight toward the highway.

"Going through town?" asked Osborne.

"If you don't mind," said Lew. "Looked to me like Ray might be a few minutes behind us."

Several turns later, they were heading down Ojibway Drive towards the Rodericks' house. Lew slowed as they came up on the school and leaned over to look past Osborne. "Lights on. Good." She pulled over to the curb to study the building. All the classrooms on the second and third floors were lit up.

"What are you thinking?" asked Osborne. "Ed Raske is the janitor. He was a patient of mine."

"So you know him? I've been wondering if he's noticed anything unusual around the neighborhood recently."

"I haven't seen Ed since I retired. Nice enough fella. Golly, he's been the janitor here for as long as I can remember. C'mon, let's go in, I'll introduce you."

"No, Doc. You have to get over to Ray's."

"I can take ten minutes. To be perfectly honest, Lew, I am not looking forward to the next hour of my life, and a ten-minute delay is quite welcome. Anyway, it'll give Ray time to set the table and shake those blue gills in a little seasoned flour."

Lew was already out the door of the truck.

They had to bang hard on the side doors to get Raske's attention. When the old man finally pushed the doors open, he had a look of severe irritation on his grizzled face until he saw Osborne. Dressed in dark brown cotton pants and a long-sleeved shirt to match, the old man couldn't have been more than five feet tall. With the bright lights casting shadows across his bony features and watery, red-lined eyes, he looked like he had been cleaning the school floors since the turn of the century.

"Dr. Osborne," he said in surprise, "I thought youse were a buncha kids tryin' to make my life miserable. What—do you need to use a phone or somethin?"

"Ed, this is Lewellyn Ferris, our local Chief of Police. We were hoping you could take a minute for us to ask you a few questions."

"You mean them kids that broke into the computer room? All I know is what I told Mr. Adams." The old man backed off nervously.

"No, no, nothing like that," said Lew. "I noticed you work evenings quite a bit, and I'm not sure you're aware there's been a problem in the neighborhood."

"Oh, sure," the old man nodded, relaxing, "I know. My wife was telling me jus' today. You mean Mrs. Roderick's sister getting killed. That's the Roderick house over there, y'know." He pointed behind Lew to where the Roderick house stood on the other side of the lilacs and the street.

"I was wondering if you saw anything unusual around there recently," said Lew. "Mrs. Roderick told me she thought someone tried to break into her house the other afternoon, late afternoon."

"Oh she did, did she?" A sly look stole across the old man's face. "She tol' ya that, did she? Ain't she somethin' huh?"

"Don't keep me in suspense, Ed," said Lew, half kidding but anxious to urge the old man along.

"Depends on how you look at it, I guess," said the old man. "Breaking in is all a matter of who owns what in my book."

"Ed, you lost me," said Osborne.

The old man stood bent over in the bright hall lights, arms swinging loosely at his sides as he said, "You know Mr. Roderick?"

"Yes . . ."

"He's the one. He's been hangin' around those bushes almost every night for the last month. Lookin' in his own windows, for Chrissakes. I noticed he's drivin' a different car, see. Parks it over in the Pizza Hut parking lot, then walks over to spy on his own house. I'm always walkin' down there for my coffee, see. He doesn't notice me, of course. I'm just a little ol' man, y'know."

"Why do I get the impression you don't think much of Mrs. Roderick?" said Lew.

"Hell," said the old man, "nothin's right for her. She's complained 'bout where I park my truck because she can see it out her window. She don't like how the lilacs are trimmed. I have to carry the trash barrels all-l-l the way 'round the building thanks to her. Wasn't any problems before she moved in. I been here nearly forty years, y'know. Had to change all my ways to suit her."

"So what do you think is up?" asked Lew.

"Only one reason a man ever has to spy on his own wife,"

said Ed. "Anybody here don't know what that is, I sure ain't gonna tell 'ya."

"Food for thought," said Osborne walking back to the truck.

"Yep," said Lew. "I'm beginning to think that for such an organized woman, Meredith Marshall left quite a mess behind her."

"Now, Doc," said Lew as Osborne got out of her truck eight minutes later. "You be careful what you say to your daughter tonight. She's likely to listen to you."

"Thank you, Chief. Is that spoken as a mother or a police officer?" Or, he thought but did not say, as a woman who can see I'm having a hard enough time trying to figure out my own life.

Lew gave him a tired but sympathetic smile. "Just think before you talk. You men think you have to have all the answers. You don't."

She waved and he shut the door. Before walking down to Ray's trailer he took two minutes to finally check his phone messages. He had three from Ray calling in from Thunder Bay and one other message. Cynthia Lewis wanted to see him or Lew at their earliest convenience.

twenty-five

Osborne walked down the leaf-covered drive to Ray's trailer. Lights shone warmly in the windows, and the perfume of blue gills sautéing in butter drifted across the night air. He could see Ray's curly head in the window and knew he was standing over the cast iron frying pan on the gas stove, expertly nudging and flipping the tiny fillets. Credence Clearwater Revival suddenly boomed into the lakeside silence, and Ray's head nodded in time.

He paused a few feet from the trailer, watching as Mallory walked into the frame of the small window. He saw Ray give her some kind of instruction. Then she vanished from view. Probably setting the table.

He wondered why he felt so blank. Here he was walking into a time of crisis in his daughter's life, and he really did not know what he could do. At least he didn't feel fatigued. If anything, the conversation with Ed had generated an adrenaline rush that still held. He felt poised for something, but he had no idea what. The only advice he could think of at the moment, he knew she wouldn't want to hear.

He pulled open the screen door and stepped inside quickly to keep the mosquitoes out. Mallory was seated at the table where Ray was in the act of handing her a plate heaped high with lightly browned blue gills.

"Hey, Doc, grab that hot pad and pull up those French fries,

will you, please? Mallory, make room on your plate—my fries
are twice-fried. You've never tasted anything like it."

Osborne executed the familiar procedure as he smiled over
at his daughter. "My contribution to Northwoods cuisine—
emptying the French fry basket."

"Hi, Thad," Mallory's eyes were amused and bleary, her
head weaving in a drunken attempt to look sober. Her first
forkful of blue gills missed her mouth slightly, hitting her
cheek. She wiped at it quickly with her napkin.

"Eat," said Ray, delivering plates for himself and Osborne.
And so they did, washing the fish and French fries down with
big gulps of ice water from a large pitcher set in the middle
of the table.

"So, Doc," said Ray. "For reasons you are about to understand, I am very . . . very . . . disturbed. George was supposed
to show up at the bar by eight tonight with the keys for those
boats tomorrow."

"Right," said Osborne. "You've got the pre-fishing starting
in the morning."

"Yep. Guess who was a no-show."

"Don't tell me." Osborne set down his glass of water and
looked at Ray in disbelief.

"I called John Murphy over at the marina, and he'll loan
me some renters for the morning, but that's not what's been
promised the walleye boys. I've got to have those boats by
Thursday night at the very latest. I have to tell ya, I'm starting
to get a little freaked about this, Doc." Whatever his state of
mind, it didn't keep Ray from enjoying the blue gills on his
plate.

"These professionals usually have state-of-the-art boats from
their sponsors," Osborne explained to Mallory, "but they like
this tournament because they demo the newest models and rate
them for national magazines. Ray is in charge of the boats this
year, and they were supposed to be up here last week. Do you
remember George Zolonsky?"

"Who doesn't know George?" said Mallory, continuing to
wolf down her buttery fillets.

"He sure is making Ray's life miserable."

"Can I have a few more?" asked Mallory, lifting her plate
toward Ray.

"Plenty more," said Ray, returning to the stove for another
full platter of fish. They finished it off and counted. "I had

thirteen," said Mallory, sounding a little better. "Sixteen, for me," said Ray, and he burped loudly.

"Jeez, Ray," said Osborne, "we've got a lady at the table."

Mallory closed her eyes in rapture, "My god, Ray, this has been delicious." She opened her eyes, "Will you marry me?"

Ray, leaned back in his chair and studied her, a gentle look of interest on his face. "What's wrong with that hardworking husband of yours?"

"Oh, he has a girlfriend," said Mallory nonchalantly, reaching for a French fry.

"Really," said Ray, his voice soft.

"Yes," said Mallory, "one of the executives he works with. I filed for divorce."

"You seem very matter of fact," said Ray. Pushing her plate slowly away, her face wooden, Mallory started to say something else, then she stopped. She choked back tears.

"Not much I can do. Never was. He has never wanted to do things with me. We lead separate lives . . . like he doesn't like to play tennis, he won't travel. He doesn't read, he never works out. We never talk. We never have a good time like you have a good time, Ray."

"Mallory, don't tell me about his life, his mistakes. What about you, your life, your future. What do you want? What do you want from life?"

Mallory looked at him in utter silence. She looked so confused. Osborne felt his heart breaking.

"Not what your mother wanted you to want," Ray said, "I want to know what you want."

She set her chin defiantly like a little kid, "I want to dance. Steve refuses to dance with me. I want to dance!" Her words rang out over John Fogarty's voice in the background.

"So dance," said Ray, "it's never too late to start dancing."

"I can't dance alone."

"Yes, you can."

"But what if he won't."

"Mallory," Ray chuckled softly, "we all have our own dance, and we all have to dance alone.

"I like how you dance. Why can't I join you?"

"Hey, kid," said Ray, "you don't want to dance with a digger of graves."

"Yeah, but, Ray, I'll be wealthy after my divorce. Dance with me, and you'll never have to dig a grave again."

"Mallory. That's the difference between us." Ray looked hard at her: "I *like* to dig graves."

The look of confusion crossed her face again. "Why?" she whispered.

Ray shrugged, "Who knows? Maybe 'cause it keeps me honest. One thing I know," he chuckled again, "we all leave the world the same way—with the clothes on our back and twenty bucks worth of embalming fluid."

"Even Meredith Marshall with all her millions," chimed in Osborne.

Mallory turned to him, "Dad, you've been awfully quiet today."

"I'm worried about you."

She laughed a tight, hard little laugh, "That's positive."

"What does that mean, Mallory?" From the corner of his eye, Osborne saw Ray pick up the remaining plates, drop them in the sink and quietly leave the room.

"Dad, did you love Mother?"

"At first, very much. Later... your mother was never happy, Mallory. I never knew quite why. All I know today is I like to be with happy people. Perhaps a better way to put it is I like to be with people happy with themselves."

"That's what I want. You and mother, you wanted me to marry a stable man, one who lives inside the lines. Well, Dad, I did what I was supposed to, and I am so lonely. Look at Ray, my God, he doesn't just enjoy his life—he goddam sparkles. I'm sorry. I'm so drunk, Dad."

"I was going to suggest you consider re-hab, kiddo. I did."

"I'm in therapy... My therapist asked me if I could ask you a question." Mallory paused. Osborne waited.

"Dad, do you love me?"

It was the question he didn't want to hear. Osborne dropped his head. He felt a kind of pain through his chest. He knew Ray was in the other room, and he knew Ray knew his answer. It was a hard one that he had had to answer in order to survive. He had answered it once before in the company of his daughter, Erin, during the intervention that saved his life. He had a choice now: he could be kind and tell a lie or be honest and brutal.

"No, Mallory, I don't. I... I've had a difficult time liking you."

His daughter heaved a great sigh. "O-o-h," was all she said. "Can you tell me why?"

"You asked me if I loved your mother. Well, the early years of our marriage, when you were born, you were her focus. It sounds silly, but I felt pushed out of the way. Everything you did was perfect. I was always wrong or late or doing the wrong thing. I feel bad telling you this, Mallory . . ." Osborne raised his hands in a gesture of helplessness. "Can you forgive me?"

"Dad, just knowing the truth is a huge relief," said Mallory, nearly sober now. "Subconsciously, I think I've always known how you felt. Don't feel bad. I'm paying a shrink to ask me a lot of questions. I'm happy, I'm getting some answers. At least, now I know why I married Steve."

"What do you mean?"

She sighed again. "He doesn't really like women, Dad. He doesn't like me. I was comfortable with that."

"So what do you do now?"

"I'm not sure. Ray turned me down," she gave a rueful little smile. "I guess I have to start over. You know, Dad, life is so unfair. Look at Meredith. Everyone loved her. Her father adored her—"

"Maybe that's why she died," said Ray, standing in the doorway. "She took love for granted."

"We need to head home, hon," said Osborne, standing up.

"Let me use the bathroom quickly," said Mallory. She left the room, and Osborne helped Ray clean off the kitchen table.

"Call me if I can help with anything on those boats," said Osborne.

"Hey, you two," said Mallory as she walked back into the room. "I almost forgot. I got some good gossip from Randy tonight. You mentioned George Zolonsky earlier? Guess who he's having an affair with?"

Ray turned around from the sink where he had started to wash dishes. "Not 'who,' " he said, " 'how many.' "

"Not this time," said Mallory, "this one may be exclusive. Randy said he finally hit the big time."

"How does Randy know so much?" asked Ray.

"George bragged about it all around Thunder Bay, I guess."

"So who's the lucky lady?"

"Alicia Roderick."

•   •   •

As Mallory walked towards her bedroom after brushing her teeth, Osborne stepped into the hallway. He held his arms out and she walked into him. He felt her head against his shoulder.

"I want you to find your way to being happy, sweetheart."

"Thanks, Dad. Are *you* happy?"

"I'm close."

As he spoke, he felt a new firmness in his heart as if a kinship was blooming. Could he and Mallory use this awareness of sorrow and neglect to find a bond, maybe even a stronger friendship than they might have had? Maybe even love? What was that Ray said? It's never too late to start over.

twenty-six

McDonald's was bustling when Osborne walked in at twenty to seven, a few minutes later than usual. The regular crowd was sitting over in one corner in groups of twos and threes and fours. Some days, he might find just one group of six but not today. Jerry, the manager, saw him coming. He had Osborne's Danish and coffee out before he reached the counter.

"Mornin' Doc."

"Thanks, Jerry."

He walked over to the threesome that included Ray, Wayne, and Jake Mettersly. As he arrived, Ray and Wayne stood up to get refills and their orders. Although he was decked out in brand-new fishing boots, Wayne still wore the same jeans. Osborne was relieved to note the detective had changed his T-shirt. He never did understand why so many guys up from the cities assume spending time in the North Woods has to include a sabbatical from clean clothes and deodorant.

Ray set his steaming cup of coffee alongside Osborne's as he bent and folded his lanky frame into the booth. He unwrapped the tissue around his Egg McMuffin, ripped off the edge of a pepper packet and dumped the contents on his egg. Then he sat back and eyed the fat-laden, greasy unit hungrily. As always, Osborne's stomach lurched at the sight.

"Tell me this, my friend," said Osborne, repeating a question he asked at least once a week. "How can the connoisseur of the perfectly sauted fish fillet justify scarfing down an Egg McMuffin with exactly the same enthusiasm?"

"Same principle applies to Alicia Roderick boinking our buddy, George, I guess," said Ray, taking a big chomp. He wiped a dribble of fake butter from his curly beard, grinned at Osborne and rolled his eyes skyward, waiting. His words had the desired effect: Jake Mettersly, sharing the booth with them, looked up.

"George who?" asked Jake. He was a phamacist who knew every individual in a three-county range needing a prescription over the last thirty years. He also knew most of the druggists in nearby towns who filled the prescriptions he refused on the grounds that he knew they were forged. Now that he was nearing retirement, Jake was a little less reluctant to share his inside information on various members of the Loon Lake community, particularly those of whom he didn't approve.

"Zolonsky," said Osborne. "Doesn't fit, does it?"

"I don't believe it," Jake returned to the Milwaukee Journal sports page.

"Doesn't matter if you believe it or not," said Ray, finishing off his muffin with one last bite, "the source is pretty darn good. The big question is what is in it for Alicia." He took a sip from his steaming coffee cup, "Gotta head back to the marina."

"Everything go okay this morning?" asked Osborne.

"Fishing stinks. With all this heat, the minnows and the mayflies are laying low, so close to the bottom the walleyes don't have to go far to get happy. These pros are gonna be tearing their hair out. Otherwise, okay. Had everyone on the water by five" said Ray. "No complaints so far.

"You planning to see Lew with the news on George, Doc?"

"You betcha," said Osborne. "I'm stopping by the jail to see her right after I leave here. She's usually in by seven."

"Mallory doing okay?"

"I think so. She's sleeping in this morning. Her flight's at four. Thanks for your help last night, Ray."

"You tell her if she still wants to marry me this morning—I accept."

Jake had it with that. He lifted his head from his newspaper and looked at the trio as if they were all going mad. He was a very large man, pushing 300 pounds, with a moonlike, pleas-

ant face and a bald head ringed with a halo of straight white
hair. He had crisp blue eyes, pink cheeks, and a white blond
mustache that reminded Osborne of the little silver-handled
broom Mary Lee had used to brush bread crumbs off the dining room tablecloth.

He also had a rollicking sense of humor, an excellent head
for logic and professed to having experienced only two surprises in his lifetime. The first was discovering one of his sons
loved to sing country music and did so professionally; the
second, was when his best friend of twenty years announced
he was divorcing his wife for another woman, and Jake had
had no idea anything was wrong.

Other than that, Jake considered himself an expert on community relations in Loon Lake. And ducks. He was a fanatic
duck hunter and collector of duck decoys. Any conversation
you had with Jake was always going to end with ducks somehow.

"Doc's daughter interested in you, you goombah?" He
shook his head and folded the paper in front of him. "Now
what's this about Zolonsky and Alicia Roderick?"

"No details," said Ray, "just a rumor. What do you think?"

"I've lived here long enough to know anything's possible,"
said Jake. "He scored with the wife of that dentist from Eagle
River, remember. Who knows what women are thinking. Then
he took up with the wife of that fella that opened the brew
pub in Rhinelander. Alicia, huh? That might explain why
Pete's been looking so bad lately."

"He told me he's exhausted from traveling," said Osborne,
"said he's been on the road for months."

Jake had a thoughtful look on his round face. "That reminds
me. Pete's got a twenty-gauge side-by-side I'd love to buy
from him. Browning. Beautiful gun. The carving on the butt
is really something. Boy, would I like to get my hands on that
before duck season opens." Then he remembered the topic of
conversation.

"Poor Pete," said Jake, "Zolonsky's never been anything but
trouble, y'know," he said. All three men nodded in silence.

"I've had it with the guy," said Ray, and he shared with
Jake the on-going saga of the missing fishing boats.

Jake nodded when he was finished. "But why would Alicia
Roderick want anything to do with that guy? She's smarter
than that."

"That's what I'm trying to figure—what's in it for her," Ray mused, tipping his empty coffee cup around on its edge.

"Now George is easy to read," said Jake. "He's got drug and alcohol problems going way back. His routine over that last couple years has been to fake nervous breakdowns, check into the hospital and con those fourth-floor girls into giving him prescriptions for uppers and downers."

"The fourth floor is the mental ward," Osborne explained to Wayne.

"What about cocaine?" said Wayne to Jake. "Any locals try to get some of that out of you?"

"George." said Jake. "He only tried once, though. Showed up with a prescription supposedly written by a doc out of Minneapolis. I just gave him the eye, y'know. Pushed that little piece of paper right back over the counter."

"How long ago was that?" asked Wayne.

"Last year sometime."

"You see many legitimate prescriptions for cocaine?" asked Wayne.

"Not too many. Most of the local MDs prefer morphine," said Jake, "it's a easier on the system. Last cocaine prescription I filled was for Alicia Roderick after she had eye surgery last year.

"Oh . . ." Jake realized what he had just said.

"Local MD write the prescription?" asked Wayne.

"No, surgeon out of Marshfield. They have a big clinic over there."

"Did you check it out?"

". . . No."

Wayne turned to Osborne, "I'm helping Ray this morning, but I plan to drop by the police department later. Will you let Chief Ferris know? Ask her if she can pull Zolonsky's file for me. Maybe, see if there's one on this Mrs. Roderick, too."

"Gee, I doubt you'll find anything on her," said Osborne. "What time do you guys have to be back at the marina?"

"Six-thirty. What time is it?" said Ray, standing up. "Doc, you wanna help me? I've got two lawyers coming down from Land o' Lakes, two amateurs that qualified to fish with the pros. I sure could use a hand helping them pre-fish."

"Sorry, Ray. I need to see Lew, then take some time with Mallory before she leaves."

• • •

Osborne strolled leisurely over to Lew's office outside the new jailhouse, a short block and a half from McDonald's. The morning was warm and sunny and pleasant. He stopped to watch a hummingbird dart among the Stella de Or daylillies blooming in front of the Court House. The good feeling of the morning made him feel years younger than sixty-three. It struck him suddenly—he could make a habit of this. "Deputy." He liked the sound of the word.

Bounding up the stairs lightly, he headed down the hallway to Lew's office. He was learning that few things made his day better than the sight of her lively face looking up at him from her morning paperwork. This little visit to her office had become almost a regular habit of his on Mondays and Wednesdays.

Lucy, the switchboard operator, turned around as he entered. She lifted her headset from one ear, "Hey, Doc," she said. "Lew's out. Having coffee with Ralph. She said she'd be back in an hour or so. You'll find them at the pub if you want."

Osborne's mood changed with a thud. Ralph? Again? The very sound of the man's name grated on his nerves.

"I'll leave her a note," he said glumly.

The day sped by. Erin showed up at his place by ten with little Cody in tow. The four of them drove up to Kristine's in Three Lakes for pancakes and more coffee. Osborne was quiet, enjoying the sound of his daughters' chatter. From time to time, he would catch Mallory's eye. She returned the look with a friendly smile. He was probably reading too much into it, but she seemed more relaxed. She definitely seemed to be carrying less of a burden than when she arrived.

"Mal, do you really have to go back so soon?" asked Erin at one point.

"I do," said Mallory, "now that I'm determined to get my degree from Northwestern. Orientation starts tomorrow, remember?"

Erin had planned to drive her to the airport, but at the last minute Osborne decided to intervene. "Let me drive," he said to Erin, "I'd like to take her if you don't mind." The mixture of surprise and pleasure that crossed Mallory's face was one he wouldn't forget for a long time.

On the way out to the airport, Osborne apologized, "I wish I could take back what I said to you last night, but I can't."

"Dad, you don't understand," said Mallory. "You helped me understand myself. It's fine. I'll be fine. It's going to be a hard year, I know, because I've got to leave this marriage." Then she laughed the lightest laugh he had heard from her in years. "You know, I can't divorce you, but I sure can get rid of the other guy."

"Does it have to be divorce?"

"Steve is who he is, Dad. I married him for reasons that no longer exist. I want to be a different person—he doesn't. I can't ask him to change."

"You know, Mallory, if this had come up before your mother died, do you know what I would have said? I would have told you you have no business leaving your marriage. I would have quoted Thoreau: 'The mass of men lead lives of quiet desperation.' "

"Thank god, we didn't talk, Dad. That's a terrible thing to say."

"You know who talked me out of that mindset?"

"Ray?"

"Yep."

"So, Dad, Erin tells me you're seeing that woman."

"Oh, no," said Osborne. "Not really. She's just a friend, a former patient, y'know." He tried to sound casual. "The coroner is on vacation so I'm helping out with forensic dental exams when she needs it. And we've fished together—but only two times."

"*Fishing* together?" Mallory's emphasis implied an intimate act. Osborne felt a blush creep up his neck. He tried to camouflage his feelings with a stern, fatherly tone: "Lewellyn Ferris is an expert fly-fisherman, Mallory. She has been coaching me on my casting."

"I see." His daughter turned to him with a teasing look in her eye. "Are you falling in love?"

"Heavens, no." Osborne felt his entire face flush with embarrassment. Mallory didn't press, but she didn't drop the teasing expression either. "Just keep me posted, Dad."

He hugged her closely when her flight was announced, feeling again that sense of firmness deep within. After she boarded, he tried the police station from the pay phone. Lew was still out.

As Osborne drove home, he thought about Mallory's question. Love Lew? He certainly liked her. He knew he liked looking at her, he loved the lines around her eyes.

Back at the house, he took a few minutes to throw the ball to Mike who made it clear he had been severely neglected in recent days. Then he walked out onto the porch. The windows were wide open to the lake breezes. He settled into the old velour sofa in the corner, pulled up the afghan his mother had crocheted fifty years ago, and fell sound asleep.

He didn't wake up until the phone rang three hours later.

It was Ray. "I tried to reach the chief, but she just left to go fishing with Ralph. I've got some interesting news on the Sutliff estate, Doc, I'm coming over." He hung up before Osborne could say anything.

"We have got to get this to your friend as soon as possible," said Ray as he banged on the back screen door, his choice of words implying his opinion that the relationship between Osborne and Lew was more than professional. Osborne ignored the implication. Ray wiped his feet on the mat, walked into the kitchen, opened the refrigerator, and grabbed a can of ginger ale.

"Help yourself," said Osborne after the fact. "I just tried her for the umpteenth time. She hasn't been in all day. What's up?"

"Well . . . ," said Ray, relishing the moment. "You know those lawyers from Land o' Lakes? One of 'em turned out to be old man Sutliff's lawyer, the one who drew up his will. Very, very interesting development . . . ," Ray raised a finger.

"Now correct me if I'm wrong," he continued, "but are we not under the impression that the estate was split between the two sisters?"

"That's what I've been told," said Osborne.

"By whom?"

"Well, by Alicia, I guess. Yes, Sunday, when Lew and I told her about Meredith's death."

"Not so. Sutliff left all his money to Meredith."

"Everything?" Osborne was astounded.

Ray nodded and took a swig of his soda. "Everything.

"Now . . . if Meredith died without a will, which no one has yet found, what do you think happens?"

"The money goes to the next-of-kin . . ."

"Who is . . ."

"Alicia."

"Though it would have been Ben if those papers weren't signed."

"We have got to reach Lew," said Osborne.

"I said that," said Ray. "Let's go."

Roger was dozing, feet on his desk. He looked up as they ran in.

"Lookin' for Lew? She's gone fishing," he said.

"Where! We've got to find her," said Osborne.

"Y'know, all she said was somewhere north of Watersmeet with Ralph," said Roger.

"This is critical—can't you reach her?" asked Ray. Osborne knew the answer to that.

They ended up driving out to Lew's farmhouse and leaving a note stuck in her door. Osborne knew she wouldn't want a word of this spoken on his phone so he asked her to call if she got back before eleven, and they could rendezvous or meet him at McDonald's first thing in the morning. Then Ray dropped him off back at his house.

Osborne turned on the TV and tried to find something that would take his mind off Lew. Not to mention Ralph. Ten o'clock rolled by, then eleven. No phone call.

He gave up and went to bed. He must have fallen asleep instantly.

Ralph's Trading Post was brightly lit. Osborne walked through the front doors, skirted a man and a woman selecting postcards, and turned left down the aisle with fishing rods. At the end of the aisle was the counter where Ralph kept ammunition and his custom-made flies under lock and key.

From behind the tall shelves stacked with reels and lures, Osborne could hear Ralph's nasal British accent. The sound of that pretentious all-knowing voice pushed him over the edge. Hatred, pure and black, coursed through his arteries, pumping up his already racing pulse. No turning back now, he knew what he had to do.

Osborne examined the fly rods carefully. He selected a Sage rod, a 4-weight, 8½ feet, with a long cork handle. No, too light. He put it back. He picked up a Winston 5-weight, 8½ feet. Ah, the rod with the thumb groove on the handle, the

Joan Wulff Favorite. That's the one Lew had. He held it. Felt good. He looked around.

Ralph never saw him coming. His back was to Osborne as he adjusted a .22 pistol in the display behind the counter. Osborne raised his arm and brought the fly rod down hard on Ralph's head. Again, he raised the rod, grasping it this time with both hands to slam it down with all his might. His anger was so intense, his arms so powerful, the man's skull had to split in two.

Then his hands melted, the rod turned into a glutinous sac of fish eggs.

Ralph stood up, turned around and smiled his condescending smile.

The banging that woke Osborne wasn't the authorities arriving to lock him up. He was still in his own bed, Mike barking loudly at the back door. Osborne threw off the light cotton quilt and stumbled from bed. It was dark, from his living room window the lake surface was invisible behind an early morning fog.

Ray was at the door. "Get dressed, Doc. We're driving south."

twenty-seven

They sped down Highway 45 in Osborne's station wagon. With a thermos of hot coffee and some donuts they could pick up on the way, Ray figured they could reach the boat warehouse and be back in Loon Lake by three or four o'clock that afternoon.

"Dick Johnson, the tournament chair, is calling ahead this morning to make arrangements for the boats to be loaded and ready to go," said Ray. "He's as upset about this as I am."

"Where the heck is George?" said Osborne, "you told me every day this week he was on his way."

"That's what they kept telling me," said Ray, shaking his head. "His daughter promised me yesterday afternoon that George had picked up the remaining boats and was due at home at dinnertime. His sidekick, Ned Larson, drove one rig. He showed up yesterday with five boats. Guess who never showed with the other five."

"Did you call the warehouse?"

"I called the warehouse, Dick called the warehouse. Doc, the entire pro-am tournament has called the warehouse. George has been in possession of a hundred thousand dollars worth of boats since Monday afternoon. Only no one has seen him since. So the head office for the national walleye tournaments has gotten involved. Otherwise, there would be no boats.

"Even when I get the darn things, Doc, I still have to have

help removing the packing, installing motors, locators, and acqua cams—not mention being sure everyone's got cold drinks
and snacks on board."

"Ohmygod," Ray ran his hands through his hair, "why did
I ever agree to do this? What a nightmare. Don't slow down,
Doc."

For six short blocks, the highway became the main drag of
the town of Crandon. Two construction workers were setting
up barriers in the early morning haze, preparing to work on
the traffic light that dangled over the crossroads at the center
of the small town. The haze promised another hot day.

"Ray, the speed limit is 25 mph. We do not need to com-
plicate matters running red lights and maiming innocent citi-
zens."

"Yes we do."

"Try to settle down. I need to stop at the next open gas
station to call Lew," said Osborne. "I wasn't able to reach her
yesterday. As far as I know, she's still in the dark on the affair
between Alicia and George, and what you heard from the lawyer on the Sutliff estate. I'm worried I'm letting her down."

"Doc, get us to the warehouse first. Then call. Okay? This
boat situation has me in knots."

"Ray, I have never seen you so tense."

He sympathized with Ray. The Loon Lake Pro-Am Walleye
Open had become the biggest fishing event in the region. They
had fought hard to wrest it from a town in North Dakota, and
the last thing anyone wanted was to see the regional prestige
and a million tourist dollars slip from their fingers. All because
of George Zolonsky.

As they neared the tiny hamlet of Laona, the Beaver Lake
Casino came into view at the base of a long, winding hill.
Even though it wasn't even 7 A.M. yet, the parking lots were
full. As they drew closer, Osborne had to slow for a car turning
onto the highway in front of them. He always marveled at the
steady stream into the casinos day and night. The parking lots
were never empty, not even on the most beautiful of days.

Suddenly, Ray sat up straight, yanking his head back to look
behind them. "Whoa, whoa, whoa! Stop! Turn around, Doc. I
see a rig with boats back there. I'll bet that's George."

"Okay, okay, settle down. I'm going to pull over then swing
back around. I don't need to kill us both in the meantime." He
pulled onto the shoulder and let the one car behind them pass,

then crimped the wheel to turn around and head back to the casino. He took a right turn into the parking.

"Over there."

Ray pointed to a semi-trailer rig parked in the RV section. It was loaded with walleye boats. George Zolonsky was nowhere in sight.

"Are you sure this is George?" Osborne parked the car. They got out and walked around the rig.

"Tracker boats. Has to be. You stay here, Doc. I'll see if he's inside."

Ray ran across the parking lot to the main entrance of the casino. He was inside less than a minute before running back out.

"Yep. It's George all right. He's at the blackjack table. Looks like hell. I'll bet the guy hasn't slept in days."

Ray walked around the front end of the rig. The trailer was as shiny and new as all the boats. "Can't believe they trusted this to Zolonsky after they took one look at him," muttered Ray.

He knelt to run his fingers along the inside of the front bumper. "Let's hope he follows tradition, Doc."

Osborne hoped, too. North Woods sportsmen, whether hunting or fishing, have a habit of tucking their car keys up under their bumpers or on top of the rear wheels of their vehicles. It may be a bad habit but it is the only way to be sure you don't drop your car keys in water or lose them in the woods. If you hunt and fish enough, it becomes an automatic response, especially if you have your mind on something else.

Ray walked to the back of the rig. Once again, he knelt and slipped his fingers along the back section of the trailer to which were attached the brake lights and the license plate.

"Bingo!" Ray stood up, a set of keys in his hands.

"I'm outta here," he said as he unlocked the door of the rig and climbed into the driver's seat. "Meet me at the marina and help me unload these will 'ya?"

"What about George?"

"What about George."

"Doc, where are you?" said Lew, "I stopped at McDonald's hoping to catch you this morning."

"I'm in Crandon. Calling to report a stolen vehicle."

"What? Your car was stolen?"

"No, no. Ray and I found Zolonsky and the boats about a half hour ago. Parked at the Beaver Lake Casino. Strictly speaking, Ray stole the boats and the rig—with my help."

"Without telling George?"

"He was at the blackjack table. Neither one of us wanted to get into it with him, know what I mean? As it is, Ray will be working all day and night in order to have those boats ready in the morning."

"I'll take care of it on this end. Wasn't he due in here days ago?"

"Oh yeah."

"I'll tell the state guys that if George calls in, he's the offender. Don't worry about it. But, Doc, I've got Peter Roderick coming in late this morning. Is there any chance you can join us? Having you here might loosen him up. I've got to be hard on him, Doc. I've got to break him."

"I'll be there," said Osborne, checking his watch. "Then I'll give Ray a hand getting the boats set up. But I have some information you need, Lew." He gave her the details of Mallory's report of the affair between George and Alicia, and Ray's news on the Sutliff estate. When he was finished, Lew gave a low whistle.

"Cynthia Lewis left a message on my machine, too," said Osborne. "I haven't had a chance to get back to her."

"She's coming in at ten," said Lew. "She called me, too."

"Lew," said Osborne, "before you go, how was fishing last night?"

"Good, not spectacular. Ralph got six brookies. I got two on my salmon stone fly. But tonight should be better. We're supposed to get some rain and a cold front. I'd like to get back up on the Deerskin."

"Going up with Ralph?" his voice felt tight.

"I don't think so," said Lew.

As Osborne drove back up Highway 45, he thought over his dream. Hammering Ralph with the fly rod was as close as he had ever gotten to homicide. He sure understood the urge.

Lew's office was an airy, well-lit room with generous windows along the south wall. The window ledge held six clay pots brimming with nasturtiums in full bloom. On the opposite wall, she had juxtaposed a series of framed photos of sunsets she shot on the lake where she lived in a tiny farmhouse. Just inside the doorway, on an old square wooden table, sat a Mr. Coffee. Beside it was the Loon Lake telephone book, the cover featuring a close-up color photo of a sleeping fawn. The photo credit read "Ray Pradt."

Today, the windows were pushed up as far as they could go, and warm breezes ruffled the papers on Lew's desk. She had centered her desk against the west wall, leaving space behind for a long table that held her computer, two framed pictures of her children, and several neat stacks of paperwork and files. Two wooden armchairs with dark green leather seats had been pulled up in front of her desk, another was set off to the side along the inside wall. She had directed Osborne to that chair.

Cynthia Lewis sat facing the desk. Behind it sat Lew sat in a high-backed swivel chair. She was leaning forward on her elbows, hands folded under her chin, attentive to every word of Cynthia's.

"I'm not sure why I didn't tell you this the other day," said Cynthia. "I guess I was still in shock. But I talked it over with Bud, and we agreed I better let you know about this.

"When Meredith learned that I do the books for Bud's office, she asked me to help her out. Balance her checkbooks and set up a basic accounting system for the restaurant and for the property. She had three separate accounts that I managed for her. Even though I only did the books for two months, we'd made a list of everything she needed to get taken care of. One was her will, the other was her health and life insurance. She had me do all the insurance paperwork . . ."

"I believe the divorce agreement cancelled her previous will," said Lew, "isn't that correct?"

"Right," said Cynthia. "She had an appointment next week to have a new one drawn up. I knew that, and, I think, Alicia knew that, too. But her life insurance we did take care of. I don't think Alicia knows about that." She looked at Lew, "I . . . Clint Chesnais is the beneficiary."

"How much is the policy?"

"A million dollars."

"And he knew that."

"No, he didn't. That's just it. He didn't know about the policy, nor did he know she was planning to marry him . . . eventually."

"I see . . . ," said Lew, nodding thoughtfully.

"She told me she wanted to be around him for another year before she said anything, but she really liked him. I do, too. That's why I held back, I guess." Cynthia looked stricken as she talked. Her face was white, her manner very deliberate.

Osborne said nothing. It intrigued him the two women could talk about Meredith's plan as if keeping Chesnais in the dark was totally acceptable. It made him wonder how many men had their marriages planned out for them long before they knew anything about it.

"Alicia found two of the checkbooks," continued Cynthia, "but I hid Meredith's personal checkbook. I shouldn't have, I know. But something about her frenzy that morning made me cautious. I need to tell you where it is."

"I found it, Cynthia," said Lew. "What about those checks to Alicia? The two for twenty thousand each that Meredith wrote last week. Do you know what were those for?"

"I have no idea what you're talking about."

"When was the last time you saw Meredith's accounts?"

"Friday before she died."

"And no checks had been written to Alicia at that time?"

"Not that I'm aware of. She was a co-signer on the restaurant account, but she had no privileges on Meredith's personal account."

"Did you know that Mr. Sutliff cut Alicia out of the will?"

"Meredith told me," said Cynthia. "She felt badly about that. I was under the impression she was planning to gift some of the money back to Alicia."

"Had she talked to Alicia about it?"

"I don't think so. Don't forget Meredith had that complicated divorce settlement going on. Between her divorce, the restaurant opening, and the work on The Willows, she was stretched pretty thin."

"Well," Lew rocked back in her chair. "Some of what you say points a finger at Clint Chesnais . . ."

"I hate this," said Cynthia. "I just . . . I don't think Clint Chesnais murdered Meredith. And I don't know how he would have known he was a beneficiary because Meredith asked me to keep it confidential."

"She could have told him, and you wouldn't know."

Cynthia's black eyes rested on Lew's, her shoulders slumped. "What a terrrible situation."

* * *

Twenty minutes later, Peter Roderick sat in the same chair. Osborne still occupied the chair against the wall.

"Mr. Roderick...," Lew leaned forward as she opened their meeting, "thank you for coming in this morning. I know this is a difficult time for you."

Her face was set in a pleasant expression, her dark eyes centered on Roderick's face. Peter looked away and cleared his throat.

He was wearing a gray business suit with a shirt and tie. If Osborne didn't know him as well as he did, he would think he looked like a successful business man: authoritative, yet casual; unconcerned, yet attentive. However, Peter Roderick was normally not that way. He was a sloppily casual man, given to slacks and open-collared shirts with the sleeves rolled up, his belly rounding over a loose belt. Even the clean-shaven crispness of his appearance was offset by a rheumy redness around the eyes. And Osborne detected a sweet whiff of whiskey circulating with the breezes in the room. This was not the Pete Roderick that he knew and liked.

"May I call you Peter, Mr. Roderick?"

"Certainly," Peter cleared his throat and re-crossed his legs.

"Peter, I know you have not been telling your wife the truth. No...," she raised her right hand as he started up in his chair, "... let me finish. I know, Dr. Osborne knows, we both know that you have not been travelling as you said you were. You have been staying at The Willows. We know you have been distressed. We know...," she enunciated her words carefully, keeping a gentle tone in her voice, "your sister-in-law was helping you, *trying* to help you anyway. You can save us all a lot of time if you'll tell us about it."

Peter just stared at her, his left eyelid flickering.

"The game is over," said Lew simply, filling in the silence.

"I'm broke," he said in a dead voice. "I'm flat broke, and my wife hates me." He did not take his eyes from her face. "Now you tell me. Where do you go with something like that."

The pain in the room was palpable. The heavy cheeks had never looked so pale, his skin so loose and waxy.

"Do you mind?" He stood up, took off his jacket, loosened his tie and unbuttoned the top of his shirt. "It's a rather brief tale," he said, carefully laying his jacket on the seat of the empty chair beside him.

"My wife took up gambling two years ago. I didn't pay

attention at first. She would go to the casino with some of her
women friends. But that was the beginning of the end. I didn't
know until it was too late that she had run through our joint
savings account. Then she managed, somehow, to get access
to my profit-sharing from the company. Our retirement savings."

As he spoke, Osborne felt helpless and hollow, witness to
an accident he could see coming but do nothing to stop.

"I didn't know until the money was gone. After a while,
she lied about her trips to the casino, telling me she was playing bridge or shopping in the cities with friends. For the last
few years, she has made a big deal of my letting her pay all
the household bills, a feminist kind of thing, so I was in the
dark until the bank called one day."

"How long ago was that?"

"Oh, nine months ago. Not too long after her father died.
Then she banked on her inheritance to get us out of the hole.
But at the same time, she kept gambling. I take responsibility
for this, by the way. I should have been able to help her."

"How bad is it, Peter?" asked Lew.

"We are well over a million in debt," he said softly. "Well
over."

"And you're losing the house?" Lew continued.

"I'm not sure. Alicia told me the other day that she had
managed to make a payment out of her salary from her little
business with Meredith."

"Were you surprised that she was cut out of the will?"

"So you know about that." Peter's eyes shifted in surprise
at Lew's comment on the will.

"Yes."

"That was a blow."

"Why did the old man do that?" asked Osborne from the
side.

Peter looked over at him. "I have no idea, Paul, except that
Alicia was always treated unfairly by her family. Her stepmother played favorites and would deliberately leave Alicia
out of family events. She had a very unhappy childhood. Her
father was cold. I have never understood how two adults could
be so miserable to a young girl but they were downright mean
to Alicia. This will, this leaving everything to her sister—that
was unconscionable."

Peter sat up straight now, his face flushed with anger, "All those years that Meredith was living in Lake Forest, who took care of the old man? Alicia. And I helped her. We were there for him. And he was not a pleasant man. Doc, you know that old codger was a crotchety sonofabitch."

"Yes he was," said Osborne. "He was a patient, and I agree with you. He was a miserable human being."

"Why were you staying at The Willows? Did Alicia know you were there?" asked Lew.

"Oh no," said Peter, "she had no idea. I haven't had the heart to tell her that I tried to get my old job back, but they didn't want me. I'm too old, y'know. The company doesn't want a guy in his sixties on the road. I couldn't tell her. I just couldn't."

He dropped his head, "I couldn't bear to see the look on her face. So instead I lied and said I was traveling abroad." He looked up now, his cheeks waggling, "I went up to my old hunting shack, and I drank. That's all, I just drank. One day, I needed some food so I drove over to Land o' Lakes to the little convenience store there and ran into Meredith. Or she ran into me. She knew right away I had been drinking.

"She and I have always been able to talk, you know. She got the truth out of me and then she insisted that I come stay with her. She made me get into rehab but I . . . I'm not well yet.

"You must know one thing," he said suddenly, emphatically, "I love my wife. This is not her fault. She is an addict, she is sick. Her gambling is an addiction just like my drinking. But things are going to be okay now."

"They are?" said Lew. "How on earth can that be?"

"Because we'll have the money. Alicia is next of kin—so she'll receive her inheritance after all. Don't you see?"

Lew looked at him long and hard. "Is that why you killed your sister-in-law?"

"No. Of course not . . . I didn't . . . why . . . ? Oh. Oh . . ." he said again, the logic of his statements dawning on him. "No, I did not kill her. I really didn't have reason to even if it looks that way. See, Meredith told me she would help us financially. So I knew things were going to work out if only . . ."

"If only what?" asked Lew.

"Ah," Peter hesitated, he inhaled deeply, then repeated himself, "if only . . . if only . . ."

"If only what, Peter?" said Lew quietly.

"... I stopped drinking." A swell of despair in his voice made Osborne think those weren't the words he had intended at all.

"Believe me, I could never have killed Meredith," said Peter, his eyes beseeching Lew, "she was helping me. She was a good and kind woman. She loved Alicia, and she loved me. I loved her ... like a sister."

Osborne caught Lew's eye to make sure it was okay to interrupt. "Pete," he said, "how did Alicia feel about Meredith?"

Again, the eyelid flickered.

"Paul," said Peter, "how can you even ask such a question? Alicia adored Meredith. She worshiped her from the moment she was born. She was her big sister, her guardian angel."

"Peter, there is always some resentment among siblings," said Lew. "It's perfectly natural. Alicia had more than enough reason—"

"Alicia had nothing to do with Meredith's death," said Peter. "I know she didn't."

"How do you know that?" challenged Lew.

"Because she was home that night. All night."

"And where were you?"

"Watching her."

"You were at the home?"

"I was ...," Peter closed his eyes and spoke slowly, "I was ... outside ... my home."

The office was perfectly still. In the distance, through the windows, Osborne heard a car honk down on Main Street.

"I love my wife," Peter said again. "This has been a hard time for us. In my drunken stupors, I imagined she was having an affair," he raised his head as if proud that he had finally confessed. "I was spying on her. That's how I know she was home."

"You realize you are a suspect in the death of your sister-in-law, Peter?" said Lew, standing up and walking around her desk.

"I can understand that," said Peter, his eyes looking off into the distance as if he was waiting for yet another blow.

"I want you to stay in Loon Lake," said Lew matter-of-factly. "I may have some more questions."

"I'm not going anywhere except home."

He pushed himself up from the chair, reached for his suit

coat, raised his hand in a slight wave and started to let himself out the door. Then he turned back. "I haven't told Alicia that I don't have a job. Would you let me handle that?"

"That's your business, Peter," said Lew.

"Poor Pete, said Osborne once the door had closed, "what a sad, beaten man. But certainly not dangerous . . ."

"No?" said Lew. "I'm not so sure."

"I just . . . I feel so sorry for him," said Osborne.

"Doc," said Lew straightforwardly, "we choose our delusions just as we choose our addictions."

"I guess you're right," he said, wondering how it was she and Ray knew so much more about people than he. He may be older, but wiser was in question. "Do you think he did it?"

"I really don't know."

With that, Osborne stood up to leave her office. Lew walked over to refill her coffee cup. Watching her pour, he resisted the urge to ask why, since she had her own pot, she had to have coffee with Ralph every morning?

"Say, Doc," said Lew, opening the door for him to leave, "I'll be by the marina later. I've never seen one of those acqua cams, and I just heard the DNR is planning to ban them. We have a meeting on it next week. Ask Ray if he would have time to give me a demonstration later, would you?"

"Sure."

Then it dawned on Osborne, this was his opening. "Maybe he would loan us one after the tournament is over."

"Really? Why?"

"Well . . . ah," he stammered, "I'd like to pay you back for all your help with my fly fishing. I was wondering . . . I mean I know Ralph is first on your list, of course . . . but if . . . when . . . if you ever want to I would really like to take you out on my weed beds with a musky rod. And the reefs, we can test the acqua cam on the boat. See what we see, y'know. Got some 50-inchers in there, Lew. Oh well, you're probably booked solid with Ralph . . ." He finished lamely, trying to figure out exactly what it was he had just said.

An expression of amusement had settled on Lew's face. "Doc," she said, "I don't know what you're getting at exactly but Ralph Kendall is not 'first on my list.' He is a good, good friend, but he's not my type. You know Ralph—he talks too much. And it's always about Ralph. If he's first on anybody's list, he's first on Ralph's list."

"Really? That's how you feel about the guy?"

"Yeah. A little bit of Ralph goes a long way, but he knows his stuff, so I put up with him. He has his good points, y'know?"

"Oh sure, sure," Osborne couldn't agree more.

"I'm not booked solid with anyone. Yeah, sure, I'd love to do some musky fishing with you—but after trout season winds up next month, okay?" She seemed pleased with the invitation. "I fish musky in deep water myself. Gave up on weedbeds years ago. Maybe you can change my mind."

"I'd like to try," said Osborne. "See you later." Shutting the door behind him, he resisted the urge to skip down the hall.

As Osborne drove through Loon Lake to the marina, he reflected on the meeting with Peter. In his opinion, Lew had let the man go without asking any number of key questions, not the least of which was what led Peter to think his wife was having an affair? The more Osborne mulled it over, the more the spoken word paled beside the unspoken.

The unspoken was like a fishing line left loose. Like the technique for drawing in a trout that is called "dancing the fly." That delicate move in which the fly fisherman chooses not to reel in but simply dance the dry fly across the downstream currents to tantalize the big ones lurking below. Yes, indeed, casting no shadows that might frighten her prey, Lew had let out just enough line to dance her fly across the current.

The question: who would strike and when?

twenty-eight

The parking lot at Murphy's Marina was crammed with huge cardboard boxes, some ripped open, others still taped shut. Ray had just walked outside, Wayne beside him, as Osborne drove in. He pulled up, his window down.

"Hi, Doc," Rivers of sweat were running down Ray's face. Wayne, too, looked flushed and hot. "It's coming together, but I need you to give me a hand with these outboards, okay?"

"Sure. Lew asked if you would have time to give her a demo on one of those acqua cams later."

"I don't think I'll have those hooked up till pretty late this afternoon."

"That oughta work." Osborne parked and walked back to where Wayne was struggling to pull one of the big moters from its packing. He reached for the sides of the engine, steadying it as Wayne tossed the styrofoam forms aside.

"We install these first," said Wayne. "Ray got a couple of the guys from the marina to help us get the boats into the water inside the boathouse. John is letting us use all ten slips so we can lock up tonight." He wiped the sweat from his face with the sleeve of his T-shirt. "I'll tell you, this is amazing stuff these tournament guys get to use. Digital everything and *expensive*. Jeez, ya gotta be a millionaire to fish walleyes these days!"

"I don't know about that," said Osborne, tugging away on

a few final strips of heavy strapping tape. "You always have choices, Wayne. I know plenty of fellas are happy with little Lund boats, twenty-year-old casting rods, and a carton of nightcrawlers."

"I hear ya, Doc. Funny, y'know," Wayne kept talking and grunting as they hoisted the outboard motor onto a dolly, "I like this area. Did Ray tell you yesterday I put a deposit down on a little cabin over there by you guys?"

"No kidding, Bob Baker's place?" Osborne knew there was only one lakefront lot with a cabin available on Loon Lake. He also knew only a Chicagoan would even consider the list price. They walked the dolly through the boathouse entrance and down to one of the slips. Wayne cut away the protective padding on the stern so they could ease the big outboard onto the boat.

"Yep," said Wayne, "I really like it up here. This is the time for me to make a move if I'm ever going to. I'm single right now, and I love to fish. I really never took the time before . . ."

"You never had Ray Pradt to get you hooked," grinned Osborne.

"You're right," laughed Wayne. "Takes a guy like Ray to show you what the good life really is, y'know? It isn't money, it isn't the big job, it's being able to hear the wind in the pines as you fall asleep at night."

"Listen to the loons while you have your morning coffee," added Osborne.

"Break open a cold beer after racing off the lake before a thunderstorm hits," said Wayne.

"That's why I decided to practice up here," said Osborne. "I'd have made a lot more money elsewhere."

"I talked to Chief Ferris, too," said Wayne. He had a happy gleam in his eye. "She said a full-time position may open up when that deputy, Roger, retires. Something could come up in Wausau, too."

Osborne chuckled softly as they headed back to the parking lot for the next engine. "Wayne—you're changing your life."

"I'm tryin'."

"But won't Loon Lake be boring after Chicago?"

"Hey, with what I saw in the police files, I'd say not. You got plenty action up here, Doc. By the way, did Chief Ferris tell you I checked out the Sutliff family—that was quite interesting." It was Osborne's turn to grunt as they hoisted an-

other outboard. "Watch your back, take it in your knees, Doc,"
cautioned Wayne.

Osborne stepped back and wiped the sweat from his forehead. "The Sutliffs had a file?"

"Just one item. Police report from years ago. A Mrs. Sweedberg reported seeing Alicia push her baby sister's buggy into
an oncoming car from the sidewalk in front of the family
home."

"I never heard this," said Osborne.

"The file was marked confidential," said Wayne. "The driver
of the vehicle was able to stop so nothing happened. Alicia,
who was fifteen at the time, didn't deny it, but she said she
was hurrying to cross the street, stumbled, and the buggy flew
out of her hands. However, this Mrs. Sweedberg insisted she
saw the girl wait for the car to approach, then give it a deliberate shove.

"Interesting detail in the report. The father was very upset
and accusing of his daughter. Apparently, he made quite a
scene in the police station, and he wanted to file charges."

"Be careful what you believe," said Osborne, "much as I
am not fond of Alicia Roderick, Helen Sweedberg was nasty.
She was a vicious gossip. I imagine John Sloan, who would
have been chief of police at the time, did not consider her the
best witness."

"In this business," sighed Wayne, "we learn early on the
worst witness is an eyewitness. Still, interesting, huh?"

Ray walked up with two large plastic cups filled with ice
cubes and ginger ale, "Break time, you razzbonyas."

Osborne took his cup and sat down on a bench just inside
the boathouse. He looked around as he inhaled the cool drink.
The old boathouse was a classic, built in ways no longer allowed by new shoreline restrictions. Essentially a large
wooden barn jutting out over the water, the exterior was a deep
blue-red, a hue common to many of the old structures found
along North Woods shores and impossible to duplicate. Time
and weather burnishes the underlying coats of paint with a
glow that can't be duplicated. The interior walls were black
with age.

Built at the turn of the century, there was space for a dozen
boats inside, each with its own slip and double doors opening
out into the lake. The building stood at the end of a wide
twenty foot dock and cantilevered out over the water yet an-

other thirty feet. Because it was in a bay on the northeast side of the lake, it was protected from winter winds and ice floes. This year, the summer rains had been so plentiful that the lake was much higher than usual. So much so that the floor inside the boathouse seemed to float a bare two to three inches over the lightly lapping waves.

"Why is this water so black?" asked Wayne, standing at the edge of one of the slips and looking down.

"Tannin from the pine trees," said Osborne, "plus we're in the shade. This lake has a mucky bottom, too, which doesn't help."

"How deep do you think it is?"

"Right here? Five feet, maybe deeper." Osborne studied the water, "this dock was built for a water level a good six inches to a foot lower than what you see. This is so high they may have winter damage when it ices over."

"Do fish swim in here?"

"Oh, sure. Rock bass, suckers—you'll hear them jump. They come after any insects the wolf spiders haven't eaten."

"Wolf spiders," said Wayne. "So you get those up here, huh."

"Oh yeah, hundreds of 'em under a dock like this and big as a puppy," Osborne teased. He relented when he saw the distress on Wayne's face. Funny what reduces a tough guy to jelly. "Don't worry, Wayne. You'll get fair warning. From tip to tip, a wolf spider measures four to five inches—you won't miss one," said Osborne. "They aren't poisonous, but they are a very good reason to watch where you put your hands when you work around a dock."

Wayne shook his shoulders in a mock shiver. "Ee-yuck. Give me a car thief any day, Doc."

By five-thirty, they had almost all the boats outfitted. Outboard motors were hooked in and tilted high, fuel tanks readied, locators and acqua cams plugged in, tested and operating. Ray assigned one final chore: remove all the packing tape from the storage units and fill the livewells with fresh water.

Osborne was just uncoiling a length of hose, when Wayne shouted from where he crouched in one of the boats, "Hey, wait a minute. Doc, you better take a look at this."

"Got a problem?"

"Somebody's got a problem." He held open a livewell, and

Osborne looked down. It was full, neatly packed with packages wrapped in white freezer paper. Wayne had slit open one of the packages with his jackknife. He pointed with the tip of his knife: "Ever see bulk cocaine before?"

They checked the next boat. That livewell was empty. The next one was full. In all, four of the ten boats had livewells that needed emptying.

"Ray—get out here!" shouted Wayne.

"Ho-o-ly Cow! So that's what old George was up to—he was waiting for his connection," said Ray two minutes later. He was standing in one of the boats, staring down at the cache in front of him. The look on his face changed from amazement to chagrin.

"Now what do I do?" He threw his hands up in disgust. "Next you'll tell me you have to put everything in quarantine or something stupid like that? That's it, y'know. That wrecks the tournament. We'll have to cancel. Thank . . . you . . . George."

"Not so fast, my friend," Wayne put a comforting hand on Ray's shoulder. "You pulled some strings for me, I can pull a few for you. You got that camera of yours in the truck? Go get it. While you do that, I'll call in. I want someone on George Zolonsky's butt right now.

"We'll shoot photos of these for evidence. Since you and Doc are deputies for Chief Ferris, you can unload. But we have to get her out here right away. We need her to document the unloading, and, of course, she needs to take possession. She and I can handle the paperwork on this."

"What do you think, Wayne?" asked Osborne. "Is this what you came up here for?"

"We hooked a big one, boys," said Wayne. "No catch and release on this mother," he looked at Ray and Osborne with a wide, wide smile of satisfaction. "This is a career-maker, men, this has to be one of the biggest coke busts north of Milwaukee. Ever."

"*Ever?*" said Ray, starting to lighten up. "Jeez, I may be on TV again."

"I guarantee you'll be on TV," said Wayne, "but we need to hustle if you want to be on the lake in the morning."

"Okay, okay," said Ray, jumping up onto the dock from the boat.

Just then the door to the boathouse swung open. Osborne

saw the barrel of the shotgun before he recognized the figure holding it. By the time, his brain had registered the face, the force of the deer slug had blown Wayne over the back of the boat and into the dark, oily water.

Osborne never did remember making a conscious decision to do anything. All he knew was he was flying, too, over the edge and down into the murky blackness.

Opening his eyes, he strained to see through the dark water. Even though the afternoon sunlight lent a brownish glow to the surface, he could see less than twelve inches in front of him. Reaching down he pulled at the laces of his fishing boots. Up he went for a quick gulp of air, then down again. Boots off, he thrust his hands out and around, desperate to find Wayne before the detective's boots and sodden jeans would drag his unconscious form down to the muddy bottom.

Arms flailing through the dark water, he searched until he couldn't stand it any more. He burst through the surface for air. A slug thudded into the water by his right ear. Down, down, he pulled his arms furiously. Looking up, he could see the bottom of the boat but no sign of a floating body, no Wayne. Nor could he touch bottom, it was so deep. The muffled crack of two more slugs hit the water over his head.

He kept kicking, reaching around him, hoping to make contact with something. His foot hit a piling. Quickly, he grabbed the slimy timber. Grasping desperately with both hands, refusing to let his fingers slide off, he pulled and kicked until he knew he was under the dock, then eased up slowly, slowly. He had to breathe, but he didn't want to die doing so.

Struggling to keep all movement minimal, knowing that the slightest change in the sound of the lapping waves would give him away, he let himself float up and up. Just when he thought his lungs would burst, the top of his head bumped the underside of the dock. Easing back, he raised his chin, letting his face break the surface. There couldn't be more than two inches of clearance but it was a life-saving two inches. Silently, he hoped, he exhaled, then inhaled, then waited.

Submerging his mouth and tipping his head back and forth to breathe through his nose, he looked around between breaths. Cracks in the boards overhead let light sprinkle through. A wooden lip along the edge of the dock made it impossible to see into the slips, but he could hear the nearest boat rocking.

Heavy feet shuffled as someone banged their way through the
boat.

Osborne backed into the black recess under the dock, pushing overhead with his hands. The soft body of a wolf spider
moved beneath his fingers, and he felt cocoons that he would
have avoided any other time, crumbling as they dropped into
the water around his face and eyes.

With a sudden roar, the outboard motor in the slip beside
him revved up, churning the water with such force that it put
anyone within a fifteen-foot range at risk of being sucked into
the powerful blades. It also churned a wake that would have
drowned Osborne if the ledge along the edge of the dock
weren't there to break the wave action. As it was, the water
lapped up against the undersurface of the dock, forcing him to
take hasty breaths between the swells. The swells were a bless-
ing: their steady rhythm helped Osborne force down the urge
to panic.

The outboard stopped as suddenly as it had started. Silence.
Osborne tried to remain perfectly still, pumping only his legs
to tread water, hands loosely circling the piling. He waited and
hoped to hell Wayne had regained consciouness and was out
of danger. In his gut, he knew otherwise.

"George . . . take it easy, George . . . ," he heard Ray's
voice, steady, reasonable.

"Shaddup, Pradt. You're next," the boots clumped on the
boards directly over Osborne's head. "I see one floating out
there. Where's the old man? Where's he, huh?" said George,
speaking so fast Osborne could barely understand him.

"I think you took 'em both out, George," Ray drawled
evenly. "That last slug, I saw blood, you got 'em."

"Yeah? Nah, you're foolin' with my head, Pradt. That sonofabitch is down there." George's boots clumped along the
planking. Osborne could see him through the cracks in the
dock. Or rather he identified him from the waist down: bow-
legged in Levi's worn low on his lean frame. A white band
of Jockey shorts showed above the waist of the Levi's.

"I don't see any blood."

"I saw the hit, George, you can't see blood in this dark
water. You know that."

"But I don't see his body. I oughta see two floating out
there . . ."

"Doc was wearing my tool belt, George. I guarantee he went straight to the bottom."

"Huh." George had stripped off his shirt, and Osborne could see the sweat stream off his shoulders and run down his back. Zolonsky was a wiry, small-boned man, well-muscled across the shoulders and down his back from years of working home construction and tile laying. But it wasn't that warm in the boathouse. The profuse sweating was a bad sign. Knowing what he knew about pharmaceuticals and knowing George may have been doing cocaine for days, Osborne figured the man's paranoia level had to be so intense that the slightest sound, the most minimal movement would set him off.

Osborne gritted his teeth and held on, expecting the worst. Nothing like a paranoid psychotic with a shotgun.

George loped back towards Ray, who stood on the dock just inside the doorway, his back against the wall, his hands held conspicuously high. Suddenly, a fish jumped, the soft plunk breaking the silence of the boathouse. George spun around, shotgun waving wildly towards the lake through the open doors of the boat slips, "They're coming! They're coming! Where are they!" he shouted.

"George," said Ray, his voice soothing, almost singsong, as if he was telling one of his over-long stories at the bar late on a Saturday night, "that was a bluegill. A tiny bluegill. An *unarmed* bluegill, George. Besides, *they* aren't after you, *they* are after me. You called the cops on *me*, remember? You called and said I stole your rig. So settle down, George. You, my friend, are in the driver's seat."

"Yeah?" George's highstrung voice was doubtful as he stood waving the shotgun towards the open doors to the lake.

"Say, Georgie—did you get a tax stamp for this crap?"

George swung back around to level the shotgun at Ray.

"Just kidding, just kidding." Right or wrong, Ray was doing his best to act naturally, to calm George down. Osborne was not at all sure it was working. The one factor in Ray's favor was the simple fact he was well-liked by most North Woods men, no matter what their economic status. Osborne knew, too, that Ray had spent more than a few hours in the musky boat with George when they were younger. Maybe the sharing of secret fishing holes would count for something.

Stopping in front of Ray, George nudged the muzzle of the shotgun under Ray's chin. Osborne had a full view through the cracks in the dock flooring. He could see the man's entire body vibrating so violently that the gun shook where it pushed into Ray's neck.

What did that say about the trigger finger? Osborne tipped his head back for a quick exhale and inhale. Moments like this made him glad he still attended Mass, that he covered his bets just in case there was a Greater Power. He ripped off a series of Hail Mary's like he hadn't since he was a kid with a bad report card. Ray needed all the help he could get.

"George . . . what happened fifteen years ago?" With the gun against his throat, Ray's voice sounded a little strained.

"Shuddup, Pradt. The last thing I need is one of your stupid jokes."

Osborne couldn't agree more.

"Now listen, I'm serious, George. We got caught smoking weed over on the Willow Flowage ice fishing. You, me, and Patty Boy Vinson, remember that?"

"What's the point? This ain't weed I got here, dumkof."

"I'm trying to tell you. Remember how you and Patty Boy got away? But Smiling John collared me, remember?" said Ray referring to the former Loon Lake police chief renown for his lack of humor.

Ray's voice was steady again, smooth and soothing, reminding Osborne of the day they were scouting beaver dams and found a red fox with one leg caught in a trap set for fishers.

Staying in full view and moving with graceful slowness, for an hour Ray had advanced on his hands and knees, his voice low and singsong, lulling the fox until, trusting, it lay still long enough for Ray to reach over and release the trap. Expecting the fox to leap and run, Osborne had been amazed to see the animal lay back, lick its wound, then sit up on its good haunch to stare at Ray with a long, measuring look before limping slowly off into the brush.

"I never squealed on you, George. Remember that? My dad wouldn't bail me out, and I had to stay two weeks in the slammer, but I never gave Sloan your names. Never did, remember?" Ray's voice pressed on, as mellow as if he was in his musky boat chatting in a muted drone so as not to disturb nearby fishermen.

"Okay, okay, what's the point?" George dropped the muzzle from Ray's neck.

"That's what I'm tryin to tell you. Take your stuff, and get outta here. I won't say a word. I can tell the cops some jabone I never saw before rolled in here and hammered us."

George dropped the gun and turned sideways so Osborne could see his expression. Zolonsky's face was pale beneath his reddish tan. His eyes bulging more than ever. With his left hand, he pulled a packet of Camels from the back pocket of his jeans, shook a cigarette into his mouth, reached for a lighter in his front pocket and lit the cigarette. Cradling the shotgun in his right arm, the barrel still pointing at Ray, he inhaled deeply, spit, then stuck the cigarette between his lips and leveled the rifle in both hands. He seemed a little less shaky.

"I don't know, Pradt. You've been bugging the hell outta me—calling my house, hassling my daughter. I had a big deal going down. You almost made me blow it—"

"I know, I know, and I'm sorry about that. But me, too, George. I have the biggest deal of my life. I'm on ESPN for chrissake. Look, George. We're just two guys trying to do business, trying to make a living, y'know?"

"And it's damned hard."

"You betcha. We're in the same boat, man. So let me help you outta here. Then you get your money, and I get mine. Deal? I got a dolly right over in that corner. I can help you load up."

"Yeah? Yeah, okay . . . wait, how do I know you won't call the cops after I'm gone?"

"See that roll of duct tape over in the corner? Just tape me up after we get you loaded. No one shows for the tournament until four-thirty in the morning. That's more than eight hours from now. You got a long drive to make delivery?"

"Long, long drive. None of your business how long a drive."

"Of course not. But you can be across the Canadian border before anyone finds me."

"That's true," George tossed his cigarette into the water. "Gives me time for the pick-up at my other place, too. Yeah, that's good. I didn't want to shoot you, Ray. You know that. You helped me catch that 52-inch musky what, six, seven years ago? I got that musky on my living room wall. No, this is good. You I don't want to shoot."

It took less than ten minutes for the two men to pull out the bags, load them onto the dolly and wheel them out. George had pulled his truck right up to the door, making it easy to load. It also indicated to Osborne that he must have bided his time earlier, waiting for the marina staff to leave for the day.

The loading completed, Ray sat down on a bench near the entrance to the boathouse. Holding the roll of duct tape in his right hand, he started to wind it over his pant legs and around his ankles.

"Gimme that," said George, stashing another cigarette between his lips and squatting in front of Ray.

"So, George," said Ray casually as his knees and ankles were being bound, "that you taking those big bucks off the back forty behind The Willows?"

George threw the roll of tape down and jumped to his feet, "That's it! You want my business. That's what this is all about, isn't it. Damn you, you crumb bum!" He stomped over to grab the shotgun from where he had set it on its butt against the wall. Osborne's pulse accelerated.

"Georgie, Georgie, Georgie," Ray spoke rapidly but still with a cool calmness. "Settle down, pal. How much coke did you *do*? You must've blown your sensors out your ears. No, I don't want your business. Why would I want *your* business? I got my hands full with my minnow operation. I intended a compliment."

"Whattaya mean?" demanded George, cigarette bouncing between his lips. He set the gun down and walked back over to Ray.

"I mean you have a very nice set-up. Very nicely hidden, very efficient. Just a compliment, George."

"Hands out," George demanded, wrapping the tape around Ray's wrists, "what took you back in there, anyway?"

"I was looking for beaver dams. You know how I break 'em down and seine for minnows."

"Yeah, you sonofagun," George started around Ray's mouth with the duct tape, "when was the last time you took a legal minnow, huh? Hee, hee, hee." He laughed at his own nonsense as he ripped the tape, slapping one end against Ray's cheek. The sound of Zolonsky's wheezy signature giggle came as a positive omen to Osborne. It meant Zolonsky was his usual self, at least with Ray.

"Hee, hee, hee," Zolonsky chortled again as he stepped back to admire his handiwork. "Sleep tight, Pradt." Then he reached for his shotgun, gave Ray a friendly pat on the shoulder, and headed towards the doorway.

At the sound of the ignition turning over, Osborne's heart

pounded at a slightly more reasonable rate. The drone of a distant outboard motor made it impossible for him to hear the sound of tires moving across gravel outside the boathouse so he stayed submerged until he could be absolutely sure Zolonsky was gone.

Ray's body leaned against the wall, cocooned in duct tape. It looked as if he could breathe through his nose but even his eyes were taped shut.

After a long, long couple of minutes, Osborne started towards the boat slip. Just as he prepared to duck past the outer ledge and surface, he heard tires grinding towards the boathouse. He knew it: Zolonsky had realized the stupidity of his move. With one swift stroke of his arms, Osborne shot back towards the piling and safety.

twenty-nine

Osborne tensed, lifting his chin for yet another silent exhale and inhale. This time, his hands found a knot on the slimy piling that made it easier to hold on. This time, he would be sure Zolonsky was gone before leaving his anchor. Just the sound of a body moving through water would echo in the silent boathouse. One slug through the flooring, and he'd be fishing with Wayne.

The interior above was darkening as the early evening sun moved away. Peering up, he could see nothing, hear only the scraping noise made by the boathouse door as it was pushed open. His eyes strained through the cracks in the flooring. The twilight sky behind the opening door offered a silhouette he could not identify.

"Jeez!" cried the figure that hovered in the doorway for a millisecond before rushing forward.

"Lew!" Osborne shouted, pressing his mouth against the sodden underside of the dock. Ducking his head under the water, he jackknifed forward and down, propelling himself into the slip. His head banged into the boat moored there as he surfaced. He grabbed for the ladder to the dock and yanked himself up, water pouring from his clothing, his wet stocking feet slipping as he ran.

Lew was already kneeling beside Ray, ripping the duct tape from his eyes. Looking past her at Osborne, Ray's eyes widened in relief, then clouded with a question. Osborne knew he was thinking of Wayne.

"I couldn't help him," said Osborne, "I am so sorry, Ray. I tried . . ."

"Doc," said Lew as she worked on the tape, "what the hell happened here?"

"Zolonsky," said Osborne as he knelt to help with Ray. "He was smuggling cocaine in the boats. That's why he was so late delivering—he was waiting for a connection down south. We found it when we went to fill the livewells—"

"Why the hell didn't you call me? You're lucky I came by to see those acqua cams—I almost didn't come, dammit."

"We found the drugs at the last minute, Lew. Couldn't have been ten minutes after we found the stuff Zolonsky barges in here with a shotgun firing every which way. Poor Wayne never had a chance. I don't think he even knew what hit him—"

"How long ago was all this?"

"Last half hour. Zolonsky pulled out of here maybe six, seven minutes ago. I thought you were him coming back to finish Ray off."

Lew pulled out a Swiss Army knife. She slipped it under the tape binding Ray's mouth and ears.

"Sorry, Ray," she said, "you're about to get a cheap shave." She ripped.

"I love it when you hurt me," said Ray, shaking his head free of the strips of tape. Lew cuffed him on the shoulder then tackled the tape binding his wrists.

"Hey," Osborne grabbed Ray's shoulder, "that shaky trigger finger had me worried."

"You, Doc? I thought for sure I dug my own grave this time."

"I still can't believe you talked him out of here." Osborne patted and rubbed Ray on the back, convincing himself his good friend really was alive and well. Lew continued slicing and yanking at the tape around his wrists and ankles.

"He owes me, Doc. He's got a 51-incher on his wall thanks to me. A guy like George doesn't forget that, y'know."

"Can you stand okay, Ray? I think I got it all," said Lew. She stepped back, her eyes anxious, "I am real sorry, boys. I have to leave you two here if I'm going to nail Zolonsky. Roger's on the desk, I'll radio in, ask him to get someone out here for you.

"You are not going alone," said Osborne. "Not after that madman."

"No sirree," said Ray, "George is wild with that shotgun. You need back-up, Lew.

"Okay." Lew seemed relieved. Her eyes darkened, "You sure Wayne is . . . ?"

"No question," said Osborne. "I tried to find him just after he took the slug but no luck. Jeez, y'know, I still can't believe Zolonsky didn't get me—all I did was hide under the dock."

Lew walked over to the edge and looked down, "This dock? Is there room to breathe under there?"

"Barely. It's not a performance I care to repeat."

Lew turned to Ray, "Do we have any idea where Zolonsky's headed?"

"My guess? Canada. He's got the drugs in his truck, and he's coming off three or four days on coke," said Ray. "He left here thinking he's got eight hours to make his move. I got the impression he might be stopping by his place first, then heading north to make his drop."

"Okay, let's give him just enough time to think he's pulling this off," said Lew. "I would like to follow him up to the border with an alert to the Canadian authorities to take over from there. For Wayne's sake, we should give them a chance to see if they can nab George and his contacts. What do you think?"

"Wayne would appreciate that," nodded Ray. He turned to look Osborne up and down, "Doc, before you go dancing, you need shoes. You want dry clothing?"

"That'll take too long, I'm fine."

As Lew climbed into her cruiser to radio in, Osborne and Ray ran up to the marina.

"I know this place like the back of my hand, what size?" said Ray as he opened the door. Once inside, he rummaged through boxes. Within seconds he thrust a new pair of boots at Osborne. They hurried back outside where Lew had pulled up in her cruiser.

"What are you doing?" said Ray. "Zolonsky's place is up on the other side of the chain. We can get there faster if we take one of the boats up to Evan's Landing. You have somebody waiting for us with a car, and we're less than five minutes from George's place. Save us fifteen, twenty minutes, Chief."

"Done," said Lew.

•   •   •

The walleye boat hummed across the glassy surface like a loon flying low. With the sun setting behind the shoreline, each balsam spire was etched sharp against the sky. Clouds scudding overhead captured rays of sunlight and threw them onto the water in pools of peach and silver blue. Beneath the flying boat, the lake was a plain of stillness.

Leaning forward, elbows on his knees as he sat in a bucket seat at the rear of the boat, Osborne let a sadness flow through his bones. The elegant peace of the water masked the violence and tragedy lurking below. Violence in the rock-jawed musky, the "shark of the north" that lured men like George Zolonsky into the North Woods. Tragedy in the death of Wayne, his lifeless body down there somewhere, tangled in muck and reeds.

Before leaving the boathouse, Lew had arranged for a crew from the volunteer fire department to drag for Wayne's body even if it meant working through the night. Roger had located a state trooper operating radar from an unmarked car on Highway 17 who agreed to meet them at Evans Landing. All they needed now was to find George at home.

No one had spoken since Ray pushed the outboard motor to its limit. At 150 horsepower, it was touted to do 50, maybe 60 mph, but Osborne guessed the absolute stillness of the lake made it possible for the boat to fly at a speed closer to 70 mph. Whatever the speed, the warm air blowing at him had rapidly dried his wet clothing.

The chain of lakes, eight miles long, had two shallow channels where they were forced to cut the engine and raise the propellor in order to pass. Even so, less than twenty minutes later Ray had the watercraft drifting into Evan's Landing. The unmarked car was waiting. Leaving the trooper to return the boat, Lew took the wheel and spun gravel up the lane to the country road.

As they started down the road, Osborne shook his head, "Ray, I was just thinking how George warned you off his poaching operation. Like he thinks he's coming back to that? What on earth—? Does he really think he can shoot two men in cold blood, get caught with hundreds of thousands of dollars in cocaine and waltz back here to run a two-bit poaching operation?

"That's his game, Doc," said Lew with a wry tone in her

voice. "Just you watch. He'll be back, whether we get him or not. He behaves like a crazy man, then he pleads insanity. The Wausau boys will make me check him into the hospital for a couple months. Then he's out—"

"And he's on disability," Ray shouted. "He's a crook, he's a looney and the Feds pay him for it."

"Jeez," said Osborne. They drove on in silence.

"Here we are," said Ray, pointing at the fire number and mailbox identifying George Zolonsky's property. From the road, they could see down a short drive into the yard surrounding the small log home. No cars or trucks stood in the drive. The door to the one-vehicle attached garage was open, the garage empty. A fishing boat on a trailer, covered with a blue tarp, was parked along the outside of the garage.

"We missed him," said Lew. "Are we too early?"

"I don't think so," said Ray, "he should be here by now."

Lew turned into the narrow drive and pulled up to park in a clearing by the front door that passed for a driveway. Up close, the log house appeared well-kept.

"Nice place," she said as she and Osborne climbed out of the car. "I'm surprised."

From the back seat, Ray climbed out behind them. "When he isn't drunk or high, George is a very careful man. Besides being the best tile layer in the county, he's a good carpenter and an excellent finish man—when he shows up. The problem with George, see, isn't doing a good job, it's getting the job done."

Lew tried the front door knob. It was unlocked. Standing off to the side with Osborne and Ray behind her, she pushed the door open calling, "Hell-o-o." No answer. They stepped into a small vestibule. To their left was a handsome wooden rack holding six fishing poles. A large tackle box was set beside the rack.

To their right the modest living room held a large screen TV, an orange plaid sofa with a magnificent musky mounted over it, and a black vinyl lounge chair. Against one wall was a beat-up maple desk covered with bills and mail. They walked through the living room into a small kitchen. A chrome lunch box and thermos stood on the counter.

"Tidy," commented Lew.

"You should see his tackle box," said Ray. "Every lure has

its place, always shined up, too. The guy's obsessive—the ti-
niest detail matters to George."

"Too bad he never learned how to keep his nose clean, too,"
said Lew. She turned around wih a sigh of exasperation. "I
think we got a dead end. Now what?"

"I'll check the basement," said Ray, opening a door to a
stairway leading down. Osborne left Lew checking the bedrooms. He walked back through the living room, looking
around. The rod stand caught his eye. It was as nice as any
he'd ever seen, made from a lovely dark wood he didn't recognize. The fishing rods were good quality. Osborne knelt to
unlatch the tackle box. Ray was right, the man was obsessive
all right. The box was pristine, each lure had its own slot in
the trays, polished, not a trace of rust anywhere.

Like Osborne, George favored surface lures. He had some
nice ones, too. Osborne reached for an antique surface mud
puppy. He didn't see the drill lying beneath the clear plastic
tray until he had lifted the lure. He stopped, lure and hand in
mid-air, "Lew!"

The drill was his old one. The one he had used when he
made house calls on handicapped patients. Mary Lee, damn
her, had sold it at a garage sale after his retirement. Never
asked his permission. Just scooped up all his instruments and
equipment and sold everything one day while he was deer
hunting.

"Doc! Ray! Get in here—fast!" Lew answered his call with
one of her own. Osborne grabbed the drill, put the lure back
and latched the box shut. He ran to the bedroom where Lew
leaned over the bed, holding down two sides of a large square
of paper. Rolled up tubes were scattered on the floor around
her.

"I was looking at this box of fishing maps," she said, "and
I found this. She held down the edges of a large architectural
rendering. Grabbing one side, Osborne helped her flatten the
diagram across the bed.

"The Willows," said Lew, "looks like a copy of the architect's building plans."

"He must have been using this for the tile work he was
doing up there," said Osborne.

"Not only that," Lew pointed to a red circle drawn in marker
on one end of the large rectangle. "he's circled The Stone
House. And he has X'd sections of the interior walls."

'Hey, you two," Ray stepped into the room, "found something interesting downstairs." Osborne and Lew looked back. Ray was brandishing a four-foot length of black spruce. "He's got a woodworking shop downstairs and a nifty stack of this wood. Where do you think this came from?"

"Ray," said Lew over her shoulder, "what's between here and the marina?"

"The Willows."

It was a long ten minutes to the road leading into The Willows. While they drove, Osborne explained the importance of the drill. Battery-powered, it would have made it easy for George to remove fillings from a corpse. So easy it was worth it.

The sun was just dropping below the horizon as their car crested the last rise before the dip into the circle drive. The Stone House rose up in front of them. Literally. In slow motion, the square stone building launched into the air. A fiery base illuminated the base then spread up and up, radiating out the small square windows and erupting through the roof in a shower of flame and rock.

"Now . . . why . . . did he do . . . that?" asked Ray from the back seat.

thirty

George died smoking his last cigarette. That's what the city engineer from Rhinelander confirmed two days later. Osborne suspected as much as he approached the smoking rock and debris that remained of the old waterworks building.

Gases rushing from the bowels of the old storm sewer system towards the open doorway where George had been standing initiated a series of explosions, building in intensity to a central blast that lifted and shattered the building. George himself was blown back into a pine grove thirty feet away by the first fireball, believed by the engineer to have ignited when George flicked a lighter towards his cigarette.

"I'm not sure if the impact that killed him was the force of the explosion in his face or these trees that he hit traveling at pretty good clip," said Osborne as he knelt beside the body, which lay face down. George was not in good shape, the state of his body parts reminding Osborne of auto accident victims he had had to identify using dental charts.

But they didn't need a face to know it was George. Both Osborne and Ray recognized what remained of the Levi's. Lew was able to pull a wallet from an exposed back pocket. The driver's license confirmed the victim was indeed George Zolonsky.

"Do you need me to check further?" asked Osborne.

"Do you mind?" Lew turned away, rifling through the wallet. "All the pockets if you can. I'd sure like to find some indication of where he was going with the drugs." He wondered if she was hiding the fact the sight made her a little queasy.

"I'll help, Doc." Ray stood behind him, "this isn't too different from dressing a deer."

Together, gently, they rolled the body over. Ray checked the blood-soaked Levi's pockets while Osborne patted the sodden shirt. Ray found change, Osborne a small plastic box similar to a trout fly holder. At first glance, he thought the one-inch square held shot pellets for weighting a fishing line.

"Oh, oh," he said on opening it for a closer look, "We just found Meredith Marshall's gold fillings."

"What are you thinking?" Osborne asked Lew as she studied the contents of the box.

"I'm thinking George may have been working as a courier for some time, skimming a bag or two each delivery and stashing them here. Meredith caught him, confronted him and he killed her."

"But why hold on to these fillings?" asked Osborne. "Why go to all the effort when he's got access to big bucks from the drugs?"

"If you want my two cents," said Ray, raising his hands, fingers extended, as if ready to tell one of his stories, "and I'm not sure that you do."

"Go ahead," said Lew, "I'm listening."

"George is a detail man and a pennypincher. Fishing for crappies, I never saw him waste a minnow. I think he saw those fillings as real gold that would have pretty high value. Doc said himself, the drill made it an easy operation. Easy to a guy like George anyhow."

"Maybe," said Lew. "Maybe he was here to pick up what he had hidden earlier, then swing by his place, then head north to hide out for a long time. If he was just a courier, he didn't get that much money. Maybe he thought he could use those fillings to blackmail someone."

"I don't like this," she kicked at a rock, "this is too easy. If you ask me, George was set up. He's a chain smoker. If he was using The Stone House as a hiding place, wouldn't he have lit up in here before? Why didn't the place explode then?

"You got the plans in the car, Lew," said Osborne. "Let's take another look." They walked quietly back up the driveway

to the cruiser. Lew had radioed to Rhinelander for assistance
right after the explosion, now they could hear sirens in the
distance.

"Sure enough," said Osborne, running a finger across the
architectural rendering. "See along the main corridor here?
These manholes were built so any plumber working in the
building would know to open them in order to vent the gases
before entering. This is exactly what Cynthia Lewis described
to us the other day."

"Now if someone closed those manholes before George got
here, if someone knew that he was likely to be smoking while
he was in or around the building . . ."

"Someone turned The Stone House into a time bomb," said
Lew.

"But who besides me and Doc would want to kill George?"
asked Ray.

"I can name an angry husband," said Lew.

"Sad," added Osborne, "because if it really is Peter, then . . . ,"
he looked at Lew and Ray, "it is Alicia's fault." He knew Peter
was capable, too. He understood the urge.

thirty-one

Late Friday afternoon, Ray called Osborne at home. He was overflowing with good news: the walleye tournament had launched without a hitch. Every boat was fueled and ready, every locator and acqua cam worked as planned, every livewell carried only water, and, to top the day off, the ESPN crew returned to shoot some more B-roll of Ray demonstrating his custom walleye jig. The clicks of party-line listeners only added to his pleasure.

"Dinner's on me," he said grandly, "I've invited Lew, too."

"I sure won't turn that down," said Osborne.

He arrived at Ray's shortly before six, contributing tortilla chips, salsa, and an expensive root beer he rarely purchased.

"Check the cooler," said Ray from where he stood at the sink husking corn. Osborne lifted the lid of the blue and white box to see three beautiful northern pike. Only Ray could always find the time—and the perfect fishing hole—to hook these tigers. Dining would be exquisite.

"I ran into Lew at the gas station just before I called you," said Ray, "she was not a happy camper."

"Really?" said Osborne.

Just then Lew's truck drove down the lane to Ray's place.

"Let her tell you. I'm staying out of the line of fire." Ray lifted the first northern into the sink.

Lew banged open the door to the trailer. She stomped in

without knocking, a paper sack in her arms. In spite of the glowering expression on her face, she looked fit and healthy in a close-fitting pair of khakis and a long-sleeved forest green shirt open at the neck. Her dark hair glistened, curlier than ever in the humidity. Osborne remembered her description of Clint Chesnais and applied to her at this moment: "easy on the eyes."

"What a lazy bum," she slammed the sack down on the kitchen table as she yanked out a chair and threw her body into it. "I cannot believe what happened today. I absolutely cannot believe it. Ray—did you tell him?"

"Nope." Ray flushed bits of something down the drain.

"What—who are you talking about?" Osborne asked as he sat down across from her. Lew leaned forward across the table. Her eyes grim, her cheekbones flushed with color, her lips pressed tight. Osborne could feel the tension. Mary Lee's anger had always been a passive-aggressive stew of pouting and whining. Not this woman. What you saw was what you got. Right now, she was ready to slug somebody. The way Lew was built, Osborne agreed with Ray: keep out of the way.

"The lab director down in Wausau. He closed my case. Done. Over. End of investigation. For no reason other than he's a sonofagunlazybum! Nogoodgettingreadytoretirelittle-creep!"

"Settle down, Lew."

"I've been trying to settle down, Doc! For the last two hours I've been trying to settle down. I know you two don't drink. I brought my own beer do you mind?"

If they did, they sure as heck weren't going to say so.

She didn't wait for an answer but reached into the bag to pull out a six of Leinenkugel's Original in the bottles. Osborne took the six-pack from her hands, handed her one and put the rest in the refrigerator. She also pulled out a plastic quart container—"Potato salad." She set the potato salad on the table a little harder than necessary. Then she twisted the cap off the bottle, took a swig, and followed it with a deep breath.

"I've been told that George Zolonsky was responsible for Meredith Marshall's murder, that finding those fillings on him was plenty proof to close the case and that his death was accidental. Over and done."

"You disagree with that?" said Osborne.

"Don't you?" Lew looked at him, her eyes piercing.

Osborne felt an intense need to say the right thing. He did the best he could: he opted for complete honesty, "This may sound silly, Lew, but I think George was hired to kill Meredith by . . . ," Osborne halted, he hated to say it because he felt so sorry for the man, ". . . by Pete Roderick. For the inheritance. And he killed George to cover himself and because he knew George was fooling around with Alicia."

"*George* was fooling around with Alicia? I'd say it was the other way around, Doc."

"Lew . . . I know what I saw in my friend's eyes over the thirty years I've known him: how happy he was when he made her happy. And how did he do that? With money. Lots of money.

"I saw something once, years ago. A fella from Madison came up for deer season as a guest in our shack. Mary Lee and I had a dinner party the night before the hunt started, and the Rodericks were there. Now this Madison fell was quite well-to-do, old lumber money, and you would not have believed Alicia that nigh. Even Mary Lee said her flirting went a little to far.

"Now," Osborne leaned across the table and tapped his right forefinger to emphasize his point, "I saw the look on Pete's face that night. Let me put it this way—I wasn't going to be surprised if there was a hunting accident that week. A little problem of a gun going off while climbing into the deerstand, if you know what I mean. As it was, nothing happened—but Pete was capable. I saw it in his eyes and it scared the bejesus out of me.

"If I have learned anything in all my years, Lew, it's that good people are not always rational. As much as Pete might have appreciated Meredith's help—and you heard him say this: he still believed Alicia when she accused her parents of favoring Meredith, of shutting her out. I think he felt her hatred of Meredith was justified somehow, that Meredith, kind as she was, was still the source of the problem. Then, when he learned of Alicia's affair with George—he lost it. That pushed him beyond reason. All Pete could see was his whole life, everything he loved, everything he had worked for, being stripped away. I think he did it, Lew. I really do."

Lew studied Osborne for a long thirty seconds, "You are dead wrong, Doc. Alicia hired George. Alicia baited George. Alicia is a vicious, grasping woman. I don't care what she says, she hated her sister. Always did. But I have no solid proof. I've sent the checkbook out for a handwriting analysis, which will take weeks. I would love to find she forged those checks. But that's as close as I can get right now. If only I could catch her in one little lie . . . what do you think Ray?"

"Jeez Louise," said Ray from the sink where he was filleting the pike. "I take the fifth. My mission is to fry these fish and be sure you two watch me on ESPN tomorrow morning at seven."

"That's all you have to say, Ray?" Osborne couldn't get over how tense and angry Lew was.

As if she knew what he was thinking, Lew threw her hands up in the air. "Okay, okay, why am I so upset? Who really cares? Bozo down in Wausau has a nice clean desk on Monday, George Zolonsky won't be breaking up any more marriages, the dope dealers got screwed . . ."

"Peter Roderick gets to keep his house," Osborne reminded her. "What happens to the drugs and those names and phone numbers we found on George?"

"Wausau told me to turn it all over to the Illinois authorities. But that doesn't bother me."

"Anybody else come out ahead on this?" asked Ray as he plopped a quarter pound of butter into his black cast-iron frying pan.

"Mallory is making a few life changes after being up here for the funeral," said Osborne.

"Really," said Ray, looking over at his friend with a quizzical smile.

"Clint Chesnais will be a very rich man," said Lew matter-of-factly. Her words hung in the kitchen, which was suddenly quiet.

"Does he know yet?" asked Osborne.

"I'm not sure."

"We should tell him."

"Yes," said Lew, leaning forward again. "Excellent idea. May I use your phone, Doc?

"With my party line?"

"This call is harmless."

She reached Chenais at the casino. He said he would be at the Farmers Market in the morning. Could they talk then?"

"But you'll miss me on ESPN," said Ray, distressed, when she hung up.

"Tape it," said Lew. Her face had brightened considerably.

Osborne inhaled deeply as he pulled into the McDonald's parking lot just after seven-thirty the next day. This Saturday morning was North Woods perfect: the sky deep blue to match the lakes, fluffy white cirrus clouds drifting high. Green was still dominant in the leaves and pine needles, though the tamarack was hinting of change. In just a few weeks, the entire countryside would be golden . . . then white for many, many months. Yes, thought Osborne, this was a morning to savor.

Lew was waiting at a bench outside the little building, capped cups of coffee in hand. She marched quickly towards his car, official in the smooth beige tones of her summer uniform, black-holstered revolver strapped to her belt. Osborne saw three of his coffee-klatch buddies watching through the window. He chuckled. He would have to answer a few questions tomorrow morning.

"Am I late?" asked Osborne as she climbed in.

"No," she said, "I was early. But I want to see Chesnais before the market opens at eight. Thanks for coming along, Doc. I want your take on his reaction."

The Loon Lake Farmers' Market was set up in a bank parking lot just two blocks away. They parked across the street and walked over, strolling briskly past the card tables set up by local farmers. The last of the summer corn was heaped in bushel baskets, mammoth zucchini lined the tables, orange-red tomatoes, their skins bursting, were piled everywhere. And the first apples of the season caught Osborne's eye.

At the very end of the line, they spotted Clint, the back of his truck open to showcase with pots of mums, packets of gladioli bulbs and a few evergreen shrubs that Osborne didn't recognize. He looked relaxed as he leaned against his red pickup, sipping a cup of coffee. He was talking to a slender, sandy-haired man.

The two were laughing together as Osborne and Lew walked up.

"Hello, Chief," Clint straightened up. He didn't look like a man who had just inherited a million dollars. He was casually dressed in jeans and a worn navy-blue T-shirt. "I'd like you to meet Jeffrey Winick here, he sells chickens."

"Chickens, pork, bacon—I've got fresh eggs, too," said the sandy-haired man with a lively smile.

"Chickens, huh?" asked Lew. "Raise your own?"

"You bet. Free range, grain-fed. I got an eight-pounder if you're interested."

"Jeff was raising the chickens for Meredith's restaurant," said Clint.

"Boy, I sure hate to lose that business," said Winick, his smile fading. "I built up my operation this summer, planning ahead. What's the story? Will Alicia be opening the restaurant?"

"You know Alicia?" asked Lew.

Winick raised his eyebrows in an expression of pain, "Unfortunately. Thank goodness her sister taught her a few things about the wholesale butchery industry before the accident. That woman—whew! I still have five birds on ice that she ordered two weeks ago, and she refuses to return my phone calls. She owes me whether she takes 'em or not."

Lew had been walking around as he spoke, peeking into his freezer, opening a carton of eggs that set on the table with his cash box. Now she stood staring at the side of his truck. "You are 'Winick Farms'?" she asked, reading the magnet sign attached to his door.

"Yep, that's me. Freshest eggs, finest chickens you can find out Starks way."

"Whereabouts in Starks?"

"Down aways from Kubiak's Landing. I moved up here from Chicago five years ago. I got forty acres, some cows, a few pigs—"

"Meredith drove all the way out to buy from you?"

"You would be surprised how many people do," he said. "All the chicken in the grocery stores today is prepackaged. Here, take my card," he handed cards to each of them. A bright green rooster perched on a fence that carried the words "Winick Farms" in orange lettering. "I have wonderful turkeys coming along for Thanksgiving."

He continued, "I did steady business with Meredith and Alicia. That day she died, they stopped by for some blackberries my kids picked for Meredith. They were going fishing, the three of them. I figure I was one of the last people to see her alive. Kind of an eerie feeling, y'know."

"Three of them?" Lew's voice stayed markedly casual.

"Some guy named George was with them. Never saw him before," said Winick, "but I don't know many people around here."

"What time of day was this?"

"Late Sunday morning. I remember because it was a beautiful day before that storm rolled in."

"Did you know about this?" Lew turned to Chesnais.

"No," he said, shaking his head. "I work the casino Sundays, that's a big day for us. Meredith and I usually fished during the week."

"Hmm. Did she fish with her sister very often?" said Lew as she walked over towards Clint's truck.

"I didn't know that she ever did. She didn't mention it," said Clint.

"Clint," said Lew, "may I speak with you in private?" She stepped towards the cab of his truck, leaving Osborne standing with Winick.

"That George fella looked out of place with those two women," said the farmer. "I kind of wondered what was going on, but Mrs. Marshall seemed okay with it all, so I didn't say anything."

"Were they in one car?" asked Osborne.

"Two. Meredith's Jeep and a black pick-up."

From the corner of his eye, Osborne could see Lew talking with Chesnais. Looking up at him, she said something that caused Chesnais to step back quickly as if startled. Seconds later, she shook his hand, then turned to walk towards Osborne. Only her eyes gave away her excitement. Behind her stood Chesnais, watching her walk away with a stunned expression on his face.

"Good," she said. "He had no idea he was the beneficiary on the life insurance policy."

"You changed his life, huh?"

"The good farmer changed mine. I feel so stupid, Doc. From the get-go I assumed Meredith Marshall had to be fishing earlier that *night*. It never occurred to me she might be on that river in broad daylight. Nobody fishes the Prairie in the heat of the day. Nobody."

"Lew, don't beat yourself up. You and I both know that the most elementary-level fly-fisherman knows better than to waste a casting arm on a hot, sunny day."

"Maybe they weren't fishing."

thirty-two

Lew pulled the cruiser into the school parking lot. Across the street, through the screen of lilacs, they could see the Roderick house, the garage, and the driveway. Both garage doors were up. One stall held Alicia's Mercedes, the other was empty.

"I don't like it," said Lew. "Peter's car isn't there. This is one conversation I do not want interrupted. We could wait for him to come back... but who knows where the guy is. He could be gone all day, I suppose."

"Do you want me to wait outside while you talk to Alicia?"

"No, I want you with me, Doc. I need a witness. You put pressure on her, too. I like how she tries to behave when she's around you. What's Ray doing this morning?"

Osborne checked his watch, "Watching re-runs of himself on his VCR."

Lew flipped on the handset to her radio, "Lucy—patch me through to Ray Pradt, will you please?"

"Yo-o," echoed Ray's deep voice over the speaker, "who goes there?"

"You sound happy," said Lew.

"Chief... I... am savoring... the moment, my slice of stardom."

Lew grinned at Osborne as Ray's deliberately paced words filled the cruiser. "They cut your bad jokes I take it?"

Ray ignored her needling. "You and Doc won't believe your

eyes. Really, this ESPN show will put Loon Lake on the map."

"Congratulations, Ray." Lew's voice turned serious. "Are you dressed? How soon can you meet Doc and me in the Carlton School parking lot?"

"Seven minutes."

Almost seven minutes to the second, Ray's battered blue pickup bumped up over the curb. Quickly, Lew explained the problem.

"If Peter arrives while we are with Alicia, I need you to keep him out of the house. I don't want him interrupting us. I don't want to talk to him until I've finished with his wife."

"What if he doesn't show up?" asked Ray.

"Then I don't have a problem. Now, Ray, I'm parking my cruiser in front of the house. He'll know I'm here on official business, that's okay. But if he asks, you say I'm just tying up a few details on the final report, nothing serious. I want to keep him off guard. Got it?"

"Yep." Ray nodded, then raised his right hand to wave an oblong box at them.

"I'll bring him over to the school here. I see old man Raske's truck out back. Maybe he'll let me play this on one of those big screens they got in there."

"Ray . . ." Lew didn't smile.

"Just pulling your leg, Chief. Yes, I will do as you say."

Lew led the way as she and Osborne opened the wrought iron gate leading into the yard between the house and the garage. Six rings of the front door bell had produced no one.

"Maybe Alicia's off with Peter," said Osborne as they trudged down a slate walkway past shoulder-high white hydrangeas in full bloom. Turning the corner, they saw Alicia in the garden behind the house. She was bending over a bank of profusely flowering gladioli, cutting away.

"Good morning," said Lew striding towards her. "Beautiful glads."

Startled, Alicia jumped and turned.

"Ohmygod!" she said. "I didn't hear you come in the gate." Then she waved a gloved hand over the blooms in front of her. "Yes, aren't these lovely? Peter grows them. I thought I would fill a vase in memory of Meredith this morning. Maybe take some over to the church for Sunday Mass, too."

She flashed them a winning smile. A classic Alicia smile. A smile Osborne no longer found charming. A smile that chilled even in the warm morning sun.

Alicia looked as fresh and light as the summer breeze blowing across the blooms. She was wearing dark green plaid bermuda shorts with a black T-shirt tucked in neatly to emphasize the outline of her breasts. A red baseball cap sat perkily on her head and matched her red leather garden gloves. A tall metal pail beside her was filled with stems of cut flowers. Now she walked towards them, pulling the gloves from her hands, brushing her tawny hair back from her face with one hand.

She was a picture of peace and happiness. Not bad for a woman who had learned of her lover's death within the last twenty-four hours, who had lost her only sister days earlier. Osborne resisted extending a compliment on her resilience. He did not want to compromise that crucial moment when Lew set the hook.

"I cannot thank you enough, Chief Ferris, for all your *hard* work," gushed Alicia in a condescending tone. She managed to make it sound as if she was thanking Lew for vacuuming her garage.

"What a *relief* to know we have the killer, though who would have ever expected George Zolonsky. I feel so badly. I feel so *responsible*. After all, I hired him after he did such a fabulous job on our kitchen here." She gave a deep sigh, "Peter and I are still reeling from the news—but then, life goes on, doesn't it."

"Yes, it does," said Lew briskly. "As does paperwork. I have a few details we need to review. Could we step inside, Alicia?"

"Really? Right this minute?" said Alicia, obviously reluctant to take much time with them. She checked her watch. "I'm due at Cecile's for a golf brunch in half an hour. "How long will this take?"

"O-o-h, not long I should think," said Lew.

"All right then, come on in," she motioned for them to follow her into house. She led them through the back entrance into the kitchen. "Anyone for a cup of coffee?"

"Where is your husband?" asked Lew as they followed her.

"Who knows? I think he went to one of those dumb flea markets of his," said Alicia, voice dripping with disdain. "I keep telling him I don't want any more of his junk around here.

"Cream or sugar anyone?" she asked as she hastily pulled down two china cups, banging them unceremoniously onto saucers. She reached for the half-full coffee pot, touched it and poured. Though the coffee was tepid, she made no effort to heat it up. Alicia was making it very clear that she had an important engagement pending, much more important than wasting time with them.

"Nothing for me," said Lew. As she reached with her left hand for the cup and saucer, her right hand pulled the narrow reporters' notebook from her back pocket. The card from Winick Farms, which had been tucked into the notebook, dropped face up onto the white tile floor, the green rooster hard to miss. Lew stooped swiftly to grab it. Alicia made no reaction.

"Black for me, too," said Osborne. "Aren't you having any, Alicia?"

"No, I already drank half that pot. Speaking of coffee, excuse me one second while I use the restroom, won't you?" She flashed a gracious smile and walked quickly into the outer hall before they could respond.

"Go right ahead into the living room, it's nice and cool in there," called Alicia as she ran up the stairs.

They waited for her in the shadowed silence of the long room, sitting at opposite ends of the leather sofa in front of the ornate French mirror, exactly where they had sat the night they informed Alicia of her sister's death.

Alicia returned immediately, checking her watch as she strode quickly across the room. Just as she had before, she took her place in the green armchair across from them, crossed her legs, slipped her hands into her pockets, braced her head against the back of the chair and fixed her eyes on the two of them. She did not smile. Her right front foot bounced impatiently.

"This will just take a minute," said Lew briskly, a ballpoint pen poised over her notepad. "Did you know Clint Chesnais is the chief beneficiary on a million-dollar life insurance policy taken out by your sister less than a week before her death?"

Anger mixed with shock transformed Alicia's face. "What!" Her eyes widened. She leaned forward, uncrossing her legs. "Say that again," she demanded. The expression on her face at this moment was identical to the contained fury Osborne had seen in the family photos.

Lew repeated herself.

"Damn," said Alicia, sitting back slightly, a grim steeliness in her tone. She seemed suddenly preoccupied. For a brief period, it was as if she forgot they were there. Then her gaze shifted back, moving between the two of them, unsmiling. "It's obvious. He and George planned this together," she spoke curtly. "That money belongs in the estate."

She picked at a piece of lint on her shorts, "I am sure, between us, we can find proof they planned this together." She crossed her legs again. Again the right foot bounced.

"Alicia . . ." Lew leaned forward, elbows resting on her knees, the closed notebook palmed between her hands, her eyes drilling into the woman seated across from her.

"Why did you lie about Meredith driving out to Starks?"

Alicia's eyes cut to the side swiftly, then shifted back to meet Lew's, direct and unsmiling. The foot stopped bouncing.

"You think I lied?"

"I *know* you lied," said Lew, her voice quiet and deliberate. "I know *you* were out there, too. A number of times. Buying chickens and eggs from that fella that runs Winik Farms . . . and I know you and George and Meredith stopped there, together, the day she died. I know you forged those checks in your sister's checkbook after she died. To pay George off?"

Alicia looked over their heads as if an entire new landscape existed in the mirror, one that didn't include Osborne and Lew.

"I *know*, Alicia. Now why don't you tell me the whole story." Lew's voice was firm, ready to understand.

Alicia's hands slid from her pockets. The barrel of the small revolver gleamed in the soft morning haze that lit the room. Right fist rested on the left. "I know how to use this." A sly smile crept across her face.

"I can see that," said Lew.

"George taught me. He said I'm a natural. Now move slow and place your gun on the floor at your feet, Ferris."

Lew did as she was told. Alicia stood to nudge the gun towards her with the heel of her right foot. Then she kicked it back under the chair where she had been sitting.

Then a smirk crossed her face, an evil little twist of a smile. Maybe it was the need for someone to appreciate her brilliance, maybe it was as simple as relishing this moment of complete control over two lives, but she decided to sit back down in her chair. She held the gun in one hand now, the legs crossed, the foot bouncing again.

Osborne shifted ever so slightly. Her eyes let him know she was watching. He waited. Each minute she took gave them a chance to find a way out. Only he did not see a way out. He knew only he did not want to die, most certainly not at the hands of a woman he despised.

How life changes, he thought. Just eighteen months ago, right after Mary Lee died, he would have welcomed death. Trying to find it in the bottle, he thought his life had ended then. But he was wrong, habits had ended. Now he had new habits, a new life. His children were new to him, his grandchildren. Lew. He refused to die.

Adrenalin surged in his gut making him acutely aware of every object around him, every sound and silence, every angle, every opening.

"I hated Meredith. I hated her the day she was born," Alicia spoke flatly, honestly, without emotion. "You have no idea what it was like to grow up with that spoiled brat. My father gave her everything. Everything. Never once did he have a pleasant word for me. He didn't even see me."

Osborne heard her as if from a great distance, wondering as she spoke if he been as cruel to Mallory. He had to live if only to change his daughter's life. It was not too late. He refused to let it be too late.

Eyes focused on Alicia, without moving his head he explored his peripheral vision, checking to the right and to the left. Was there anything he could knock over to distract her? Could he take a bullet without being killed? That would give Lew time to tackle the woman. One thing he knew for sure, Lew would not let this end easy. But with no lamp table at his end of the sofa, the only close object was foot-tall jade Buddha on the coffee table at his knees.

"She got everything I ever wanted. A handsome husband even if he was a dolt. Money. Fame. Every damn thing. *Loved* by everyone," she sneered.

"Even my idiot husband drooled over her." Now the face changed, eyes narrowed into slits glittering with hate. "But Dad leaving her all that money was the last straw. She got *everything*.

"Every . . . damn . . . penny. Until I got smart." The rage that twisted her face was so raw, Osborne felt panic low in his belly: she could not be stopped. Nothing would stand between her and the money. Not him, not Lew, not reason.

The muzzle of the gun did not shift. All that moved was her right foot in a steady rhythm, up and down. Osborne watched the foot. When it stopped, she would pull the trigger.

The anger had transfromed her, reminding him of a rabid raccoon, fur standing on end, wild eyes bobbling, that had stalked him in his own backyard. The animal had cornered him by his car until he made a frantic dash, barely making it through his back door in time. Osborne wondered if this fierce female was what Peter Roderick faced every morning.

"Can you imagine my humiliation?" her voice a low growl. "You know, Paul, you know how people in this town think."

"But, Alicia, I heard your sister was planning to give you some of that money." To buy time, Osborne risked saying the wrong thing.

"I don't need *some* of that money," she mimicked him, "I need it all. Every penny."

"Why did you kill George?" asked Lew quietly.

"Hah!" Alicia shook her head in disbelief. "He was an accident waiting to happen. Believe me, George was the right man for the job but after that—a liability. Would you want an alcoholic drug addict whom you paid to kill someone running loose? I'm not stupid, Ferris.

"Just look what he did taking those gold fillings. I never asked him to do that? Who the hell needs a few gold fillings? God knows what else he was doing. I had to stop him before he hallucinated some night and spilled his guts."

"The fillings closed the case for Wausau," said Lew, "tied him irrefutably to the body."

"An accident and a bonus. I had planned for Meredith's death to look like a drowning. George told me he had perfected his swing so he could snap her neck. Instant death. Then, poof, we let her float away. Everyone knows the Prairie is a dangerous river. Only he hit her too hard. Then he told me he could hide the body without anyone seeing. That was the last I knew until you two arrived."

"You would have fooled me," lied Osborne. "Those missing fillings were the only reason I suspected foul play."

"I had a back-up plan," said Alicia with a tight little smile.

"Don't tell me," said Lew. "Blame it on Clint Chesnais, and if that didn't work . . . your husband?"

"There you go, Ferris. See, the secret to success in life is to know what you want and have faith you'll find the way to get it. You must be alert to opportunity."

"Like George," said Lew, nodding in appreciation.

"George was *Mister* Opportunity," said Alicia. "I hired him to work on my kitchen here. He taught me how to win at blackjack. We went to the casino a couple times. George and I . . . well, we had other things in common. Didn't take long, he would do anything I asked him to. Anything.

"So I offered him a percentage, and he decided to take the risk. He did quite a nice job, too. Aside from the mess it made, one blow was all it took."

"Oh, that afternoon was something," said Alicia, her voice appreciative of her own cleverness. "It was piece of cake to get her out there. I asked her to give us casting lessons. She was so proud of her technique. As if I really cared, you know?"

"Very smart," said Lew. "No one fishes the Prairie mid-afternoon."

"I knew that. I knew we had a window from morning until five o'clock. So there she was in that damn river, going on about tippets and leaders and all that baloney, fussing over her stupid trout flies. I will say she knew her stuff. She raised a fish in spite of the flat light and the heat. She got so excited playing a big brown, she never even saw George behind her. Merry never knew what hit her. She'd still be under that damn log if it weren't for you, Paul. Nope, George was great until he became such a pest."

"He wanted more money?"

"He wanted more money, and he wanted *me*," said Alicia. "Ugh," she shivered, "he couldn't get it through his stupid head he was just a tool. Right now I miss him—I could use his help with you two."

"I imagine you'll figure it out," said Lew drily.

"I have," said Alicia, her foot stopped at the height of its bounce. She uncrossed her legs and stood up, "we're going to take a little walk now, back through the kitchen and down the basement stairs."

A door slammed suddenly off in the direction of the kitchen.

"Don't move," she hissed, her eyes fixed on Lew and Osborne, the pistol unwavering.

"Peter?" Alicia's voice took on a shrill note as she called out, "Peter! Would you please run to the store for some dog food? Right away, we're all out. Hurry, hon. Chief Ferris and I are still busy with some paperwork."

"Howdy, howdy," Ray came loping around the corner into the room from the hall, a sheepish look on his face and his hands high in the air. Peter Roderick was right behind him with a shotgun aimed at his back.

"What the hell—?" Alicia backed away as Ray walked through the living room as if pushed. Alicia gave a slight wave of the revolver, indicating an antique wooden chair to Osborne's right, "Pull that close to the sofa next to Paul and sit down," she ordered.

"He told me he had to let his dogs out of the back of the Rover, next thing I know it's target practice," muttered Ray in a low voice as he followed orders. You never mentioned he keeps a twenty-gauge in the back of that hog he drives."

"My fault, Ray," said Lew. "Sorry."

Peter Roderick had stopped just inside the room. He held the shotgun high as he studied the group. "I'm sorry, but this is my home. You don't shut me out of my own home. Whatever you have to say to my wife, you can say to me."

"Mr. Roderick," said Lew. "Let me explain—"

"When I'm finished," said Peter, his face flushed a dangerous dark red, cheeks swinging as he spoke in a hoarse, strained voice. Osborne expected him to have a heart attack any second.

Keeping her revolver trained on the three sitting on the sofa, Alicia turned slightly, in the direction of her husband. "Peter— just what the hell do you think you are doing? Move over here where I can see you."

"No, dear. I heard everything you said. I thought I understood you . . . but I don't even know you, Alicia. All these years and I do not know you." Peter's voice cracked. "Why? Can you tell me? Why?" Osborne saw him looking over their heads, searching to meet his wife's eyes in the mirror.

"Oh Peter, shut up." she said derisively.

"I loved you so much. We could have had a good life. I was putting it all back together. Together we—"

Facing the mirror, Alicia rolled her eyes in disgust, "I do not need——"

"Stop," said Peter softly.

Before she could finish, the shotgun blast tore through the room.

The twenty-gauge didn't carry a slug. The impact carried Alicia towards them, a look of total surprise on her face as she flew forward, knocking over the coffee table. She hit the floor and did not move.

Nor did Osborne and Lew, they sat perfectly still in stunned silence. Ray lowered his hands to his knees.

"Pete, old man," he said softly. "We are friends."

"Stay where you are." Peter walked over to look down at Alicia's still form. He fired again.

Then he reached into his pocket for two cartridges. He loaded the shotgun.

"Yes, you are friends," he said. "Please, I am not going to shoot anyone." He waved one hand weakly as he sat down heavily in the chair where Alicia had been moments earlier, the butt of the shotgun on the floor, the barrel pointing to the ceiling.

Peter looked at Ray and Osborne, "No grave, boys. Cremate both of us. I don't care what you do with her. Me?" He breathed deeply. "Me, I'd like to blow in the wind by our deer shack, Doc. Maybe you would take me back by the blue heron rookery?"

"I can do that for you, Pete." Osborne didn't raise a hand to wipe the tears rolling down his cheeks.

"Pete, c'mon," Ray's voice was soft, "you don't have to do this."

"It's my call, Peter," said Lew. "Justifiable homicide."

"No," Peter shook his head slowly, a deep sadness in his voice, "it's my call. I call it 'nothing left to lose.' Please, all of you. Leave the room."

Before they could enter the hallway, they heard the gunshot.

Twelve hours later, they sat at the Loon Lake Pub. It was nearing midnight after the long, long day. Even though a lively Saturday night crowd buzzed around them, no one at their table of three had spoken since ordering. Now they sat staring at their dinners: luscious cheeseburgers, cooked medium, buried under slabs of Wisconsin Cheddar Cheese.

"I reached Wayne's mother," said Ray. "It wasn't easy. I told her he felt no pain. Maybe that helps."

"Thank you, Ray," said Lew. "I'm sure you handled it well." She sighed, "I'm relieved the crew found him as quickly as they did. Did I mention the Wausau lab called late this afternoon? They estimated the time of death for Meredith Marshall between two and five P.M. Sunday."

"What did they say when you told them about the Rodericks?" asked Osborne.

"I didn't yet. The weekend team was on duty. I'm saving my report for Monday morning—and making sure it arrives on more than one desk."

"That should ruin someone's day."

"I certainly hope so," Lew shook the salt shaker very carefully.

"Why do decent people have to die because of the craziness of others?" Osborne squirted ketchup over his french fries. He wasn't sure he could even eat them.

"May I have that when you're done?" asked Lew. He handed over the bottle. Lew slammed her palm against the base of the ketchup bottle, making a small pool in one corner of her plate, "Some days life is unfair, Doc. Other days it works out. No one gets more than a 50-50 chance."

"I don't accept that answer, Lew," said Osborne. "Wayne was a good man. Meredith had just put her life together. Pete—he tried so hard."

"C'mon, Doc," said Ray matter-of-factly as one finger tap-tapped the pepper slowly over his side dish of cottage cheese. "The water is always dark. You never know. Now Wayne. His last days were quite fine. It's not like he died of cancer. Me? I would not mind going by surprise."

"Don't forget, Doc," Lew finished with a thin swirl of Dijon mustard on the inside of her bun. "Meredith had hooked a big brown, remember? You and I both know you don't see many browns in the Prairie. She had to be thrilled.

"The way I see it," Lew raised her burger towards her mouth, "the victim died happy."

About the Author

Victoria Houston lives, works and fly fishes in Northern Wisconsin. She also hunts grouse with her black lab, Cyber. Currently plotting her third Loon Lake mystery, she can be e-mailed at *victoria@newnorth.net*.

Enjoyed *Dead Angler?* Be sure to pick up *Dead Creek*, the next book in the Loon Lake mystery series!

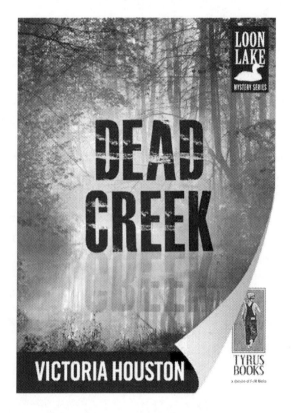

Fishing aside, there's nothing Doc likes better than helping Chief of Police Lew Ferris, a world-class fly fisherman in her own right, delve into Loon Lake's criminal underworld. He's looking for any excuse to spend time with the only woman he knows who likes to fish as much as he does. So bloodthirsty killers and backwoods bandits be damned, Doc will take the quiet risk.

Praise for Victoria Houston

*"With this fine novel, Victoria Houston will hook readers
and make them seek her previous stories."*
—Painted Rock Reviews

Please enjoy the following brief selection.

Osborne scanned the edges of the brook for a firm hillock. Much of the area was swamp and wetland, and the shadows from the towering firs made it hard to see. He spotted a good, wide, firm clump and revved the motor toward it.

Suddenly a sickening, grinding noise from under the boat caught him off guard. He switched off the motor, unhappy to hear the grinding continue until the propeller blades had stopped.

"Oh boy," he said, dreading the sight of a broken blade on his brand new motor. Gently, Osborne moved his fishing rod so he could lean forward onto his knees to peer over the left edge of the boat.

He froze, so stunned he couldn't breathe, then he lurched back, almost tipping himself out of the boat. Deperate, he grabbed for both gunwales, terrified he was going to fall out and right into the horror beneath him.

The boat steadied, and Osborne looked up at the crystal blue sky. Not a sound did he hear except his own harsh breathing. Even the dog sat silent, watching him, his head cocked inquiringly. Osborne got himself up straight on the boat seat and reached for both oars. Arms shaking, he finally got them into the oar locks and, barely dipping the oars below the surface of the so as not to touch anything under him, turned the boat around and gunned his motor out of the hidden brook.

Mike, looking back, started to bark loudly.

"Goddamn it, piss in the boat," said Osborne. He had to get to a phone. He had to get the sight out of his head. Never in his lifetime of cleaning fish, gutting dear, drilling root canals had he ever seen anything like it.

The sparkling clear water had magnified what he saw: a black wire care about ten feet long and four feet wide with bodies floating in it. The photographic imprint in his mind was so sharp he could still see the blue denim jeans, the sodden dark woolen shirts. But what he really couldn't forget was the one face staring up at him, its mouth a black hole with a tongue protruding and cloudy eyes bulging directly at him. Instinct told him it was dead, but his pounding heart made him feel like it was rising up out of the water, lumbering after him.

All freezes again
Among the pines, winds
Whispering a prayer
—Riei, 18th century Japanese poet

"You can't say enough about fishing.
Though the sport of kings, it's just what the deadbeat ordered."
—Thomas McGuane, *Silent Seasons*

"It is just possible that nice guys don't catch the most fish.
But they find more pleasure in those they do get."
—Roderick Haig-Brown, 1960

A few words from the author:

I was born and raised in Rhinelander, Wisconsin, in the heart of the fishing culture that backgrounds my mysteries. I grew up fishing for walleye and bluegills and muskie—and when I turned fifty, I learned to fly fish!

I've always had an aptitude for writing (not singing, for sure, as the nuns at St. Mary's told me to "just move your lips") and won a full scholarship to Bennington College in Vermont. Went on to have three children, marry and divorce twice. My second husband was 9 years younger, hence my non-fiction book, *Loving A Younger Man*, which I wrote 25 years ago. We broke up for reasons that had nothing to do with the age difference.

After a decade of magazine and newspaper feature writing—the source of my non-fiction books—I directed promotion and publicity for Andrews & McMeel/Universal Press Syndicate, during which time I had the privilege of working with outstanding writers and cartoonists such as Abigail Van Buren, Gary Larson, Erma Bombeck, and Garry Trudeau. Later I joined Jane Mobley Associates, a public relations firm based in Kansas City.

I moved back to Rhinelander in 1996 (having been gone for more than 30 years) where I now hunt, fish, and write mysteries. Over the years, I have published 23 books—a fact that surprises the hell out of me as I never finished college. I am just starting my fourteenth Loon Lake Mystery.

My influences are the happenings in the world around me and I continue to be a fanatic newspaper reader, devouring *The New York Times* and *Wall Street Journal* daily. My favorite authors are Willa Cather, Edith Wharton (Rhinelander is named after her uncle who brought the railroad through in late 1800s), early Hemingway and early John Updike, Raymond Chandler, and Ross Thomas. Growing up I was an avid Nancy Drew/Agatha Christie fan. Oh, and G.K. Chesterton's Father Brown series, too. I'm not a card-carrying member of Oprah's Book Club. However, I do enjoy biographies such as the one about Steve Jobs. And poetry! I don't think I could get through the day without some Mary Oliver and Billy Collins to name a few.

I love movies—*Argo, Zero Dark Thirty, Silver Linings Playbook, The Descendants, Pulp Fiction*, and *Gone With the Wind*—and music. I'm currently listening to Calexico, Avett Brothers, and Sea Wolf. Other favorites range from Elvis, The Beach Boys, Roy Orbison, Bob Dylan, and The Beatles to Adele, Emmy Lou Harris, and Aimee Mann. Classical music and jazz round out my listening.

When it comes to the books, I have always worked on a Mac and just treated myself to an iPad. When not writing, I run, play tennis, and do Pilates. Oh, and I fish!

A Guide for Book Club Readers of the Loon Lake Mystery Series

Q. *How does the author use fishing as a device within the mystery?*
- What happens while characters are fishing?
- Are there differences in personality types between the people who fly fish and those who bait fish (as in fishing for muskie, walleyes, bass, and bluegills)?
- What is the role of the female characters who fish?

Q. *What role does water play in the mystery?*
- Are there differences between lakes and rivers and streams? Do they attract different types of people?
- Is the water always safe and lovely?

Q. *What role does dentistry play in the mystery?*
- Is that valid in contemporary investigations?
- What other characteristic of Dr. Paul Osborne helps to solve the mystery?

Q. *Are you familiar with the regional vernaculars used; i.e. "razzbonya," "goombah" and "jabone?"*
- What do they mean?
- How are they pronounced? (Hint: two of the words are pronounced with a long "o" sound.)

Q. *What role does the northwoods landscape, which has the second-highest ratio of water to land in the world, play in the stories?*
- Would you want to visit the region?
- If you did visit, would you want to go fishing?
- And would you prefer to fish *on* water in a boat—or *in* water with flyfishing gear?

Q. *How does Point of View (POV) figure in the mystery?*
- Is it clear and satisfying?
- Do you agree with the author's approach?

Printed in the United States
By Bookmasters